CRUISIN' ON DESPERATION

This Large Print Book carries the
Seal of Approval of N.A.V.H.

CRUISIN' ON
DESPERATION

PAT G'ORGE-WALKER

THORNDIKE PRESS

An imprint of Thomson Gale, a part of The Thomson Corporation

Detroit • New York • San Francisco • New Haven, Conn. • Waterville, Maine • London

LIBRARY OF CONGRESS CATALOGING-IN-PUBLICATION DATA

G'Orge-Walker, Pat.
  Cruisin' on desperation / by Pat G'Orge-Walker.
    p. cm. — (Thorndike Press large print African-American)
  ISBN-13: 978-1-4104-0269-1 (hardcover : alk. paper)
  ISBN-10: 1-4104-0269-X (hardcover : alk. paper)
    1. African American women — Fiction. 2. African American churches —
Fiction. 3. Revenge — Fiction. 4. Female friendship — Fiction. 5. Single
women — Fiction. 6. Cruise ships — Fiction. 7. Large type books. I. Title. II.
Title: Cruising on desperation.
  PS3607.O597C78 2007b
  813'.6—dc22   2007034095

Published in 2007 by arrangement with Dafina Books, an imprint of Kensington
Publishing Corp.

Printed in the United States of America on permanent paper
10 9 8 7 6 5 4 3 2 1

ACKNOWLEDGMENTS

Some are called, others just show up!

> And God hath set some in the church, first apostles, secondarily prophets, thirdly teachers, after that miracles, then gifts of healings, helps, governments, diversities of tongues.
>
> — 1 Corinthians 12:28

I give all my love, praise, and honor to my Heavenly Father, the beginning and ending of my faith.

To my husband, Robert, I can never thank you or show you enough love for your generous love and support. When the chemo and the stem-cell transplant to treat your multiple myeloma should've left you weak, you always summoned the strength to encourage me to go on. Continue the good fight.

I thank my children, Gizel, Ingrid, and

Marisa. My precious jewels, Kecia, Desean, Jerome, Nyasia, Shareef, Donald, Gary Jr., Denzel, Maya, Aniyah, Brian, Shyheim, Jada, Sharday, and India, and my future granddaughter-in-law, Patrice Edwards. To my remaining siblings, remain firm. Aunts Ovella and Mildred and Uncle Elbert, God bless and keep you.

My eldest daughter, Jah Queen Gizel, I thank you for your beautiful poem. From wisdom and experience, you've told us to *Just Get Over It.*

Ms. BerNadette Stanis (Thelma/Good Times), I so appreciate your support, and I can't wait to work with you. Ms. Dawn Carter, Producer, Fox Pictures, I thank you.

New York Times bestselling author Zane, *Essence* bestselling authors Tia McCollors, Stacy Hawkins-Adams, Angela Benson, and Jacquelin Thomas, I thank you and appreciate your comments and support.

To my third-grade teacher, Mrs. Bobby Mackey, God bless you for putting up with me. You're still as pretty inside and out now as you were then. Your continued support is amazing.

I give a special, heartfelt thank you to Karen Thomas, who followed her heart in 2003. Sister Betty and I will always be grateful to you, Latoya Smith, Jessica McClain, and the entire Dafina family.

My new editor, Selena James . . . Hang on, we're about to fly. Robin Caldwell, who edited tirelessly, I thank you. Content editor Monica Harris, I thank you.

To my pillars of constant support, Jacqueline Thomas and Tracy Price-Thompson, thank you.

My agent, Renee Byrd and Vanessa Morman along with the entire Sheba Media Group; a thank you is barely enough.

I thank one of the other hardest working women in the business, besides me, Ms. Vickie Winans. I'm still shaking loose during every performance.

Maurice Gray, author, thank you for the "Oh Lawd, Why Am I Still Single" singles group.

Thank you to my attorney, Christopher R. Whent, Esq., my pastor, Reverend Stella Mercardo, and the Blanche Memorial Baptist Church family.

I give thanks to my first church, which remains my love, St. Paul's Tabernacle, as well as Bishop John and Lady Laura Smith. Thank you.

To Bishop Noel Jones (Fresh Oil), I love and admire you so much. To the Reverends John and Diana Cherry (From the Heart Church Ministries), you've taught me to hold fast and not compromise and I thank you for that.

To Tyler Perry, who could've known how well known Madea, Sister Betty, and Ma Cile would become? I certainly didn't. I offer a big thank-you for finally knocking down doors and taking those hits for the comedy ministry teams that came before and will follow after.

I give a special thank-you to my lifelong friend, Akia Shangia. I applaud you. I feel it is a privilege and an honor to have known you for over forty years. I will continue to support the enormous task that you and Sister to Sister International, Inc., have undertaken to ensure the collection and distribution of Maama Kits throughout Africa to eradicate neonatal fatalities.

In addition, thank you to the Depend Company, for your dedication to helping millions of men and women who suffer from the embarrassing but curable affliction of incontinence.

Finally, to the many book clubs and bookstores; my readers; the radio, print, and television media; the many churches, libraries and organizations; and so many others too numerous to mention, I thank you for your continuous support. It is always appreciated and very much necessary for my comedy and writing ministry. For those I've not mentioned, please blame it on the head and not the heart.

For more information regarding Akia Shangai and Sister to Sister International, Inc.'s efforts in eradicating infant mortality in Africa, please visit: *www.stsi.org*

Please log onto *www.depend.com* for more information regarding incontinence. You don't have to suffer with its embarrassing effects.

Please log onto *www.mskcc.org* (the Memorial-Sloan Kettering Cancer Medical Center) to learn more about multiple myeloma and other cancers. Please remember to give blood because there is never enough. There is also information regarding using your own blood for its stem cells.

For Pat G'Orge-Walker, log on to: *www.sisterbetty.com, www.myspace.com/sisterbettycomedy,* or *www.cruisin-on-desperation.com.*

The same day I wrote my acknowledgments, my husband learned that he was in remission. He'd only been given a year to live and didn't God just show out!!!

I give all praises to God.

DESPERATION . . .
JUST GET OVER IT
NEEDY'S LAMENT
BY JAH QUEEN GIZEL

Just get over it. Just get over it!

You mean all the mistakes I've made and all the times I've been played?

You mean to tell me I'm supposed to *just get over it?*

All those relationships where I sacrificed everything, even my dignity.

All the times people smiled in my face and behind my back, they talked and told lies about me, am I supposed to . . . *just get over it?*

Speaking of back, I'm sick, I'm tired, and I'm desperate, so when can I get my life back? I've tried almost everything to be free.

Just get over it. Four simple words were the key. Desperation left when I discovered truth . . . just getting over it will keep life from getting all over me, and truth be told . . .

YOU NEED TO *JUST GET OVER IT, TOO.*

PROLOGUE

It was 2005 and in the town of Pelzer, South Carolina, during the month of June, weddings sprang up faster than gas prices.

It seemed that bouts of desperation had taken over the many physically and mentally challenged who seemed destined to remain unmarried. The why and how of the sudden marital surge was a mystery, except to those who were getting married. They didn't care why, and for the most part, really didn't care how.

However, most of the other town folks, tired of boredom, were happy to have something to celebrate. And, of course, having plenty of free food to eat on Saturdays when no one wanted to cook at home, in all the heat, was always a good thing.

There were a few of the folks not happy for the newlyweds. They were the just-couldn't-get-a-man-to-save-their-lives members of the Oh Lawd, Why Am I Still Single

Singles Club. Those women had never so much as received an obscene phone call let alone a marriage proposal. But for propriety's sake, they tried to keep their opinions quiet, preferring to gripe among themselves.

They indulged and wallowed in self-pity. Their unhappiness didn't bother the other Pelzer residents until there was one wedding that finally sent them over the edge. They could stand it no more.

The beginning of their push for freedom from unmarried misery began when suddenly one of their former members, Sheila Shame, got a man.

Fifty-year-old Sheila with chronic post-nasal drip, and one of the worst church soloists in the "A" choir history, announced she was getting married. Before folks could recover from her news, a flood of other wedding invitations poured into mailboxes all around town.

The wedding deluge spread out over several gorgeous sunny Saturday afternoons. The first one, which was Sheila's, started like something straight out of a Disney movie. There were colorful birds chirping, smiling bees buzzing, and it was all for a woman no one thought they'd live to see walk down the aisle.

There was standing room only when

Sheila married Pookie Bowser at an IHOP Restaurant. Sheila could barely control her joy at her good fortune. She grinned and cried endlessly at the altar, causing her makeup to smudge all around her bulging brown eyes. She stood at that altar looking like Pookie had given her a shiner. But before their "I do's," Sheila boasted to her guests.

"Y'all didn't think I could get a man, but I did," Sheila gushed, causing her makeup to spread and making her look like she wore a half-mask. To further her point, she turned and snapped her fingers at the guests.

Pookie quickly snatched Sheila's burqa-shaped veil and covered her pimply face before he changed his mind.

Although they wanted to laugh, the guests could do nothing but nod in agreement. Some did bother to cover their mouths and muffle a snicker as Sheila stood, slightly askew, on her one leg hidden by her extravagant, long, off-white gown. And, with a quick shout of "Thank you, Jesus. I sure do," when asked if she'd take Pookie, Sheila grabbed and leaned on her new husband.

Pookie, on the other hand, was elated because he finally had a chance to get his bucked and crooked teeth fixed. Sheila had both dental and medical benefits. The image of his name on an insurance card made Pookie scream out in joy, "Hallelujah."

Although Sheila and Pookie's marriage was the straw that broke the camel's back for the singles group, they weren't the only unlikely pair to wed that month.

There was Sister Patty Cake, the eighty-year-old, reed-thin co-chair of the Senior Choir. She had celery-colored teeth and breath so bad she could peel paint off a wall. She married a twenty-five-year-old Jamaican man nicknamed Kool Aid. He had dreadlocks that flowed like branches from his head. When folks tried to warn her that her soon-to-be husband was only marrying her to get a green card, Patty didn't listen or care. Having never been married, she was so happy she gave him a matching green American Express card. Whatever he did to her on their wedding night pleased her, because even though he left the following morning, she continued to send him a weekly check. And she was happy to do it.

There were others. Southside Annie was forty with arthritis so bad she couldn't thread a needle, but she snagged her a man. She married a thug named Klepto from the north side. They married quickly because he was only out on temporary parole. She declared she didn't mind conjugal visits.

And then there was Two-Ton Sally who married a fella from Alabama named Big Louie. He was about three times smaller than Sally. Despite the odds, those women had snagged husbands.

After that last wedding, which the members of the Oh Lawd, Why Am I Still Single group took as a slap in the face, they became downright shameless and, of course, even more desperate. They perpetrated daily sunrise jogging sprints. They sported natty but expensive hair weaves that were neon-colored. They even enrolled in "nouvelle cuisine" cooking classes. There wasn't a ploy or a trick that was off-limits.

None of their schemes worked. Since it was still early in July and they weren't willing to give up their manhunt, they decided to try something new. They would open the door to new membership.

They didn't have to wait long after the call out to the lonely and desperate before someone answered.

That next Saturday was their first meeting for new members. As always, Sister Need Sum held the meeting at her house as she had since the group's beginning. It was at that meeting that they welcomed into their chaotic mix the group's first caucasian member, Sister Birdie Tweet.

None of the members suspected that Birdie's huge heart and even larger, overflowing bank account would catapult them into a journey that they were ill prepared to take.

Moreover, the women went to new heights to prove that desperation creates strange bedfellows when they also welcomed a former ex-con and current memory-challenged member of their church's Mothers Board, Mother Bea Blister.

There was a little more than a month left of summertime, and there wasn't any time to waste.

Desperation made these women act crazier than a swarm of intoxicated butterflies stumbling for ten miles, instead of flying. They were just that lost.

1

"Do you think this old gas-guzzling clunker can go a little faster?" Cill asked, impatient and loud as she leaned towards the steering wheel of the 1993 red Camry from her seat on the passenger side.

Cill and her childhood friend, Petunia, had just left the wedding reception for a fifty-year-old woman with an oversized glass eye, nicknamed Blind Betty.

Blind Betty had landed a wealthy real estate mogul who, for reasons no one could understand, had fallen deeply in love with her.

Cill and Petunia, along with some of the other single women at the reception, tried to be happy for Blind Betty but they couldn't. None of them had ever found a poor man who owned a bag of dirt, let alone a rich real estate mogul.

The single women sat around wearing plastered smiles, and had almost accepted

Blind Betty's good fortune until it was time for her to toss a bouquet of colorful forget-me-nots. They'd swarmed out onto the floor kicking, pinching and screaming. Suddenly from out of nowhere, a twenty-something shapely woman with lemon-colored skin and an ebony, store-bought wig with its price tag showing, just happened to pass in front of the crowd of desperate crones. "Get out the way," someone from the crowd shouted at her. When the young woman, whose name was Miss Fitt, turned around, she accidentally caught the wedding bouquet with her French-manicured, claw-shaped nails.

The sight of those long nails ripping the colorful forget-me-nots to microscopic shreds brought a hush all over the place. Like the other single women, Cill and Petunia thought they'd lose their minds. However, when they saw the young woman toss the remains of the bouquet into a nearby garbage can as she screamed, "Ooh, I don't want this. I don't want to get married, ever," they wanted to strangle her shapely neck.

Going to jail for murder would certainly hamper their chances of marriage, so they decided to grab a few petals as souvenirs. With their heads held high, and a single tear rolling down their cheeks, they left with a scrap of dignity and a renewed vow not to remain alone or attend another wedding unless it was their own.

Petunia's old car lurched out of control as though it was trying to throw up its last little bit of gasoline. All the while its speedometer seemed to stand still, even as the steering wheel spun erratically. It clanked and inched down the right lane of Pelzer's Highway 29, while black smoke spewed out its muffler like smoke signals. Yet it was in better shape than the lives of its occupants.

Petunia pushed Cill's hands away. "Touch my steering wheel with those ashy paws, and I'll fight you like the man you want to be," she snapped as her sunglasses bobbed on the tip of her pointy nose.

Petunia was skinny and banana-shaped, and she was just as pale, almost to the point of looking jaundiced. At the age of thirty-six, she was an on again and off again anorexic with breasts the size of acorn seeds. She stood about five foot nine and weighed about one hundred and five pounds, and that was only after gorging on a Happy Meal.

Cill took another glance over at Petunia and sucked her teeth as she pointed at her. "Girl, please. I'd love to see you fight me or

21

anyone for that matter. As a matter of fact, stop tripping. You've never won a fight against anything, and from the looks of this puddle-hopper, certainly not the war on poverty."

Cill watched the steam escape from under Petunia's peach-colored, floppy hat. She laughed and then pulled her oversized, beige Apple cap further down over her doe-shaped, brown eyes. Cill wore a big Apple cap everywhere, and had even worn it to the wedding that day. The hat covered her micro-short dark hair, giving no clue as to her gender, despite a stubborn, long chin hair.

Cill and Petunia fought constantly and made up just as often. Arguing about how slow Petunia drove was the springboard for most of their arguments. Next was whether Cill truly wanted a man or just hung around the other women pretending she did. Those were the same arguments they'd had for the past several years on the first Saturday of the month, as they drove to the singles meeting.

"You just make sure that there's some padding in the backseat before we let Mother Blister sit down when I pick her up," Petunia said as she pointed to an old comforter balled up in the backseat.

Cill let her shoulders drop and shook her head. "I don't know why we always have to pick up that old woman to go everywhere," she mumbled as she reached over the headrest for the blanket. "I know for certain that they have free shuttle service from that seniors' home. She could use it if she wanted and stop inconveniencing us. And, you know good and well, she has a problem with her bladder. It just ain't sanitary to have her in the car with people that normally pee in toilets."

"You got a lot of nerve, Cill Lee," Petunia argued and rolled her eyes. "I only live a block away from Mother Blister, but I had to drive three miles from my house to pick you up and take you to a meeting that's right next door to you. I'm going out of my way because your car is in a shop that's on this side of town. So, who's an inconvenience?"

Petunia totally ignored the reference to Mother Blister's uncontrollable bladder. After all, she had the blanket in the back seat for that very reason.

"I'm your friend. We go way back like salt pork and collards," Cill answered as she again shook her head in annoyance and watched old folks on the sidewalk in their motorized wheelchairs speed past.

"Why don't you be a better friend and chip in for some gas?" Petunia asked. She knew Cill wouldn't do it but she still needed to remind her.

"Well, let me look in my pocket for a quarter. At the rate you're driving that's about all the gas you'll use."

Petunia was just about to lock horns again, but Cill spoke up too quick.

"Look, there she is in the front of her building standing under the awning," Cill said as she avoided Petunia's impending rebuke. "Have mercy, will you look at that old woman?" Cill was about to burst with laughter. "I wished she'd come to the wedding wearing that orange and red striped blouse and that maroon wool pleated skirt. She'd have made us look good."

Petunia, forever the cautious one when it came to the maintenance of her precious car, kept her eyes and mind on parking it, completely ignoring Cill. When Petunia was satisfied that she'd parked exactly twelve inches from the curve, she looked over at Mother Blister, and accidentally hit her mouth on the steering wheel when she leaned over. She almost chipped a tooth to keep from laughing, too.

"Lord, please don't let me be and look that crazy if I live to be that old." Petunia whispered the prayer, laughing as she did.

"We ask in your name, dear Father," Cill added as she crossed her chest and her fingers. She almost caught a cramp when she tried to cross her toes, too.

Mother Blister hadn't looked in their direction. Instead, the seventy-plus senior stood under her building's awning with a jar in her hand. At five foot nine, with a hefty frame, she looked like an overripe dark raisin with twice the wrinkles, bent almost in half like the letter C. Her entire body looked uneven when she stood.

As the blazing hot sun poured through the cracks in the awning's cover, she spooned fistfuls of sunscreen from the jar and smoothed it on her dark skin. But it was when she lifted her skirt, to dab a little on her knobby knees, that she spied Cill and Petunia. She dropped her skirt and waved to let them know she'd seen them.

"Look at her," Petunia said. She pointed towards the building's awning quickly so Mother Blister wouldn't see her as she approached. "She's one of the senior heads of our church's Mothers Board." She dropped her head again pretending not to laugh as her bony shoulders shivered. "That's too sad."

"Sad ain't exactly the word I'd say. Downright ridiculous is more like it," Cill chimed in as she suppressed another giggle. "Listen. Do you hear it?" she asked.

"Hear what?" Petunia asked. She turned her head from side to side while holding one of her ears.

"The sounds of snaps, crackles and pops," Cill answered while snapping her fingers. "Mother Blister was standing there broiling in that sun and sounding like a geriatric bowl of Rice Krispies. I can still hear the sounds echoing in the air."

"Hello, Mother Blister." Petunia stopped laughing long enough to call out as Mother Blister ambled towards the car. She opened her door and stepped out to give the woman more room to enter on the driver's side, when she finally reached there. "You're going straight to hell for that," she leaned back inside and whispered to Cill.

"How y'all doing, today?" Mother Blister asked as she finally arrived. She squeezed her hefty body into the back seat of Petunia's car, pushing aside the blanket Cill had carefully laid out.

"How was Blind Betty's wedding?" she asked, but didn't wait for an answer before continuing. "Forget about a wedding, I hope we get to the meeting on time, today," Mother Blister said as she finally found a comfortable spot, despite the concerned look from Petunia and the smile on Cill's face.

"Well, they can't have a singles meeting without all the most promising singles being present," Cill offered. "You do remember that we are going to discuss what other things we can do to meet our soul-mates, don't you?"

"You do remember that I've probably forgotten more about men than you've ever learned or will learn no matter how hard you try to be like one," Mother Blister snapped.

"I like keeping in touch with my masculine side. You gotta problem with yours?" Cill'd always liked tattoos and keeping folks guessing about her gender. She never questioned why. She just enjoyed the game.

Mother Blister was old, but not stupid. She knew Cill would always try to get an argument going with anyone she could. "Watch yourself, youngster," Mother Blister continued as she adjusted her false teeth as if she were going to take them out and use them on Cill.

For the rest of the ten-minute ride to Sister Need Sum's house, the three women alternated between arguing and apologizing. And, of course, Cill and Petunia had to give their edited version of Blind Betty's "fiasco of a wedding," as they called it.

And *they* were the sanest women in the Oh Lawd, Why Am I Still Single Club.

2

It was Saturday morning and several sweat-stained gardeners were scattered throughout the Pelzer suburbs of the rich and wish-they-were rich population.

Most of the men were young, willing workers, and arrived in small trucks and multi-colored vans. Their well-toned bodies were tanned from the hot sun and dirty from the hard work of mowing lawns and spreading fertilizer. That morning they came prepared to prune and to plant.

Light testosterone whiffs of dripping sweat intermingled with the fragrance of jasmines and yellow lilac bushes that dotted the lawns of several plush homes. The homes of the rich and snooty residents of Hope Avenue were definitely not the homes of the single, but often desperation still came to visit.

As they pushed their roaring lawnmowers, the gardeners' sleeveless T-shirts clung to their bodies. Although the sight of the young men intimidated the well-dressed men struggling under the weight of their golf clubs, it wasn't enough to keep them from driving off in their luxury cars and leaving their wives behind.

Standing in the doorway with each hair in its place and nails polished to a shine, the left-behind wives leered at the workers. The sight of the promising young men caused the spoiled wives to daydream of slinging the golf clubs and their husbands over their shoulders, and depositing them at the curb.

A little farther away the intoxicating mixtures of flora and perspiration had wafted towards the corner and into one of the homes on Drudge Road. It was a house where an old flowery faded mat with the furrowed face of a winking cherub, resting lopsided on the front porch, welcomed visitors.

Townfolks always described Hope Avenue as looking "well-off." They said that Drudge Road just looked "far off."

Inside the small, cluttered wood-framed eyesore on the corner of Drudge and Hope avenues, where the smell of Icy Hot for back pain and Clairol plum hair dye was certain to attack a visitor's nose, lived Sister Need Sum. Her close friends called her Needy. Moreover, even those who didn't know her at all took one glance and called her that, too.

Needy leaned out of her narrow bedroom window with a chipped pair of binoculars and inhaled the morning air for the umpteenth time since awakening from a restless night. *I'm long overdue for some pruning and planting,* she sighed as she mentally tore off with her teeth the shirt of one of the young gardeners. With her free hand she began to fan furiously with a torn Aretha Franklin album cover. Her heart fluttered as her mind began to entertain fleshly thoughts that she'd thought she'd overcome at a recent prayer meeting.

Since she had her first kiss at the age of twenty-five, Needy struggled with issues of the flesh. "God's still working on this building," she always testified.

"Buenos diás, Carlos. Que pasa?" Needy shamelessly yelled across and up the street at one of the workers who came dangerously close. She prayed her voice rose above the constant high-pitched buzz of the hedge clippers. "Oh you fine, young thing," she muttered and then quickly looked skyward and added, "Lord, please forgive me for that flesh-ridden thought about what I'd love to do with that young man."

As happy as she was to see the bare

chested young Spanish men flexing their toned and sun-kissed muscles, she was even happier to know that God would forgive her for her inappropriate thoughts. She knew this because she'd asked forgiveness far more times than she probably deserved.

Needy was in her late thirties, if she'd been telling the truth. Unlike most of her single friends, she owned her home. There was nothing outstanding about her one-story green and brown frame house except that it sat cushioned between two trailer homes that teetered precariously on whittled cinderblocks.

After a few minutes of inhaling as much air as she could without wheezing from the rag weed in her back yard, Needy shut her bedroom window and went towards the front of the house. Her huge head-wrap, a tattered dark linen towel spotted with hair dye, slowly began to unravel. She moved about as if she were trying to dodge flying objects as she quickly sprayed her living room with long misty streams of Old Spice cologne. The odor of Old Spice was as close to having a man in her home in the middle of the day as she'd been in the past year. And she was not happy about that fact at all.

Needy had barely finished spraying the

room with the odor of false hope when the urgent sound of her doorbell clanged though her home.

"Hold your horses, I'm coming," she yelled, angrily, even though she knew her visitors couldn't hear her. She quickly looked at her wall clock and realized that her guests were almost thirty minutes early. She was annoyed but certainly wasn't surprised. Plotting to catch a man was serious business. Blind Betty's wedding had sent them into overdrive.

The six female club members had become a tight-knit group. They hung out together and even planned their vacations together. They all worked in the same area of town and they still checked in with each other at lunchtime, every day, just in case one of them caught more men than she could handle. That never happened, but they still clung to hope.

"Cill, Birdie and Mother Blister, come on in. How are you ladies today? Excuse the mess." Needy feigned surprise and the appropriate agitation as the women entered in various stages of desperation, decay, and annoyance into her living room. "Y'all have a seat. Is Petunia parking the car?"

"Yes, she's outside trying to find a suitable parking space for that mess on four wheels," Cill said, cheerfully. "We ran into Birdie while we were coming up the walkway."

"You look wonderful," Birdie said softly to Needy while giving her a quick peck on the cheek.

Needy returned the kiss, showing her appreciation for Birdie's thoughtfulness. "Y'all came earlier than I expected. I'll try to get dressed as fast as I can. After all, one can't rush perfection."

She put a little something extra on the perfection comment feeling that she most certainly had to look a lot better than the hot messes, with perhaps the exception of Birdie, she saw seated around her.

Every month for the past five years, Needy led the single and childless meetings in her tiny, cluttered living room. The only thing she'd gotten out of those get-togethers was the title of Madam President and about a twenty-pound spread of unwanted fat on her hips and thighs, along with a bushy mustache on her upper lip that if left alone, most men would've killed for. Needy carried around a pair of tweezers that were as necessary to her physical survival as the air she breathed. If she didn't keep that busy, bushy top lip weeded, she wouldn't be able to breathe or gossip.

Needy had barely turned to leave before she heard the not-so-subtle whispering followed by snickering begin behind her back.

"Forget about perfection. We don't have the hundred years to wait," someone said.

Needy quickly spun around. She let her angry brown eyes spray accusatory bullets at the women and dared them to flinch. None of the usual suspects moved. It was as if whatever words had been spoken were frozen in time.

Needy decided to let the snipe go unchallenged for the time. "Why don't y'all just go ahead and read the minutes from the last meeting." A wide menacing grin appeared on her face before she continued. "Birdie, why don't you do it since you and I are the only ones here that are college-educated."

Needy gave the insult a minute to hit Cill and then she added, "Oh, I'm so sorry, Cill. I keep forgetting you decided to drop out and play in some Middle-East sand lot." She didn't wait for Cill to reply or throw something at her. "It's only a few paragraphs at the most so y'all decide who'll do it while I go and change."

A collective sigh filled the room as each woman, thinking silently of what Cill had said aloud, came back to life.

"We'll do that while you change," Cill

purred through her clenched teeth. "Take whatever time you need to pull yourself together."

Needy could feel her chubby fists involuntarily open and close. She suspected that Cill had made the earlier dig. Although this time the comment was said softly, the voice still had the same venom that had spat out the unkind words earlier.

"Girl, you know I love you . . . all of you," Cill said, gesturing to Needy's wide hips.

"You wish," Needy said as she sashayed past.

Like Petunia, forty-year-old Cill Lee was one of Needy's oldest sometime-friends. Their friendship was on and off more times than a light switch. They'd reconnected while attending Hampton University.

College didn't sit well with Cill. She'd always wanted to study automotive design. Although Petunia wouldn't let her touch her prize Camry, Cill could, back then and even now, take apart and put together any engine. She'd thought it would be an easy degree to obtain in college. After a time, she began to feel differently about school, because it was all books and no hands-on. She thought the studying was too hard and definitely too boring.

Cill decided she'd join the army and spent

four years trying to be all that she could be. Then she spent nine months in Kuwait. All the sand, one-hundred-plus-degree days in the sun, and lack of toilet facilities caused her to rethink her choices. She still wanted to be all that she could be — just not in Kuwait.

Six months after Cill had left the army, she returned home. She reconnected with Needy, and moved into a doublewide trailer next door. Somehow, she never noticed that she'd only traded Kuwait for Pelzer, because her trailer sat on a lot that seemed to have as much sand. During the summer, the humid temperatures were unbearable and she was in constant need of plumbing services. Sometimes she'd wished she was back in Kuwait.

Ten minutes passed and Petunia still had not come inside from trying to park her car, but it was enough time for Needy to prance back into her living room. She'd changed into a beige sleeveless housedress that covered her oversized blouse. She always wore something beige or in the beige family because she thought it complimented her muddy-brown skin. Her rather large legs and feet seemed an afterthought as they poked out from an even larger pair of khaki pants that didn't seem to fit the rest of her body. But that was her normal, indoor, warm weather wear.

With all eyes on her, Needy placed her hands on her wide hips and began to bark at the other women like a sergeant in Boot Camp. Normally, she wouldn't speak in such a manner but when it came to the singles meeting, she took on a different persona, and this time she wanted to insult Cill by imitating Cill's masculine manner.

"Okay, I know you've had enough time to poke your noses into whatever I've bought lately for my house as well as into my business. Let's get this meeting started properly because in about twenty minutes we're gonna bring this pitiful gathering to an end."

Her skin suddenly spouted prickly heat bumps brought forth by her rising anger. The other women looked on in horror, as Needy's dark eyes bulged while her bountiful bosoms heaved in and out like jaws on a puffer fish.

Needy pulled together the top button on her blouse when she saw Cill Lee pointing towards her.

"You might wanna handle those," Cill said, struggling to keep a straight face while pointing to Needy's escaping breasts.

Needy tried not to act embarrassed. Not only was the top of her blouse unbuttoned;

so were several buttons that appeared to zigzag from the uneven fastening. She was showing a lot more cleavage than the other women wanted to see.

"Stop gawking. Y'all should be ashamed of yourselves, you're just jealous of my two gifts," Needy laughed, nervously, and laid her hands on her chest. She suddenly forgot that a moment ago, she was barking orders at them.

When Needy was younger, the attention paid to her ample bosom often embarrassed her. She'd learned to cope by embracing them, because that's all she could do. According to Needy, her size 44DD breasts were a gift that more than made up for her lack of beauty. However, when she wasn't bragging about her double-D ammunition, secretly she'd complain about her stooped shoulders and constant lower-back pain.

Needy gathered her wits and continued in a kinder and more even tone. "Each of us, in our own minds, is the epitome of woman-hood. We're self-sufficient, with jobs and benefits. So, why is life still giving us the middle finger?" Without realizing it, Needy was ranting again. "Why does life sometimes seem to just toss us crumbs?"

The other women, all of them seasoned and unsuccessful manhunters, began to nudge one another, nodding in agreement.

They were physically different, yet they had one thing in common; armed with an arsenal of low self-esteem bullets and hair-trigger raging libidos, they were desperate, and extremely lethal.

They were also, with the exception of one, women with their biological clocks locked and set on "Right now, Lord."

Although Mother Bea Blister was the oldest spinster and should've received the most respect, she was often the crankiest.

When she'd responded to the group's open invitation to join, she'd said that she was in her late sixties or early seventies. This vagueness really depended upon her memory or whether she felt people were just being nosy. Unlike the others, Mother Blister didn't have a hormonal clock. She'd been on the prowl the longest, so she had a sundial.

With dementia slowly yet daily settling in, she sat motionless with a concerned look etched on her face while the others listened to Needy's rage. Without meaning to do it, she let her mind wander any place it chose to go. Her wandering mind finally settled on trying to figure out why and where she was.

Mother Blister, who for most of her adult

life had worked as a housekeeper for the rich and infamous, continued her mental trip through fantasyland while nestled in a corner. She sat hunched over looking like the letter C. She was sandwiched next to the wall clock, which was shaped like a black and white grinning cat; its obviously broken pendulum hung instead of swinging. On her other side hung an oversize calendar with a grinning Japanese woman pouring tea.

"Do you smell that men's cologne?" Cill grabbed Birdie's arm and asked, while pretending to sniff the air. "You know she sprayed it so that we'd think she had a man in her home. Any man that would wear that skunk smell, she can have," Cill said as she tightened her grip on Birdie's arm, causing the skin to redden as she laughed at her own joke.

"Ouch! You're hurting me," Birdie winced.

"Sorry," Cill whispered. "You're so skinny I thought I was holding on to a climbing rope." She laughed again.

"I'm sure any man that any of us gets is most appreciated," Birdie hissed, ignoring Cill's comment about her weight. At that moment it was more important to quickly extricate herself from Cill's unwanted and too familiar grip.

41

As usual, Birdie's observations about life were murky. Some folks laughed behind her back, whispering that she reminded them of the character Rose on the television show *The Golden Girls.* No one knew what to make of her kindness, generosity or naïveté.

Birdie was also the latest woman to join the singles after their open invitation. This was her second meeting. She was forty-two years old, clueless, and the only white woman in the group. She and Needy were old college friends. They'd met at college shortly after Cill had left to join the army.

Birdie and Needy were also co-workers at the Pinching Pennies Brokerage House.

Birdie stood at least six feet tall in her bare feet, and her body was as straight as an arrow. Although she had more money than the others, with the exception of Needy, and had a bachelor degree in business, Birdie didn't have a man, so they let her join.

Under different circumstances, the women were usually quite a vocal group. Yet today they continued to sit like a row of dominoes, stoic. Whenever Needy threw a rant their way, each looked back with their chins rising, nodding in agreement. As soon as she moved onto the next person, the last would drop her chin again. They looked like bobble-head dolls as she ranted on about the unfairness of life.

No one in the room would argue that Needy didn't have a reason to be angry. She'd recently celebrated her thirty-ninth birthday — alone — just as she had for the last fifteen years.

With the exception of Brother Lead Belly, no one called, including the regular yet annoying telemarketers.

Needy was angry when she'd answered and heard him wheezing instead of singing a verse of "Happy Birthday." In truth, she couldn't stand the short, box-shaped, chocolate-complexioned, middle-aged man with jowls so fat and long they look like bat wings hanging from both sides of his nose.

The feeling of abandonment left Needy in a lingering foul mood.

Get a grip, Needy, she thought as she inhaled to regroup before continuing. "Soon it will be August," she spoke softly as though she'd never raised her voice.

"We've only just begun our three-week vacations and so far nothing has changed. I'm so sick and tired of us meeting with no new or decent man sightings or dates to report," Needy whined, quickly abandoning her composure.

"Oh my goodness," she blurted out, suddenly grabbing the edge of the sofa. She was about to topple over from trying to be cool and collected and realized just how long it'd been since she'd had a date.

Again, Needy tried to play it off and avoided the looks from the other women by pushing away with a dramatic hand sweep a wandering hair-weave track that covered one eye. She knew it didn't work, because the women were looking on as though hypnotized, and she fought to take control of another escaping piece of hair that had come undone. She finally tossed it back over her ear as she swung her head back and forth like a pendulum.

"It's a shame," Needy droned on. "I don't know about y'all, but I can't even find a decent man anywhere that's fit to take out my trash, let alone me." Needy's head started to bob and weave again, like she was fighting something invisible and evil in the air. Her eyes suddenly narrowed as her voice rose almost to a shriek.

She continued with her hands still on her hips. "What's wrong with these men?" She asked the question without really expecting an answer. "When I used to act like trash I got taken out all the time."

"That's true. Everyone knows that a lot of men will take out a trashy woman, especially when she begs them to do it —" Cill yelled out from the foyer. She'd only heard part of what was said. She'd left for the bathroom as soon as Needy started her second rant, yet she felt the need to voice an opinion.

"You're right about that," another voice added with a little too much confidence. It was Petunia. She'd found a suitable spot and kept parking until it was her habitual twelve inches from the curb.

When did she get here? I didn't see her come in. Needy's eyes narrowed so Petunia wouldn't mistake her anger for anything more than what it was.

Petunia ignored Needy just as she had when she'd opened Needy's front door and let herself in without ringing the bell. Up to that moment, she'd sat quietly in the corner. Late or not, she still felt a need to put in her neurotic two cents.

"I've seen on more than one occasion how Needy and her trashy, trifling ways got her big butt kicked to the curb. It happened, mostly, after the first date." Petunia, too, had known Needy since childhood and always pushed her buttons. She did it because she knew she could get away with it but she truly loved Needy, in her own way.

Petunia looked Needy up and down, showing her pretend disdain, and then nodded towards the other women for emphasis.

Needy couldn't respond the way she wanted to because she didn't want to get blood on her rundown orange carpeting, and because she had bobbed her head in self-pity one time too many, and had come dangerously close to being stabbed in her eye by one strand of her stiff, gelled, artificially plum-colored hair.

"Yeah, you was definitely a bag of trash back in the day; first-class trash at that. And, you were certainly freaky-nasty too, but like you said, you did have a lot of dates."

Cill had reentered the room and continued down bad-memory lane. "The way I remember it, you even made a decent amount of change from a few of them dates."

Cill was on a roll; however, she suddenly stopped and threw a conspiring wink at Needy as she pretended to be only teasing.

When Needy didn't reach over and slap her silly, Cill boldly continued. "Of course, it was a good thing you were getting paid because I remember each time you got locked up for trying to sell *what yo' mama gave you,* you needed bail money."

Cill droned on like a bee with a bad lisp. "But back then you weren't saved or paying tithes to a church, so you were only doing what came natural to you."

The room got eerily quiet as if the other

women knew a volcano was about to erupt and didn't want to set it off quicker than necessary.

Cill was satisfied that she'd turned the spotlight off Needy so she turned and nodded towards the others, making sure she still had their attention. She had them by the hairs of their chinny-chin-chins. "Of course, I've known you since we were toddlers together," she said, quickly looking back at Needy before returning her attention to the others. "I remember your mama saying that, even back then she knew you were gonna be a sorry hussy, because you used to tear the slit in your diaper just a little bit higher than it should've been, just to show off more of your fat thighs."

None of the women remembered moving, yet there they were — all bunched together. They looked like an Oreo cookie with Birdie as the white creamy center.

Naïve as she was, Birdie magically produced a set of car keys and dangled them from her hand, ready to move out of harm's way if she needed to.

Needy's patience was about to snap. She was so mad she could've tossed a pot of hot grits at Cill, and pinned each searing grain into her. Instead, she dismissed the insults to her character when her wandering hair track fell forward, again. She quickly leaned over the arm of her chair and snatched a bobby pin from atop the tall black beehive hairdo of Petunia.

Petunia yelled as if she were singing an aria.

"Ouch!" Petunia winced, grabbing the side of her elongated head. Unfortunately, the bobby pin was the only thing holding together her short au-natural hair that peeked through a ratty, discounted, burgundy-colored weave.

"Dang girl! Do you mind?" Petunia snapped, leaping from her seat as if she'd sat on a pin. She snatched the precious bobby pin from Needy's hand before Needy could use it. "Everybody knows you got dandruff the size of cornflakes. So don't put nothing of mine in your hair and then try and give it back."

Petunia made her move just in time to pin up several tresses of her own coarse, un-naturally black hair that threatened to escape, split ends and all. Every bogus strand of that weave would've landed in her lap if she hadn't.

If there was ever a time that Needy was happy that she knew a little something about being a Christian this would be it. She mumbled a quick "Thank you, Lord" before she glared over at Petunia and thought, *she's a pain in the butt but I need someone around who is even more pathetic than I am.* Instead of turning the affront into more of a big deal, Needy decided to let the comment go. She still had bigger fish to fry.

While Needy gathered her thoughts to continue with her self-important oration, Mother Blister, who'd sat motionless and looking completely bored on one of Needy's matching, wobbly wooden chairs with one missing slat from the backrest, interrupted her.

"I'm bored. Let's get it started before my bladder kicks a mud hole in my behind." Mother Blister was always straight to the point. She'd tell anyone that she neither had money to spend on frivolous things nor unnecessary words.

"What did you say?" Petunia asked Mother Blister, thinking that perhaps she'd missed something, particularly since the meeting was almost over and she hadn't had a chance to start her usual drama.

Mother Blister tried to jump up. She couldn't because of her age, and that mud hole her bladder had started was kicking like a mule on uppers. "Needy, where's your bathroom?"

"It's in the same place it was when you

last said you needed to use it." Needy's voice dripped with agitation. Old or not, that elderly spinster was working her last nerve.

"You know you can lead a horse to a bucket of water but you still gotta show them where to pee," Birdie chimed in with a wide grin plastered on her pasty face. She'd finally found the nerve to join in but as usual all she got were questioning stares from the others. She ignored the obvious and continued, "It looks like Mother Blister is looking pretty intently at your geranium pot over there as though it might need watering." Birdie pointed and then leaned her head towards the flowerpot as though no one knew what she meant.

They didn't.

It took a lot of effort on her part, but Mother Blister finally got up. She claimed her poor posture and back pain was the result of osteoporosis.

Some folks who knew her from way back whispered it was from her years of bending over when she worked as a house cleaner or cleaning out houses. The facts depended on who was telling the tale.

Mother Bea Blister had at one time spent some quality time in minimum security prison for theft and swindling. That well-known fact gave credence to the rumors of her extra-curricular, illegal, income-making ventures, and that the back pain resulted from bending over and picking the locks of several prominent homes where she'd worked.

Of course, there were others that had the misfortune of crossing Mother Blister's path. They had another theory. They claimed that she was just Rosemary's baby all grown up.

No sooner had she stood than Mother Blister plopped back into her seat. "Aw, I feel so much better now." She smiled innocently before adding, "Please stop gawking. At my age, you have to go — when you have to go."

The problem was that she hadn't gone anywhere, so where was the pee?

While the others sat dumbstruck and sniffing the air for any tale-tell ammonia smells, Mother Blister dropped her head, which allowed one of her several fleshy chins to rest on her chest as she returned to her self-imposed state of denial.

As was her nature, no sooner had her head dropped than it rose again. She began fidgeting and was wide awake with renewed energy. She pulled a wrinkled, folded paper towel from one of her pockets. She opened it and after rechecking the gummy adhesive on her beige-colored dentures that lay uneven in her hands, Mother Blister replaced the dentures quickly in her mouth and then decided to toss in her two cents.

At her age, her opinion was worth about two cents and a ten-percent off coupon for a box of industrial-strength bladder control pads, but for now, it was all Mother Blister had to offer.

Mother Blister continued staring at the others as she suddenly blurted out, excitedly, "So what do y'all think of my idea?"

Of course, she hadn't given an idea but to avoid embarrassing her they all nodded and smiled. Everything would've been just fine and the meeting could've continued if Petunia hadn't decided to rock the boat.

"Would you please repeat your wonderful idea?"

"I don't feel like repeating anything," Mother Blister replied, harshly. Every word she spoke was cloaked with annoyance. "Let someone just read it from the minutes."

She fidgeted in her seat before continuing. "Y'all go ahead with the meeting. I've got to use the bathroom again."

Mother Blister never moved from her seat but soon, a look of satisfaction spread across her face before she let her head drop back onto her chest.

Like the others, Needy quickly began, again, sniffing the room for any signs of Mother Blister's real or imaginary watery *gift*. She didn't smell anything unusual so she decided to ignore the obvious. "Why don't we just go ahead and give any reports on dates, good or bad, since the last meeting," Needy humbly suggested.

It took all the little strength she possessed to act as if she was being considerate and had nothing better to do than to humor and respect their eldest member, especially since she suddenly began to hear a squishing sound every time Mother Blister moved around on her cushioned seat.

So while the other women chatted and bickered, Mother Blister just sat and daydreamed. However, unlike the lonely and desperate women lounging around Needy's small living room in various stages of hormonal decay, Mother Blister was the only one who really had a date waiting for her back at the Old Ben Gay Arms Assisted Living home. Even in her advanced years, she'd seen more action than a soldier with several tours of duty under his belt.

Every third weekend of the month Mother Blister and her long-time friend and undercover bed-buddy, seventy-year-old Slim

Pickens, got together for a little "show me and I won't tell anyone" inside the home's fully stocked medicine room. It was where they always tasted the fruit of their illicit rendezvous so just in case they needed medicine or medical equipment to revive each other, it was handy.

The only reason Mother Blister ever left the confines of her secure assisted-living home other than to attend church, a bingo game or the singles club meetings was to keep the other women from nosing into her business. She needed to make sure none of them had any designs on her man.

As far as Mother Blister was concerned, Slim may be old, even a little phobic, since he spent a great deal of time trying to snap his crusty arthritic fingers and click his false teeth for no good reason. And certainly Slim was also quite cranky when he didn't get his lunchtime prune-flavored applesauce cobbler, but he was still more man than the rest of the other women had.

With all the medications she took by mouth and otherwise, it was only fitting that delusions were one of the many side effects.

Mother Blister decided that she'd toyed with the women in the pathetic group long enough. She checked her watch and saw she still had about thirty minutes before she was to meet Slim. She and Slim met at least three times a month. With her memory becoming more and more faulty every day, she wasn't sure if today was the first time since last month or not. She wasn't taking chances, so she needed to make sure she had her strength. A nap was in order. She raised her head and then let it drop slowly, making her curly gray wig slide down onto her forehead.

"Have mercy," Cill mumbled and snickered, using her thumb to point towards Mother Blister.

"Don't be so mean," Birdie rebuked her again. "She's old and we ought to respect the old. We may one day become retarded, too." Somehow, she always managed to reprimand and confuse, all in the same sentence.

"For you, someday is today," Cill hissed under her breath. She was too through with Birdie. *If Birdie weren't a white woman with money, I'd have voted her out as soon as she joined,* Cill thought.

For the next few moments, Needy continued to bark orders. Birdie tried to sound sympathetic to Mother Blister's faulty state of mind, Cill sulked and Petunia whined about not being able to find her bra size.

Ten minutes later when Mother Blister

awoke from her power nap, the women were still going at it, and they still hadn't discussed any of their dates, real or imagined.

Mother Blister's patience was growing shorter than a flea's facial hair. There didn't seem to be an end or an answer forthcoming to the women's plight. With one dark leathery hand sporting long veins forming the shape of a road map, and age spots resembling routes, exits and all, Mother Blister pulled back her tatty wig. She fumbled around and picked up the Bible beside her that lay open to the "Song of Solomon," resting with her other hand on the end table. She could tell that it was a passage that Needy must've read often because the ink was faded, the page folded repeatedly, and the verses highlighted while the rest of the Bible looked brand new.

Mother Blister grinned as she remembered the essence of the erotic verses before she hurriedly closed the Bible. She didn't want to let the words of love go, so she hugged the Bible tightly to her sagging breasts as if to bring heaven a little closer.

Mother Blister's pink rubbery gums supporting her dentures looked like two thick pieces of hard Bazooka bubblegum, laying one atop the other as she smiled and nodded, "I agree with Needy. I want to hear about your dates; if you've had any." She squinted over her bifocals and pointed around the room. "I'm hoping that some-body in this room had a chance to be with a man lately —"

Needy interrupted Mother Blister that time, not caring that the woman was the senior member. Needy needed to regain control of the meeting so she added impatiently, "In addition to relating or lying about your dates, please for once let's not give the man's last name. We don't need another fight like the one at the last meeting when Petunia and Gracie Charles thought that they were going after the same man."

"I agree," Cill butted in. "Y'all know it's a shame that it wasn't until Gracie was released from the emergency room that we found out that she and Petunia were actually chasing father and son." Cill sat back proudly and pointed at Needy. "I'm sorry. You were about to get somewhere with this sordid trip down memory lane."

Needy's muddy brown skin was beginning to turn beet red but she was also determined to show a little decorum and not sink to Cill's level. "Now, let's get down to it," she said with her lips curling, "because our common denominator is the *we still need a man* factor."

After all, it was Needy's house and until things changed, she was the man of it.

While Needy began to recount the several imaginary encounters she would've had with men she'd never met, which was unnecessary because none of them had a man, Birdie found herself looking over at Petunia.

As physically challenged as Petunia might've looked at thirty-six, Birdie wasn't much better at the age of forty-two, with just a little more meat on her bones.

Birdie suddenly started feeling uneasy. A twinge of jealousy was invading her spirit, and she wasn't comfortable about it. She sat farther back in her chair and started to sulk when she realized why. She was afraid that Petunia might get a real date before she did.

Petunia wasn't aware of Birdie's discomfort as she rolled her eyes and sucked her teeth at Needy. She held up one skinny palm so Needy could talk to it, instead. With her position silently stated, Petunia wiggled in her seat, eager to start the lying fest. Looking like a nervous and anemic worm on a hook, she was so busy trying to be dramatic that she didn't see Birdie jump from her seat, trying to be the first one to set it off.

Birdie shuffled her feet from side to side, ready to deliver her news. "While Petunia is getting her act together, I've got something to tell."

Knowing that she had all eyes upon her, Birdie took time to flick away an invisible piece of lint from her green couture dress. She wanted to give the other women a chance to envy her new matching green Manolo Blahnik shoes. Which was something she'd never have done before joining this very vocal group.

The way the other women, including Needy, smiled and gave appreciative nods towards Birdie now angered Petunia. *No, this heifer did not dismiss me,* Petunia thought, as her eyes narrowed into two slits. Evil thoughts of what she'd like to do to Birdie weighed heavy on Petunia, causing her to sink lower in her seat. She sank until she almost disappeared into the cushions. Any farther and she'd have looked like a needle stuck in a pincushion.

Making sure she had everyone's full attention, Birdie's voice took on a phony seductive tone as she spoke her words, hushed and raspy. "It was simply amazing —"

"Say what!" Cill blurted, her words tinged with a taste of jealousy. She'd decided that just a nod of acknowledgment would not do. "Please don't play with us." She leaned forward while twirling a stubborn chin hair. "How did that happen? Are there any other details?"

The room was quiet as everyone leaned forward. Birdie thought they were about to hang on her every word but the other women's attention was really captured by Cill's unyielding chin hair that she twirled like a baton.

No one was ever sure if that was the only chin hair Cill had, or just a hair that she'd missed while shaving. But then again, the women were never sure exactly why she attended the singles ministry meeting since she looked like she loved being a switch-hitter in the game of life and a good one at that.

"Well, until he recently contacted me, it was about two years ago since I'd seen him," Birdie said slowly as she watched the other women's attention return from Cill's stubborn chin hair back to her. "I'd gone to the prison —"

"You mean to tell us that you got a date and a marriage possibility while up there at the prison?" Petunia interrupted. Thinking there was more drama coming, she was giving Birdie her full attention. She could hardly contain her excitement as she thought, *Imagine, meeting a man working in the prison? Why didn't I think about going to prison?*

"Anyway, like I was saying," Birdie continued with a little annoyance in her voice as she tossed her long brunette hair over her shoulders with an exaggerated head shake, "it was while I was talking to one of the guards and he was commenting on how nice my outfit was —"

"Now, ain't God good? You wore something decent for once and you were rewarded by meeting a nice man with a job," Mother Blister quipped, cutting Birdie off as she stood to answer the nonstop urge from a non-cooperating bladder. By the time she realized it wasn't sweat dripping between her legs she really needed to go. All those false alarms finally caught up with her. She was rushing out of the room so fast she looked like a speeding shadow.

Before Birdie could reply, Needy quickly picked up where Mother Blister left off. "You sure are blessed. You went up to that prison — no doubt to do some prison ministry — and as a reward you got a date two years later with a guard with job benefits. Do you know what that means?"

"If she doesn't know then I certainly do,"

Cill answered for Birdie. "That means that Birdie gonna be able to use some of those benefits when she marries that guard. She can get gold crowns placed on her teeth so that she'll look like she belongs. And, of course, that will take care of that halitosis she got."

Cill was proud of herself for taking the opportunity to throw that mention of bad breath into the mix. She could tell by the sneaky grins on the other women's faces that she'd said what they'd been thinking.

At the mention of her having bad breath Birdie cupped her hands to her mouth and blew into them. She was stunned. No one had ever mentioned that she had bad breath. When people leaned away from her, she always felt it was because her essence was so overpowering and folks wanted to give her space. Now she knew, and the foul-odor truth was trapped in her hands, floating up her nostrils and momentarily making her dizzy. She clutched the end of the bookcase for balance and continued speaking with one hand covering her mouth as if she suddenly had a toothache.

"That's not exactly what happened," Birdie murmured into the palm of her hand. She didn't want to take a chance of speaking too loudly and having more of her bad breath escape.

Mumbled or mangled, the words were clear to the others as the sudden, revised revelation spread around the room. In an instant, the women stopped their chatting and envying.

"If that's 'not exactly what happened,' " Cill asked as she slowly stood, "then what 'exactly' did? And you can remove your hand so we can hear you clearly. You can't help your medical condition. Check out Mother Blister," Cill continued. "Her breath can stop a Mack truck."

Cill wanted to know the real story, so she decided to sacrifice Mother Blister's reputation since the old woman had finally gone to the bathroom and couldn't defend herself. "Go ahead and tell us what really happened."

Birdie wasn't sure if she believed Cill's sudden interest and particularly the part about Mother Blister since she'd never smelled the old woman's breath. But then again, she hadn't smelled her own either. With her dignity hanging by a thread, Birdie continued explaining.

"Like I said, I was talking with one of the guards." Birdie stopped. She was momentarily distracted by Mother Blister reentering the room and sitting down. "As I was saying, the guard only mentioned my outfit once as he wrote out my visitation pass. No doubt he knew class when he saw it."

"We already know you went there to visit. So if you didn't get a date with the guard, who was it?" Needy asked with a touch of agitation in her voice as she dismissed Birdie's mention of *class*.

"It's not that I couldn't have had a date with a guard; but it was with a guy that was being processed for release," Birdie replied almost apologetically. She let her head drop in shame.

"Say that again," Petunia said, rising like a stalk of wheat from her seat. "You got us all riled up and hopeful and your date was with a man that was just getting out of jail?"

"It wasn't exactly that simple —" Birdie hesitated before going on.

It was starting to get ugly as if ugly wasn't already present in the room.

"I didn't know at that moment that he was a guest of the state."

"I betcha they didn't treat him like a guest," Cill snickered.

Birdie let that remark slide. She needed to hurry and finish telling her side of the story. "It was while he was waiting for his papers to leave, and I was waiting for mine to go in, that we started talking. He seemed so nice. All the guards that passed by seemed to know him and they called him by his first name. I didn't find out until many months later that at that time he was being released from prison. On that day, we just never talked about it."

"You've got to be joking," Cill said as she slumped back in her seat. "What in the world were you thinking?"

Birdie's face reddened as she tried to explain. "At the time, with him being so popular, I figured he just came up there a lot."

"You mean came *in* there a lot," Needy snickered while getting high fives from Cill and Petunia.

It was like watching a speeding car wreck waiting for Birdie to finish. There would be casualties but it would have to wait for the story to end.

Birdie ignored Needy and continued. "Anyway, after about ten minutes of sweet conversation that day, we exchanged telephone numbers. And, he also gave me a snapshot. I'll show it to you —"

"A snapshot or a mug shot?" Mother Blister interrupted. She had returned around the time Birdie mentioned something about a man in prison.

It was only about the second time that

Mother Blister had bothered to interrupt because Birdie's story was too familiar and she wanted to see how much so.

While the others snickered and nudged one another Mother Blister leaned forward in her seat to hear better. Although the clicking sound made by her false teeth distorted some of Birdie's words, she listened anyway. Mother Blister only mildly began to feel sorry for Birdie's apparent predicament. She wasn't sure if Birdie would know the difference between DeCon or an ex-con.

"I think I have it right here in my pocketbook," Birdie said, rumbling through her purse still searching for the questionable photo and, hopefully, a Tic-Tac.

"Don't feel bad honey," Petunia said, "I had one of those experiences too. I even went so far as to accept some collect calls from a fella in prison. He sent my phone bill up so high I thought I'd have to use a carrier pigeon to keep in touch with folks."

"Been there and done that," Cill added.

Needy was the first one to ask Cill what the others were suddenly thinking. "You had a man in prison, too?"

"Girl, please. No way. I was talking about having a high telephone bill," Cill said, laughing so hard her chin hair was starting to wiggle. Her laughter seemed to lighten the tension that was starting to build.

"Here it is!" Birdie said, excitedly. It wasn't just because she'd found the photo, it was also because she'd found an old dinner mint. She quickly popped the mint in her mouth and continued.

"It will be difficult to see his entire body because it's only a side-view shot of him from the waist up. Although it's his left side, you can believe he is a fine-looking man." Birdie used the photo as a fan to show just how hot she thought the man was before handing it to Needy.

Needy's reaction was hard to read. Her jaw fixed, she looked at the picture of a young, honey-complexioned man with jet-black wavy hair. He looked to be somewhere in his late thirties. She studied the photo long and hard before she finally spoke. "Birdie, dear. I know this is only a side view but why does his eye look so teary?"

"Oh, I ain't no ordinary fool. I asked him the same thing. He said he'd had some drops put in his eyes because they were dry," Birdie replied, impatiently.

It looks more like he'd had drops of liquor. This man looks high, Needy thought before continuing. "Birdie, dear. What is he being measured for? There are height measurement lines on the wall behind him."

"I asked him about that too," Birdie replied in a huff. What had started out to be a brag session was quickly turning into an inquisition. "He said he took the picture in a doctor's office. He said the doctor's office was really small so instead of a scale with a height pole on it the lines were drawn on the wall."

"Birdie, dear," Needy asked, slowly that time. "These numbers along the bottom of this photo, I guess they are his medical identification information?"

"In fact, Needy, that's exactly what it is." It dawned upon her that the others might start to think that she wasn't hip so she quickly added, "Well you know I'm quite sharp. Like I said before, I ain't no fool so I asked him about those numbers on the bottom of the photo, too." Birdie was quite pleased with herself. Apparently, she'd asked all the right questions.

"And why is the last name smudged off?" Needy asked. She ignored Birdie's last enthusiastic response. "I can still read the first name. It looks like his name is Lyon," Needy added while holding the picture at an angle to see it better.

"Oh that. I asked about that too because I wanted to know his last name."

While Needy and Birdie carried on with their foolish question and response routine, the other women looked on, totally captivated by what was happening.

"So, what did he say? How did he explain it?" Needy asked, slowly. Suspicion was riding her like a jockey with his butt glued to the saddle trying to sprint in the mud. Each step, like each question, was getting dirtier and harder.

"He said that they had misspelled his last name so rather than leave it that way, he decided to erase it." Birdie was starting to get an eerie feeling like perhaps they thought she wasn't telling the truth. "But, he did tell me his last name," she offered.

"Really," Needy pushed. "Care to share it?"

"L.I.P.P.S." Birdie recited each letter slowly. "His last name is Lipps."

"Lyon Lipps? Is that his name?" Needy asked while still studying the photo. She was about to ask another question when the quiet in the room was suddenly disturbed by the sound of rustling and scurrying. She looked up just in time to catch Cill, Petunia and even Mother Blister rambling through their purses and pockets, as if their very lives depended upon it.

"Got it!" Petunia yelled out ahead of the

others. She'd pulled out a frayed Polaroid picture and within seconds both Cill and Petunia had joined Birdie with their own photos in hand.

"Hold up," Mother Blister pleaded and continued searching through her bag. "Give me a moment."

"No time to wait," Petunia cried out as she held her other hand out towards Needy. "Let me see that picture, please."

Needy looked at Birdie, who gave her a nod of permission.

"I want to see it too," Cill chimed in.

"It had better not be that same fellow that tried to scam me about two years ago," Mother Blister snapped under her breath while still searching. "I can still see that sunburned, greasy-looking, wavy haired . . ." Her voice trailed off as she continued her search through her messy pocketbook.

"That shameless son of a monkey who tried to rip me off had pitch-black wavy hair," Petunia said, shaking with anger while still waiting for Needy to hand her the other photo. She was anxious to confirm her suspicions.

"The one that sent my sister Jessie and her credit sky-high and off into outer mental space was a Creole-looking piece of —" Cill stopped short of cussing. She'd prayed hard to be delivered from a foul mouth but it didn't mean that at that moment she wouldn't feel better letting out a few choice words. However, it was the pained look on Petunia's face that had her momentarily unnerved, and saved her from an unscheduled trip to the altar for forgiveness for that particular sin. "What's wrong, Petunia?" Cill asked, this time with real concern.

"It's just that your sister's scallywag of a man sounded just like that piece of honey-complexioned garbage that sent me free-falling into Chapter 11," Petunia said as she glanced down at the worn photo in her hand. She'd rubbed the picture so much until the ink was one layer away from being a smudge. Needy needed to hurry and hand her that other photo before she exploded.

Not one to waste a moment, Petunia's face suddenly reddened. It was a clear sign that time was up and she was out of control. She suddenly snatched the bobby pin that held her weave intact and started stabbing the photo in her hand as she yelled, "That man got my credit so messed up until I have a hard time getting the stores to even accept my coins."

None of the women had ever seen Petunia explode and it wasn't pretty, particularly when her weave started flying off its track, again, from the lack of bobby pin support.

The women never claimed to be rocket scientists but they didn't need to be to connect these dots. Lightbulbs started going off under wigs and weaves like candy Pez's from a Pez dispenser.

Cill reached over and snatched the photo from Needy's hand, which still seemed frozen in time. Heated anger shot from Cill's body, colliding with the anger of the other women, causing another explosion in Needy's living room.

"That reprobate!" Cill shouted after snatching the photo. It wasn't a clear picture of his face, but it was enough for her. "If I ever get my hands on this slime-ball, I'll pull out every hair on his body, one by one, with a rusty pair of tweezers."

Cill's chest heaved as she held up the photo for the other women to see. "Why would any woman let this piece of jackal flesh touch them?"

Birdie wanted to be the first one to explain Lyon's allure but the silence and awe of the other women at Cill's ridiculous question silenced her. The sight of Cill ripping the photo to shreds kept her quiet.

"What the ham and cheese!" Mother Blister finally added, after remembering why she'd gotten involved with Lyon Lipps. She wanted to cuss, too, but decided that the others knew that already. It took her a moment but she finally caught on to the full magnitude of the situation.

"I can't believe I've been such a fool," Birdie whined as she lowered her head in shame. She'd really been looking forward to the date. "I didn't mind that he'd done time, I could've forgiven him about leaving that bit of information out. But I'll be doggone if I'll be happy about him serving time and serving all of you."

Birdie's hair started fanning as she pounded Needy's thrift-shop coffee table until it almost splintered.

"Well, what are we gonna do about it?" Petunia asked. She didn't care if her weave totally derailed. She was out for blood.

"I still have the telephone number he gave me. And I know the number is good because he and I are supposed to get together soon," Birdie said as she massaged her aching fists.

"Soon, you are seeing him soon?" Needy echoed while visions of whacking off the man's heads, both of them, top and bottom, danced in her head.

Needy went over to the corner of her living room and lifted a telephone book from a shelf and started thumbing through the smudged pages so fast her fingers looked like wings on a hummingbird. She'd never met the man, Lyon Lipps, but she didn't need to do that to issue a little payback.

"What are you doing? Why are you rifling through a telephone book at a time like this?" Cill asked, suspiciously. "We got a situation that needs fixing."

"Back in my day" — Mother Blister hissed and wobbled while pounding the side of her stool, which made the hanging skin under her upper arms flap so hard they sounded like a helicopter taking off — "we'd send his trifling butt straight to hell and then have a party to celebrate." She stopped abruptly and furthered her point by pointing one of her fingers downward.

As Mother Blister moved, her sagging breasts fell forward, releasing a fluffy piece of cotton that suddenly floated out. She'd been looking for it earlier that morning when she'd dusted her body's nooks and crannies with talcum powder. The sight of the free-falling cotton suddenly seemed more interesting, outweighing any embarrassment she should've felt, and she lost her train of thought, again.

"I second that motion," Petunia said before adding, "I say throw a pot of hot grits on him and a pail of glue to make sure it sticks!" She'd forgotten how vicious she could be, and the feeling of revenge made her feel good and important.

"How about we just catch him in a back alley and we'll each use a bag of marbles to crack his bones? I say we clock that sucker from his tooter to his rooter. We can say that he fell or tripped, if anyone walks in on us," Cill chimed in. She became animated to the point of pulling her stubborn strand of chin hair straight. If she hadn't looked over at Birdie with concern, she might've yanked it completely out, which would've made her look less masculine.

"Birdie, are you okay?" Cill asked. "Don't be ashamed. We've all been made a fool of by that mangy piece of masculinity." She stopped to amend her declaration. "What I meant was that all of you have been made a fool of by that lying Lyon."

"What do you mean? That dude has never made a fool of me," Needy barked as she continued to thumb through the pages of the telephone book. She'd recovered just in time to retain her phantom reputation as a classy lady. "I don't even know him, so get your facts straight. After all, y'all still carrying around your torn and smudged photos, so he must've either set your sails a-flapping or all of you are just gluttons for punishment."

Of course, Needy failed to mention that perhaps not that particular man had made a fool of her, but rather there were others who had.

"I'm sorry. You're right. I guess you and me are the only ones untouched by masculine deceit," Cill replied.

Needy ignored Cill's apology and reference to her lack of sexual activity as she stopped thumbing through the pages she'd taken from Mother Blister's hands and cried out, "Okay. I think we should take Mother Blister's suggestion and send that supposed lover boy to hell. And I've found the perfect way to do it."

The meeting had taken a sudden strange and dangerous turn. They were riding high from the drama. The smell of a jive-talking, lying man's blood became their driving force.

Needy had their attention. Even Mother Blister stopped concentrating on the piece of cotton to raise her head and show an interest.

"How are we going to send him to hell?" Petunia asked. She leaned forward in her seat, which made her look like a leaning banana stuck into a pincushion.

"And what's your definition of hell?" Cill asked. She was in the mood to pay Lyon

Lipps back for what he'd done to her sister, Jessie, her friends and to the whole human race.

"What's with the telephone book?" Birdie asked as her pride and courage slowly began to return. "You ain't trying to hire a hit man, are you?" From the looks on the other women's faces, she wouldn't be surprised if they wanted to do just that and of course, make her pay for it.

"Of course not," Needy snapped. "Why kill him quickly when we could make him suffer slowly? I said let's send him to hell, not to the grave. I ain't trying to do jail time."

"It ain't all that bad." Cill had spoke out before she thought. "I mean, that's what I've heard."

"Well, it made me the woman I am today," Mother Blister said proudly. "Don't nobody wanna mess with me." Her voice trailed as she took another peek at the Polaroid that lay with its sides bent, secreted in the palm of her hand. She didn't want to tell the others that she'd found the photo she sought. She was almost certain that it was that same Lyon Lipps that had sweet-talked her out of three months of her pension. At the time it happened, she felt it was payback because she'd stepped out on Slim with a much-too-younger man.

"I thought nobody messed with you because you were old and you had God on your side," Birdie said, interrupting Mother Blister's sudden silence. She'd never heard Mother Blister get so riled up.

"It is because I'm old and I have God on my side that demons, spiritual and human, will try," Mother Blister answered and balled her wrinkled fists. "Who do you think gives me the strength to knock somebody out if they mess with me?" She didn't wait for an answer. Instead she concentrated on the cotton ball that lay at her feet as she eased the frayed photo back into her pocketbook. She didn't know why she'd continued to keep it. It was barely recognizable.

"Can we please get back to my plan?" Needy shouted. Her patience was about as thin as a piece of thread. "Think about it. If we want someone to wish they'd never been born, and to be left without a shred of dignity as they drown in payback hell, what should we do?"

A smile started to spread across Needy's face as she saw the looks of understanding come forth, one by one, from the other women's faces with the exception of Birdie. "Who do we know who is so cold-hearted that when she walks into a room the furnace kicks on automatically?"

"You wouldn't," Cill said without much conviction, as a wide grin appeared on her face.

"I wanted that Lyon Lipps to suffer, but do we have to go that far?" Petunia asked as she started to chuckle.

"Come on now, Needy. What that man did wasn't all *that* bad to put him in that situation, was it?" Mother Blister had reached down and grabbed the cotton ball from the floor. She smashed it repeatedly in her hand as she started to giggle as her memory and some sanity returned. "Have mercy."

"I don't know if I want any part of this," Birdie said as she nervously rubbed her hands together. "I don't know if we, as praying women, should be involved in something that's evil. After all, vengeance does belong to the Lord."

"Well, I tell you what. When it's all over we'll pray for forgiveness," Needy replied without conviction. "We'll just make four reservations at the altar. After all, God knows our hearts, and He knows that we're just weak sometimes."

"Aren't you talking about premeditated sin?" Petunia asked as her smile started to fade.

"Connect the dots, Petunia," Needy said,

79

exasperated. "If it wasn't planned or pre-meditated, would we need to make reservations at the altar for forgiveness?"

"Well, I don't know about the rest of you but I haven't used up my seventy-times-seventy quota yet. So, I guess I'm down with the plan." Petunia went back to grinning; this time with a smile that threatened to split her face.

"Anybody that wants to back out should leave, now." Needy looked at each of the others. Not one foot moved. The look on Needy's face went up a notch past diabolical as she folded her arms over her double-D arsenal and continued. "So the plan to destroy Lyon Lipps is a go."

Even the temperature in the room seem to rise as it finally set in that they were about to go where most women will when disrespected by a man.

"Simply destroying him ain't good enough for me, but if it's all we got then it will have to do," Petunia replied as the other women nodded in agreement.

"Good." Needy put down the telephone book and reached for the phone. She started pushing the buttons. "You know once we start this there'll be no turning back." She let one chubby finger rest in the air for a moment before letting it slowly come down to push the last button.

"I don't care. Let's just do it! I don't know what the plan is but I'm in," Birdie said. "Let's get it started so I can go home and anticipate the final date with Mr. Lyon Lipps."

Suddenly, the old broken clock in the corner started to vibrate instead of chime. The entire room took on an atmosphere of urgency as Needy finished dialing. Several flies dashed themselves against half-opened windowpanes as they tried to escape as if they, too, preferred to die than buzz around those lethal women.

"Ooh, he's gonna get it!" Petunia whispered to no one in particular as she twisted her skinny hands into the shape of a pretzel.

"Shush. It's ringing . . . Hello. May I speak to Sister Ima Hellraiser please, if she can receive phone calls?"

A few seconds later Needy turned towards the other women as she cupped the telephone receiver. "We're in luck. She made bail but she hasn't left the precinct yet, so she's available. When I hang up we're gonna have to hold hands to pray and thank the Lord for helping her to get out."

"You know that woman has her own private suite at the jailhouse," Cill whispered to the others. "She's a regular there."

Needy raised her finger again for silence as she spoke.

"How are you doing, Sister Hellraiser? . . . That's wonderful. I'm glad you're going home. How much probation time did you get, this time? . . . A year? That's not too bad. Anyway, listen. I have a problem. It's a man problem . . . Can we come over in about an hour? . . . That's great . . . Of course, I know the address."

Needy winked and raised one thumb as a sign of success to the other women. "By the way, do you now take credit cards for your services? No. It's not my credit card." Any other time she'd have been insulted but she'd taken this one on the chin. "It belongs to Sister Birdie Tweet — she's that new white woman in our group."

Needy gave the women the "okay" sign instead of giving Ima specifics over the precincts telephone. She hung up. Apparently, everyone knew that Ima Hellraiser always thought that a white woman's ice was always colder than a black woman's.

That reprobate Lyon Lipps didn't know it but he was in for the fight of his life. Ima Hellraiser, the gorgeous and only daughter of the infamous Sister Areel Hellraiser, and the niece of the infamous Mother Sasha Pray Onn, was one of ole Satan's prizefighters and her record was still 100 to 0. She was so dangerous that it usually took an act of Congress and a huge monetary deposit just to get permission for her to visit another country.

If the women of the Oh Lawd, Why Am I Still Single Singles Club had never been on a manhunt before, they were now.

3

After Needy finished her conversation with Sister Hellraiser, she replaced the telephone in its cradle, seemingly in slow motion. Like a queen with well-trained servants, she relished the attention from the others. The silence was thick in her living room, making time stand still.

"Okay, the deal — as well as that Lyon's behind — is sealed." Needy's smile started slowly. No one knew how hard she tried to contain her enthusiasm.

"We need to stand and hold hands," Needy continued. "Let's ask the Lord to bless our plans."

"That's a good idea. It's always good to have the Lord on your side when you getting ready to dish out a righteous retribution," Mother Blister said as she struggled to stand. "I also think we need to thank the Lord for Birdie. After all, we ain't got the money to hire a hit man, and she does."

Birdie wasn't quite as sure as the others if her financial contribution to the plan would be looked upon favorably on Judgment Day, but she didn't want to discourage her new-found home girls. She decided to seek God's counsel on her own, later.

Cill thought they were taking too long to get heaven on the line so she started dialing by cutting to the chase.

"Heavenly Father who art the bright and morning star, we're calling on you. We need you to give us the strength to dismember a man who has done harm to your faithful women . . ."

Petunia became caught up in the fervor of the prayer. Her head started bobbing side to side with enthusiasm as she held on to Birdie's hand tight enough to cut off its circulation.

Birdie struggled to extricate herself from Petunia's grip. She thought Cill had gone too far in asking God to step aside and let them do His work. She didn't want to be counted among the number when God started slaying them in Needy's living room, one by one.

". . . And if you do these things," Cill implored, "Lord, we promise to give you the honor and most of the glory, amen."

When Cill proudly lifted her head, thinking she'd prayed better than a bishop at a revival service had, she discovered that the others had taken a few steps back, virtually leaving her standing alone.

"It was a good thing that y'all stepped back. I was in the presence of the Lord, and it was just Him and me while I prayed." She was quite pleased and at that very moment, she decided that praying for retribution was her calling and purpose.

The complacent look upon Cill's face spurred Needy to bring the meeting to a complete halt. "Well, we certainly don't need to add to Cill's prayer."

"You can say that again," Petunia quipped as she rushed to gather her pocketbook and other belongings. She thought Cill was being selfish in only offering to give God *most* of the glory.

"I, personally, don't want God to even know I was here when you called on Him," Mother Blister added as she dragged her stiff hips towards the front door. She turned towards Cill, pointing directly at her. "You've really lost your mind."

"I'm not crazy. Doesn't the Word say that we need to come boldly to the throne of Grace?" Cill said without a hint of remorse.

It was the first time they'd actually seen any sign of weakness from Cill.

86

"Boldly, yes, but He certainly didn't tell you to come before Him acting crazy," Petunia shouted as she slammed Needy's door hard enough to make the screen door rattle.

Cill almost knocked Mother Blister down, causing her belongings to spill from her hand, as she raced past her to catch up with Petunia. There wasn't a doubt on any of their minds that Cill was rushing to lay hands on Petunia and it would be Petunia calling on the Lord.

Mother Blister seemed dazed as she gathered her things.

"I'll need to call a cab," Mother Blister told Needy. "I'm not riding in the same car with those two nut cases."

"Don't worry, Mother Blister," Birdie cut in. "I'll call a cab for you and pay for it, too."

Instead of acting grateful, Mother Blister became even more annoyed. "You should pay for it," she barked. "This is all your fault, Birdie."

"How is it her fault?" Needy asked. She was genuinely surprised at Mother Blister's ungratefulness.

"If that woman," Mother Blistered yelled while pointing at Birdie, "knew the difference between a duck and a swan, we wouldn't be swimming in this cesspool . . ." She stopped yelling and adjusted her wig, thinking she'd completed the sentence and made her point.

Both Needy and Birdie looked at Mother Blister with their mouths gaped. They were shocked.

The taxi couldn't arrive fast enough for Needy and Birdie. Mother Blister had spent the past ten minutes ranting and raving in half-sentences. One minute she'd call them idiots and the next minute ask Birdie for money to tip the driver. Needy almost broke out in applause when she finally left.

With all the women except Birdie gone, Needy retreated to her bedroom to change her clothes, leaving Birdie alone with her thoughts.

So now, this is what it's like to be like one of the sistahs, Birdie thought. She exaggerated pronouncing the word *sister* while trying to calm down after Mother Blister's unwarranted tirade. *I can see where it could be a very expensive relationship.* She laughed softly to herself more out of disappointment about the lack of solidarity, than happiness. Whatever the price, she'd pay it.

In truth, Birdie would've hocked her mother's lung machine to get back at Lyon Lipps.

It didn't matter to Birdie that, unlike the other women in the group, Lyon Lipps had yet to take full advantage of her and that it had been two years since they'd laid eyes upon each other. He was still going to pay for all the other men who had broken her heart. And, besides, now she had help. The other women from the singles group would see to it that she got her money's worth. She was going to rip a page out of the Sistahs' Revenge Handbook and use it until the ink wore off the page.

"If you want something to drink just help yourself," Needy shouted from the bedroom, interrupting Birdie's thoughts. "I'll be out in a moment. I just need to wear something appropriate for our visit to Sister Hellraiser's house."

"Why do you need something special to wear?" Birdie shouted back as she started towards Needy's kitchen for a glass of cold water.

"I forgot. You've never met Ima Hellraiser. Do you own a bullet-proof vest and a cross?" Needy asked with a nervous laugh. Her words were starting to fade as she struggled to get into a nylon slip that kept clinging to the perspiration on her body, brought on by her fight to get it over her wide hips.

Birdie wasn't quite sure she'd heard Needy correctly so she just answered, "Yes. I do have a cross and whatever else is needed." She wondered why she needed protection from a church sister. The humidity in the house quickly nudged away any further thoughts of concern as she held down the lever on the refrigerator's ice dispenser, allowing small chips of ice to fill her tall glass completely, then she added water. The taste of the refreshingly cold liquid quickly erased her need to ask any more questions.

"Are you going to be much longer?" Birdie shouted as she made her way through the cluttered hallway and back into the living room. Her costly blouse felt clammy and the water offered no relief. *I wonder if Needy would be offended if I bought her a new air conditioner as a pre-Christmas gift while this weather is still hot. I'm about to melt.*

Birdie chuckled as the liquid raced down her throat. She remembered that she hadn't sweated this much since she'd tried to dance the Macarena at an all-black after-hours club back home in California. It was before she'd joined any church.

This heat is affecting my mind. She'd almost forgotten about that fiasco. Earlier, on the dance floor trying to do the Electric Slide, she'd already stepped on toes and turned in the wrong direction. Birdie learned quickly that black folks could get downright nasty when someone messed up the Electric Slide. She recalled that when she'd felt brave enough to return to the floor to dance the Butterfly, she'd ended up with bruised knees from trying too hard. She'd worked her knees like they were wings.

On her third attempt at blending into the sea of black faces Birdie accidentally slapped a young woman when she tried to coordinate her Macarena arm movement. The woman, whose complexion was so pale she looked like she spent all her time inside the dark club, quickly placed her hand on the bright red spot where Birdie had decked her on the cheek. The woman inched slowly closer to Birdie while the sea of black faces parted.

With the crowd chanting over the loud music, "Fight, fight," the perspiration of fear poured from Birdie like she'd been shot with buckshot. She wanted to die before the woman killed her. Still caressing her bruised cheek, the woman leaned over and hissed in Birdie's ear, "Take your no-dancing behind off this dance floor before I mop it with you —"

Birdie didn't realize that if that woman

could've fought she would've fought. She sold Birdie a wolf-ticket at a discount and Birdie bought it.

"I'm so sorry." Birdie's halting apology cut the woman off as the smell of alcohol and cheap cigarettes accompanied the woman's whisper.

"The only reason I don't return the slap is because *I'm* white, too. You can't dance and you're messing it up for us."

Us. Birdie thought. *What us?* She'd been to that club a few times before, enjoying the sounds, the smells and the company of blackness. Had she been too absorbed to notice other whites? She strained her eyes and suddenly saw, even with the low lights, pale faces sprinkled in among the other dancers. Each of the pale faces squinted their eyes and gave a quick head nod towards the door to tell Birdie all she needed to know. She almost slipped in her own puddle of sweat as she dashed out of the club without as much as a goodbye to anyone.

This didn't stop her from going to after-hours clubs in the Compton area, it only made her determined to learn the Macarena. It was shortly after that awful experience that she'd found God to be more important to her, but every now and then she still felt the urge to do the Macarena; sometimes even as she shouted in church.

"Just give me a few more minutes. It's so hot everything I put on is clinging." The high-pitched voice coming from Needy's bedroom suddenly interrupted Birdie's bad memories, replacing them with a smile.

What you really mean is that you're so big and that's why everything you try to put on is clinging. Squirts of water spurted from Birdie's mouth as she laughed at her observation, which she'd never make to Needy's face. "Not a problem," Birdie replied. "I'll just make myself comfortable."

Birdie took the liberty of adjusting the old air conditioner. She reset it twice, trying to get it to blow out colder air. When nothing but a rattling sound happened, she made up her mind that Christmas was coming early to Needy's house — whether Needy wanted it to or not — or they'd have to hold their singles meeting elsewhere.

Birdie sat down on the sofa. It was her first opportunity to look around Needy's living room without the constant chattering of the other women distracting her.

It was the old, broken cat-shaped clock that first grabbed Birdie's attention. She compared it to the grandfather clock in her mother's home when they were back in

California. Her mother's house was filled with antiques handed down from her mother's parents, who never found anything they wanted to throw away.

Birdie was so absorbed in her thoughts that she almost didn't hear Needy call out again.

"I'm almost done putting my clothes on," Needy yelled. "I just need to do something in the bathroom and I'll be right with you. At least it's closer to my living room and I won't have to shout for you to hear me." Needy wanted to stop shouting because it was making her sweat more. She also didn't want to be a bad hostess by not paying attention to Birdie.

"Birdie, there's something I've been meaning to ask you ever since you joined our church and our singles club," Needy said as she waddled down the hallway to the bathroom with her slip riding up her hips. "I know we've known each other since college, but I don't know a lot about you — the real you." She stopped speaking and waited for Birdie to reply.

Birdie said nothing.

"It's been a while and I can't remember where you're originally from." Again, Needy heard nothing. She continued the pressure. "Where are you from?"

"Really?" Birdie finally replied. "I thought everybody knew everything about me since my money seems to be so well known."

"Well, you know I try and stay out of folks' business," Needy lied.

"I'm from Old Money," Birdie said, proudly.

I knew she had a ton of money! Needy thought with excitement riding her like a Saturday morning bill collector. "Is that so? I would've never thought that," she lied again. "You're from Old Money? That must be so nice." *It's going to be wonderful to have a friend who is financially stable. I'm so tired of the poor, living from paycheck to paycheck crowd —*

"It's wonderful," Birdie replied, interrupting Needy's delusional thoughts.

Suddenly Birdie started feeling a little homesick. The small community of Old Money, California would always have a place in her heart no matter where or how far she moved. She'd been happy there for most of her younger years. It'd only taken one unfortunate incident for her to leave the comfort of her mother's eclectic home, piled high with a vast assortment of memories. The memories, some good and most bad, were jammed haphazardly between crumbling pages in numerous leather-bound scrapbooks that cluttered every corner.

Despite the chaotic décor inside, outside the two-story house the one-acre ground was well-kept, dotted with orange, lemon and palm trees that always seemed to bear fruit when others on the tree-lined street did not. Her mother, Kanair Ree Tweet, worked diligently to keep some semblance of order outside. It seemed to help Kanair Ree cope with her confused life.

Unlike her mother, Birdie lacked any of life's gardening skills to help her cope with her surroundings. So there was one innocent error in judgment and the next thing she knew, she was on a plane, that time headed for South Carolina. It was about as far away from the West Coast as she could get with limited funds in her hands and unlimited embarrassment at her back.

Coming to South Carolina where she knew no one was the only option Birdie thought she had. After all, besides living in Old Money, she'd only gone to Hampton University in Hampton, Virginia.

Her mother was against her leaving Old Money to travel across the country for an education. Birdie'd tricked her mother by having one of her then-best-friends, Muffy Brewington, say that she too was going to

Hampton to seek fame and fortune. That's all Birdie's mother needed to hear.

Kanair Ree considered the Brewingtons to be the *crème-de-la-crème* of the community because they were one of the founding families. If Muffy batted her large green eyes and tossed her long blonde hair, and said that she was going to Afghanistan to wear a burka and become head of the Taliban, Birdie would've been encouraged to do likewise.

Birdie hadn't totally lied. Muffy was traveling to Hampton, Virginia. She just hadn't told her mother the truth about why Muffy was going.

The real reason Muffy had gone there was to shack up with one of the up-and-coming football players. He was a young black man by the name of Lance George who was only twenty-one and had the physique and looks of a young Fred Williamson.

Birdie had met Lance first. He'd briefly visited Old Money to work at a pre-college job the previous summer. Birdie took to him immediately but he didn't seem interested, so she moved on. She didn't know *he'd* moved on to Muffy until a few months later. She saw them together walking down Rodeo Drive. It wasn't the thing to do back then, with the color difference being a barrier.

Muffy cared little for conventionality or their racial differences. She said it was love at first sight when Lance changed a flat tire for her at the Sears shop. They struck an instant friendship and her plan was to do anything to make sure that Lance made it to the NFL.

Birdie and Muffy had parted company when they landed in Virginia. Birdie moved onto the Hampton University campus and that's when her life truly began.

Unfortunately, Lance suffered a career-breaking knee injury and ended up working at a Columbia, South Carolina post office. Muffy then decided that if the NFL didn't want Lance there was little chance that she would either. She disappeared from South Carolina without telling either Birdie or Lance. At least that's what Lance told the authorities when Muffy's mother hadn't heard from her daughter.

Hampton University always held a special place in Birdie's heart. It was on that small campus that she'd lived and learned racial harmony, which was the total opposite of her exclusively Caucasian community in Old Money.

As she twisted and turned on the sofa trying to catch more of the uneven breeze from Needy's old air conditioner, Birdie suddenly felt as if she could almost recall the aroma from the orange blossoms from the garden blending with the perspiration of her mother. It was as though time had transported her back to Old Money from Needy's living room, and she didn't want to return just yet.

However, she had to. It was just the smell of Needy's cheap orange fragrance and her perspiration as she entered the living room.

"Are you ready?" Needy asked. She needed to make sure that Birdie was up for the job. When Birdie nodded yes, Needy became excited. "When we get finished with old Lyon Lipps, he's gonna wish for death."

Again Birdie nodded in agreement and then said, "I'm ready but I do have one more question."

"What is it?"

"What's in this for you? Other than being the president of the club and seemingly destined to remain single, what do you get out of helping us to destroy a man you've never met?"

Birdie's anger at Lyon Lipps was beginning to fade as common sense revisited, accompanied by too many questions. But she didn't want to use common sense, she wanted to stay angry. She needed Needy's inspiration.

"What do I get out of ripping a new hole for this man?" Needy repeated the question while balling her fists. "Well, my biggest reason is that men shouldn't treat women the way he's doing, and he should pay for all the times men have treated me badly." She stopped abruptly as her hairy top lip began to quiver. "They don't seem to want dark-skinned women like me," she continued. "So what if I have a little more on my chest and butt than most women. I'm a good person. I have feelings . . ." She seemed about ready to cry and that lip was doing its own thing.

"And what are the other reasons?" Birdie's need to get answers from Needy was quickly replaced by her anxious need for Needy's hairy top lip to stop shaking, so she didn't know why she bothered to ask another question that would require a reply.

"My other reasons are the same as my first reason," Needy snapped as she dabbed at her moist eyes.

Birdie decided not to ask more questions, particularly when Needy, on the way out of the house, became so agitated she slammed her fist against the old air conditioner. She hit it so hard the machine gave out one last sputter and died.

It was the perfect opportunity for Birdie

to offer to buy her a new one, but she didn't. Instead, the two women walked to Birdie's pink Lexus in silence.

The death of an innocent air conditioner should've been a sign to Birdie to just leave well enough alone but she wasn't carrying her *Signs for Dummies* handbook.

Birdie should've had that book stapled to her hand, because she was about to learn that both Needy and Ima Hellraiser had their own handwritten chapters in it.

4

The feminine blight on Pelzer's otherwise stellar reputation lived about ten miles from Needy. She occupied a bright red, single-family house with its black shades perpetually drawn tight. From a distance it appeared haunted, sitting in the middle of a wide patch of tall brownish grass, with a small rock garden of Devil Snuff shrubbery as the only outside decoration. Neighbors often avoided the home by walking across the wide street void of traffic lights but busy with traffic. They'd rather risk being run over than walk in front of the feared residence.

Ima Hellraiser lived inside the house that sported the décor of a dungeon. No one visited unless they were coming for the torture.

Behind her back Christians and atheists alike, particularly those who could barely stand her, called her a reprobate witch. To her face, they called her Ima.

Inside her bedroom, which was decorated and patterned after old Hollywood horror flicks, Ima could barely contain her excitement after the phone call from Needy. So, with more force than she'd meant to use, she'd tossed her cordless telephone onto her round bed, barely missing her pet cat, Evilene.

Contrary to what most people thought because of her surroundings, Evilene was a cat with a smidgen of feline sense, but not much direction. When Ima found her, as a kitten, scrambling through the garbage in the back yard, she was the color of midnight black. Now Evilene at the age of two was almost completely gray. Ima had scared the black right off the cat.

Instinctively, Evilene squealed loudly, just as the large pillow Ima playfully threw sailed by close enough to part the fur on her back. She jumped off the bed, snatching her remaining lives, and fled.

The call from Needy came just in time. Ima had barely been out of her latest stint in the local jail a good two hours, and was bored by the time she'd driven out of the precinct's parking lot.

Ima stood about five-foot-six in her stocking feet. Her flawless mocha-colored complexion accented curves that were so perfect and lethal they were secretly registered with the Pelzer, South Carolina police department. Most of her registration information was written in the little black books of Pelzer's bravest in Pig Latin.

Despite her obvious beauty, Ima had severe issues with self-esteem. She'd been a child with a body that blossomed early and belied her age. She'd never known her father and with no qualified man to guide her, she learned by trial and error, on her own.

There was no rest from the sexual harassment. During school hours she used her limited wit to withstand the constant advances from her male teachers and even a principal. There was no rest at home, either. Ima had fought off every sexual advance from her mother's live-in boyfriends, who plied her mother with alcohol to disguise their deeds. Not even in church was there safety. Ima stopped going to Sunday school and Youth Meetings because she was betrayed by those supposed men of God, who orated piously from the pulpits.

By the time she was in her late teens, Ima both hated and loved men, but she never trusted them. When she fully discovered what they really wanted from her, despite her need for their full love and affection, she was on the defense, repaying them with treachery and false promises of her own. Ima purposed that never in her life would she give a man the chance to hurt her first.

Standing in front of a long mirror she carefully scanned the outfit she held in her hand. *This purple two-piece Donna Karan with the plunging neck and back should do the trick,* Ima thought.

She grinned at the flimsy purple outfit consisting of a top so tiny that it could barely cover the N in "nipple." The skirt was form-fitting and was so short that it only came to her mid-thigh. If she dropped anything she'd have to depend on the kindness of others to pick it up, or risk landing in jail for indecent exposure.

Ima spent a lot of time locked up because people weren't always kind and that's the way she loved to dress.

After taking Needy's call and listening to the singles group's dilemma, it didn't take but a second for Ima to decide that she'd take the job dismantling Lyon Lipps. She loved being able to take a credit card for payment. It made getting undercover jobs using her unique "revenge" skills a lot easier than she'd imagined. Ima could make Steadman forget about Oprah. It also increased her frequent jail time points. However, at the rate she was racking up the jail mileage, she hoped a long stretch in the penitentiary wasn't in her future. Her nasty mouth and spiteful attitude had long ago voided her "stay out of jail" card with the local police department. Until recently, just flaunting her sexuality was enough to keep her out of a line-up.

Ima hurried with the finishing touches to her man-killer look. She sprayed some cologne called "Pain" around her neck and shoulders and inside her belly button.

Evilene's short memory had caused her to creep back into the bedroom and jump onto the bed. Unfortunately, she was in the line of fire again, and Ima accidentally — or purposely — doused her, too.

Of course Evilene didn't like it and sprinted from the bed again, this time tearing the bedspread in the process. It was the fourth time the cat had torn a bedspread.

If Ima saw it, she didn't show it.

Evilene's back hunched with fear. Understanding and forgiveness were not a part of Ima's persona. Evilene's bright green eyes turned red as she went, just that quick, from having nine lives to having five.

Ima applied several layers of shea butter lotion to her body, on top of the cologne, and then slid into the purple outfit. She chose a dirty-blond colored, short and sassy wig to complement her mission.

Short and sassy was perfect for getting down and nasty, she thought as she surveyed her body from all angles.

Pleased with her first line of combat wear she then went into the bathroom. Ima carefully put on a pair of lavender-tinged contact lenses, which gave her a more exotic look and took the edge off her otherwise hypnotizing hazel eyes.

While Ima lay the finishing touches to her make-up she went over the plan in her mind. Needy was very specific in the outcome she wanted. According to Needy, the women wanted the victim, Lyon Lipps, to lose not only his mind and finances, if he had any, but to lose every shred of dignity.

The ladies wanted his "Y" chromosome whittled down to a "V." With that last thought in mind, Ima grabbed a small pair of scissors from her vanity drawer and secreted them in a hidden lining inside her purse.

A lady always needs a little extra protection.

Ima went towards her living room still checking out her every angle in the mirrors that lined the walls of the hallway. *"Perfect,"* she purred.

A few moments later and Ima was in full combat mode. She turned on her radio just in time to hear the late Marvin Gaye's "Let's Get It On." She gyrated and strutted around the room as though Marvin was right there with her.

Marvin was better off wherever he was.

When the song ended, Ima checked her watch and at the same time, the doorbell rang. She tiptoed over to the window and peeped outside at her porch. As brave as she liked to think she was, she unconsciously released an audible sigh when she saw that it wasn't the police again, or an irate wife or girlfriend with a weapon.

Ima opened her door grinning like she didn't have a care in the world.

"Needy and my new friend, Birdie. You ladies come on in."

Both Needy and Birdie looked at Ima Hellraiser in awe. Birdie loved and admired the outfit. Needy gawked because Ima suddenly acted, now that there was a white woman in the room, like she'd had some type of polished upbringing. Needy then remembered that Ima was getting paid and she was probably just being nice because of that.

Needy was right. If the credit card had been denied Ima would've rip those women asunder — and then asunder again. Whatever was left she'd have torn apart.

"It's sort of hot in here." Needy said as she noticed the fire in the fireplace. It was hot enough to melt the wax that was holding the last bit of her weave in place.

"No it's not." Ima quipped, "you must be flashing. You did just have a birthday and I bet that you got menopause as a gift and nothing else." Ima started laughing at her joke.

Two minutes haven't passed since we entered this she-demon's lair and already she's started with the insults, Needy thought as she struggled not to take the fireplace's poker and beat Ima with it.

Birdie didn't want their plans to go awry and when she saw the look on Needy's face her mind raced to find a way to cool things down, but she was too late.

"I guess you're probably used to living in an Easy Bake oven," Needy shot back as she struggled to decide which she wanted more — Ima poked with a poker or Lyon Lipps destroyed.

Needy shot another nasty look at Ima and

Ima did the same in return. Then both women came together and gave each an air-kiss on each cheek, followed by a hug.

"Girl, you are so crazy," Ima said, with a false lilt in her voice.

"You're a nut case, too," Needy shot back, honestly. "And you ain't ever gonna change until you die." Needy stopped and gave a conspiring smile before adding, "And we know evil don't die."

"You know it!" Ima exclaimed. "I'm so glad to hear from you."

"Birdie, just in case you standing over there wondering what is going on, don't panic. This is how we do it. Ain't that right, Ima?" She didn't want to take a chance on Ima being too honest, which was a rarity, so she quickly added, "And, when she said that she was glad to hear from us, that only meant that your credit card payment went through."

"Break it down for that white girl, Needy." Ima laughed so hard one of her contacts threatened to fall out. She stopped only long enough to grab a tissue and extend a well-manicured hand to Birdie. "Don't take offense. I've known Needy for years and we just tolerate each other."

"She's right," Needy remarked. "Ima Hellraiser takes a lot of prayer and toleration, but like air, she's necessary for our mission." Needy let out a spiteful laugh equal to the one from Ima as she walked over to Birdie and whispered, "Just follow my lead. We can always try and kill that heifer later."

The thought of possibly killing Ima Hellraiser — someone she'd just met and already didn't like — calmed Birdie as she went over and extended her hand to her. "I take no offense," Birdie said. "Can we get down to business now?"

Suddenly Ima didn't quite like the new complacent attitudes of the visitors. Normally, she'd have had them shaking in their boots within five minutes. However, they were paying for her services, not her approval or friendship, so down to business they would get.

"Here's the way I see it," Ima said. "We all need to take a vacation."

"A vacation? You're gonna get this man with a vacation?" Birdie asked.

Needy was beginning to think Ima had finally lost her mind, but she'd known the woman long enough to hear her out. If Ima did things the traditional way she wouldn't be so much in demand. "Let her speak," Needy told Birdie. "After all, she ain't normal."

Again, Ima knew that Needy had slid in a nasty comment but it was okay. She'd make Needy pay later. With Birdie standing in her living room, Ima just knew she'd hit the motherload. The hurt, anguished and embarrassed look on Birdie's face told Ima all she needed to know.

Ima was about to get paid.

It took the three women about two hours to come to an agreement about the disposal of Lyon Lipps' mental, financial and, possibly, physical being. All during that time Needy and Birdie had moved from room to room, opening windows trying to catch a breeze before Ima immediately closed the windows behind them. It was disturbing to both Birdie and Needy that while they sat drenched in their clothes, Ima kept saying that she was chilly and the cat kept cowering over in a corner like it knew something dreadful was about to happen.

"So then, it's agreed that we will take a vacation?" Ima asked with authority. She knew the answer but asked the question anyway.

"It makes sense once you lay it out. That Lyon Lipps certainly won't turn down a vacation — especially a free one," Needy added. The paper she'd grabbed to fan herself with was ripped to shreds from her frantic use and little bits of paper were shooting around the table. In fact, there was so much shredded paper flying around the three women sat there looking like they were trapped inside a snow globe turned upside down.

"Let me get this straight," Birdie finally said. "Lyon Lipps has made a fool of Cill's sister, Jessie, Petunia, and me, but I'm the one who has to pay for your services and for this vacation?"

As Birdie spoke, she realized that she also suspected that somehow, Lyon Lipps had done something to Mother Blister, but she couldn't prove it. All she had to go by was the extra-disturbed look on Mother Blister's face earlier and perhaps that's why she didn't throw her name onto the victim list. "I just don't see why we can't split the expenses."

Birdie looked around at Ima and Needy. They had blank looks on their faces like she'd asked them their true ages. She finally said aloud what she'd started to suspect. "Am I being asked to pay this entire bill because I'm the only white woman in the group and y'all think I can afford it?"

It was out in the open now.

"I thought you knew that," Needy answered.

"Of course we'd ask you to pay for it." Ima added, "It's all part of the Reparations Act."

"Huh?" Birdie said in amazement. "What Reparations Act? What does it have to do with me?"

By the time Needy and Ima finished with their customized version of slavery and its awful consequences as it pertained to them, personally, Birdie had thrown in a set of Louis Vuitton luggage for the three of them. She also spent the next ten minutes apologizing for the horrific acts of her ancestors. Birdie was so caught up in her supposed guilt that she'd forgotten that her grandparents hadn't arrived in America from Europe until 1908.

Birdie's relief at absolving her guilt took her into generosity overdrive. She promised to take Ima and Needy shopping for new outfits at the Cost A Plenty boutique. When she finally slowed down enough to take a deep breath, she realized that she really didn't mind that perhaps her new best home girls were taking advantage.

"We accept your apology and the gifts of luggage as well as the new clothes," Ima said, sheepishly, after determining that Birdie wasn't much of a fighter. She was about to choke from trying to keep her laughter from escaping.

Needy wanted to feel guilty about taking advantage of Birdie, but she couldn't. Seeing someone else become the butt of a joke was a welcome relief. Hearing Ima apologize almost sent her over the edge. She slapped one hand over her mouth to stifle the losing battle with her laughter and pushed a pile of papers towards Birdie. "Take another look at these brochures. Just pick one and we'll take it from there."

"You pick one. After all, since I'm paying for all this it's the least you can do."

Needy's eyes locked with Birdie's. *Now is not the time for her to grow some courage.* Birdie wouldn't look away. Reasonable doubt tugged at Needy, but she decided to ignore it.

Ima's sense of drama ignited. If she read the two women's body language correctly, and she was sure she did, there was a seed of confrontation germinating. Evil gardener that she was, she'd water it later with a few well-placed lies.

Needy carefully scanned each brochure, finally settling on the one with the most colorful cover. As she slammed the brochure down in the center of the table, diabolical smiles spread across Ima and Birdie's faces.

"Oh yeah, this is gonna be wonderful."

Birdie suddenly felt invigorated. "Getting even may be expensive but you can't put a price on what I'm feeling right now."

"Why shouldn't we go on a breathtaking cruise? And, I mean that literally." Needy's fat cheeks plumped with joy.

"It's sailing to the Southern Caribbean. I've never been to that part." Birdie's thin fingers flipped through the brochure and her enthusiasm mounted. "It starts off in Miami, Florida and sails to Mexico, St. Maartens and Jamaica."

Needy pushed her chair back and leapt up. "This is a gift from heaven."

"It's not really a gift if I'm paying for it," Birdie reminded her.

Birdie might've as well have used sign language because Needy didn't hear a word said as she reveled in her imagination. "We'll be on the high seas eight days and seven nights on a ship. Elbow to elbow with an abundance of single and available men. I'm getting that old feeling again." Needy had a smile that seemed to emanate from her very core.

"Listen up! Earth to Needy!" Ima roared, slapping the back of Needy's chair to startle her, which caused her to take her seat again.

"This is not about getting you a man." Ima continued, "Keep to the plan. It's about payback."

The smile vanished from Needy's face faster than her money around the first of the month. How was she going to stick to the plan of getting back at Lyon Lipps when she could be getting a man? That particular cruise was very expensive. In her mind, any man who could afford it had to be someone of substance and financial stability, and she didn't care if he came aboard in a wheelchair or on a skateboard. She wasn't sure how she was going to pull it off. No way was she going to go on a cruise and return without a man.

Time was running out and that's probably why they chose to sail on an ocean liner called *Desperation of the Seas.*

5

Needy and Birdie went their separate ways after the meeting.

By the time Needy returned home she felt invigorated, and yet at the same time, a little guilty. Her conscience pricked her. She hoped they hadn't gone too far when they convinced Birdie to underwrite their venture. Although Birdie was, without a doubt, one of Lyon Lipps' victims, so were the other women. Nevertheless, they didn't have the finances to bring that scallywag down.

"Get it together, Needy," she scolded as she peeled off her perspiration-drenched clothes. "You're doing what you gotta do."

A tall glass of iced tea took the edge off her guilt, so she immediately dialed the others for an emergency meeting. She told them that after Sunday morning service, everyone should return to her house, and she'd give the news.

6

Ever since the former pastor of the Ain't Nobody Saved But Us — All Others Goin' to Hell Church, the Reverend Knott Enuff Money, got saved *for real* and truly found the Lord, the church's pulpit overflowed with visiting pastors in an effort to find a new one.

Several of the unscrupulous board members wanted to have the Bishop Was Never-called, a carbon-copy of the reverend's former egotistical self, take the job so they could keep control of the church. However, he was away in another city, secretly trying to get both his GED and his act together. He desperately wanted to further his sixth grade education, so he could one day return and read the Bible without maiming every word, verse and chapter.

There were several other prospects. The buzz had already gone around the church about one in particular — how tall and handsome and single he was. The board hadn't given out his name yet but it didn't seem to matter. Since the female members outnumbered the male, it was almost a certainty they'd chosen him based upon those three qualities.

The next day after the meeting with Ima, all the single women went to church. That Sunday morning service was, if nothing else, revitalizing. The visiting pastor bringing the message was the renowned Bishop Noel Jones, a television celebrity pastor from Gardenia, California.

Though a divorced man, Bishop Jones said he never regretted his staunch Pentecostal family background. Most believed he was the brother of a 1970s disco diva named Grace Jones. If it was true then they were total opposites; he wore more clothes.

Today, his theme, A New Oil, placed him among the most celebrated speakers in the world, alongside Bishop T. D. Jakes from Dallas, Texas and Pastor Jamal Bryant from Baltimore, Maryland. He loved to preach about the pros and cons of being single or married, so the church brought him in to preach at the Singles Sunday Service.

As was their custom, the ladies arrived twenty minutes late but proceeded to march, heads held high as most Christian soldiers would, down to the third pew. There was no room on the first two pews or they'd have sat there. Every available inch of those first pews was occupied by the visiting dignitaries' spouses and the members of the Mothers Board.

Needy had led the pack. She wore a neon-red two-piece suit. The top, gathered together in wide pleats supposedly to fit her ample bosom, failed to contain them. She looked as though she had two midget sumo wrestlers fighting on her chest as she proudly turned sideways, because she had to, and entered the row.

Petunia and Cill followed. They were a little more subdued in their attire. Petunia wore a long white gauzy dress. She'd long ago accepted the fact that any dress she wore would make her look like a teepee. Today, she'd boldly added a gray straw hat with several dark gray feathers poking through the top. She still looked like a human teepee, one with a smokestack attached.

Cill, with her short-cropped hair slicked back with extra mousse, wore a chocolate-brown, pinstriped, double-breasted suit with a beige shirt and chocolate brown necktie. She'd added a beige brooch to the jacket to throw people off her gender scent even though she'd still worn a pair of men's beige Foschini shoes. She still refused to believe that most people had either figured her out already, or truly didn't care.

Birdie walked just a little ahead of Mother Blister. She was dressed in green from head to toe, with the exception of her favorite accessory, an oversized cross. She'd had the twenty-carat diamond cross especially made for her by Jacobi the Jeweler. It was the one luxury she'd never part with, no matter what. Every time that heavy cross hit one of the buttons on her dress, it rang out. She sounded and looked like a human cash register or a walking bell.

Mother Blister trailed behind as usual. She was very eclectic in her church attire. She wore a little of this and sometimes none of that. Today, in the hot weather, she wore a blue cotton blazer, a pink skirt without a lining (and everyone could see through it) and a wide-brimmed purple hat with a polka dot ribbon. She'd worn the same pair of shoes from the past Sunday. The difference was that last Sunday the shoes had a two-inch heel. She'd shouted so much that Sunday that her heavy girth had turned them into flats.

"Ya'll gonna move over or are ya gonna keep gawking," Mother Blister barked. She didn't care if she interrupted the service or not. Nobody was gonna give her a little eye-criticism and get away with it, real or imagined. She was having her say.

Fortunately, no one responded. Not even the elderly mothers on the Mothers Board pew said a word, lest they alert Mother Blister to the fact that she was supposed to sit with them.

Mother Blister had sat on that Mothers Board for years. However, often she'd just sit in church wherever she felt like sitting. She'd probably sat on the second pew only five times, and those five times were not without drama. So, her absences from the pew never bothered the rest of the Mothers Board.

Just as Mother Blister's heavy bottom hit the pew, all heads turned back to the pulpit to rejoin the service already in progress.

Bishop Jones was an impeccably dressed, slender, handsome man in his fifties who sported a five o'clock shadow every day and all day. Where on some men the stubble would've made their skin look dirty, on the bishop it seemed to bring out an otherwise underplayed sexuality that looked out of place in a pulpit. With his dark brown eyes ablaze and his chocolate skin glistening, he preached about the rewards of waiting on

God for a mate until the church building seemed to elevate off its foundation.

"The minus of being a single man is that often you want to be with someone, and you want to have someone. If I take a trip to Jamaica, where I was born, for example, it would be nice to have someone with me to share all the delicacies. The plus side of being single is that I can be in Jamaica and not have to worry about someone thinking I shouldn't have those delicacies."

He stopped and smiled, drinking in the congregation's appreciation of what he'd said.

"Ooh, that man is handsome," Petunia whispered in a voice low enough to sound more like a cow mooing. She should've turned into a smoldering skinny heap of ashes for what her mind started to imagine. The strength in the bishop's voice brought her back to the present and reality.

"So I am flexible." Bishop Jones continued, still smiling and walking back and forth, creating a path in the deep, plush, beige pulpit carpet.

"But at the same time I am running myself into the ground because of that freedom. I think it would be good to have someone in my house to say, 'you know what you need

— rest.' I think marriage preserves your life."

"Oh yes it would," Needy blurted as she looked around, unashamed, for confirmation. "It'd sure save my life."

Her sudden outburst caused Bishop Jones to laugh, which gave permission to all the others to laugh at Needy as though they needed permission. Most of them laughed at her all the time.

When the laughter died down, the Bishop continued. His smile evaporated as he leaned forward with his finger pointing accusingly at the congregation. With a look of worry suddenly replacing the smile, he added, "The difference between being married or single is like going to a city for a vacation or going on a cruise —"

"Did he say cruise?" Birdie asked Needy under her breath.

Needy could barely contain herself. "Yes, he did." Ignoring the rebuking stares from those around her, Needy added, "You know that it's a sign. God is well pleased with our plan."

Birdie and Needy, in their rush to take whatever tiny bit of confirmation from heaven, completely missed the rest of Bishop Jones' story where he'd added a very crucial part.

"In a city, you get to pick and choose what you're gonna do. On a cruise, there's no mystery. Most activities aboard ship are scheduled. For example, you know when and what you are gonna eat. You are locked into that schedule. Because of that it is narrow and you get more done."

If any of the congregation understood or cared about the rest of the Bishop's remarks, they didn't show it. Instead, practically every female — and a few of the males — envisioned themselves in Bishop Jones' famous television living room. It was a place where they, too, could sit. A lot of them particularly wanted to relax in that beautiful orange-colored futuristic chair where the Bishop always had one leg slung over the arm.

"Put your need for a mate on hold. The Bible says to take hold of Holiness and be patient. Let God fix you first, so you don't become unequally yoked. Til then just do this. Grab the happiness you need for yourself, right now." In an instant, he slid from behind the lectern and rushed to its edge. "Grab it!" His hands made a fist and he opened and closed it firmly demonstrating what he preached. "Grab it and hold on to it. Do it now!"

Like popcorn, everyone jumped to his or

her feet and started reaching into the air and grabbing at their invisible dreams. Some grabbed and slammed their balled fists to their chest so hard until they almost punched themselves out.

A few of the women became so caught up in the moment, they ran over to some of the married men and whispered, "I'm putting you and me in the palm of my hands and I'm closing it. I got you, Boo."

Of course, some of that whispering didn't sit too well with a few of those husbands who knew they had a lot of explaining to do when they got home. Those same men just went ahead to the altar to pray for strength for the whuppin' they were about to receive. Shamefully, they kneeled in spots where they'd worn groves in the floor. The front of the altar resembled the sidewalk in front of Grauman's Chinese Theatre in Hollywood, where the foot- and handprints of the rich and famous are preserved.

"If you wait on God, you can have it all."

Bishop Jones kicked it up a notch. He preached until he almost passed out. Several of the women did pass out. And, of course, the ushers made use of the pandemonium and passed the collection plates around.

Through it all, Needy and the other women sang, shouted, and asked God, again, to bless their wicked scheme.

When it was over they all rushed towards the door. "Oh my goodness, that man sure can preach!" Petunia shouted over the din of outgoing church folks.

"I was almost persuaded not to go through with our plan but I overheard Needy asking God to bless it, so I'm still in," Cill added.

"Where's Sister Hellraiser?" Birdie suddenly asked as she started to walk towards her car. She, too, had given in to the frenzy of the congregation and only just then noticed Ima's absence.

"She never comes to church when she's preparing for a job. She doesn't want her demons compromised by the truth." Needy tried to speak with a straight face, but failed when she winked. "She only comes to church when she's looking for work," she added.

"And, there's always someone here at church service willing to use Ima's special services," Mother Blister whispered as she finally caught on that the conversation was about Ima.

As it had for some of the other churchgoers, Bishop Jones' message had started to prick a hole in Mother Blister's supposed holiness. She had felt the beginnings of a tiny pang of guilt about her nursing home affair with Slim Pickens and being unequally yoked. She was all too happy to turn the conversation around and make it about Ima Hellraiser.

After the service, outside on the sidewalk, if the Bishop noticed Needy and the others, he didn't show it. He was too busy shaking the hands of the other parishioners, surrounded by some of the deacons who'd hoped to catch a falling crumb from his holiness.

To make sure that their plan would be successful all the women rushed towards their cars, avoiding the still outstretched hand of Bishop Jones as they dashed past. They didn't want to chance that he might discern what was really in their hearts, and ask God to intervene.

These women wanted God on their terms only.

7

Needy had barely driven two blocks from the church, still savoring the spirit-filled sermon, before the first taste of drama unfolded. The battery in Petunia's old clunker had died so Petunia, Cill and Mother Blister were riding along in her car.

"I'm so glad we ain't meeting over to that she-demon Ima Hellraiser's house, especially after I heard such a wonderful and uplifting sermon." Petunia sat hunched over in the back seat of Needy's old Civic. Her skinny arm twirled like a baton, coming dangerously close to knocking off Mother Blister's new wig and hat.

"If you raise that toothpick wrapped in flesh one more time and touch my new wig," Mother Blister hissed, "you gonna need help from that she-demon because all the angels in heaven and prayers on earth ain't gonna be able to put yo' bony behind together again."

Before Petunia could say anything in her defense, Mother Blister had turned from her and moved on to another topic, parroting what she'd forgotten Petunia had just said.

"I don't know about any of you but that sure was a wonderful and uplifting sermon coming from Bishop Noel." Mother Blister stopped, pointed and glared at Petunia. "It's a shame that this beanpole didn't appreciate it. I'm sure glad *I'm* saved."

"It was just what we needed," Needy said softly before breaking out into song. "Yes, Jesus loves me. Yes, Jesus loves . . ."

Cill was about to say something but she didn't. It wasn't reflection about the message that kept her silent. It was her military training. Something was amiss. She could feel it and she didn't like being kept in the dark. Her eyes almost burned a hole in the back of Needy's fleshy neck as Cill tried to figure out why Needy was singing and in such a good mood.

Petunia ignored Cill's silence and Needy's singing. She was about to protest but then she stopped. Unless she'd blanked out for a few minutes, she couldn't figure out why Mother Blister was angry with her. She was about to ask but then she spied Needy's face, seeming to turn darker by the second, in the rearview mirror as she continued to sing. Hundreds of times, she'd seen that look and she took heed. It was a familiar and ominous look from Needy, so silence took her over.

Whenever Mother Blister started to show even a subtle hint of dementia, Needy seemed to be the only one of the women who knew it was a wasted effort to challenge the old woman. As a signal to the others, she'd make her eyes squint and shake her head like a toy rattle, then a sound like air escaping from a balloon would be followed by the sucking of her teeth.

"Mother Blister, you know, you are so right. I should be more spiritual, since we did hear a wonderful sermon this morning. I don't know why I didn't think of that." Petunia chewed viciously on each word. By the time she'd finished placating Mother Blister, she'd almost gnawed off her own tongue.

"That's okay." Mother Blister turned towards Petunia and sweetly replied, "We just need to stop sometimes and give God thanks when we hear His word brought so well." She dabbed at one eye and lifted her head towards heaven to let God know that she was on His side. Her homage to heaven only lasted a moment before she quickly added, "Now let's see how we gonna cook that goose's behind for making a complete fool out of Birdie and Petunia." She started squirming in her seat. "Hurry up, Needy. I got to pee."

If Needy stopped at a stop sign or a red traffic light, the women didn't see her do it. Just the thought of what Mother Blister could do to her Civic's upholstery was enough to make Needy's foot turn into lead as she shifted into warp speed. They arrived at her front door ten minutes faster than normal and before Mother Blister did any damage, real or imagined.

"Here, take my keys," Needy urged as she reached back and pressed the keychain into Mother Blister's hands hard enough to make an impression. "Get inside and use the bathroom."

"Why?" Mother Blister asked, innocently. She leaned back in her seat with confusion plastered on her face.

Neither Cill nor Petunia waited for Needy to answer. Both women rushed to exit the car, spilling out onto the sidewalk.

Meanwhile, it took another five minutes of sniffing and a coat of Lysol spray before Needy was convinced that her car was unspoiled by Mother Blister. She led Cill and Petunia into her house.

Birdie finally arrived about twenty minutes after the others. She ran bobbing and weaving as if chased by a mob up Needy's front walk. By the time she made it to the front door, she was completely out of breath.

Birdie didn't take the time to knock, instead rushing through the front door, slamming it hard enough to make the screen door shake. Barbs of shredded mesh wire snagged her expensive cotton blouse but Birdie didn't care. These were her churchy home girls and she was still ecstatic they'd accepted her and wanted to help her reap retribution.

Birdie sailed down the narrow hallway still clutching her chest and trying to avoid the sharp stings from her hair whipping at her face. "I made it," she said as she flung her pocketbook on a nearby chair and plopped down on another. "Sorry I'm late," she added.

"It's about time you got here," Petunia snapped. "We're trying to help you out and you just can't be bothered with details, such as getting here on time." She hissed as she spoke. She was still peeved about not being able to correct Mother Blister, so she was going to take out her frustration on Birdie.

As usual, Needy ignored Petunia's drama. "Did you happen to see Ima when you came

134

in?" Needy asked Birdie, and craned her neck as she tried to look past her chair.

"No, I didn't," Birdie replied, still trying to catch her breath. "I would've gotten here sooner but there's several patrol cars blocking the street so I came around the back. If Ima was on her way, she might've gotten held up by the cops."

The women looked at Birdie as though she'd just prophesied. To prove just how close Birdie was to unwittingly doing that, Ima bounced through Needy's front door chased by enough of the Pelzer Police force to make the ten o'clock news later that night.

"Okay, I'm here. Let's get things started," Ima barked as though the women had held her up. She peeked out of each living room window and then quickly started closing the curtains before she continued, "Ladies, our plan has progressed quicker than I'd planned. We're gonna need to leave for our cruise a little sooner than later."

There was an eerie quiet that suddenly enveloped the room, stopping any impending chatter. The only thing that moved was Mother Blister's arm flaps as she suddenly bolted from her chair. "What cruise?" Her false teeth nearly plunged from her mouth. "When did we decide about a cruise? Who's paying for a cruise? I didn't agree to a cruise." She stopped and adjusted her wig and her teeth before she asked, "Did I?"

There was no holding Petunia back. "Ya'll have a lot of nerve using my pain to go on a doggone cruise."

"Hold on," Cill interrupted. "It might not be such a bad idea to sail the high seas. We can cut him up and throw his bloody carcass over the side of the ship and let the sharks finish him off." She started laughing. "I think it's splendid. He'll still get to hell but he'll arrive piece by piece."

Cill jumped up and tried to get high fives from the other women. None moved. Instead they looked at her as if she'd had lost her mind.

When Ima saw the shocked looks in the room, she couldn't be happier. Not even fifteen minutes had passed since she'd escaped the clutches of the Pelzer police, and already she'd stirred up more drama. To her, life was good.

Needy held up her hand to quiet Cill and the others. She decided that she needed to speak up before Birdie joined in with the truth. Needy knew exactly how to end the confusion: she chose to lie. The whole truth would only add more fuel to the already blazing fire.

"The cruise is going to cost about two thousand dollars plus airfare," Needy said nonchalantly as if the cost meant nothing to her.

"Count me out!" Petunia squealed. "I don't have that kind of money." She was mad and sad. She couldn't have raised two thousand dollars even if someone had paid her cash for all her dreams and five future dates.

"I certainly will not pay that kind of money when this man has done nothing to me," said Cill, who was the thrifty one in the group. "My sister will get over her hurt."

Birdie started to feel the pangs of guilt. She wanted all her churchy home girls to go on the cruise. However, she didn't want it bad enough to pay for all of them. She could settle for just having Needy and Ima along. The only one who hadn't spoken up was Mother Blister.

As though they had read Birdie's mind, the women turned towards Mother Blister with a questioning stare.

"I don't know why y'all looking at me. I got a man —" Mother Blister almost slipped up but she recovered quickly. "Mansion on high and my God will provide." She let out a nervous laugh. She was determined that none of them would know about Slim Pickens.

As much as Mother Blister wanted to remain in Pelzer and protect her relationship with Slim, she also wanted to see Lyon sent packing to hell much more. Luckily, she knew Ima's credentials and they were impeccable.

"I'm going on that cruise," Mother Blister said, enthusiastically. *This means that I'm gonna have to take Slim into the medicine cabinet tonight and give him a little sleeping medicine.* Mother Blister was old but she still had skills. She'd have Slim snoring and handing her his pension money, both at the same time, before the sun rose.

It was apparent to the others that Mother Blister was blanking out again, but the sly smile that quickly spread across the old woman's face made Needy nervous.

While Mother Blister smiled and basted in her daydream, Needy gently guided her off her good sofa and onto a chair with a plastic cushion. It was better to be safe than sorry.

It took a bit of ingenuity and downright lying but between Needy, Ima and Birdie, they got Petunia to accept their decision to take the cruise without her.

"We're gonna make that reprobate pay

extra for what he did to you," Ima promised Petunia.

Ima thought she saw Petunia's body relax just a little. That wasn't good enough for her. She decided that diplomacy was not the way to go. Why leave someone with dignity when she could put it through the shredder with a few carefully crafted words?

"I'm sorry, Petunia. I have to tell the truth," Ima said slowly.

Without the gift of discernment, Needy knew that Ima was about to throw her and Birdie under the bus.

"What neither Needy nor Birdie is honest enough to tell you is . . ." Ima lied with a false look of repentance, ". . . is that you're broke, and you won't be able to dress sexy enough to trap that grease monkey or any other human or zoo animal. Your lack of fashion sense and your skinny body won't look decent enough to hang with us and our finery."

The look of fear and defeat on Petunia's face was satisfying, so Ima turned around. "And, don't let me get started on you, Cill."

Cill sprung to her feet and planted them close enough for her toes to touch Ima's. Like a tree planted by the waters, she would not be moved. "Please give me a reason why I don't kick your butt," Cill said angrily at being snubbed, forgetting that Ima never fought a clean fight.

Just like Houdini, Ima produced one nail file that just happened to be serrated, and Cill's memory magically returned.

Needy saw an opportunity to defuse a situation that would only end badly. Although she was concerned for the others, she was more concerned about keeping her living room and a few pieces of furniture from the Rent-a-Center intact.

Needy bolted between Ima and Cill and rushed over to Petunia's side. The width of her hips knocked Cill and Ima off balance, sending them to neutral places.

"You've been hurt enough," Needy said, laying her thick arms on Petunia's shoulders hard enough to make her lean lopsided as she glared at Ima.

"That's so true," Birdie chimed in. She was becoming a quick learner, and on her way to becoming quite a liar.

At that moment, Birdie wanted to contribute to the peacekeeping. She also wasn't feeling quite as guilty as she should've and decided that she'd repent later.

Birdie walked over and stood on the other side of Petunia, smiling warmly. "We love you, Petunia. We feel your pain as if we'd been wronged ourselves to the same level as you." She hadn't totally gotten the lying game down, momentarily forgetting that she'd been hurt, too.

Needy reached around Petunia's shoulders and pinched Birdie and shushed her. "Quit while you're ahead," she whispered.

Wrapped up in her pain, Petunia, too, quickly forgot that Lyon had hurt the others, and Birdie in particular. She preferred to believe that they were seeking revenge strictly on her behalf.

Petunia took the crook of one finger and dabbed at an invisible tear. "Now, I want daily updates," she insisted through several pretend sobs. "They have computers aboard those ships and I want to receive an e-mail every day detailing how ya'll dismantle that weasel!"

"In fact," Needy interrupted. She really had gotten enough drama and her patience was wearing thin. "Why don't you and Cill go on home. Ya'll don't need to be implicated in our little plot." She winked at the women, not caring that they didn't return the wink or smiled.

"Well, I for one am no criminal," Cill boasted. "So I don't have a problem with leaving ya'll's little soirée."

"Hold up and I'll share a cab with you," Petunia added. "I know that with Ima heading things the job will be done proper." She was lying more than Cill.

With the exception of the scratching sound made by the dragging of Cill and Petunia's chairs as they stood up, it was quiet. Not even Ima made her usual nasty remarks, which disturbed Petunia and Cill.

"They could've at least pretended that they were sorry that we aren't going on that cruise," Petunia whispered angrily to Cill as they gathered their things to leave.

"That's okay," Cill mumbled. "It ain't over 'til it's over."

"We'll be in touch," Needy called out as Petunia and Cill stormed out the room without saying their goodbyes.

They still said nothing even as they slammed Needy's door hard enough on their way out to shake up the neighborhood and the nearby cemetery.

Needy and the others ignored the slight and began to plot. They chatted and schemed until almost sundown. After sorting out their differences of mainly who would share a cabin with whom, Ima demanded that she have her own cabin, so she could have privacy to lure Lyon.

It made sense to Birdie, so she and Needy decided that they would share a cabin. That left Mother Blister without a cabin mate.

Mother Blister humbly said that she didn't mind sharing a cabin. "That way, either you or Birdie can have your own cabin too," she suggested.

"That's quite okay," Needy said, strongly.

"We want to honor you because you're our senior member," Birdie insisted. *Lying is becoming quite too easy. I've got to pray,* Birdie thought. But she still didn't want to share a cabin with Mother Blister so she let the lie stand.

Again, Ima spoke up and lit the proverbial match for a messy shipboard explosion when she offered to find a cabin mate for Mother Blister.

"Don't you worry about being alone on board the ship, Mother Blister. I have someone in mind that will be perfect to share your cabin. I'm going to make sure that you don't have a dull moment."

Ima was starting to act a little too friendly. That should've been Mother Blister's first hint. However, Mother Blister hadn't seen a hint, or dropped a hint, in years. She was already losing touch with reality, and with Ima involved, that left her in a dangerous situation.

"Won't that cost more money?" Mother Blister asked.

"Our benefactor will cover it," Ima said

quickly as she winked towards Birdie, who had her back turned.

"Benefactor is a good insurance company," Mother Blister said, smiling.

"Don't you mean Beneficial?" Needy corrected her.

"That's what I said," Mother Blister snapped. "Benefactor."

"Have mercy," Ima said, shaking her head.

A few minutes later, Mother Blister was put in a taxi and sent home. For the next several minutes, Needy and Birdie anxiously waited for Ima to tell them whom she'd picked to share Mother Blister's room.

After a number of servings of iced cold lemonade for Birdie and herself, Needy finally got Ima to tell them what they needed to know. "I'm not giving you any hot tea until you answer my question," Needy threatened. "Who are you putting in the cabin with Mother Blister?"

Just as Ima opened her mouth to fake a protest, several claps of thunder crashed through the sky, followed by the sound of heavy raindrops.

While Needy and Birdie jumped around in fear, neither liking loud noises, Ima stayed completely calm. She loved hearing the snapping sounds of thunder and seeing quick streaks of lightning.

"You two are beginning to work my last nerve. I should just give you half of your deposit back and let y'all work it out."

Both women put their hands on their hips and looked at Ima in disbelief. Then Needy and Birdie calmed down.

"Now that you two have relaxed a bit. I'll tell you my plan. I thought it would be a lovely idea to put my aunt in the same cabin as Mother Blister."

Needy was the first one to recover from the shock. "Are you truly that evil?" Needy asked suspiciously. "Even the devil wouldn't be that mean."

The question from Needy caused Ima to start laughing so hard she had to hold on to the edge of the bookcase to keep from falling.

"Of course I'm that mean. That's why you hired me."

It only took a split-second for another clap of thunder to sound, and in that same second Ima's face changed. Her eyes slowly slanted and even her voice dropped two levels past bass as she muttered, "And, as for that old Devil, I'll tell him that you complimented him when he comes crawling to me for his next meanness lesson."

Birdie, as usual, had a hard time keeping up. With so much going on, she felt as though she would need a scorecard. "I think that's a lovely idea, Needy. Why do you have a problem with it?" *At the very least, it will be someone who can keep Mother Blister occupied while we work on destroying Lyon,* Birdie thought.

"Thank you, Birdie. I knew you'd understand. I want to give you your money's worth," Ima smiled and then turned to give Needy a look that read, *Mind your business or suffer the consequences.*

Needy's dark skin took on an ashy color as she stammered, "I guess . . . you're . . . right, Ima." Her need to stick with the plan while finding a man was whittling away at her self-esteem.

In the back of Birdie's mind, she quickly calculated how much the vengeance was going to cost her. She could see it was already over the budget. They hadn't left Ima's living room, let alone boarded a ship, and already she was thinking about having to mortgage her house.

Birdie decided she needed to take control before Needy said or did something further to thwart their plans. "Just give me your aunt's name and I'll get her a ticket."

Suddenly, at the sound of Ima's aunt's name, Birdie's brunette mane started shaking. That meant she was either nervous or doing something she really didn't want to do. That time it was both.

Poor Birdie didn't know what hit her. One minute she was asking for the name of Ima's aunt and the next minute, she lay sprawled out on Needy's living room floor.

While Needy grabbed a wet towel and dabbed at Birdie's forehead to bring her around, Ima stood and watched in fascination. Her heart was pounding, not out of fear for Birdie's welfare, but from the sheer ease it took to knock her out.

While the room continued to spin, Birdie felt as though she was spiraling through a tunnel accompanied by Dorothy and Toto, with the bad witch waiting at the end. It took much effort, but somehow she managed to mumble a few quick words. "Did she say her aunt's name was —"

Needy dotted Birdie's head again with the wet towel, cutting her off in mid-sentence. "Don't get yourself riled up again, Birdie. You heard her right the first time. I thought you knew who her aunt was."

"I don't see how she could be so surprised," Ima snickered. "After all, my aunt and I share so many family traits. How could anyone not know? Healthy doses of good looks and confidence run in my family."

Needy helped Birdie to stand. She steered Birdie over to the sofa where Ima stood.

Needy pointed at Ima and asked. "Birdie, do you know anyone who is just as cranky and ruthless as Ima?"

"Yes," Birdie replied, sheepishly. "I just never put the two of them together as being related."

"I can see how that might happen," Ima said as she gently took Birdie's hand. As much as Ima enjoyed tormenting her new benefactor, she didn't want to scare her away before extracting more financial gains. "I'm five-foot-six inches of pure gorgeous femininity. My aunt is about four-feet-six inches of elderly sagging skin and bones crammed into an awful white dress. And let's not forget, that tight gray bun that makes her look like a spinning top." Again Ima turned on her thirty-two watt smile. "Aunt Sasha and I are not nearly as bad as people say."

Needy started coughing to keep from retching. The motive for Ima's sudden sweetness was lost on no one. *Even Birdie can't be that dumb,* Needy thought as she folded her arms to watch Ima's magic show.

Nevertheless, Birdie *was* just that dumb. By the time Ima finished spinning tales of how she and Mother Sasha Pray Onn's little acts of mayhem were so often misunder-stood, she had Birdie apologizing.

"I'm so sorry. I should've given her the benefit of doubt. After all, she is one of the mothers of the church." Birdie sighed. "Please forgive me."

"That's okay," Ima countered. "I'm curi-ous. What did my aunt do or say to you that was so terrible?" She managed to ask the question without so much as blinking, caus-ing the words to sound even more sincere. She really didn't care about Birdie's apol-ogy. She only wanted to hear the details of how miserable her aunt had made the church's resident white benefactor.

Needy couldn't take any more. She was literally throwing in the towel. She grabbed another and handed it to Birdie, so Birdie could wipe away her tears. *I gotta give Ima props. That heifer is too good!*

While Birdie composed herself as best she could, Ima and Needy listened to Birdie explain her fear of Mother Pray Onn.

"The first time I entered through the hal-lowed sanctuary of the Ain't Nobody Right But Us — All Others Goin' to Hell Church, I felt at ease. So I decided that I would return for another service night.

"On this particular night, I returned and had a chance to fellowship with some of the

149

other members who came to the Wednesday night test-a-lying service. Most of them I didn't recognize from that Sunday service, but it was crowded, so I wasn't surprised.

"One of the first people to welcome me was one of the oldest members of the church. You may know her. Her name is Sister Betty."

The mention of Sister Betty's name caught Ima off guard. "Of course, we know Sister Super Saint," she uttered as she let her eyes roll. She followed by letting her finger circle her head to show how crazy she thought Sister Betty was.

Birdie completely ignored Ima and when she saw Needy wasn't going to chime in, she continued.

"I was so impressed with her as she stood and spoke of her love for her church members and, especially, her God. Her voice boomed. That's the best way I can describe her because it didn't seem to fit her size . . ."

The more Birdie spoke about Sister Betty the more she regained her composure. Needy and Ima couldn't believe her transformation right before their very eyes.

Birdie lay the towel aside and slid to the edge of her seat as she continued speaking.

"Sister Betty was short and skinny with the loveliest brown skin. She looked like she would be a sweet woman.

"That night she was dressed completely in white with a large cross dangling from her neck. It wasn't as nice as mine, but it was still nice. I just could not get over how soft-spoken she was and yet had a powerful presence . . ."

"If that bird-brain don't get to the point I'm gonna have to rethink taking this job. I can't take all this drama," Ima whispered angrily to Needy.

Another generous clap of thunder roared, causing Needy to jump again. Ima stood flatfooted and belligerent as though she'd heard nothing. Needy could only imagine that it was Satan asking Ima to stop embarrassing herself and him with her outrageous behavior.

Needy didn't bother to answer Ima, instead she kept her eyes on Birdie.

Birdie had kept talking the entire time, so Needy wasn't sure what part of the story she'd missed when Ima interrupted.

". . . It hadn't escaped me that I was the only white woman there that night; although if you want to add the Bishop Nevercalled as the other white person, I guess it's okay.

"I also noticed that Sister Betty seemed to be an outcast and yet she didn't seem to mind it. She introduced me to some of the

other members. Everything was fine until
—"

Suddenly Birdie's hair started fanning as
she grabbed the towel and started bawling
into it.

Neither Needy nor Ima were surprised. It
wouldn't be the first time the mention of
Mother Pray Onn's name drove someone
over the edge.

*"She . . . said . . . she . . . was . . . gonna . . .
make . . . my . . . life . . . a . . . living . . . hell!"*
Birdie was almost hysterical. "She didn't
say why."

Before Needy could comfort Birdie and
let her know that she wasn't the only one
the tiny terror in orthopedic shoes haunted,
Ima spoke up.

"Well now Birdie, calm down." Ima laid
her hand on Birdie's hand in comfort. "You
have me and I promise that since you have
become my new best friend and benefactor,
I won't let my grouchy Aunt Sasha threaten
you again."

Needy almost believed Ima until she heard
her use the word "promise." She immediately looked over at Birdie who was not only
on the edge of her seat, but was about to
fall off the edge of her mental health.

"Ima," Needy warned, "please."

Ima turned her attention away from the

still bawling Birdie and winked at Needy. "You know I got things under control. Don't worry."

Needy's hairy top lip shook like it was doing the Laffy Taffy. "Oh, God, help us."

8

The hard-hitting, but brief storm had passed by the time Ima left Birdie still crying at Needy's house and arrived home. Her perfectly pedicured feet barely touched the carpet as she grinned and danced through her living room. She was floating on air as she reveled in what was sure to be one of her best schemes ever.

Ima was so self-absorbed she didn't realize that she'd almost stepped on her cat. But Ima was in her bedroom taking off her clothes before Evilene had a chance to retract her claws and hide.

Evilene was terrified of Ima, but it didn't stop her from getting into trouble in her absence. Evilene had left a little gift for Ima behind the sofa in a mound that would've impressed any Great Dane. The cat sensed Ima didn't smell anything since Ima hadn't grabbed a rolled newspaper and gone to whacking her. Evilene sprinted out of the room while she could.

Meanwhile, Ima's mind was on something other than her pet. She still hadn't figured out why her aunt hadn't mentioned any little nasty encounters with Birdie. They usually bragged to each other about the havoc they'd raised in someone's life. It was a ritual that the entire Hellraiser clan enjoyed performing. It was tradition.

The fact that Mother Pray Onn didn't particularly care for Birdie and truly hated Mother Blister might cause a problem if she found out she had to spend a week sharing a cabin. Ima plopped down in her recliner to think.

For most of her teenage years and on through into her late twenties, Ima was influenced by her aunt, Mother Sasha Pray Onn. Ima witnessed her aunt's duplicitous behavior, which was honed almost to perfection. The way Sasha would testify at the various services about the goodness of the Lord was a work of art. She'd weep and gnash her teeth as she related how Satan had tried to intervene between her and her God.

She had the congregation trained. If she didn't hear the appropriate amount of "amens" and "hallelujahs," she'd just keep on test-a-lying. Most of the members started yelling out her praises soon enough. Sometimes it wouldn't be ten minutes later before she'd claw someone's eyes out if they didn't show reverence to her the way she thought they should. Even the pastor and the elders were not exempt from her wrath.

No matter how many times the Reverend Knott Enuff Money or the Bishop Was Nevercalled got up and yelled that God was the head of their lives, it was Mother Pray Onn that was the head of that church.

Ima's mother was Sasha's oldest sister. Much taller than Sasha by at least a foot, with an hour-glass figure, the bronze-colored, hazel-eyed Areel Hellraiser was another force to be reckoned with.

Between the nefarious deeds of a cautious but just-as-mean mother, and an outspoken, all-up-in-your-face aunt, Ima was bound to be a mess. And she was. Whatever meanness she'd witnessed during her youth she learned to master.

Ima lay back on the recliner. She started with a small giggle that suddenly turned into a full blast of laughter as she recalled one incident between her mother and aunt.

It was Christmas. Ima was nineteen and proud that she'd used her charms to wheedle a little extra offering from one of the older deacons. The way he'd explained it, he was "sowing a seed" into whatever she'd wanted.

She'd taken the money and bought her mother a beautiful lavender wool suit that clung to Areel's shapely body like a glove. Of course, Areel liked to dress inappropriately, often like a hooker, including when she attended church. She did so because it always caused some type of jealous chatter from the women and a rebuke from the pulpit to the back door. She liked that kind of attention.

That morning when Sasha and her daughter, Carrie Onn, came by Ima and Areel's house, Sasha saw the beautiful suit and was instantly jealous. Sasha turned on her daughter without blinking. "You're a poor excuse for a daughter — my only child at that. Why couldn't you buy something that nice, instead of always making a mortgage payment as a gift?"

All Carrie Onn could do was stand in the middle of Areel's living room in tears and embarrassment.

Sasha first asked Areel if she could wear the outfit to church that day. It didn't matter that it would never fit her small, shapeless body or that it was a gift. She wanted that suit.

The first warning to Areel should've been when Sasha backed down and apologized for even suggesting such an outrageous thing on Christmas. But Areel, caught up in putting on too much make-up, wasn't on her guard.

It was a huge mistake.

About ten minutes before everyone was to leave for the service, Sasha started joking around. She started slowly with a small lie. Sasha knew it would get Areel's attention as well as cause her to start laughing.

As confident as Areel was, in most areas, she still had a weakness. She would always break out in a drenching sweat when she laughed.

Before Ima and Carrie Onn caught on to what Sasha was doing, it was much too late.

Areel started laughing hard but not hard enough for Sasha. Sasha rushed her big sister and started tickling her. Sasha was on Areel like a swarm of bees. She was grabbing and tickling her sister like a madwoman.

The inevitable happened. Areel started sweating and, of course, ruined the new suit. There was no way she was going to church with sweat stains on her clothes. She didn't have time to change into something just as inappropriate. So she got dressed in a long dress that would make the church happy and sulked.

Areel also put Sasha out of her house. That didn't bother Sasha at all. She made it to church just in time to holler, "Hallelujah, Christ is born."

Sasha was so pleased with herself that she almost shouted out of her own clothes.

Of course, Areal served up a huge plate of payback. The following Sunday, she gave Sasha several bars of Ex-Lax disguised in Almond Joy wrappers. It was one of the few times that Sasha ever missed church. She couldn't go anywhere for several days; she was too weak.

Ima was laughing so hard remembering that day until she, too, realized that the apple didn't fall to far from the tree. She leapt from the recliner and rushed into the bathroom.

By the time Ima finished showering she'd concocted a plan. If things went the way she'd wanted, she'd have Lyon's manhood on a spit, her aunt and Mother Blister ready to be committed, and Birdie would pay for all of it. She hadn't decided what or if she was going to do anything to Needy. After all, Needy had referred her. Obviously, she was a fan.

Before Ima got in her bed, she looked again at the faded and almost shredded picture of Lyon lying on her nightstand. The Scotch tape that Needy used to put the picture together again only made the man more unrecognizable. It didn't matter. She had the telephone number and tomorrow she'd put her plan for Lyon Lipps into action.

In the meantime, she still had to get her aunt to go on the cruise. The dial on the clock read ten. It was probably too late to call Mother Pray Onn. *Old crabs do need a lot of sleep.* She laughed softly, thinking that perhaps the old woman was dreaming of a new and vicious way to torment someone.

Ima was suddenly in an even better mood and decided to share it with her cat. She reached over and grabbed Evilene, who had managed to cower beside the nightstand. Ima was going to let Evilene sleep in the bed.

The cat, thinking that Ima had found that little mound of poop in the living room, started clawing for its life.

"Ouch!" Ima screamed as she tossed the cat. She jumped from the bed and checked her finger for blood. "Are you crazy?"

Like two gladiators, they circled one another. Ima hissed and reached out while Evilene hissed too, and backed up. They were about to start spitting but the ringing of the telephone sent them to neutral corners.

"I'll deal with you later," Ima threatened, bringing her index finger across her throat for emphasis as she picked up the telephone receiver.

Evilene turned away from Ima. The cat hunched her back and raised her tail as she slinked away.

"Who is this?" Ima snapped. "It's too late to be calling my house."

"Oh give me a break," the raspy voice on the other end snapped back. "It ain't like you got a man in your home or you're doing something nice for someone." The voice quickly turned from vicious to sweet as it suddenly laughed and cooed, "What was I thinking, teasing you like that? Everybody knows you don't even have a man. You can't even get a man. You can't keep one even if you snag one by offering up some of your feminine goodies."

"I love you, too," Ima replied and laughed. "You gonna live a long time. I was just thinking about you."

"I have already lived a long time. I try to never think about you, but you're family."

"Who would you harass, Aunt Sasha, if you didn't have me?"

"I'd harass anybody and everybody. The good Lord didn't bless me with these good looks, sweet disposition and wisdom if He didn't want me to use it."

"He didn't bless you with any of those things and what He did give you, you use as weapons."

"You know it!" Sasha cheerfully replied.

"Why are you still up and calling me at this crazy hour?" Immediately, the feeling of well-being fled. Her aunt was up to something. A Hellraiser will always know when another Hellraiser is on the prowl. It was a DNA thing. Ima just needed to know five things from her Aunt Sasha: what, when, why, how and who.

Mother Pray Onn knew when she called Ima that Ima would be easy to taunt at that time of night. She'd only called her because she'd taken a nap earlier and was no longer sleepy.

"I'm just checking in on you." Sasha was lying but Ima was family, so it was okay. "How's that old cat of yours?" She smirked and hoped the double sexual meaning behind the word cat wasn't lost on Ima. That's what the women in her time called their private feminine parts.

"She's okay. Right now, she's dragging her butt around on the floor. I think she's in heat."

Mother Pray Onn could hardly contain herself as she innocently served Ima a Hellraiser double-diss special. "Well then, I guess both of you are leaving burn marks in the carpet. Suppose we just take the both of you and get you neutered or spayed, which-ever one they do." She could no longer hold it. She started laughing and stammering. "We . . . can . . . get . . . a . . . two-for-one . . ."

That was a slam-dunk served lower than low.

Ima's vicious reply was already on her tongue, locked and loaded for fire, yet she held back. Her aunt had just given her the opportunity she needed to haul her old behind on the cruise.

"You are just too cute, Auntie."

She's not yelling and she called me Auntie. Something is not right, but what? Sasha said nothing. She turned her hearing aid up to full volume and continued to listen.

Ima knew she'd caught her aunt off guard and was relishing having the upper hand. "Your mentioning of a two-for-one deal just brought something to mind." She stopped to let it sink in. It was Ima's way of letting her aunt know that she heard the insult and would probably deal with it later.

"I've been given a trip for two on an ocean liner and I was wondering if my favorite aunt would like to come along."

She'd thrown Sasha the line and now all she had to do was reel her in and toss the old fish in the cabin with the other old fish,

Mother Blister.

"What's the catch?" Mother Pray Onn was not about to walk blindly into something. Yet, the idea of taking a cruise was definitely appealing.

You're the catch, Ima thought, but instead she replied, "You're too suspicious. I just want my favorite auntie to come along with me on this fabulous, fun-filled cruise."

There's that word again, "auntie." I'm her only aunt so I know this imp is up to something. I'm gonna find out even if I have to take a cruise to do it, Sasha Pray Onn thought.

"I'm sorry, honey. Of course, I'll think about going." She carefully added, "You're my favorite niece, too."

Ima knew her aunt was suspicious so she tried to sound more confident. "That's wonderful. I'm so excited. I'll call you tomorrow with the details." Ima couldn't help but toss a log onto the fire by adding, "You get some rest. I'll take a shower, again, and cool my burning *cat.* I meant body."

How was Mother Pray Onn supposed to get any sleep behind Ima's cutting remark? It was going to be a long night and if necessary, she'd use the time to plot just in case Ima was really up to something evil.

Ima was about to hang up the phone when

her aunt stopped her with one more question.

"Ima, what is the name of this wonderful ocean liner?" She needed to verify the legitimacy of the offer. She wasn't taking any chances.

"It's called the *Desperation of the Seas*," Ima answered.

"Of course, it is," Mother Pray Onn remarked, chuckling.

The next thing Ima heard was the dial tone.

She was beginning to have doubts. That was not like her. How was she going to pull off waylaying Lyon Lipps *and* keep her eye on her aunt?

All she'd wanted was for her aunt to come along and torment Mother Blister.

It took Ima several hours before she finally drifted off. While she tossed and turned, Evilene kept watch. Just the sight of Ima bouncing around the bed in discomfort caused the cat to purr, lick its paws and curl up.

With everything that was about to go down, it was a good time to be a cat.

9

Mother Sasha Pray Onn willed her tired body from her bed. With feet the size of a small child's, she slid them, bunions and all, into a pair of her favorite Sponge Bob slippers, and inched her way into the bathroom.

She slowly refilled the small jar that held a pair of off-color false teeth with warm water and a Efferdent cleaning tablet.

I know my niece is up to something, but what? That question plagued her through most of the morning. It seemed that no matter what she did or was about to do, the same question invaded her mind. *What is Ima up to?*

In the Hellraiser family, no one did or said anything nice unless there was something they wanted or needed. It was their custom.

She poured a cup of tea and felt very full. "Did I have a cup of tea already?" She couldn't recall if she had. She'd asked the question not expecting an answer because she lived alone.

For the past few months it seemed that Mother Pray Onn's memory had started slipping. If she wasn't repeating herself or misplacing her house keys, she was over-watering her plants.

A little later that morning she was on her front porch rearranging her cacti. She'd forgotten that she'd watered them the day before and was about to drown them with more. She moved cautiously from pot to pot, breathing in the fresh air while trying to decide which of her chores to do next, or remember which she'd done already. At that moment, her arthritis wasn't acting up too bad so, perhaps, she would run errands in town.

"Hello." The voice had a tinny tone to it, and could only belong to one person.

Mother Pray Onn turned slowly with her trowel in one tiny hand and glared. She wanted to say something sharp but she'd left her teeth soaking in the bathroom, so she mumbled, "What do you want, Petunia?"

"I don't want nothing much. I was just out walking and saw that you were out on such a lovely day. After all, you're one of our sweetest church mothers and Ima's favorite aunt."

Mother Pray Onn's gums almost clacked together from the shock of Petunia's remarks. She walked a few inches forward and lay her trowel down on one of the porch chairs. Her eyes squinted as she adjusted her glasses while thinking and looking around. *This twig must've been out in the sun too long. She don't even live around here and I don't see that junk with a steering wheel. Something's not right. God is showing me that something just ain't right.*

Finding out what was really going on suddenly became more important than showing her unsightly dark speckled gums and her missing teeth.

"That's so sweet of you to say, daughter." Mother Pray Onn kept her eyes on Petunia, looking for some kind of sign.

Just like both Ima and Mother Pray Onn, Petunia had her motives, too. Honesty among the women was as scarce as a hen's tooth and a rooster's lip.

Mother Pray Onn and Petunia muddled through their niceties without any casualties. During the conversation Petunia let it slip, on purpose, that Ima was going on a cruise paid for entirely by a white woman. But not just any white woman: Birdie Tweet.

After Petunia's whining and working

Needy's last nerve, she had gotten this information, and ran directly to Mother Pray Onn. She would've never thought to venture into this dangerous lair if Needy hadn't thrown in the part about the rift between Birdie and Mother Pray Onn.

Before Petunia could say more, Mother Pray Onn grabbed the trowel and started slicing through one of her beloved cactus plants.

Petunia took it as a sign, said good-bye and retreated down the pathway winding like a snake as she went. If Mother Pray Onn became that mad just knowing that Ima had made alliances with someone she didn't like, what would she do to the messenger if she discovered that Mother Bea Blister was going on the cruise, too?

Mother Pray Onn willed herself to calm down. She needed to teach her niece a lesson about family loyalty. After several cups of hot, thick black coffee, she called her niece.

After several rings, an irritated and groggy voice finally whispered, "Hello."

Mother Pray Onn looked at the kitchen clock. It was almost noon. "Ima, sweetie, I'm sorry if I woke you."

Mother Pray Onn suddenly realized that she was about to give away her hand by being too nice, so she quickly added, "I'm sure you needed the extra sleep. You looked terrible the last time I saw you." She could almost visualize Ima's face twitching from the insult. She might as well drive her over the edge so she said, facetiously, "A man in your life would help you sleep better."

"I love you too, Aunt Sasha." Ima didn't sound too convincing. "So now, old woman, what do you want?"

"I told you that I would get back to you on whether or not I would take you up on your lovely offer."

"And . . ."

"I'm going with you as your all-expenses-paid guest."

"That's lovely, Auntie."

Suddenly Ima perked up. She hadn't expected it to be that easy, but she wasn't going to look a gift horse in the mouth.

10

Ima relaxed on her living room floor with her legs folded in the lotus position. She sipped and nibbled from a wooden tray holding a piping hot cup of orange-spice ginseng tea and peanut butter cookies.

She was quite pleased with the way her plans were preceding. And so, with a week and a half to go before the cruise, Ima made the most of her day. She set about meticulously designing Lyon's downfall.

On about the third day, she was ready to make contact with Lyon. During the previous two days, she'd done some snooping. It had taken a lot of effort because, unfortunately, at the time, Lyon was out of town.

Ima wasn't one who gave up easily, if ever. Along with several skillful lip lickings and eye battings, she'd used her sultry voice to massage information on Lyon's whereabouts from the security guard at Lyon's apartment building.

Ima also found out that depending on who inside Lyon's building she asked to describe Lyon, she'd get several different descriptions. The security guard thought Lyon was Hispanic. The neighborhood grocer swore that Lyon was Italian. It turned out that everybody she asked thought Lyon was something different.

Just when she was about to give up, she found a flyer folded under one of her windshield wiper blades. Normally, unwanted flyers would've made her angry, but not that time.

This one she'd seen before. "This is just what I need." Ima wasted no time in finding the address printed on the flyer.

Ima eased her rented, pearl-red 2005 Escalade, a temporary gift from Birdie, into a parking space that she made fit by nudging the cars in front and back with the Escalade's firm bumpers. She didn't care that it left slight dents on the other cars; she was on a mission.

Ima took in the paper-littered street of Divers Row as she strutted towards her goal. She had to walk around young girls dressed in the latest fashions pushing dirty strollers and babies. Two elderly pimps dressed like they were on a budget in polyester jumpsuits and baseball caps accosted her.

"Yo mama," one called out as he tried to pimp-walk. Arthritis made him look more like he was playing hopscotch.

"You look real good," the other chimed in with his long head bobbing and weaving. "You make the five and we let you keep three."

Both men stopped and slapped high fives, thinking they still had game as they shamelessly promised her the world. One evil stare from Ima promised to end theirs quickly. They scurried away into an abandoned building with the other vermin.

Ima saw the woman standing in the doorway. She looked the same as the picture on the flyer. A smile spread across Ima's face as she saw the sign hanging by a rope over the storefront doorway.

The sign read, MIZZ LAFONKA — LIFTING SPIRITS AND WALLETS.

"I should've thought of this before. She can tell me what I need to know and eliminate the stress," Ima murmured. She was well pleased with the idea.

The fortune teller, Mizz LaFonka, advertised that she was a purebred Gypsy. What she was was about five feet tall and well over two hundred and fifty pounds of pure con artist.

Showing her yellow speckled teeth, she stepped toward a designer-clad young man rushing past who looked like he had a few dollars. "I can lift that curse that your great-grandmother placed on your grandfather," she offered. ". . . Or I can place a bigger curse on you," she promised when it looked like he would ignore her.

He didn't ignore her but returned a string of cuss words that made the bold Mizz LaFonka blush. She was about to retreat when she spied Ima rushing purposefully towards her.

Mizz LaFonka recovered quickly after giving the approaching Ima the once-over. She automatically sensed a kinship with the strange woman.

After dispensing with all the little niceties, the two women entered the darkened room and sat.

"I need some information," Ima pressed. She never thought this would happen, but she found herself very leery.

"I know what you need," Mizz LaFonka offered. "That's why you come to me for help with your financial situation." She lifted one eyebrow for effect.

"No," Ima replied. "That's not it."

"Of course it is. You just don't know it yet," Mizz LaFonka urged.

"Before we go any further," Ima said, slowly, "how much is this little fact-finding mission gonna cost me?" She placed a twenty dollar bill on the table.

"We don't discuss money, yet."

Mizz LaFonka hopped up, nearly toppling the table and grabbed something from under a ragged towel. She placed the object on the table directly in front of her.

It was supposed to be a crystal ball. It was actually an old disco ball that had dulled with age. Her eyes slowly closed as she perpetrated a semi-trance while spinning the ball like a top.

"I see a very handsome man. Perhaps he is a Geechie or a Cherokee. I can't determine which, especially since I only see twenty dollars on the table," she said, peering over the twirling ball.

Suddenly Ima felt intrigued; she couldn't be totally sure that she wasn't becoming hypnotized by the spinning crystal ball. Perhaps it was all the multi-colored lava lamps or the cinnamon-perfumed incense sticks that held her captive.

The Gypsy also had Al Green playing in the background for no apparent reason other than she liked his voice. So while switching her hips in her seat to the sexy tones of Al Green, Ima laid out another fifty dollars of Birdie's money.

"I see that this man is a preacher," Mizz LaFonka added cheerfully as she swiped the money off the table and stuffed it up one long sleeve. She rose and pointed at Ima and then towards her door. "I see nothing else for this little bit of money."

I can't believe I paid this crazy woman seventy dollars to tell me that Al Green is a preacher. Who doesn't know that? Ima was about to go off on the woman and get a refund but then she heard the voice of James Brown warbling, "It's a Man's World," from the stereo speakers.

It was an unwritten rule. If one was down with James Brown then any stupid thing one did or said received an automatic pass.

Instead of attacking Mizz LaFonka, Ima decided that she'd bill Birdie extra for the time she'd spent on the investigation. As much as she still wanted to slap the woman and shatter that crystal ball, Ima mumbled her goodbyes and started to leave.

The sneer on Ima's face along with the mumbled and hissing goodbyes made Mizz LaFonka suspicious. Ima's words sounded more like a curse.

To be on the safe side, Mizz LaFonka grabbed a small bag and rushed past Ima. She blocked the door with her legs parted, ready to tackle. She then returned Ima's hissing with some of her own and spun like a top. From her bag she started tossing black chicken feathers and purple jellybeans out the door and onto the sidewalk. Tossing her head back, she started screaming obscenities while placing a curse of her own on Ima's entire family for generations to come.

Ima flew out the door. She hopscotched over the spilled candy, laughing all the way to her car. "Woman, you've lost your touch." Ima stopped long enough to squash a jellybean with her shoe. "Your curses mean as much to me as this jellybean."

Like a spoiled child having a fit, Ima continued to squash the jellybean. In the heat, the waxy substance stuck to her sandal. The words she let out had nothing to do with LaFonka. At that point, she was just angry. She'd just gotten those sandals. It looked as though Birdie would have to buy her another pair.

"You never gonna find love. Nobody will ever love you or your entire family, ever," LaFonka predicted. She was so mad she started twisting the chicken feathers until they became as small as a wren's wing.

The sight of Mizz LaFonka reshaping chicken feathers temporarily caused Ima to forget about the sticky mess she was tracking inside the car. Several people had gathered around Mizz LaFonka in disbelief. They'd never seen her so riled. Everything she said commanded obedience on that block and now this strange and beautiful woman had her losing control on the hot sidewalk.

As Ima drove away, a line of gawkers now emboldened by her strange behavior lined up to get a refund from Mizz LaFonka. She was so beside herself she actually started handing out dollar bills and chicken feathers.

On her drive back to her side of town, Ima drove erratically, sometimes slow, and then speeding up, and narrowly missing other cars. The persistent honking of car horns, on both sides of the street, interrupted her thoughts. She responded with either an irreverent back flip of her hand or, to those even more annoying, she gave the middle finger salute.

By the time Ima pulled into Needy's driveway, she had forgotten about the little slight, the cryptic curse and the bad information she'd received from Mizz LaFonka. Ima slammed the car door hard enough almost to break the glass. "With or without help, I'm gonna find this man. He will never know what hit him. I'm gonna break him in two, and then in two, again."

Ima had formed a new plan and knew exactly how she would get Lyon to fall in line with it.

11

Needy's pacing was beginning to work Birdie's nerves. Needy had done nothing but pace and complain for the twenty minutes since Birdie's arrival at her home. And it didn't help that it was still hotter inside the house than outside.

Ima dashed into the room. Although Needy had stopped pacing, it took a moment before the rest of her did.

Ima completely dismissed the aggravated look on Needy's face as well as the questioning stare from Birdie.

"Ya'll will not believe what I found out." Ima was in her element as she watched the itch for more information spread from Needy to Birdie.

"Are you going to tell us or do I tell Birdie to get a refund?" Needy's patience was evaporating faster than the deodorant under her clammy armpits.

"Our boy is rich!" Ima gushed. "I mean

he's loaded and he's ready for the picking."

"What in the world are you ranting about? How long were you out in that hot sun?" Needy questioned. There was something different about Ima's disposition. It wasn't necessarily something good or bad, just different.

Ima dismissed Needy's questions with her usual flip of the hand. She took her time as she gave them, piece by piece, the information she'd uncovered.

Ima told how she'd discovered from her secret sources that since Lyon's release from prison, he'd done very well financially. "Where that trifling piece of garbage lives," she said, "everything from the flamboyant sculptures in the building's lobby to the well-dressed tenants and even the snobby doorman screams *We've got tons of money.* Nobody had to tell me that he was getting paid."

By the time Ima finished giving her report they were convinced that the building and the area was definitely too upscale for an ex-con to live, unless he was still into something illegal.

For the next two hours, the women plotted and prayed. Their Christian-lite conscience seemed comfortable with alternately asking God for a man to come into their lives and having one eliminated from the planet. By the time they'd finished holding hands and petitioning heaven, complete with sobbing and shouting, they'd asked God to release all seven of the known plagues on Lyon. Ima asked God to make it impossible for him to have children and to snip off the tool needed to do so, slowly.

By the time Ima finished with her pleas to heaven, Needy knew that God must've needed a Tylenol.

But Ima was just getting started in her quest to sway God over to her side. She was praying like Hell was nipping at her behind. With her body and hands outstretched on Needy's living room floor, she promised God that she'd give Him the honor and the glory if she could watch Lyon's demise.

Needy and Birdie quickly backed away from Ima. Suddenly they didn't want to be too close to the feminine demon they'd hired to do their dirty work. If Ima could plead for God's wrath on a person she'd never met, how would *they* fare against her?

By the time Needy and Birdie summoned enough courage to move and help Ima from the floor, minutes had swept by.

"Take your hands off me, I don't need or want your help." Ima shoved them away. She never liked women who didn't have a man in their life to touch her. Anything more than a handshake felt a little too strange.

Just sniping at them made Ima feel much better about being seen praying, which she took as a sign of weakness or desperation.

It wasn't that Hellraisers didn't pray — they just didn't need everyone to know that they did so.

Tension flooded the room riding high on a wave of suspicion. The chatty women suddenly didn't know what to say. To lighten the situation, Birdie suggested that they go out to dinner — on her, of course. She'd hoped that a change of scenery might remind them of their mutual purposes.

"Well, if you're paying, I'm going." Needy's laugh sounded more like hiccups.

"You know how I'll support you in your effort to atone for your people with reparation acts anytime you ask," Ima smirked. She meant every word she'd said.

Again, Birdie was being held financially captive because of her skin color, and even more so because of her generosity. Becoming one of the churchy home girls was becoming very expensive. But, if she backed out they'd rescind their offer to let her be a part of their unique clique, and she needed them as much as they needed her.

Not one word passed among the women as they rode in Needy's Civic, but it didn't last long enough. As soon as Birdie let down the passenger-side window for some air, peace flew out, snatching any semblance of unity with it.

On the way to the restaurant, the women bickered about everything from the ridiculous to the sublime. Who would make the first move in snaring Lyon? How far did they need to go in snaring Lyon without collateral damage? They even argued over who they thought could become the next Mrs. Noel Jones, as if Bishop Jones had sent each a silent invitation during that Sunday's service.

After gorging themselves on filet mignon and strawberry cheesecake they complained about the evils of weight gain and solidified their plans.

12

It was Thursday morning and about a week to go before they sailed. Ima awoke in one of the best moods she'd had in quite a while. Just the thought of what she was about to perpetrate made her swoon with delight. The timeframe was a little close but still doable.

That entire day she sang and played a Yolanda Adams song, "The Battle Is Not Yours," repeatedly as she cleaned her house.

She didn't necessarily believe all the words but she loved anything the woman sang. In Ima's eyes, Yolanda Adams was the only gospel singer who was as sexy as she. She could live with that as long as Yolanda stuck to singing.

Evilene crept into the room and when the cat spied Ima's over-the-top giddiness, it caused her to chime in with purring. The cat hadn't felt that relaxed in quite some time. She also hadn't felt that hungry. Ima had forgotten to fill her kitty bowl.

By that evening Ima should've been ready to fall out tired, but instead she prepared for phase two of her day.

Ima went all out. She showered and dressed in a sleeveless orange dress that seemed to bless her mocha complexion. The dress fit Ima as if she'd been wearing the material when it was sewn together. Her hair, freshly washed and curled, gave her a look of elegance. Even her open-toed sandals showing her orange pearl-polished toes looked inviting.

The bait, all five foot six of her, looked fetching and the hook was about to drop. In Ima's world, she used sex appeal as a weapon, so she always dressed sexy, even to place a phone call.

There was a lot of purring going on inside Ima's bedroom. Some of the purring came from Ima as she modeled her feminine goods in the mirror. The rest of the purring came from Evilene who was becoming weaker from hunger.

With one final look in her mirror, she was ready. Ima's fingers stroked the telephone keypad as she keyed in the numbers.

Needy and Birdie had rehearsed her about what she'd say until she almost had tears from the boredom. She knew exactly what to say, and she'd deliver the message with the subtlety of a club hammer.

No matter how rich Lyon was, he was no different than any other well-off person. He'd never refuse anything that was free. Of that, she was certain.

The plan was that Ima would call Lyon under the pretense of informing him that he'd won a free cruise that was departing in about a week. She'd pretend that his name was drawn from a mystery list of eligible bachelors submitted by an elite group of women calling themselves The Pelzer, South Carolina 100 Unattached Women of Influence.

She'd stroke his male ego until he was a lump of silly putty.

In Ima's world, she got whatever she wanted, but she wasn't prepared for what she heard.

"Hello," the male voice answered in a tone that was deep but not overbearing. It was sweet but not syrupy. The voice intoxicated Ima from its first word. It swept through every female defense she'd built for lifelong protection. For the first time in her life, Ima felt defenseless.

"Hello," he repeated. "Who's there?"

Ima slammed the receiver back into its cradle, the loud noise causing the fur on

Evilene's back to rise as the cat fled the room.

Ima's mind spun as she allowed excuses to accompany her panic. *I must've awakened him. I need him to be alert when I draw him into the plan. I'll call him back tomorrow.*

Ima's face twitched as the two-second conversation replayed in her mind. It'd never occurred to her that a voice as masculine as the one that replied could belong to Lyon Lipps. How was she supposed to know that? As far as she was concerned, Lyon was a crumbled and unrecognizable face on a faded mugshot. He was a man who'd wronged many women. That was all she needed to know to seek revenge.

As much as Ima teased the other women, if they ever discovered the truth that she was just like them, they would never let her live it down. Even Petunia might've had a date more recently than she had. That thought almost caused Ima to weep.

Ima was a broken woman who didn't trust men. She'd earned the right to be so. Trying to avoid the touching from Areel's many boyfriends, and even some of the men in the neighborhood, had turned her off at an early age.

Ima, still unexpectedly dazed from the phone call, took her clothes off slowly.

Unconsciously, she pouted as she carefully removed her makeup. Even in her distress, she moved in a way any red-blooded man would've appreciated. But there was no man in Ima's world. There was no man in her home to see her when she routinely slithered her fabulous body into a form-fitting nightshirt in front of her standing mirror. No man's body commandeered the sheets or snored loudly while she lay in her spacious queen-sized bed.

Sleep played tag with Ima throughout the night.

But, the rule of the universe was that the sun rose and set on the just and the unjust. When it rained, it rained on the just and the unjust. And, when one dug a hole for another, they'd better dig two.

The rule of the universe was about to clash with Ima's rule of survival.

13

Around 6:30 p.m., with Petunia's car still disabled, Cill picked her up in her 2003 black Jaguar with tinted windows.

They'd already decided that even if they weren't going on the cruise, they'd still be in on the plot. When it came time to announce Lyon Lipps' comeuppance they were determined to have bragging rights, too.

"Do you think any of them are suspicious?" Petunia asked Cill while donning a pair of oversized sunglasses. Any other time, she would've never completely trusted Cill, but with a common interest, she'd put her suspicions aside.

The sudden closeness of the two conspiring was lethal at the very least and extremely comical at its worst.

"Not at all," Cill responded. "You told Mother Pray Onn everything just the way we discussed, didn't you?"

"Of course, I did," Petunia replied, quickly. "You're acting like I'm not down with the plan." She didn't bother to mention to Cill how being in Mother Pray Onn's company had caused her to forget to mention Mother Blister's participation.

"Good. Let's get over to Needy's before Birdie and Ima show up." Cill laughed. She loved military-like drama because it took finesse and skill to manipulate people. Cill had skills.

"What about Mother Blister showing up? You did take care of that, didn't you?" Petunia wanted to make sure every part of their plan was covered. And she really didn't want to hear Cill brag about how she was the one who made sure that everything went well.

"When I left her this morning, she wasn't in shape to go anywhere." Cill's laugh echoed around the inside of the car.

"What . . . did . . . you . . . do?" Petunia asked cautiously. She didn't put much past Cill.

"When we chatted I mentioned that I would be in her neighborhood and wanted to check up on her. She asked would I stop by the store on my way to visit her. She needed a jar of orange-flavored Tang. I got orange-flavored Metamucil, instead."

"Oh, you are so wrong on too many levels for me to count." Petunia started laughing and placing her hands on her invisible chest and that set Cill off into hysterics, again.

"Let's just say that she'll be sitting for most of the day. If we need her we'll just follow the smell."

Petunia went along with the crazy this-can-only-end-badly plan to one-up Ima and the other club members.

As Cill and Petunia waited out of sight at the end of the block, they watched Birdie arrive with Ima. There was no way they could hear what the women were saying, but even in the dark, their cheerful looks didn't sit well with Cill and Petunia.

They waited another fifteen minutes and then drove slowly down the block to Needy's house and knocked on the door.

Needy answered her door in complete shock. She hadn't expected to see Cill or Petunia. It wasn't that she didn't want to see Petunia and she felt the same about Cill, but the sight of them together put her on guard.

Cill and Petunia each gave Needy a respectful peck on her plump cheek. It was quick as they tried to dodge her spiked top lip hair.

"I wasn't expecting to see you two,"

Needy said as she tried to read their expressions.

Their faces looked blank, giving away nothing.

"We were in the neighborhood and had stopped by Mother Blister's," Cill offered. She looked Needy straight in the face daring her to disbelieve the lie.

"We just thought we'd stop by once we found out that Mother Blister was under the weather and wouldn't be coming to your meeting. If there's anything, any little thing, that we can do, all you need to do is ask," Petunia added, quickly. She never could or would lie as well as Cill but she gave it her best shot.

"Mother Blister's not coming?" Needy was surprised since she'd spoken to Mother Blister earlier that morning and she seemed anxious to come and hear the latest.

"She decided to stay at home and disinfect her bathroom," Cill said. "You know how weak her bladder is."

That definitely seemed plausible to Needy.

"That's right," Petunia interrupted. "We've come to do our Christian duty and report everything back to her."

Needy almost bought that excuse until she saw Petunia crossing her arms over that invisible chest, which caused Petunia's back to hunch.

"Well, that's okay with me," Needy lied, almost as well as Petunia.

Almost.

"Just let me go back and speak with Ima and Birdie. We were going to have the meeting in my kitchen but since it's too small to add anyone else, I'll bring them out here. Make yourself at home. I'll be back in a minute."

Needy started to back away, not daring to take her eyes off Petunia.

However, she should've watched Cill instead. Needy's apprehension was not lost upon Cill at all.

The green army fatigues Cill wore paled in comparison to the ugly green-with-envy grin that inched across her face as Needy left the room.

Needy quickly brought Birdie and Ima up to date. It was Ima's suggestion that she take over the meeting, thereby insuring that Petunia and Cill would only find out what she wanted them to know.

Birdie didn't seem comfortable with the deceit. She didn't mind plotting to take down Lyon Lipps, he was the enemy; but she felt it was a betrayal to deceive Cill and Petunia.

On the way to the living room, Ima took the opportunity to warn Birdie. "You do know that I don't give refunds? If you botch this because you have a conscience, it won't be my fault."

It made sense to Birdie. She'd keep quiet.

"Hi there, Petunia, how are you? And, you too, hello Cill," Ima said, smiling as she circled the women like the head jackal of a ravenous pack.

It took a jackal to know a jackal. Cill started moving from side-to-side as if she were waiting to tackle Ima.

Right away, Needy remembered the scene from the movie *Cooley High* where the conked-haired thugs started fighting and tearing up the living room. She knew the two women were just as dangerous. "Okay, can we get this meeting started?" Needy asked as she bravely stepped between Cill and Ima.

A sigh of relief filtered throughout the room as Cill and Ima backed off into neutral corners. However, everyone in the room, except Birdie, knew that the fight was only postponed, not cancelled.

True to form, Ima took over the meeting. She fed Petunia and Cill a diet of half-truths of which they anxiously ate. As she spun a web of lies, the answer to her biggest problem came to her.

"I'm so happy to see that you two ladies aren't upset about not going on the cruise," Ima said as she cheesed through her perfectly lined-up teeth.

"We haven't given it a second thought," Petunia blurted.

You're such an amateur, Ima thought as she fought to keep from laughing at Petunia's child-like attempt to lie.

"I'm happy to hear that," Ima said. She was about to add more but Needy tossed in her two cents.

"That sure took a load off my mind. I felt for sure that you two would be teed off." Needy nodded towards Birdie and Ima trying to give them a look that read, *We were worried for nothing.*

Birdie's entire body relaxed as she nodded her confirmation.

Ima totally ignored Needy's stupid conclusion, choosing instead to keep her eyes fixed upon Cill as she continued speaking. "What I'm about to ask you to do may seem trite but it is essential to our plan. I'm hoping you won't say no."

Ima had Cill just where she wanted her. If Cill wouldn't go along with the request then she'd show contradiction. Checkmate.

Cill almost jumped out of her seat. The

witch had her. Cill would've rather chewed and swallowed porcupine quills than let Ima embarrass her. "Just tell what you need me to do." The words were sweet but they spewed through sour lips.

"It's no big deal," Ima said as she again came near Cill. "All you have to do is call Lyon Lipps and just read off a prepared script."

"Why don't you do it?" Cill asked. The request was a little too simple not to be dangerous.

"I can't do it because I've got other things to do," Ima said through clenched teeth. She never liked to have her orders challenged. "And I don't want him to recognize my voice later when I do the dirty deed."

"I'll do it," Petunia said as a peace offering.

"No, you can't do it," Ima barked, causing Petunia to sink further back into the chair to resume her resemblance to a pincushion. "I need to have Cill do it."

Facing Cill again Ima taunted, "I want to make sure that this is done right. Cill can speak to Lyon, man-to-man."

The only thing that kept those two from tearing each other apart was a sudden power failure caused by Needy's old air conditioner. By the time Needy found a fuse and had the electricity turned back on, tempers had cooled.

Ima carefully laid out the plan to Cill, who genuinely seemed to embrace the idea of snaring Lyon with her participation.

After careful consideration, they even gave Petunia a small part to play. A part that, they hoped, she wouldn't mess up. All she had to do was dial the telephone number.

It seemed that all of the women in the room, with the exception of Birdie, had their own agendas. Of course, Birdie didn't have a clue. She only had the money.

14

"All you had to do was dial a doggone number." Cill had her fists balled and was ready to work Petunia over. "Nobody told you to start breathing heavy into the phone."

"I'm sorry," Petunia whimpered as she picked up the telephone from Cill's floor and replaced its receiver. "I sort of lost it."

Petunia hadn't heard a man's voice that deep and sexy since she'd accidentally played a Barry White song, "It's Ecstasy," at one of the church socials instead of a John P. Kee gospel song.

"What am I gonna do with you?" Cill asked. "You seem to always mess up the simplest thing."

"I said I was sorry."

"I thought you'd learned your lesson after holding Sister Swan's bachelorette's party in the church's fellowship hall."

"Are you ever gonna let me live that down?"

"No, I won't. Do you know how bad you traumatized those folks?"

"It wasn't that bad."

"Who are you kidding? Some of those elderly mothers from the Mothers Board still haven't gotten over running into those male strippers at the eight o'clock morning service. Most of them hadn't seen that much nudity since —"

Several pictures of the Mothers Board members with flushed faces popped into her head, making it necessary to add, "Never. The only time those old women get a chance to see male nakedness is when they're changing baby diapers."

"I made a simple mistake." Petunia wanted to put a different spin on it so she quickly added, "At least the deacons liked my effort."

Cill didn't bother to reply. Instead, she shook the stiffness from her fist and snatched the telephone. She laid it on her lap and started dialing. "I hope this man doesn't have Caller ID."

"Hello." This time the voice sounded agitated and heavy but a lot less sexy.

"May I please speak with a Mr. Lyon Lipps?" Cill's voice was almost as deep. She used that tone when bill collectors called her house. Usually, Cill had them confused, and they'd end up apologizing and promising to recheck their numbers. It normally gave her an extra week's extension.

"This is his brother. I'm sorry but Lyon is out right now. Would you like to leave a number where he can call back? Or, would you prefer to leave a message?"

Cill didn't know whether to believe him or not. She decided to go on the assumption that perhaps he was telling the truth.

"I'm sorry to hear that he's not available. I'm calling from the marketing firm of . . ." Cill purposely started hissing into the phone as she pretended to say the company's name three times before continuing. "I'm so sorry. We're on a new phone system and I'm afraid we still have to work out the kinks."

"That's okay. Lyon just walked through the door. Would you care to hold?"

Of course, I'd care to hold, you idiot. I called to speak with him and not waste my time with you. That's what she thought but she was smart enough to keep it at that, just a thought.

"That would be wonderful," Cill replied. She could hear him call out Lyon's name.

When Lyon finally answered the phone in a voice not quite as masculine as his brother's, Cill went into her rehearsed speech.

Cill managed to convince Lyon that he'd

won an all-expense-paid trip aboard the *Desperation of the Seas* liner. She gave him all the rehearsed particulars about why the women's group nominated him for the prize. And he unknowingly gave her his true address, social security number and every other tool to use to destroy his life.

When Cill finally hung up she then knew something that neither Ima nor Petunia knew. The deep baritone voice that made Petunia act trashy belonged to Lyon's brother.

Lyon's voice, on the other hand, was more timid. His voice was about as threatening as a flea fighting a mountain lion.

Cill never claimed to be an authority on human nature. However, she gleaned nothing from the short conversation that would've convinced her of his guilt, except that her sister said he was guilty.

Cill decided to keep her thoughts a secret. She also determined that perhaps she needed to do a little investigating on her own. In the meantime, she'd report the first phase of the plan a success.

15

Lyon slowly replaced the phone in its cradle and laughed. "I've won a trip. Can you believe it?" He raised his hand to receive a high five from his brother, Lionel.

"I don't believe this. You get a trip and all I get is a silent phone call in the middle of the night, and another one earlier with someone breathing heavy."

"And that's a bad thing because . . ."

"It's a bad thing because if I knew who called and hung up breathing heavy, I could take her on a real cruise. Of course, that would come sometime later, after I got to know her and perhaps married her."

"That's right, one thing at a time." Lyon loved his brother's wonderful sense of humor, a trait that Lionel inherited from their late mother.

Lionel and Lyon were twins but were not always close. While Lionel excelled in his school studies, Lyon excelled in the hard-knock life lessons of the streets. However, when both parents passed away two years ago, it brought them together in a way twins should be.

"God is so good. Imagine that, I've won an all-expense-paid cruise. I've received so many blessings since I changed my life. I just can't believe it." Lyon kept laughing as he praised God.

"You can believe one thing for sure."

"What's that, Reverend Lipps?" Lyon asked, innocently. He was too happy to hear any doubts, even from his twin brother.

"When you are on a path to righteousness, you have to pray as well as watch." Lionel's heavy voice softened, as he lay his hands on Lyon's shoulder. "You're still a babe-in-Christ. You've overcome a lot. Your testimony of overcoming a life of crime and using women is why God has let you go through so much. You are now a salesman for God, yet you have to be careful."

"As much as I want to say that you don't know everything, I can't." Lyon smiled. His honey complexion seemed to lighten, as did his soft green eyes. "I'll use this opportunity to cruise and pray. I'll let God lead me."

"Well it looks like the brothers will be cruising together soon," Lionel laughed.

"Wow. I almost forgot. You're cruising too.

When will you and Bishop Jones leave?"

"Next week if he can still make it happen. If he can't then I'm sure my baby brother will permit me to hang with him."

"You need to cut out that baby brother bit. Just because you're four minutes older don't make you wiser."

"Ah, but it does — because I'm smart enough to know that it will be a week of glorious sailing, a chance for fellowship, and plenty of food." Lionel reached into the telephone table drawer and retrieved a small packet.

"That's when I'll be leaving, as well. I guess we'll have to compare notes when we return."

Lionel looked at the paper where he'd written down the cruise info.

"Where are you going?" Lionel asked, noting Lyon hadn't picked up the packet yet.

"Leaving from Miami and then on to Jamaica, Mexico, and St. Maarten," Lyon said as he quickly added, "Hallelujah. God is so good."

"He sure is. Those are the same places I'll visit." Lionel's joy increased just knowing that he and Lyon could compare their travels when they returned.

"Perhaps we can get together if we're on the same island at the same time," Lyon said. Like his brother, his cup was beginning to run over.

"That sounds like a plan. What ship are you sailing on?" Lionel asked as he did a quick two-step to show his joy.

Lyon looked again at the paper before replying, "The *Desperation of the Seas*."

Lionel continued his little dance and then again held up his hand for a high five. "Amazing, that's just simply amazing."

"What is amazing?" Lyon asked.

"Pick up the packet and read, baby brother. Just pick up the packet and read."

16

The next day Mother Blister felt exhausted from taking the Metamucil Cill deceptively passed off as Tang. Her dark skin was almost blue from dehydration. She had dark circles around her eyes from the lack of sleep and her mood was far from Christian.

Although she felt ill she still regretted not attending the Mothers Board meeting, and the one at Needy's house the previous evening.

She would've loved to fight with Mother Pray Onn. The two of them when together were like gasoline and dynamite and twice as combustible. But in her condition, she would've lost any argument they'd had.

"I'm so tired and I feel like I've lost about five pounds," she said to her ashen reflection in the mirror that hung over her bed.

It took more effort than she wanted but Mother Blister finally made it through a bath and a sip of warm tea. She was seated in her living room trying to adjust her wig when the secret knock from Slim Pickens came.

In her foul mood, she could've shot him twice. Tired or not she still needed his financial help if she was to go on the cruise, so she dragged herself from the couch, her wig slanted, and let him in.

"Bea Blister, can you tell me what took you so long?" Slim's fussing began almost as soon as he managed to maneuver his walker across the threshold, leaving the door gaping open. His oversized brown-speckled glasses sat perched upon a skinny black nose that resembled a broken beak. His glasses sat lopsided and he had to lean his head a little to the side so he could see straight.

"I'm really not in the mood for your particular kind of craziness." Mother Blister felt her voice rising and was about to rein it in, but Slim wasn't finished being neurotic.

"You must think I'm really crazy. Well, I am. I'm crazy about you." He suddenly scanned the room and looked at her strangely, as he started fumbling around in his pocket. That confused Mother Blister.

She watched as Slim felt all over the front of his pants. It looked as though he was searching for his pocket in the wrong spot, but with Slim, she could never be sure. On the other hand, he might've just wanted to get down to business.

"Slim, can't you at least come all the way inside the door before our nosy neighbors see everything I've seen often and they've never seen before?"

"How do you know?" Slim asked. He didn't like being taken for granted — at least not to his face. He clucked his false teeth and started snapping one of his crusty fingers. "There are a lot of women living here that would welcome the company of a retired New York City detective who on a bad day solved more cases than Eliot Ness could on a good day."

Mother Blister was not impressed. She'd heard it all before and at that particular moment was close to forgetting about the cruise and shooting Slim.

"Just close the door." She was about to give him the Bea Blister speech about where he could go, how fast he could get there, and how he could never return. But that Metamucil wasn't finished with Mother Blister.

The only thing she could place on hold was Slim. When she dragged herself from the room to rush to the bathroom, he was still fussing.

Slim was so busy alternating between

rebuking and boasting he never noticed that Mother Blister had left the room. And, he never closed the door. From the hallway, he looked like a dark piece of a wilted, nutty chocolate bar, thrown over a walker.

Somehow as Slim went about his ranting he found what he searched for in his back pocket. It was an envelope with cash, which shook in his hands. His intention was to give it to Mother Blister, as he always did before their little trysts. This time, he'd added more as a bonus. Now he was too mad to conclude their date.

He'd seen the circles around Bea's eyes and the sweaty pallor of her complexion. *Bea's cheating on me. She's playing me for a fool. There ain't but one thing that would make her look like that and I didn't give it to her,* Slim concluded. *She ain't the only old fish in this sea. I'm gonna pay an early visit to Mrs. Tasty in 3C. We'll see who the fool is.*

Slim was so annoyed he could hardly turn his walker around and hold on to the envelope at the same time. He looked around the room for any sign that would confirm his suspicions. He didn't find any but it still didn't stop him from concluding that Mother Blister had done him wrong.

Slim knew that Mrs. Tasty would welcome him. She always did when he wanted to cheat on Mother Blister. Of course, his little once-in-a-while indiscretions, as far as he was concerned, were innocent. After all, he wasn't married.

By the time Mother Blister concluded her latest bathroom run and returned to her living room, Slim was gone. She was about to get angry but she spied a small white folded envelope by the door.

Slim must've dropped this on his way out. She picked up the envelope and felt its weight. Without opening it she expertly estimated it to be about seven hundred dollars. *He must've wanted me to have it but saw how sick I was and didn't want to bother me with working for it.*

She wasn't about to call Slim and ask him his real intentions or whether he'd accidentally dropped the envelope. As much trouble as she'd had with the law in the past, she knew about the nine-tenths possession law. Instead, she placed the envelope between the folds of her breasts, chuckled and silently thanked the Lord.

Mother Blister suddenly felt better. She'd be away from Slim, the nosy church members, and Mother Pray Onn, in particular, for seven whole days. She couldn't wait!

What could be better than to eat, drink and be merry while watching that scallywag, Lyon Lipps, get what was coming to him? At that moment, she could think of nothing.

Mother Blister was ready to set sail on the *Desperation of the Seas.*

17

For the past several days since giving Cill her assignment, Ima hadn't given much thought to the unsettling telephone call she'd placed. The rich baritone voice faded from her memory as she made the last-minute preparations to sail.

In her rush to put everything in place for the plan to succeed, she'd forgotten about Evilene. She couldn't trust her cat to spend a week alone without clawing everything to shreds. So, later on that afternoon, she ultimately threatened Petunia into keeping Evilene. She promised Petunia that when she returned she'd treat her to a girls' night out. Ima had no intention of keeping that promise since she never kept any promises. In her mind, a promise was just a series of words strung together to indicate what you might do, if you felt like it.

Ima also felt good about the report from Cill. Under any other circumstances she wouldn't have trusted Cill to do anything. However, Cill was trying to vindicate her sister. Ima had to respect her for that because she certainly wouldn't have done it.

The only task to complete was to get her aunt to Miami on a separate flight so they wouldn't run into Mother Blister.

It wasn't going to be easy. Mother Pray Onn had never flown before and only agreed to do so because she thought she was accompanying Ima.

By late afternoon, Birdie had managed to drive into town without any drama. The sky displayed a little overcast but not enough to dampen her spirits. She and her churchy home girls would be sailing in two days and life was just lovely.

Her first stop was at the bank. With her wide-brimmed straw hat bouncing as she strode, Birdie looked like a very slender, although not as shapely, Sharon Stone. The cream-colored matching sundress drew several stares, and Birdie took it as a compliment. No one bothered to tell her that the buttons on her top were out of line and the hem on her skirt was coming undone. She felt wonderful and wouldn't have cared if they did.

Birdie withdrew several thousand dollars

from her account, without any problems. She stopped at the travel agent, paid the balance, and picked up the airplane tickets without a problem. As she crossed the street to get into her car, she saw Mother Pray Onn approaching and thought, *Have mercy. I've got a problem.*

The dampness of the weather had kicked Mother Pray Onn's arthritis into high gear. Her entire body ached as she tried to shop for her trip. Even her oversized, high-arched, orthopedic shoes pinched her tiny feet. But when she spied Birdie coming out of the travel agency all the pain fled. She was determined to reach Birdie before Birdie drove away.

"Sister Birdie," Mother Pray Onn hollered. Even with less than several yards between them, she still yelled because she knew it would rattle Birdie. She also did it because she knew that Birdie would stay, out of respect for an older person, rooted to that spot until she got there.

Birdie felt helpless, her wonderful mood completely destroyed by the approach of an old, ornery woman. She looked desperate as she spun around looking for help. There wasn't a policeman, a reverend, a thug or even a Taliban there to help.

Birdie quickly prayed, "Lord, if I've said

or done anything that was not pleasing in thy sight, forgive me."

She prayed as though she was going to die, and heaven wasn't a certainty for her. That was the effect Mother Sasha Pray Onn had on most people.

Mother Pray Onn seemed to slow down when she saw that Birdie wouldn't or couldn't move. Seeing someone in fear made her tiny stature feel giant.

"I'm so glad to see you out and about today." Mother Pray Onn's grin was wide yet child-like. She looked at Birdie as though Birdie was the Special of the Day. The only thing missing was a bib around Mother Pray Onn's tiny wrinkled neck.

Birdie willed her lips to part and her tongue to be unglued from the roof of her mouth. She finally mumbled, "Thank you."

"I've been meaning to call you and apologize for the way I mistreated you when you first joined the church. That's not like me. I was probably feeling poorly that day."

"That's okay," Birdie said. A part of her wanted to leave in safety. The other part of her didn't listen and before she knew it she'd added, "If God can forgive my sins, I'm sure I can forgive yours."

"You can't possibly be suggesting that I'm a sinner," Mother Pray Onn snapped.

Birdie could've sworn that at that very moment, she'd actually seen the tightly wound gray bun fixed on Mother Pray Onn's head twist and turn. Birdie's nerves didn't wait for the rest of her to move; they fled and left her standing by the curb, shaking and speechless.

"Of course, you weren't. What was I thinking?" Mother Pray Onn could shadow box, mentally, with the best. "You're the sinner because I know you haven't attended church for as long as I have."

By the time Mother Pray Onn finished heaping layers of guilt upon Birdie, she'd tired of the game. She finally asked Birdie the question that was on her mind.

"I understand that you're underwriting this little cruise vacation for my niece, Ima. Why would you do that?"

"You really don't know why?" Birdie dared to ask.

"Of course I know what Ima told me, but I want the truth straight from the mule's mouth."

Mother Pray Onn had lied and called Birdie a jackass to her face. And, as usual, Birdie didn't know it.

"I believe that you meant, 'straight from the horse's mouth.' "

"I'm an old woman, sweetie. I always say

what I mean."

Mother Pray Onn's stern demeanor quickly changed. Her eyes magically appeared to be as sad as the puppies in the Pelzer Firehouse painting. She was slowly whittling away at Birdie's sympathy and before Birdie knew it, she'd offered to drive Mother Pray Onn around to run the rest of her errands.

Two hours later, instead of Mother Pray Onn being thankful, she insisted that they stop and get a bite to eat at one of the upscale soul food restaurants, Chez Chitterling's.

Not asking Birdie whether she even liked or had ever tasted soul food, Mother Pray Onn ordered for her.

Over a plate of steaming barbequed ribs, tangy coleslaw, pungent chitterlings, and skillet-baked cornbread dripping with butter, Mother Pray Onn put her plan into action. She was about to gnaw away at Birdie just as she was doing to her plate of gator and grits with cheese, of course.

Mother Pray Onn was a seasoned interrogator and in between bites of cornbread, which stuck to her dentures like paste, she had information pouring from Birdie's mouth. By the time the waiter brought the dessert, a bowl of deep-dish peach cobbler,

Mother Pray Onn knew everything about Birdie except what time she was born.

And, if Birdie had not drunk so many glasses of sweet tea to chase away the chitterling aftertaste, she might've even mentioned that Mother Blister was going, too. Every time she meant to mention Mother Blister's name, she'd burp in mid-sentence.

It was almost seven o'clock that evening when Birdie finally dropped Mother Pray Onn off in front of her door. The old woman had completely worn her out, both mentally and physically. In fact, Mother Pray Onn rattled Birdie's nerves so bad that Birdie actually went into her purse and gave Mother Pray Onn gas money for a car she didn't own before she drove away.

The way Mother Pray Onn saw it; it was the least Birdie could do. If she couldn't get that promised forty acres and a mule, she'd take the gas money.

18

It took sucking up and a wad of cash from Ima to make Mother Pray Onn agree to fly.

Ima didn't care about the cash but she was angry about all the nice little things she had to say to her aunt. But if things went according to plan, her aunt would be on a flight with Needy that would leave long before the one she and the others were taking.

Ima had started out telling a half-truth to her aunt. She always did that. That time Ima had to kick it up a notch.

Ima told her aunt that she was certain that one of the church sisters, a Sister Magpie, was sneaking away with Deacons Petrie to Florida. He'd told his wife, Sister Petrie, that he was going fishing.

"With a kisser like Sister Magpie's, he must be trying to hook something he's used to seeing. Like a snapper," Ima said, laughing. "I'd take the same flight as them but I want to give my seat to you. It will be just one more gift I can give to you."

"Well then, I guess you probably want me to spy on them," Mother Pray Onn replied. "I've been waiting to get the goods on that sanctimonious hypocrite every since she had one of her kids testify that they believed that their mother was still a virgin."

"That's just why I want you to go," Ima said. Her eye twitched. It was another sign that she was spinning the tale as she went.

Mother Pray Onn almost caught a cramp in her stomach trying to hold in the laughter. *She's such an amateur,* Mother Pray Onn hissed under her breath while smiling back in Ima's face.

If Ima had still been a young child and had made up such a ridiculous tale, Mother Pray Onn would've made her stand in a corner until she came up with a better lie. But Ima was a grown woman, and although her aunt could've still sent her to a corner, it would've been hard to keep her there.

Amused, Mother Pray Onn listened on intently while Ima juggled her lies. She knew that Deacon Petrie would not be going on any flight unless it was with the angels. At that moment, he was lying in No Mercy Medical Center's ICU. Besides, even in good health the good deacon would never cheat on his wife. Now Sister Petrie tipping out of town would've been closer to the truth. And as far as Sister Magpie was concerned; she was so ugly she couldn't steal a date with Stevie Wonder. He'd have seen that much ugly no matter how blind he was.

Ima should spend an extra hour in hell for lying on that poor Deacon Petrie. She's such a hypocrite. That's what Mother Pray Onn thought as she continued showing more gums than teeth.

She'd forgotten to put in her dentures again.

To see how far Ima was going with her game, Mother Pray Onn decided to go along with just about every ridiculous trick Ima devised. If Ima was this worked up, she couldn't wait to see what scheme Needy had in mind. She kept that grin plastered on her face until it was time to fly out of Pelzer.

The morning she was to leave, Birdie awoke and immediately knew something was wrong. As she looked around her spacious bedroom, she saw that everything seemed to be half the size.

Her nose was stuffy and her skin clammy to the touch. No sooner than her feet hit the floor, she felt a throbbing headache rush through her skull.

She wheezed and coughed her way into the bathroom. Birdie screamed loud enough to have the cops come running. She peeked in the mirror, through her half-opened eyes, at her reflection.

The answer to Birdie's dilemma came straight from the television. The weatherman stood in front of a map with pictures of trees, dust and ragweed plants. "Pollen count is at an all-time dangerous level today. If you don't have to go outside, don't."

Poor Birdie. With her eyes almost shut and her nose running a snotty Kentucky Derby, she looked a mess.

She needed to get it together. Ima and Mother Blister would arrive in a couple of hours and she needed to be ready.

Birdie swallowed a couple of Benedryl tablets and chased them with a large glass of warm Coca-Cola. She didn't want to leave anything in the refrigerator to spoil so it was the only thing she had in the house to drink.

She got the idea of mixing soda and Benedryl from an old college campus druggie named Cleotis. Birdie never used drugs. Cleotis had gone on to become a senator, so she figured it was okay to mix the two.

What she didn't know was that the pill and Coca-Cola combo was the thing that set Cleotis straight after a drug binge.

By the time Ima stopped by Birdie's to pick her up for the drive to the airport, Birdie was higher than that plane would ever get.

Ima couldn't believe her eyes. Birdie wore a pair of oversized, muddy-brown pedal pushers, a see-through green blouse, and a pair of mismatched black and blue socks with open-toed sandals. Her hair looked like a comb and brush were the enemy.

Birdie had packed her bags the night before, and they sat in the living room by the front door.

"Birdie," Ima fussed. "What happened to you?"

Birdie tried to answer but the inside of her mouth tasted like linty cotton balls as her thoughts played tag and skipped around in her mind. Of all the times to have her allergies flare up!

Time was passing quickly and Ima didn't have time to deal with Birdie's drama. The half-opened bottle of Benedryl and empty Coca-Cola bottle told it all. *What idiot would mix Benedryl and Coca-Cola?*

Again, Birdie tried to focus and mumble something. She failed at both.

Of course, it was our rich idiot; she would do something like that. Ima was beyond angry. She grabbed a pair of sunglasses from the dresser and slapped them onto Birdie's face hard enough to pop one of her reddened zits.

Any other time, Ima would've used Birdie's misfortune as an excuse and nosed around her house. Today, she didn't have the time.

Ima checked Birdie's purse and found the plane tickets lying on top. She searched around several compartments and found Birdie's passport. A few moments later, she found what seemed to be an inexhaustible amount of traveler's checks.

She pushed the set button on the alarm and held the door opened while she beckoned Mother Blister from the car. "Help me with this woman," Ima barked.

"You'd better respect your elders, particularly when you're asking me to drag a body someplace," Mother Blister responded.

And, that's when a part of Ima seriously thought about giving Birdie back her money and calling the whole thing off. The thought came from a small part of her that rebelled, so she quickly regrouped and ignored the feeling. After locking the door, which turned on the alarm, Ima and Mother Blister tossed

Birdie and Birdie's luggage into the car.

They either had forgotten, or didn't care about Birdie residing in such an affluent neighborhood. Because with all the years of jail time served between Ima and Mother Blister, Birdie could've developed a mild hiccup from the door to the curb, and those women would've served time for eternity, without a trial.

Grace and Mercy were on hand that afternoon when the spectacle of Mother Blister and Ima dragging a white woman and her luggage into an expensive 2005 Cadillac 300c rental didn't draw attention from the neighbors or make the six o'clock news. However, Grace and Mercy weren't getting in that car.

In the meantime, while the others were headed towards the airport, Cill and Petunia were still playing the detective game. It was Cill's idea to stake out Lyon's upscale building and see what opportunities arose to thwart Ima's grand plan. She still hadn't shared what little she knew about Lyon's identity.

Possessed with a need for attention, Petunia got deep into the game. She wore a beige raincoat and a matching hat. It didn't make her look like a detective, it made her look more like a chipped pencil with a dirty eraser.

Cill, on the other hand, opted for something more practical. She'd worn army-issued camouflage.

Armed with the remnants of Petunia's faded photo, they waited inside their car. Two hours later, they were still waiting, only this time on the sidewalk. The only activity they witnessed was the comings and goings of several grocery delivery boys who greeted the doorman as if they were old friends. Somewhere between a yawn and nod, Petunia spied two extremely handsome men dash into a waiting limousine. There was something familiar about the physique of one of the men but before she could alert Cill, the limousine sped away.

"Well it seems that your bright idea didn't pan out too well." Petunia was not only overheated in the hat and coat but she was also annoyed that she'd let herself get involved to that point.

"That's what I get for trying to help you out. I didn't have a problem with this Lipps fellow. He used you and then tossed you aside like a piece of used toilet paper. You have some nerve to question my motives."

Cill and Petunia's arguing caught the attention of the doorman, who promptly called the police.

Suddenly, Cill stopped quarrelling and grabbed Petunia by the arm, which was hard to do because her skinny arm kept slipping through Cill's grasp. Petunia thought Cill was about to shake her to death. She immediately started apologizing.

"Shush," Cill warned, "it's the cops."

Petunia stopped struggling. "What cops?" She quickly looked around and the only thing she saw was a smiling doorman. "I don't see any police."

"Trust me. They're about two blocks away and we don't need to be here in this part of town when they get here."

Better safe than sorry, Petunia dove into the car. As fast as Petunia was, she still wasn't as quick as Cill. Cill was already in the car and putting it in gear. She had the car backed out of the parking space by the time Petunia's hips hit the seat.

Before they'd driven a block away, a police car sped past without either a flashing light or a siren blasting. The patrol car stopped directly in front of Lyon Lipps' building. Through the rearview mirror, Cill saw the doorman pointing in their direction.

Suddenly, Petunia had a new respect as well as a new name for Cill. From that point on Petunia called her Bionic Cill. She could not understand how Cill knew the police were coming and at that point, she didn't care.

Once they were on the other side of town, Cill relaxed a little. Keeping up a brave front for Petunia was exhausting. She'd hoped to have caught a glimpse of Lyon Lipps, and possibly seize an opportunity to punish him before Ima did. Slowly pulling out his finger- and toenails would've been a start. She'd make up the rest as she went along. Of course, Petunia would've been mad, because she hadn't been invited to the torture, but so what. She'd cross that bridge when she came to it.

19

The sleek black limousine wove in and out of traffic as it raced towards the Greenville/Spartanburg airport.

"I'm afraid I'll have to drive over the speed limit in order for you gentlemen to make your plane. If I'm not stopped, we should make it in time for you to board."

The limousine driver didn't receive a reply. He hadn't expected one. After several months of driving for them, he'd learned that these men always seem to run late.

A pair of expensive shades hid a pair of fluttering light green eyes. His arms bronzed and ripped, Lyon's hands were clasped together, as if in prayer. Tinted windows kept the noisy outside world from intruding on his thoughts.

"You're very quiet. Are you okay?" Concern blanketed Lionel's face. "Are you having second thoughts?"

"It's not that I'm having second or third

thoughts." Lyon took off his sunglasses and carefully folded them before placing them in his shirt pocket. "I didn't seek God's counsel before accepting this trip and now my spirit is not at peace." His pensive look deepened.

"Do you want to cancel it? You can turn around if you feel that God is whispering to you. Perhaps He does not want you to go on this cruise." Lionel, always protective of his younger brother, suddenly felt his burden but was helpless to do anything beyond prayer. "I'd stay home with you but you know I was already scheduled to take this ship with the Bishop."

"That's what I'm struggling with." Lyon turned and faced his brother. His hands again clasped as tight as his spirit seemed to be. "It's probably because I'm trying to do the right thing."

"You will. Just follow God's lead."

"I'm trying to do that. I'm so thankful that the Lord has forgiven me and turned my life around. I guess I'm struggling with feeling unworthy of His blessings."

"I understand. You know God is not the author of confusion. If you seek God and you still feel uncomfortable then perhaps you need to reconsider going." Lionel reached for his brother's hands and gently pried them apart. "Let's pray now, if that's okay with you."

"I think we should." Lyon understood that he was still a babe-in-Christ and strongly relied upon Lionel for counsel.

Lionel prayed for guidance. By the time he said, "amen," he also felt Lyon's concern, but not to the same extent.

"In my spirit, I feel that this is a test," Lionel said. "You do know that even though you've given your life to Christ you will still be tested, don't you?"

Lyon laughed a nervous but hearty laugh. "Tell me about it." He reached into his pocket and retrieved his sunglasses. "It's amazing, big brother, just how smart you are."

"What's so amazing?" Lionel asked, returning the laugh. "I'm older than you and with age comes wisdom."

"There you go. You're still trying to convince me that the few minutes you spent alone before I followed from our mother's womb gave you a wealth of knowledge?"

"Glad to see that you understand."

"It's good to know that instead of using this time to plot to get some unsuspecting woman to open her purse and other things, that I'm in prayer." Lyon's face again grew serious as he put on the sunglasses and turned to look out the car window. "Thank you, Lord."

After a few minutes of silence, the brothers broke out in laughter that lasted the rest of the way to the airport. For Lionel, it was the laughter of relief that he was able to help his twin brother.

For Lyon, it was still a nervous laugh and somehow, in his spirit, he knew to watch, as well as pray. So far, he'd not met many demons from his past and he hoped not to meet any on this free cruise.

At least he had his brother to watch his back, and God by his side.

20

Mother Blister limped and complained about her bunions from the time they arrived at the airport. She fussed about the long walk while dragging her wheel-less suitcases through the terminal. She couldn't even go through security without causing a ruckus. She refused to go through the checkpoint until somebody with a wand checked every one of the other travelers wearing either a yarmulke or a doo rag. According to Mother Blister, if a man wore a hat he was a terrorist.

Ima grabbed an abandoned wheelchair and threw Birdie into it while she attended to Mother Blister. "She's okay. She's old and just a bit eccentric. I'll give her a pill and have her quieted before the plane lifts off." Ima batted her long eyelashes at the transportation security officer as she pretended to fix the seams on her seamless stockings. She licked her lips while giving him a look of promise.

While the man was distracted by Ima's look of a good time to come, everything from razors to matches could have gone through the security undetected.

By the time Ima got them to the other side of the terminal, despite avoiding one small drama after another through security, she was ready to shut down the airport, but she kept her cool.

The thought of what Mother Blister would do caused Ima's heart to race. Her head throbbed, and it was all Ima could do to keep from snatching the tight blond wig from atop her head, so the blood could circulate properly. However, she didn't want to draw more attention than necessary.

Ima spent about thirty minutes either rushing from an airport shop or pushing Mother Blister into a bathroom, as Mother Blister waved her arms wildly, trying to ward her off.

The sight and sound of Birdie, still groggy and slurring her words from the effects of the Coca-Cola and Benedryl combo attracted many stares. She was babbling about reparations one moment and cooing like a baby the next. Most of the Americans getting on and off the flights looked embarrassed. There was no doubt in their minds, from the way Birdie was dressed, that she must be a crazy woman.

The sight of the eclectic trio rushing past the customs desk caused some of the foreign travelers to also stop and stare. Several of them just abruptly turned around and tried to get back on their flights. If those three were America's best, then they were better off staying in whichever third-world country they came from.

The flight was scheduled to leave in another twenty minutes but because Birdie was in the wheelchair, the passenger crew allowed them to board the plane first.

Ima struggled to push Birdie down the gangplank. Along the way, she managed to lose sight of Mother Blister who trailed behind along with a few other elderly passengers, several hyperactive children and a couple of airport personnel flying on their day off.

The gangplank was deeply inclined, which caused Ima to lose her balance. She threw the brakes on and almost catapulted Birdie from the wheelchair into the waiting arms of one of the male stewards. She didn't wait to see if Birdie was safe. Instead, she ran back and snatched Mother Blister by the sleeve, jerking her onto the plane.

Their tickets had them seated in the rear

of the plane. Ima wasn't happy about it but the plane was fully booked.

"I'm so sorry but we're unable to switch seats," the freckled-face, flame-haired stewardess whispered. Her smile seemed built into her heart-shaped alabaster face with a little too much confidence for Ima's taste. "We'll make sure that your friend is met with a wheelchair when we land in Miami."

Before Ima could protest, the stewardess was on to assisting others who truly needed it.

As exhausted as she was, Ima had just enough spunk left to tuck away the slight in the recesses of her overactive mind. If she was happy about one thing it was that they didn't have to share their row of seats. She made sure to fasten Mother Blister and Birdie's seatbelts securely before relaxing enough to fasten her own.

Ima was used to flying, and thought she knew everything she needed to know about emergency procedures. She had already decided to forego the monotonous dialogue to be delivered by several robotic stewardesses. She chose to rest her eyes to still the onset of a headache. And before all the passengers boarded, Ima was asleep.

Of course, Mother Blister and Birdie weren't close to sleeping. Mother Blister in her natural state had all sorts of issues that kept her awake. Birdie, on the other hand, was just starting to come down from her high.

"This is the final call for all passengers boarding Delta flight 5050 to Miami." The warning resonating from the airport loud-speaker seemed as final as it indicated.

Lyon and Lionel zipped through the airport like seasoned sprinters. They were almost out of breath as they approached a petite, middle-aged black woman who moved with a purposful strut towards the open door at their gate. They apologetically rushed up to her just as she was about to shut the door leading to the plane.

"We're here. Please wait," Lyon called over the chatter of the airport crowd.

The sight of two handsome men caught the attendant's attention. It didn't matter what he'd said, she voluntarily held the door open.

"We're in first class," Lyon said as if she needed help in reading the tickets.

"Yes, you are," she responded. She kept her eyes locked on his for another second before putting the tickets, one by one, through the scanning machine.

"Thank you and God bless you," Lionel

said as the woman quickly tore apart their tickets and handed them their boarding passes.

"I feel like I've been blessed today already," she replied. She meant it. On most days the passengers who arrived late snapped at her as though it were her fault. She was still smiling as she caught a glimpse of them running down the gangplank on their way to bless the eyes of whoever was flying in first class. The men looked as good leaving as they did arriving. *I haven't seen that much fineness in this airport at one time since Delroy Lindo and Denzel Washington came here.*

An hour before that flight took off for Miami and ascended towards the wild blue yonder, Needy was seated uncomfortably on the Acela Express to Florida. She was mad enough to chew on an alligator hide while the alligator was still alive.

"I still don't see why you would wait until we were on our way to the airport to decide that you didn't want to fly." She could almost feel the steam trying to escape from under her raspberry-colored weave. If it was the last thing she did, she was going to get Ima for sticking her with Mother Pray Onn.

"My aunt won't be any trouble. She's already agreed to fly. She never flew on an airplane. She'll be too busy begging God to forgive and protect her. By the time she finishes praying, y'all will be in Miami at the ship," Ima had told her.

"Liar!" Needy meant to keep her thoughts private but somehow she blurted them out.

"Who are you calling a liar?" Mother Pray Onn hissed. "You'd better be careful before I have the Lord rain down hail and brimstone on your big butt."

Needy took Mother Pray Onn's hands, more out of a necessity than a desire. She didn't need the old woman snapping or slapping at her as if she was a child.

"I was talking about the lying train conductor saying that it would only take us about three hours to reach Miami. We're only in Alabama. At this rate, we won't be in Miami on time."

Needy's hairy top lip was quivering. Mother Pray Onn knew she was lying about something.

"I'm so sorry. This is my fault. I guess I should not have changed my old addled mind about flying. It's just that I don't want to get that close to heaven unless Jesus is standing on one of those clouds calling out to me." She took her hands from Needy's grip and put on her best innocent look. "Unless somehow Jesus' name was changed to 'Delta,' I just couldn't board that plane."

Needy hadn't heard that much lying since she'd sent away most of her mortgage money for a jar of quick weight-loss juice hawked by a lying celebrity. Her money was the only thing she'd lost.

Mother Pray Onn made matters worse by repeating the same thing two or three times. Needy listened a while longer as the old woman complained about stiffness and imagined slights. Needy's chest was about to bust out of her bra with anxiety. She realized that Mother Pray Onn wasn't coming on the cruise alone. She'd brought both arthritis and Alzheimer's as company.

Needy was too upset to argue. She rested her head on the headrest and watched as glimpses of trees and outdated advertising signs sped by, and listened to the hollow sound of the conductor announcing the stops.

Needy didn't know how or when, but Ima was going to get hers. She looked over and gave a comforting pat on Mother Pray Onn's hand. *I can't wait for you and Mother Blister to get together. Between dealing with you two and Lyon Lipps, Ima'll be too busy to block my manhunt.* "You'll be just fine," Needy said as she withdrew her hand.

"There's no reason I shouldn't be,"

Mother Pray Onn replied. She'd only caught the very end of what Needy said and really didn't care. She carefully steepled her tiny hands and supported her pointed chin. She looked like a small angel in prayer as she plotted how she was going to wreak havoc on her niece's cruise. She took a moment to peek over at Needy and, again, smiled. She was not concerned with collateral damage.

Needy had worried for nothing. Mother Pray Onn slept most of the way there and didn't cause any further problems. And not only did their train arrive in Miami on time, they didn't have to rush to the pier. She'd have plenty of time before beginning the embarkation process and getting Mother Pray Onn settled in the cabin. After that, she'd seek out a man — that's what she came to do.

After a night of outrunning cops, hiding behind thorny bushes and wearing a hot camouflage suit as a disguise, Cill awoke the next morning in a foul mood. *I'm tired of the cat and mouse game,* she fumed as she plucked a couple of stray cheek hairs.

She needed to get to the down and dirty quick, so she could outdo Ima in the revenge game. Later on that afternoon, over a large bowl of Chunky Monkey ice cream, she plotted her next move. *I need to attack this problem the same way I would if I were spying for the army,* she thought even though she'd never been a spy.

Two hours later, Cill picked up Petunia again. They drove quietly and slowly back onto Lyon's block and parked, again, in the shadows.

Just as Cill was about to lay out her final plan, she looked over in time to see Petunia already shaking like a leaf, and the ignition hadn't been turned off yet.

Petunia was becoming undone and a hindrance. Everything that smacked of danger made her panic so hard, her teeth chattered.

The last straw for Cill plummeted from Petunia's own mouth. "Cill, look over there. Isn't that a patrol car at the curb?"

Cill suddenly grabbed Petunia and hugged her tight enough for them to look like a pair of Siamese twins. "Just act like we're giving each other a friendly hug," she whispered as Petunia tried to wiggle out of her grip.

"Would you please just be still before you have those cops checking us out?" Cill snapped as she tightened her death grip on Petunia. They looked like an oversized brown pretzel.

From nowhere the sound of the patrol

car's siren blasted. The car's dome light spun and flashed as it careened from the curb towards them.

Cill had already extricated herself at the sound of the first loud toot and backed away. Instincts and army training had taken over.

Petunia, on the other hand, jumped out and started rushing towards the oncoming patrol car, screaming like a crazy woman, "I'm innocent." She was winding and wiggling like a snake with its rattlers on fire. "It's that white woman Birdie's fault! . . . Cill is the man you want! . . . Ima is a wanted woman! . . . Mother Blister don't like me! . . . Needy is gonna kill somebody she don't know!"

Petunia was giving up her friends in alphabetical order based upon an imaginary threat. Even as the patrol car raced past them, Petunia was still shaking and testifying loudly to anyone who'd listen, all in front of an invisible court.

All the commotion she caused on that street, and the fact that Cill had sped off and left her, paled in comparison to what was waiting for her back at her house. She'd forgotten to feed Evilene and she hadn't changed that cat's litter box, either.

21

Lyon's green eyes were hazy. His lack of sleep coupled with an inward feeling of dread shadowed his handsome face. His stare was vacant as he tried to refasten his seatbelt. He'd tried twice already, and each time he'd struggled.

"Normally, my prayers tend to relieve stress and bring about blessings." The confident words said in a teasing manner were followed by a rather wide smile that was embraced by a stubbly beard.

"Bishop Jones, I've already told him that," Lionel spoke as though Lyon, seated between them, was a child and unable to speak for himself. "We had prayer in the limousine, and I'd hoped that he would be a bit more joyous."

Bishop Jones folded his hands carefully. This time his voice seemed more concerned, yet it maintained the tone of a caring teacher. "Your brother's salvation is still new to him. However, it doesn't mean that God cannot whisper to his spirit. If the light of what seems to be a gift, such as this free cruise, still renders a restless spirit within him, then perhaps he should listen to his inner man."

Lionel managed a nervous chuckle as he took the friendly rebuke from the bishop. "I guess my being the brother of a new soul, although it's been more than six months, is still a new experience for me. I've been waiting since we were both nineteen years old for him to accept salvation."

"I'm sitting right here," Lyon finally spoke up. His flat tone betrayed his upbeat words. "I can't let whatever I'm feeling steal my joy. I can only watch and pray." His smile was constrained and it showed. He clasped his hands together like a steeple and dropped his head slightly before continuing. "I believe the Word says that we are to be anxious for nothing." He smiled again, that time directing it towards Lionel.

"I'm confident that you two will have a wonderful and glorious time," the bishop laughed. "Despite the fact that I won't be coming along to experience it first hand, this upcoming singles cruise will be the best yet."

"What does that mean?" Lionel thought

he'd heard some underlying concern despite the bishop's confident words. He secretly tapped Lyon on his wrist, to get his attention, as he looked past him to the bishop. "Care to explain?"

"Of course I can explain. This was to be more than a relaxing vacation for me. I'm thinking of booking this ship for the singles cruise." His smile turned mischievous as he leaned in closer and whispered, "It seems that so far, we will have more men registered than women. And, I want you two to sail when we do and to have fun on your spiritual journey."

"So what did you hope to accomplish aboard this cruise ship?" Lionel asked. He didn't want to appear stupid but the reason for the bishop's mission was completely over his head.

"I certainly hope that this is not the type of cruise line that seems to attract lonely women and unscrupulous men," Lyon said with a wink. His mood was beginning to lighten.

Laughter erupted between the three men. Each dropped their heads as well as their voices so not to make themselves a spectacle.

"If anyone does plan to go with an ulterior motive other than fellowship and have a good time, then we will rebuke those thoughts before we sail," Bishop Jones said and laughed again.

"That must be it," Lyon suddenly said. "It would definitely be the fellowship because I've never been that comfortable around too many fellas." He sat erect, abandoning his slouch.

"I wanted to cancel the singles cruise for next year, since I couldn't check out this ship. Fortunately God spoke to my heart. He wanted me to go ahead with His plans."

"So you knew this morning when we spoke that you were not going?"

"Although I had purchased cancellation insurance, up until the last moment, I wasn't sure if I'd go. My business in Miami will keep me there for the rest of the week."

If Lionel was confused before he was even more so then. Yet he said nothing and continued to listen.

"If I don't go or we can't get the right amount of attendance of the single women, it will be okay. The cruise will still be good. We need to step up our game as men of God, and give these women a choice of saved and dedicated men."

"I, for one, will definitely need to step up mine," Lyon replied almost in a whisper. "I still can't believe that God has forgiven me for all the atrocious things that I've done to women." His eyes suddenly watered. "I'm so ashamed."

The light in his eyes dimmed once more as he slowly closed them. He let his head fall back on the headrest, as he waved away the stewardess' offer of a cold beverage.

Lionel knew his brother well. So he turned away to look out the window at the bright sun that shone through the clouds. He relaxed knowing that it was the same with God. No matter how thick the clouds, God was still the Sun of the World and would always shine through and on them. One day, Lyon would discover it too.

"Of course, Reverend Lionel, you can scout the ship for me."

"Say what?"

"You're going and so is your brother. It will be a great opportunity for you to see the layout of the ship and to determine if it would suit our needs. Perhaps you can negotiate a reasonable price with your gift of persuasion."

"Why would you want me to do that?" Lionel asked, cautiously.

"Why wouldn't I want you to do that?" Bishop Jones answered. "When you return, you'll be going before the board of the Ain't Nobody Right But Us — All Others Goin' to Hell Church. This will be a great vacation for you to relax your mind, so you can do God's work."

"You seem mighty sure that I'll get the position," Lionel said with a nervous laugh.

"What's the worst thing that can happen?" Lyon added. He'd finally decided to join the conversation.

"Yes, what is the worst thing that can happen?" Bishop Jones continued, "Perhaps you'll meet a suitable first lady."

"That's right. It's about time you settled down," Lyon kidded.

"You two need Jesus," Lionel mumbled. He was not looking for a wife. He was too busy trying to do God's work. He loved working with the youth and the singles ministry as he traveled and preached until he found a church to pastor. When it was time, God would send him one. "I'm doing just fine being alone. Besides, y'all know how particular I am. I doubt seriously if I'll find a suitable mate aboard a cruise liner."

"So just where do you think you'll find her?" Lyon asked. "Perhaps she'll be seated in a library or inside the church's fellowship hall."

"Let's not tease the reverend. After all, he knows just what kind of woman he's looking for," Bishop Jones said.

"Yes, and God knows just what kind of woman he needs," Lyon quickly added.

Lionel turned his head away from their laughter. *I'm gonna have to be real specific when I start praying for a wife. It couldn't hurt if God and I are on the same page.*

While the pilot prepared to land Bishop Jones chatted away with one of the very attractive flight attendants. She managed to flip her long sandy brown hair to the side while simultaneously producing a pad and pen. As she scribbled on the pad she told him how much she enjoyed his sermons and the impact they'd had on her life.

Bishop Jones thanked her and ended the conversation with a Bible verse. He did it just in case she was coming to a different conclusion from their brief conversation that didn't include salvation. He was not about to let his good works be mistaken for evil.

The whooshing sound of the plane's landing gear engaging awoke Ima with a start. She moved in her seat, briefly unsure if she were on the ground or still airborne. The lights from the "fasten your seatbelt" sign flashed. She hadn't realized that they were almost into Miami.

"Welcome to Miami International Airport." Although the flight attendant's announcement was loud and filled with rehearsed gaiety, it hadn't aroused either Birdie or Mother Blister.

"Come on and wake up," Ima urged as she shook Mother Blister and Birdie. "We're about to land."

It took several more moments, and even more rough tugs from Ima before Birdie and Mother Blister were alert enough to understand what was happening.

The first thing Mother Blister did when she sat up straight was to fix her wig and undo her seat belt.

"I'm sorry, Madam. The fasten seat belt sign is on and so I must ask that you refasten yours." The flight attendant's eyes appeared sympathetic as she lay a soft brown hand on Mother Blister's shoulder and pointed to the sign. A trick she used quite often to get the senior citizens to obey.

There was no fooling Mother Nature or Mother Blister's bladder.

"You better move unless you want to use those newspapers to sop up some water," Mother Blister bellowed.

"She ain't playing," Ima added.

"Let her go before she lets *it* go," Birdie insisted.

Without waiting for the flight attendant to

move aside, Mother Blister inched her arthritic hips past her. When the flight finally landed, she was still in the bathroom.

22

The cruise ship *Desperation of the Seas* sat anchored in the deep blue Miami water. Its fourteen decks welcomed the playfully rolling, foamy wavecrests that teased its iron sides. Various flags representing countries from all over the world waved, as the ship welcomed its passengers. And as a precaution, forty tarp-covered lifeboats hugged both sides of the ship.

The ship's multi-national crewmembers dotted the first three decks. There were women old and young, who wore short-sleeved shirts with the ship's logo and white skirts revealing everything from their knobby knees to their cellulite craters. The men wore the same style shirts with Bermuda shorts, and they looked no better.

Two long boarding ramps led up to the embarkation level. The anxious passengers gingerly climbed aboard the ship trying to avoid the unmerciful, searing heat, along with a security posse that appeared from out of nowhere.

The high temperatures had sapped much of the passengers' energies, causing their patience to evaporate quickly. In no time at all complaints swept over the embarkation deck in various strong languages and dialects. The ship began to sound more like the Tower of Babel than a pleasure cruise.

Although Ima was more tired than and probably crankier than Birdie and Needy, she did manage to get through the security check without difficulty.

Ima's voice was a bit shaky as she tried to continue to appear calm. "I've never sailed before. I had no idea that the ship was so big."

She hadn't meant to share that information but it was out there and she couldn't take it back.

"I thought you'd sailed before," Birdie said softly to Ima. "Needy told me that you had sailing experience."

Ima responded in a huff. "I do have some experience with water-related situations."

"I don't think a couple of rhythm and blues dinner cruises around Manhattan qualify," Mother Blister interjected. She was not about to miss an opportunity to get in on the discussion.

"What kind of cruises they were is nobody's business," Ima snapped. "I don't tell you everything because you *tell* everything." Ima rebuked Mother Blister with an arched eyebrow.

Mother Blister was about to let Ima have it but the sudden appearance and laughter from one the welcoming crewmembers drew her attention away.

The laughing voice had a lilt to it that seemed to soothe and smooth a path through the humidity as she neared. She approached clutching a clipboard in one hand and a walkie-talkie radio in the other. "Welcome aboard the *Desperation*."

The girl looked no more than about twenty with a tanned and freckled heart-shaped face. Her smile was almost infectious despite her sad, dark brown eyes. She was tall with legs that seemed to go up past her hips and she wore her flaming red hair in a bob.

"Greetings to you all; my name is Diana and I represent the great country of England." She pointed at her nametag as she spoke.

Instead of returning the greeting, Ima, Birdie and Mother Blister stood rooted to their spots. Outside of James Bond movie, they'd never heard such a thick English accent.

"In about an hour or so your luggage will be set outside your cabins. In the meantime, you may relax up on our Lido Deck or perhaps just laze about in our recliners."

Diana then reached out towards Birdie. "Madam, may I see your cruise card, please?"

"Of course you may." Birdie handed over her pale blue laminated cruise card that had all her information printed on it.

"Thank you, Madam . . ." Diana paused, read the card before continuing, and returned the card to Birdie. "Miss Tweet, everything seems to be in order. Your card indicates that you have an late dining time and tells you your cabin number. It is the same for all your traveling companions. It is also the only method by which you will be able to charge any items aboard this ship."

As soon as Mother Blister heard the word "charge," she steered Diana away from the others and asked, "Do you mean this is my very own charge card?" She held the laminated card at arm's length to see it better.

"Yes, it is." Diana's sad eyes seemed to light up with the enthusiasm coming from the old woman. "In fact, the only time you will need any money is when you want to go ashore. You cannot use the card ashore."

"But while I'm on this ship I can shop until I drop?" Mother Blister asked.

"Everyone aboard has their own card and is responsible likewise."

"Sweet Jesus, I thank You," Mother Blister sang as she stepped back among the others. A free credit card was something she could handle.

Ima, Birdie and Mother Blister listened to the welcome aboard speech and then set off to explore the ship until their luggage was delivered to their cabins.

Of course, by the time they reached the observation tower, Mother Blister had visited a bathroom on each deck.

It seemed that no sooner had Birdie and the others finished their embarkation process and left to explore the ship, the crowd of passengers increased three-fold.

The heat had finally pushed a few of the passengers over the edge and bickering began to sprout.

Mother Pray Onn had no constraints when it came to voicing her complaints. It'd started with the weather.

"Why would you bring me here on a day when it's hotter than hell?" Mother Pray Onn snapped as she tapped her cane on the boarding ramp hard enough to chip the cane's metal tip.

"It's Florida," Needy hissed, "it's supposed to be hot here."

Before Needy could say more, one of the passengers, a short black man of about fifty, standing behind them, grew tired of Mother Pray Onn's grumbling. He pointed at her and whispered angrily in a voice low enough for only dogs and reptiles to hear. "How would that old biddy know how hot hell is?" He nodded towards his wife for confirmation.

Before Needy could stop her, Mother Pray Onn had spun around, and was about to poke the man in his chest with the tip of her cane. "I heard that and you need to mind your own business. I know how hot hell is because I was just there last week for my weekly visit and consultation."

The man's wife had barely heard what her husband said and she certainly couldn't figure out how the old woman had. She wasn't about to wait around and ask. Snatching her husband by the collar of his shirt, she dragged him up the boarding ramp, cutting the lines to save her husband's life.

Needy was about to admonish Mother Pray Onn but decided it would do no good.

She'd barely made that decision before Mother Pray Onn started again.

"I ain't waiting another minute in this hot sun. Let's go." Mother Pray Onn yanked Needy's hand almost hard enough to dislocate it from the wrist.

"Ouch!" Needy winced. "Will you please let me go?"

"Shut up," Mother Pray Onn said, dragging Needy.

Needy twisted and turned as they slithered though the crowd with Mother Pray Onn giving the evil eye to those who wanted to protest. "Move out of my way. Don't y'all see a helpless old lady trying to get aboard this thing?"

She didn't care that there were many other old people whose blood pressure steadily rose as they stood in agony, marinating in their own sweat. Yet, as irritated, hot and tired as they were, not a one of the senior citizens challenged Mother Pray Onn. Instead, they made mental notes to avoid her at all costs if they ever got aboard the ship.

"I wonder what all the commotion is about," Lionel said as he wiped the sweat from his forehead and inched upward along with the others. The tan baseball cap did nothing to cool his head from the punishing hot sun.

"I don't know, but if the heat has gotten to anyone like it has to me, then I fully understand their frustration." The words faltered, as though he couldn't muster up another syllable. Lyon's body shook from a sudden chill even though his clothes were damp from perspiration.

"The line suddenly seems to have started moving rather quick. It's good to have favor with God."

Lionel truly believed he had favor with God. He'd started praying as soon as he saw the long lines and felt the searing heat. He smiled knowingly as he pointed towards the fast-moving crowd. "Ye have not because ye ask not." He laughed and pointed at the moving crowd.

His smile and confidence started to spread. The wink he gave caused Lyon to laugh. Although they'd never sailed before, they'd traveled together on several occasions to various conferences and retreats.

As usual, Lyon was happy that his brother was always the voice of reason. And even with the humidity beating them almost into unconsciousness, Lionel remained calm.

Fifteen minutes seemed more like an hour to Needy and Mother Pray Onn as they

261

finally reached the ship's Welcome and Customs booth. Needy was still exhausted, so she held on to the rope that divided the lines to keep order.

"Come on, Needy. Move your big butt." Mother Pray Onn pulled Needy hard enough to cause rope burns to appear on Needy's dark skin.

No sooner than they almost skidded to a complete stop at the booth, Mother Pray Onn's sour disposition disappeared, and an endearing sweet old lady's took its place.

Tapping Needy gently on her hand, Mother Pray Onn quietly asked, "Needy, sweetie, do you have your passport or a driver's license for identification to give to this lovely woman?"

Mother Pray Onn kicked her meanness up a notch past insincerity and locked it onto pure manure when she leaned on her cane to appear helpless. She smiled and continued addressing the woman at the desk. "Of course, I have my documents and they are all in order."

She leaned in and added in a low voice while pointing back at Needy, "She hasn't had a man in years and the sight of so many on this deck has her brain addled." She straightened up slightly and smiled again.

The woman's badge read, "M'gube from

Uganda" and she wasn't smiling back. She was hotter than she'd ever felt back home in Africa. She'd also smiled so much that day that her jaws felt locked. She couldn't have scowled even if she wanted to.

M'gube was about the same height as Mother Pray Onn. She tried to appear cool and professional despite her caramel-colored skin glistening in the heat. She was about twenty-five years old and had sailed with the *Desperation* for almost five years.

M'gube had sailed enough to know possible chaos when it boarded. And chaos was standing right in front of her, dressed in a floral seersucker dress straight from the Betsy Ross Collection, wearing orthopedic shoes. Chaos also wielded a walking cane instead of a spear, but she appeared to be just as deadly.

It wasn't a shock to M'gube when she felt her tightly braided cornrows cut into her scalp and constrict to the point of cutting off the blood supply to her brain. She knew that before the two women finished their embarkation process she'd need a healer.

M'gube dropped her pen and started massaging her temples between her hands. The more she rubbed with her short flat thumbs the more she undid the base of her front cornrow. Bits of hair and patience sprinkled onto the paper.

"Ms. Need Sum. Please hurry," M'gube said with cruise-ship decorum.

"I believe I do have it somewhere," Needy whispered. She felt embarrassed as she rifled her pudgy fists through her pockets, interrupting M'gube's pleas.

Needy sucked her teeth gently as she scrounged around. She found nothing but bits of multi-colored lint, a wad of hard gum stuck to a dirty tissue and a crusty penny. *Doggone it,* she thought as her throat went dry.

Mother Pray Onn turned aside and innocently winked at the couple standing behind her indicating that she wasn't the hold-up. "Be ye always ready. That's what my Bible says," she said, softly.

But then Needy went into full panic mode. "Help me Lord." She started rifling through her handbag, almost ripping the strap and its zipper from the seams. When it seemed that all was lost, she turned towards Mother Pray Onn and out of desperation, she humbly asked, "If I don't have my papers will you vouch for me?"

"Oh come on, Needy. You know me," Mother Pray Onn smiled, "I'm not gonna let a little thing like a long-term dislike of you ruin our wonderful vacation —" She stopped suddenly and furrowed her brow. She almost blew a brain gasket trying desperately to remember what Needy had done to get on her annoyance list. It was for nothing, because she couldn't remember and it didn't matter.

Mother Pray Onn's nasty mood barely had a chance to reignite as she watched Needy's distress level rise. She saw that nervousness had turned Needy's dark skin as red as a lobster, and Mother Pray Onn's face lit up for joy.

Despite her apparent pleasure at Needy's discomfort Mother Pray Onn mustered up a hint of sincerity. "I'll do whatever it takes to make sure that these folks know the *real* you."

Whether her assistance to Needy would be of a notorious nature or not would depend upon Mother Pray Onn's present frame of mind, which was subject to change unannounced.

M'gube glanced over the counter in time to see the ship's head purser approaching. He strutted past the other waiting passengers, sprinkling them with flashing nods of everything-is-under-control as he went over to one of the other booths.

M'gube knew the head purser was in full professional mode, so she dismissed her headache quickly and wiped her fallen strands of hair off the counter. "I'm sorry, ladies, but I must insist that you stand aside. Perhaps you'd like to go over in the corner and carefully go through your carry-on bag. It may be in there."

M'gube stood as tall as she could with authority. The appearance of the head purser emboldened her so she waved Needy and Mother Pray Onn to the side and motioned for the next person in line to step forward.

The satisfied smile spread across M'gube's face was not lost on Needy. She filed the veiled insult away in her mind where she could retrieve it later for payback.

But instead of moving aside, Needy stood her ground. In front of God, the embarkation crew, and at least ten other people waiting in line behind her, she unsnapped the first four buttons of her blouse. She never batted an eye and that hairy lip wouldn't quiver, not even when her cleavage poured out like hot lava.

Needy swung one long arm around as if she were winding up for a pitch and reached way down into her bra. She started lifting and separating her double-D breasts as they moved from side to side like a pendulum. As soon as she felt the presence of stiffness, she knew it was her passport. "I found it!" Needy said excitedly as she laid the soggy, perspiration-covered passport on the counter. "It just occurred to me where I hid it to keep from losing it."

"You put it in your brassiere?" Mother Pray Onn asked, softly. Of course, she'd done the same thing on many occasions, stashing everything important including a bag of wheat pennies, but she'd never admit to it. "Tsk, tsk. That's so sad," she said as she patted Needy on the hand.

About that time, the head purser stepped up, introduced himself as Hunter from Great Britain, and asked if there was a problem.

Before Needy could apologize for the hold-up, Mother Pray Onn decided it was payback time for the supposed snub of M'gube's.

"What do you mean, 'Is there a problem?'" Mother Pray Onn snapped as she pointed to Needy's still unbuttoned blouse. "Your employee made this poor pathetic woman with too many mental-health problems for me to name, disrobe in front of all these people." She waved her cane at the waiting passengers as if she would maim anyone who interfered and offered the truth. "Can you imagine the embarrassment of showing your dingy-looking brassiere to a crowd of strangers?"

"Say wha—" M'gube blurted with her dark eyes widening and fists clenching.

"Who's crazy?" Needy snapped at Mother Pray Onn. The reference to her dirty clothes hadn't hit her yet.

Mother Pray Onn was engineering the payback train and she didn't care who she ran over as long as she hit M'gube.

"How would you feel if someone made you search through your big, oversized breasts, that you re-mortgaged your house to pay for, just to humiliate you?" Mother Pray Onn asked as she suddenly produced a tissue and dabbed at her eyes. "We're just two single women trying to have a nice vacation with our meager savings on this beautiful cruise ship in one cramped cabin."

She stopped to see if her lies moved the head purser before going in for the kill. "For a solid week, we'll be elbow-to-elbow and with not even enough room to change our minds or our clothes in comfort."

Ooh, she's good. It must be a DNA thing, Needy thought. She'd forgotten that just a moment ago, she was about to toss the old woman into the ocean.

Mother Pray Onn could've talked Bin Laden and ten generations of the Taliban into turning Christian.

Mother Pray Onn's supposed discomfort tale worked. Along with her lie, several things started to move as the head purser, Hunter, whispered into M'gube's ear and walked away.

A wave suddenly and violently splashed against the side of the ship, but not as hard as the glare from M'gube's eyes. She sprang from behind the embarkation counter, slamming down her clipboard as she did.

M'gube hissed, in Swahili, an old ancestral curse on both women's bloodlines. She followed with a full thrust from her middle finger and a couple of tongue clicks tossed in for good measure.

Being an almost reformed cuss-ologist, Mother Pray Onn knew a good curse when she heard one, and was almost about to apologize when she saw what she thought were little chicken bones sticking out from M'gube's skirt pocket.

Almost was about as close as she came as she recognized the look of defeat inch across the face of the head purser who'd had the foresight to return.

However, the head purser had mistaken the wide-eyed looks on the women's faces as a possible lawsuit against the cruise line.

"We want you to enjoy cruising with us,

and please tell all your friends to do the same. So I will have your cabin accommodations upgraded, as soon as I finish speaking with M'gube."

With as much politeness as he could muster and his thick English brogue, Hunter barked a few orders at M'gube. He was pleased with the way he'd removed the threat of a possible lawsuit by having the women moved to a larger suite with a balcony on the tenth deck, so he turned and smiled again at Needy and Mother Pray Onn. He never checked or considered whether they were supposed to share a cabin.

Less than five minutes later, Needy and Mother Pray Onn had moved on up to the big time. They'd gone from the second deck to the tenth. It was even better that their upgraded cabin was on the same deck as the buffets, so they could even get their little piece of the pie.

Of course, Mother Pray Onn had temporarily forgotten that she wasn't staying in a cabin with Needy and was supposed to be with her niece, instead.

And Needy was not about to remind her. This time it was her turn to be happy about the upcoming misery that Mother Pray Onn would receive.

Of course, Needy, too, forgot that Mother Pray Onn gave as much misery as she received. And Mother Pray Onn stayed in a giving mood.

23

By the time Lyon had arrived in his cabin on the ninth deck, he felt like the other passengers: physically and mentally drained. Neither his nor Lionel's luggage had arrived at either of their cabins, so Lionel had gone to the observation deck.

Lyon stayed behind to shower. Yet, as tired as he was, Lyon still managed to kneel down beside the bed. He gave thanks to God for a safe arrival and asked for His guidance and strength.

Whether he realized it or not, he did have favor with God. Heaven acted quickly in answering his prayers. He'd only gotten up on one knee when the sight of a turtle fashioned out of white towels and washcloths laying on the pillow brought a quick smile and a new surge of energy.

You're an on-time God, he thought as he tried to figure out how it was constructed.

For the next ten minutes or so, Lyon

hummed melodies from one of his favorite singers, the powerful and magnetic Luther Vandross.

After serving time at twenty-two he'd once come very close to a recording deal with Epic Records. However, the label already had Luther signed and their A&R man felt Lyon's voice was too similar. When Lyon wouldn't agree to change his style or tone, the deal fell through. It was but one of his many setbacks or paybacks, as he liked to call them. Everything that went wrong during his several releases from prison, he'd blame on his prior criminal record.

Lyon shook off memories from his past by singing louder. He continued to check out his cabin as he watched the scrolling Welcome Aboard infomercial on the cabin's television.

There was nothing on the schedule happening soon that piqued his interest. So he went inside the bathroom to throw some cold water on his face and look around. He was disappointed to discover that the shower was small, but adequate.

He welcomed the cold water that caused his skin to tingle. It refreshed him and he started to take a closer look at the other amenities. *Am I losing my mind or is everything about this room too small?*

He opened and closed several of the cabin dresser drawers. There was barely enough room in the drawers and the single closet to hold all his clothes.

He ran his fingers through his hair as if to massage his thoughts. *This is a dollhouse compared to my co-op back home in Pelzer.*

It only took him five minutes to see everything that was available inside the cabin and since it was a free vacation, he couldn't be choosy. It wasn't something he would've picked but he thanked God for it anyway. *I wonder if I can upgrade to a better cabin.* He made a mental note to look into it.

Lyon plopped down on the bed and then reached for the ship's *Compass Guide* again, to read about the activities. He decided to look into a few of the offshore excursions and other ship activities.

Suddenly the unsettling feeling returned. It washed over him but he dismissed it quickly. Whatever the problem, he was leaving it up to God to handle. He was going to enjoy the cruise.

Just as he'd finished writing down all the activities he planned to do, there was a soft knock at the door.

"We have come with your luggage, Sir."

The "we" turned out to be two young,

well-built men with thick African accents speaking with precise rhythms. Each was exceptionally dark almost to the point of having a blue aura to their skin. Their teeth were perfectly aligned and unnaturally white. They carried the heavy suitcases as though they were lifting newspaper. The taller of the two seemed tall enough to be walking on hidden stilts. He held his head high as though he were of regal birth, and was lifting luggage just for sport.

The other African prince in snow-white khakis appeared to be a bit more subdued and yet he, too, had a look of understated elegance that practically astounded Lyon.

"Just place them anywhere in the room." He couldn't take his eyes off them. "Where are you gentlemen from originally?" He just had to ask.

The young man gave Lyon a broad smile. "I'm called Jaiquist. I'm from Rwanda." His words were without condemnation, as if he didn't want to make Lyon feel foolish for not reading his nametag. He said the word *Rwanda* with a pride that coated each word. "You may call me, Jai, if you wish."

As Jai stepped back, the other young man came forward. He was extremely tall, much taller than most men who weren't basketball players. He leaned over as if to bow and extended his hand. "I would be called Samuel, sir. You may address me as Sam." His words were quieter and yet they were just as strong. "I am a Karamojong from Uganda."

Just as quickly as they'd arrived, the young men said, quietly, one after the other, *"Karibu,"* and disappeared.

Wow. That was powerful in a way I can't explain, Lyon thought.

Lyon was alone again and he didn't mind it at all. He tried to conjure up a little guilt because he didn't want to be selfish; he couldn't.

As much as he loved his twin brother, he was glad that Lionel had decided to keep the luxurious stateroom cabin that he would've shared if the bishop had come along.

Happy to have fresh clothes, he lay down. Lyon's sleep came quick and was welcome, and he stayed that way even as the ship pulled away from the shore.

24

Birdie took a short power nap before she happily stepped out onto the cabin's balcony. She inhaled the salty sea air and smiled at the swooping pelicans performing flying acrobatics as they dived into the ocean. *Needy hasn't shown up yet. I certainly hope Ima's plan is going well . . .*

A soft thump on her cabin door interrupted her thoughts. It had caught her by surprise, causing her to almost trip over her own feet.

Birdie opened the door slowly. Much to her surprise and delight there stood two extremely dark and chiseled-bodied male cabin stewards. They were there to deliver her luggage. She looked them over and opened the door wider so they could enter. The men nodded and smiled as they carried each heavy suitcase as though it was newspaper. Birdie couldn't take her eyes away. Each man had a warm aura that was strong, elegant and yet, invisibly detached.

The sight of the young men reminded her of a painting she owned. It was an oil of African men with glistening black skin carrying Cleopatra, as though she was a delicate dish of beauty on a colorful tray.

"We thank you, Madam, for traveling aboard the *Desperation*," one man said politely as he bowed slightly.

"Please let us know if there is anything we can do for you," the other man added as he, too, bowed.

Their accents floored her. They said their words as if they were singing a song.

Birdie wasn't sure how long she'd stood there just looking at them before they quickly disappeared. The next thing she knew she was in the cabin alone. She wished she'd spoken to them instead of pointing to where she wanted her luggage put. Perhaps it was just as well because she hadn't spoken to anyone since she'd boarded. She barely remembered coming aboard, although she thought she'd had a conversation with a tall woman with an English accent. If she had then she wasn't sure if her words were lucid or slurred, after the headache she'd had.

Pushing her unsure thoughts aside, Birdie unpacked and checked her watch. According to the *Compass Guide Newsletter* schedule, the ship had left Miami almost two hours earlier. She decided to look for the other women. She'd not seen them since she came to her room.

Birdie had barely stepped outside her cabin door when she thought her eyes were playing tricks. She'd hoped the effects of the Coca-Cola and Benedryl had vanished after taking that quick nap. That was until she looked down the hallway, and saw an old woman on her knees.

Birdie walked cautiously towards the woman, Mother Blister. As she got closer, she could see that the old woman was trying to find the correct position to place her cabin card key in the lock. From Birdie's door, the old woman had looked as if she was trying to pick the lock instead.

"Mother Blister, can I help you with that?"

Mother Blister's arthritic fingers kept trying to make the card fit in the slot as she quickly glanced up at Birdie and answered. "Help me with what?"

"You seem to have a problem getting into your cabin," Birdie answered cautiously. She didn't want to offend.

"I don't know what kind of ship you booked us on. It's a darn shame that you can't even use a credit card to pick a lock."

Birdie stood motionless. Because she

knew Mother Blister's reputation for never forgiving a slight, Birdie's desire to help wavered between self-protection and heroism.

Mother Blister puckered her lips in disgust. Her face looked pained as she hesitated and then placed her hands against the hallway wall. By the time she carefully rose to her feet, she was almost out of breath. "I remember a time when all I needed was a MasterCard or a Visa and I could get into any door I wanted." She was angry. To make matters worse, she hadn't taken out her dentures since they'd left Pelzer. The denture paste was thinning as fast as her patience. Both her teeth and nerves became unglued and her wig looked as if it were about to abandon her and the ship.

Birdie shook her head and summoned prayer and patience. She decided to wait it out and give the old woman a few moments to gain her composure.

While Birdie stood mired in sympathy and looking forlorn in the hallway waiting for Mother Blister to get a grip on reality, Ima lounged in her expensive cabin.

All was quiet among the rich and arrogant occupants of the eleventh deck with the exception of the giddy chuckling coming from within Ima's cabin.

She was so excited about cruising and tasting the delicious Welcome Aboard champagne and fruit basket in her ornately decorated stateroom, she was giddy.

She couldn't wait to check out the cabin amenities. She started by examining the sitting room with its large cocoa-colored sofa. When let out, it converted into an extra bed. There was a fully stocked mini-bar and a small refrigerator. She liked that. If she felt like a snack, she wouldn't have to leave to eat with the other common passengers unless she wanted to. Everything about the cabin was perfect, especially the bathroom, which had a real bathtub and shower.

Ima had made sure that her exquisite deluxe luxury stateroom was on one of the higher decks. It was far off the bow, and on the opposite side and one deck up from Birdie's cabin.

The explanation she'd given for the extra expense was that she needed distance from the others so she could work her retribution and enjoy peace of mind.

In reality, she was the only one getting Birdie's money's worth. Birdie, in her less-than-magnificent stateroom, sure wasn't.

Ima hadn't seen or heard anything from either Needy or Mother Pray Onn since boarding. That wasn't a good sign. It'd taken a lot of imagination but Ima's plan to coerce her aunt into sharing a cabin with Mother Blister, she thought, was pure genius. Now she began to fear that her plan could unravel quicker than a sheep's mangy wool coat.

Whenever Ima felt uncomfortable about one of her schemes, which was seldom, she'd sing. In a husky voice that sounded more like Eartha Kitt dueling with Carol Channing, Ima suddenly started singing. She sang an old Chaka Khan hit that she'd turned into her mantra. "I'm every woman . . ."

By the time Ima finished mangling the song to her personal satisfaction, she'd begun to feel like her old evil self.

She examined the skimpy outfit she wore and was pleased with it, too. The queen was ready to join the peasants aboard, and launch her plan to make Lyon Lipps wish he'd never left his mama's womb.

Needy better not mess up. I'll whittle those double-Ds down into triple-A's, Ima thought, but then quickly rebuked the intruding doubt. *Even Needy couldn't possibly mess up such a small task.*

"We've only been on the water for a few hours and you've got a problem with this free cabin already?" Lionel's teasing smile didn't budge Lyon.

"I only stated the obvious. There's only room enough for one in here. It's a blessing that you were able to keep the bishop's cabin and for the same price. It should've cost more since it's just you in there."

Lionel lay back on the small sofa with his feet resting on the ottoman. "I tell you all the time that I have favor with God. I don't know what it's going to take to get you to believe that you do, too."

There was no way Lionel would let Lyon or anything spoil his cruise. He'd thanked God nearly every day for the past week since the bishop had invited him. "Besides, I've heard you say often to let God handle people and not people nor things handle people."

"You're right," Lyon replied as he watched his brother rise.

Lionel walked a few feet and took one last look in the narrow mirror.

He liked what he saw. He was dressed in a cream-colored cotton shirt that was opened at the neck. A small patch of thick, silky, sexy dark hair peaked teasingly above one of the top buttons.

With the exception of Bishop Eddie Long in Atlanta, he didn't know many preachers who would ever wear an outfit like his.

The pair of matching cream-colored slacks that fitted his small waist and muscled legs was tailor-made. He knew he looked good and would've challenged any who said otherwise.

"Do you think I might have a chance of looking in my own mirror?" Lyon asked with a nod. It was his way of agreeing with what he knew his brother was thinking.

"Be my guest," Lionel answered. "It's a waste of time since we're twins, but go ahead."

Lyon tried to smooth the wrinkles from his dark brown casual shirt and pants as he walked over and took his turn at the mirror. He hated ironing and didn't think the wrinkles looked that bad. Compared to the way his brother always dressed, he was sure he looked like a poor image but he didn't care that much about fashion.

"Are you sure you're on a real mission for the Lord? I don't believe that Christ ever spent so much energy or expense on his appearance," Lyon teased his brother.

Lionel laughed as his eyes swept across several expensive tailor-made suits thrown across the bed that he'd brought to his brother's cabin. "I'm trying to give you a sense of style just in case you meet someone willing to become a Mrs. Lyon."

"Trust me," Lyon replied, quickly and emphatically. "If there is to be a Mrs. Lyon in my life, the Lord himself will bring her to me and she'll be singing Hallelujah, I'm Every Woman, and thanking the Master that He did."

The brothers slapped high fives and laughed.

"I guess you learned first-hand from the bishop about not being unequally yoked. That ex-wife of his tried to clean him out but good," Lyon continued.

"Have mercy, you know I did. The bishop told me that she acted as if she was withdrawing from the First Bishop Bank of America. That woman cleaned him out so good he was squeaking when he left the courthouse."

"So because he had a bad experience now *you're* gun shy?" Lyon asked.

"Gun shy? Uh no, I'm not. Marriage shy; you'd better believe it. And, you'd better also believe that if God don't come down and escort her to me that she'd better be singing my favorite Shirley Caesar song, 'You're Next In Line For a Miracle' while on a food line piling her plate up with shrimp. That's the only way she'd get a consideration."

Lyon had that conversation often enough to know that no matter what his brother said, he truly wanted a wife but he had a particular type in mind. Lionel wanted a tall but model-thin woman with long hair (preferably her own) and she had to want to have several children, naturally or adopted. Most of all, the woman would have to love God more than she loved him.

Lionel read Lyon's thoughts and laughed again. It was getting a little too serious so he decided to change the subject. "By the way, did you notice that we are not seated at the same time for our meals?"

"You're kidding."

"I wish I were. But the good news is . . ."

"There's good news?" Lyon asked, slowly.

"Yes, there's good news. We've got the same table number." Lionel had a mischievous look that reminded Lyon of their childhood.

"Doesn't that remind you of the tricks we used to play in school?" Lyon asked, laughing.

"It does, but I think we've matured a little since then. We don't have to confuse folks anymore to avoid trouble or get extra goodies," Lionel answered with another wink.

"You're right," Lyon replied, "we're much too mature for that, and not quite as desperate as we were in school."

Lionel laughed at the observation, and it left no doubt that his brother's good mood had returned.

"Why don't you go on back to the cabin, and hang up your expensive suits?" Lyon said. "I'll wait for you."

He tried to smooth the wrinkles again but they wouldn't budge, and he still didn't care. At that moment, he just wanted to get started with his adventure. He turned and walked over to the balcony door and scanned the ocean. "Not a spot of land in sight. We're on our way . . ."

"Mexico and Jamaica, I can't wait," Lyon said to Lionel as his brother gathered the suits with care.

"I'm eager to visit the island of St. Maartens. I hear it is spectacular," Lionel replied. He had already decided that he wanted to visit the Dutch side of the island. "I've never known a place to have only two streets, appropriately named Front Street and Back Street."

Within moments, Lionel had returned to join Lyon. They took one last look around the cabin before leaving.

"God is good all the time —" Lyon turned and said to Lionel.

"And all the time, God is good." Like

most church folks, Lionel knew how to finish that particular line of praise.

They stopped at the door's threshold and
prayed. They asked God for His blessing
and guidance.

The only sound in the hallway was the
loud dull sound of the closing cabin door.
Neither man spoke as they walked, single-
file, down the narrow corridor, each brother
lost in his own thoughts.

Although they were both in their late forties
and men of God now, there was a time when
Lionel and Lyon were not. During the seventies, they'd spent their youth in New Orleans.
It was a time they'd never and couldn't forget.
It was a special time when they enjoyed
seasons of gaiety and carefree years. They
embraced those years as a rite of passage,
as did most young men.

That was a time when they'd leave their
home late in the evening and in much the
same manner as they were leaving the cabin
now. At that time, in their young lives, they
dressed to impress.

As teenagers, there was no God on their
minds. The only thoughts of heavenly things
came wrapped in stolen visits to the French
Quarter where they'd returned home and
serenaded one another with lies about sup-

posed conquests.

They'd listen to sexy promises sung by Marvin Gaye. Fast beats of high living delivered with gospel riffs by Frankie Beverly and Maze and, of course, anything by the Neville Brothers. They'd hear just enough to get them in the right mood and then go in search of their recreational drug of choice, marijuana. They'd put in a lot of effort to get into all the sinful mischief that silly young teenage boys did.

They'd often heard that most ungodly folks lived off the prayers of someone else, and it was certainly true for them. The twins' father had warned them to stay clear of the Ninth Ward.

Their father, Granville Lipps, was a Christian who always preached and prophesized to the young people about the consequences of sinful living. Of course, his sons paid no attention.

On one particular fateful night, for reasons Lionel could only attribute to prayer and an unseen Guardian Angel, he arrived at their secret spot late. Lyon did not. Lyon had arrived there too early and was hanging around, waiting.

At the age of sixteen, Lyon's life changed forever. He hadn't bought drugs but he was still arrested along with the other seasoned drug sellers.

From then on, the brothers' lives changed. Lionel went on to become a well-respected man of God who counseled young men wherever he traveled.

Unfortunately, for Lyon, the months in prison darkened his outlook on life and battered his soul. Many years later, he found God, but not before he'd wreaked havoc on innocent lives from coast-to-coast.

Lionel had almost walked to the end of the long corridor before he realized that his happy mood had given room to remorse. After all the years that had passed, sometimes Lionel still carried the guilt of enjoying life so much more than Lyon had.

Lyon turned back and saw the familiar vacant stare on Lionel's face. He decided to break the ice. "Like I said before, my brother, God is good all the time —"

"And all the time, God is good. Hallelujah," Lionel quickly added. He meant each word.

Wrapped up in their returned joy the brothers almost bumped into another passenger who'd had her back turned as they passed.

The sound of distant male laughter had caught her attention but so had Mother Blister's latest dilemma. "We need to move aside," Birdie whispered. "We're blocking the hallway."

Warning Mother Blister to move aside didn't matter; Mother Blister couldn't have moved if she'd wanted. The fragile nerves in her well-aged kneecaps felt like they were on fire. Bent over and looking like the letter C, Mother Blister looked constipated and trapped in arthritis hell. She never saw the men at all.

Focused on Mother Blister, Birdie calmed down, and tried to use the cabin keycard. It didn't work. She suggested they go to the passenger's assistance desk for help.

Mother Blister didn't argue with Birdie; she grunted in pain as she slowly straightened her body. Her old bones moaned as she moved gingerly down the corridor.

Birdie actually felt sorry for Mother Blister's position and condition. "Everything will work out. They probably forgot to computerize your cabin keycard." She hoped that was true. It was near dinnertime and she needed to get things settled, and find Ima and Needy. And Birdie definitely didn't want to be around when Mother Pray Onn discovered that she and Mother Blister were sharing a cabin.

So Birdie quickly forgot her sympathy for Mother Blister. She turned around and grabbed Mother Blister's arm, despite the old woman's grunted protests. Fortunately, the ship's corridor was empty when she suddenly started dragging Mother Blister along the corridor to the elevator.

All Mother Blister could do was whimper and moan as the corridor walls seemed to fly. Nothing went right for her. Her false teeth hung dangerously by several gummy threads from her mouth. She couldn't trust herself to argue without punching somebody out.

And, if she didn't hurry up and find a bathroom, there'd be a little extra water in that elevator.

25

Just as Birdie and the others were about to sail the high seas, Cill was arranging her own cruise. She could almost taste victory until her phone rang for the fourth time that night.

"Hello!" Cill's face automatically twisted making her look as though she had Bell's Palsy. "What in the world do you want *me* to do about Ima's cat?" Cill screamed into the telephone at Petunia. The question was rhetorical so she didn't wait for a reply. Instead she slammed down the phone, again. That time she jerked the cord out from its jack leaving nothing but red, green, black and yellow wires dangling.

She wanted to do to Petunia what Petunia should've done to that cat the first time it'd shredded her couch covers. Now she was complaining that the cat had urinated on her bed. Petunia had thrown the bed out and kept the cat.

How far past stupid is Petunia? Cill fumed. It'd been more than fifteen minutes since Petunia had invaded her peace for the last time. It was time to dismiss further thoughts of Petunia and that demon-possessed cat, Evilene, quickly. Besides, it was almost eight o'clock and the night air was smothering her. The only solace she now had lay in a brown and white UPS envelope on the coffee table. She was going to enjoy it in her air-conditioned living room.

She hadn't a chance to read the investigation file she'd ordered on the Internet. She'd found a site that only charged $9.95 for all the dirt she'd need to get to Lyon first.

Cill wouldn't have run the background check if she hadn't accidentally run into an old friend.

She'd stopped at an ATM in downtown Pelzer. No sooner had she withdrawn her money she turned and came face-to-face with Deacon Lester Pugh.

Deacon Pugh was a former member of the church who left after getting into a fistfight with the Deacon Laid Handz over some missing Building Fund funds.

Cill and Deacon Pugh exchanged pleasantries. She asked what he'd been up to and what he told her, she found unbelievable.

"I've been having a ball at Old Crissed Cross Methodology Hall," Deacon Pugh announced proudly.

"I think I've heard of that church," Cill said with uncertainty. "How long have you been attending?"

"Only a few months but I'm thinking about coming back to my home church."

"Why is that?"

"Because I've decided to be a better person and forgive that yellow hound y'all call a deacon. Moreover, I'll be following one of the young ministers. If the board votes with any sense then he might become your new pastor."

That bit of news caught her interest. "Who are they voting on as the new pastor?"

"The Reverend L. Lipps is the young handsome fella's name." Deacon Pugh's chest suddenly barreled with pride.

"What did you just say?" Cill asked as her eyes bulged and fists clenched.

"I'd say that I was surprised that you didn't know about the good looking, wavy-haired sharp dresser with the green eyes, but I'd be lying. If I remember correctly, you're not into good-looking men."

Cill hadn't bothered to say goodbye or wave as she dashed to her car and sped off.

Under normal circumstances, she would have used her cellular phone and called Needy to give her the news. However, her so-called friend was out cruising with that she-devil and there was no way she would tell Petunia.

She couldn't believe her luck. The same man that they had planned to maim was now a man of the cloth.

"I won't have to do nothing. I'll watch God take care of their sorry behinds for trying to harm one of his servants," Cill said aloud, conveniently forgetting her role in the scheme.

Cill's feeling of retribution was short-lived as she began to suddenly have doubts about Deacon Pugh's revelation.

"Deacon Pugh was accused of stealing," Cill said to her reflection in her rearview mirror. "Everybody knows that if you steal, you'll lie too."

Cill put her car into warp speed and raced home to jump on the information highway. When she'd surfed through the many websites offering the low down dirty for a cheap price, she couldn't hit the enter button fast enough. She'd spent an extra fifty dollars to have the information sent overnight by UPS.

Cill kicked the remnants of the telephone

to the side as she walked over to her bed. Because she wanted to make notes of whatever was important in the envelope, she grabbed the pad she kept beside her bed, and headed towards the living room.

Cill's smile had returned and brought with it a more pronounced pep in her step. No sooner had she entered the room than she turned on her CD player. One of her favorite old songs rang out. She hummed along with Michael McDonald and the Doobie Brothers as they sang "All in Love Is Fair."

Cill was interrupted just as she finished singing the last verse and was about to open the envelope. It was the doorbell ringing as though someone thought the house was on fire. She flung down the envelope and looked at the wall clock. *It's nine o'clock. It had better be someone with a large million-dollar check and a bouquet of flowers from that Publishers Clearinghouse.*

There was no man with a cardboard check but there was a cardboard box on the doorstep. There was no one holding a beautiful bouquet of flowers, but there was someone wearing an ugly floral floppy hat.

It was Evilene circling her tail in a box of shredded newspapers and Petunia dressed in her nightgown trying to conceal her face with an ugly hat. Her arms were folded tightly, causing her to look like a praying mantis standing on its hind legs.

Cill's fist balled and became as tight as her facial muscles. She could have killed Petunia.

And Petunia wanted to kill Evilene, but didn't have the nerve, so she brought the cat to Cill, who did.

Evilene watched the whole thing unfold as she jumped from the box. She inched down a couple of steps, circled and wrapped her tail around Petunia's ankle, tight enough to cut off the leg's circulation.

"Get off of me, you mangy mutt," Petunia screamed at Evilene as she tried to shake off the cat and get some feeling back into her leg.

Evilene wasn't letting go until she felt like it, but she finally did after she'd punished Petunia enough for calling her a mutt. The cat arched her back in a manner that made her look almost regal. Evilene slowly raised her head, letting her jaw open to show her sharpened feline teeth. She gave sort of a half smile and a half sneer.

"That doggone cat is possessed," Petunia whimpered.

"Well, she's in your possession, so deal with it," Cill replied. She wasn't about to let Petunia or the cat in. She had to get back to that envelope.

While the standoff unfolded, Evilene did it as only an old, set-in-its-ways, and truly evil cat would. The cat looked on as though it actually enjoyed watching the drama unfold. With that much excitement happening, she wouldn't miss Ima much at all.

While Cill and Petunia continued blasting each other with menacing stares in the doorway, Evilene sashayed past them. The cat stopped briefly to check out the hallway before proceeding. It spied the UPS envelope on Cill's coffee table.

Cill hadn't seen Evilene slink past as she stood immovable with her legs parted, blocking Petunia from entering. "If you don't move your skinny behind from my doorway and take that feline with you, I'm beating the mess out of you. And, then I'm gonna have what's left of you arrested for trespassing."

"I wish you'd try it." The quiver in Petunia's voice betrayed her supposed bravery. "I don't have anyplace to sleep tonight. You can't be a Christian and turn me away," she pleaded. The tears swelling in her eyes were real, even if her bravado wasn't.

The clicking sounds of paper-thin window shades echoed up and down the block as the sounds of threats and venom poured from Cill's front porch. Some neighbors used discretion and sneaked a peek, while others grabbed lounge chairs and watched from their lawns.

While Cill and Petunia verbally sparred in the doorway, Evilene was inside doing what she always did. The first thing the cat did was paw the envelope off the coffee table. The first several swipes with its retractable claws ripped the envelope in half. By the time Evilene finished using her claws to play a game of Tic-Tack-Toe across the front of the envelope, its contents had turned into confetti.

Evilene grew bored with her latest mischief. The cat's fur bristled as if electricity had run through it while she watched the rain of slivered paper fall onto the carpet. With a low growl and its head bowed, Evilene jumped on and off of Cill's couch before racing towards Cill's bedroom. It was there that the cat found the allure and resting place of a pile of fresh clean sheets.

It took a few minutes before Cill and Petunia finally heard the muffled laughter from the neighbors and realized they were the cause.

"Girl, you are so crazy," Cill laughed, nervously and loud, so her neighbors could hear her plainly. She jerked around and gave

Petunia an insincere wink and a scowl that needed no further explanation.

"I know. We don't seem to ever get tired of playing jokes on each other," Petunia yelled back. She could almost hear the jokes that would be told around town about their squabble.

Cill pushed Petunia so hard through the front door that Petunia's back almost pushed through her chest. Petunia's shoulder blades would've looked bigger than her small breasts.

"Stop shoving," Petunia protested. She was mad enough to risk the awful beatdown that was surely coming her way.

Petunia didn't have time to wallow in either self-pity or fear. The screeching sound coming from Cill shook Petunia to her bones.

"That cat!" Cill was snatching tiny bits of paper from off the carpet. "That cat!" she repeated.

Petunia couldn't help but smile. Now Cill would understand what she'd been through cat-sitting Ima's demon-feline. "At least that cat didn't urinate on your sheets and mattress."

In between hysterical sobs and clipped words, Cill poured out the consequences of what Evilene had done. "Now we have nothing. I paid good money for that information on Lyon Lipps."

"Why didn't you tell me you had information on that disgusting pig? Can't we get it again?" Petunia couldn't stay calm when Cill was out of control.

"Ima and the others are already sailing and having a good time," Cill bawled. It was the first tear she'd shed in quite a while.

"How do you know that?" Petunia only asked because Cill's sudden display of emotion had her rattled.

"What would you do if you were on a cruise?" Cill asked as she suddenly cut off the waterworks from embarrassment.

"I'd have a ball." Petunia's face lit up as she started to relay all the activities and the men she'd meet.

"Shut up!" Cill couldn't take it. A misfit cat that destroyed what was surely a victory, and a skinny, clueless old maid had witnessed her crying.

Petunia didn't know why she did it. It was something she'd never thought to do if she were in her right mind. Petunia suddenly grabbed Cill and held her tight. She whispered softly to her. "Cill, go ahead and cry. It's alright. I know about the child that died two years ago in Anderson County." Petunia's grip tightened as she felt a sudden stiffness in Cill. "I know that you wanted to adopt that child."

"How — ?" Cill couldn't finish because she was crying too hard.

"Shush now," Petunia pleaded. "I've known for a while that you love children and can't have any."

Petunia led the stunned Cill to the sofa and sat her down.

"Cill," she said while handing her a fistful of the shredded paper to wipe her tears. "I've never told anyone about what a softy you truly are. And, I promise you that I never will." Petunia meant it. As often as Cill pushed and prodded, threatened and fussed, Petunia did love Cill. Cill had about as much masculinity as Petunia was bound to get, and she accepted Cill for what she was.

"I've always wanted children but I've never wanted to marry to have them," Cill confessed. "And now that I do want to marry one day, I feel too old to have children. I really don't mind adopting."

While Evilene lolled around in Cill's bedroom sprinkling her essence on the clean sheets, the women continued sharing their true feelings in the living room, unaware.

Cill's tears stopped and Petunia finally asked Cill why she'd done an investigation on Lyon Lipps since they'd already been to his neighborhood.

Cill explained about her chat with Deacon Pugh and his revelation that apparently Lyon was now a reverend. "And, he's going to go before the church board to become our new pastor," Cill revealed.

"Wait a minute," Petunia said. "I thought that they had to announce any new business in the church's newsletter."

"You're right," Cill answered as her composure returned. "I've got several around here that I haven't read yet."

Cill searched around the living room and then the dining room before she returned with an armful of papers. "The latest ones should be in this pile."

One by one they looked at the dates of the newsletters before placing them in a pile. It was in the second stack that they found it.

"This one must be it. It's dated for the first week in August." Cill's fingers scanned the print while she searched.

"It's on page five," Cill said as she turned to the page and began to read.

"Oh no . . ." Cill said as she read the notice.

During the last week in August the mem-

bers of the Ain't Nobody Right But Us —
All Others Goin' to Hell Church board
members are mandated to meet on Saturday, eight o'clock sharp. All old church
business must be concluded and a vote
for accepting the Reverend Lionel Lipps
will be held one time only. At the meeting
the Reverend Lionel will be queried and
will be accompanied by his twin brother,
Minister Lyon Lipps, as well as the Bishop
Noel Jones —

"Oh my God!" Petunia blurted.

Cill's reading was cut short by Petunia's outburst.

"I didn't know he had a twin. And he's been saved," Petunia said as she stood and started pacing.

"I didn't believe Deacon Pugh when he told me about his Reverend L. Lipps and that he was coming to pastor our church," Cill conceded. "I only did the investigation to show up Ima and let the church know what a scoundrel they were voting on."

"That would've been the right thing to do since you didn't know any different," Petunia replied.

"I wanted to be a hero," Cill confessed.

"You mean that you wanted to be a heroine," Petunia corrected, "that's the feminine form."

"I said what I *meant.*"

Cill was back.

"So what are we going to do?" Petunia asked, ignoring Cill's sudden return to nastiness.

"Well since we don't know what was in the envelope I will assume that it confirmed what Deacon Pugh told me. I'm going to try and send a fax to the ship." Cill reached over and snatched the brochure off the bookshelf. "Faxing is cheaper than a phone call."

"Do you think Needy will take time away from chasing a man to read a fax?" Petunia asked. "And, I'm sure Birdie will be too busy trying to keep up with Ima to read one."

"I'm going to send it to Ima. She's the one who will do the actual deed and she needs to be stopped."

"Hopefully she'll have a moment between keeping Mother Blister and Mother Pray Onn from killing each other, and breaking Lyon's neck to get the notice." Petunia suddenly stopped wringing her hands and pinched her nose. "Do you smell something?"

Cill jumped up and raced towards her precious bedroom, screaming at the top of her lungs. "Evilene, I'm gonna skin you alive!"

26

Needy had tried every trick she knew to persuade Mother Pray Onn to move to the cabin that was already booked for her.

The old woman had feigned everything from a massive headache to a mild heart attack. When that didn't work, she lay across one of the beds, and claimed every symptom from arthritis to gingivitis.

Needy hadn't spoken with Ima since they'd boarded. She wasn't able to let Ima know that their plan to have her aunt go quietly and unwittingly into the cabin with Mother Blister failed.

"I know my aunt. She's one of the snobbiest and most sanctimonious church mothers I know," Ima had promised. "When she finds out that the cabin the two of you have is rated a much lower class than the one she thinks I'm staying in, she'll carry her own bags to my cabin. When she gets there I'll manage to have Mother Blister out somewhere with Birdie. By the time those two old women find out that they're cabin mates, the ship will be out to sea and they'll be out of luck."

The only thing Needy was was out of was time.

While Needy fretted and fumed over what to do with Mother Pray Onn, Birdie was doing much the same about Mother Blister.

Outside the Deck Four Passenger Assistant desk, Birdie leaned against the wall with her hair cascading over her face so no one could tell that she was about to cry. She'd agonized over Mother Blister's latest predicament and the answer she found wasn't what she'd wanted.

She'd learned from the head purser, Mr. Hunter, that the reason the cabin keycard hadn't worked was because they'd tried to enter the wrong cabin.

"I'm so sorry for the inconvenience." Hunter's apology had poured out in his customary prim and proper, clipped English. "Yours and your cabin mate's luggage is now being delivered to your suite on the Owners Deck."

And that was when Birdie's head felt as if it would almost explode. Where had the mix-up started? Ima's instructions were simple enough. The plan was for Needy to deliver Mother Pray Onn to the cabin first and then after they'd set sail, she'd deliver Mother Blister. She and Needy would then disappear to the safety of their cabins and let the two old women either kill one another or accept their situation.

"The opulence of your new quarters will more than compensate for the discomfort of Ms. Blister and her friend," Hunter continued while his smile covered his annoyance. His patience waned as he waited for them to leave his station.

More than a thousand guests needed his attention, yet he continuously addressed these particular people. He knew trouble when he saw it. He took one look at Mother Blister and felt that swimming the English Channel would be far more enjoyable than dealing with her.

While Birdie handled the details of getting the correct key and filling out the Special Needs paperwork, Mother Blister sat hunched over on a nearby guest sofa. Her patience weakened as her arthritis had traveled from her knees to her hips. All she really wanted was someplace to lay her head and to take her pain medication. She needed to get to her cabin. No matter where it was.

To both Needy and Mother Pray Onn the

cabin was worth the fight. It was on a deck called the Owners Deck and away from the common folk. It not only had a private shower but also a sunken bathtub.

After stepping outside and looking at the oversized lounge chairs and the two mahogany round tables and stabilized telescope in the corner, Mother Pray Onn smiled. She was certain that the balconies on her traveling companion's decks weren't as spacious.

Some of the shelves were a little out of her reach but she'd risk standing on a chair if she had to use them. Mother Pray Onn was beyond happy. She was almost delirious.

The thought of how Needy had pounded away at the cabin door begging her to reopen it made her laugh. *That Needy is such an amateur. I can't believe she thought that I was gonna turn all this down and stay in Ima's cramped cabin.*

Mother Pray Onn glanced over at the clock. It was almost time to eat. She didn't need an itinerary to tell her that. Her stomach screamed for food. *I'll unpack and find something appropriate to wear. I'm so glad I packed my good white dress.*

Mother Pray Onn went over to the corner and looked at the luggage. She saw several strange pieces laying next to her own. *Oh, this is just great. Poor Needy's luggage is still here. I guess I can do the Christian thing and have it delivered to her cabin.*

She suddenly realized that she wasn't quite sure where Needy would stay. It didn't matter. She'd have the luggage moved to Ima's cabin. It would serve Needy right for trying to outsmart a poor, defenseless old woman into giving up God's blessing.

She looked around the cabin's living room again and then went on to explore the other rooms, including the extra bedroom. She could hardly wait to return to Pelzer and brag about her unexpected but richly deserved blessing at the next service.

Mother Pray Onn decided to take the bedroom furthest from the cabin door but closest to the bathroom. She liked solitude and it suited her just fine. She unpacked and prepared to shower before changing into her dinner attire.

Passenger lines had quickly started to build in front of Hunter's station's desk. While some passengers had whispered their annoyance at having to wait to have their concerns addressed, others loudly protested at the extraordinary attention given to the mismatched pair hogging the time.

To quell the impending revolt, several

more crewmembers appeared from nowhere. They swarmed to the desk like a covey of frightened white geese. They smiled and issued complimentary coupons for the smallest complaint. The *Desperation of the Seas* was under siege and barely out to sea.

The crewmembers did everything but stand on their heads to bring order to the confusion, although they didn't believe every complaint given.

The passenger chaos mounted by the minute. All of Hunter's proper upbringing slowly disappeared as profuse perspiration took its place. Between tightly clenched teeth, he hissed as respectfully as possible, "I've called for two cabin stewards to escort Ms. Blister to her new cabin." He continued, "As for you, Ms. Tweet. I imagine you can find your way *back* to your *own* cabin."

Before Birdie could respond, she heard somewhat familiar voices approach. She quickly looked over her shoulder. It was the cabin stewards she'd seen earlier. Her eyes, again, traveled over them. Their walk was so regal she felt as though she should bow as they came closer.

Again, they appeared and then disappeared quickly with Mother Blister waddling between them. The three of them reminded her of a scene from National

Geographic television. They looked like two Massai warriors walking beside Mother Blister. On television, Mother Blister would be a cow. By the time Birdie had completed the thought she realized, again, that she'd missed any opportunity to re-introduce herself.

The sight of several passengers dressed in formal dinner wear reminded Birdie that she too needed to dress for dinner. She hoped Needy had found the cabin and had vacated before Mother Pray Onn discovered that she was to share with Mother Blister.

For one of the few times that day Birdie smiled. She was happy that the two young men were escorting Mother Blister to the cabin. From what she'd observed about the two of those old Christian-wannabes, any proximity between them was sure to cause a declaration of war. She'd read Uganda and Rwanda on the stewards' name badges; those young men could handle war.

Birdie hurried off towards the bank of elevators back to her cabin. She wanted to look like a movie star when she entered the ship's dinning hall. Fortunately, she had late seating and that gave her almost an hour to prepare. If Needy had the same arrangement, it would be good. Birdie didn't want to spend her first night aboard the ship dining alone with strangers.

Also for the first time since she'd boarded, she'd thought about Lyon. Was she doing the right thing harboring such malice when she'd so often asked God for forgiveness?

Of course I'm doing the right thing, she thought, trying hard to convince herself as she walked faster towards the elevator.

Her hair, so neat when she'd left her cabin, had started fanning although no breeze flowed around her. The long hair swung as though it wanted to cool off the confused conversation in her mind. *Needy and Mother Blister attend church and they say that God forgives them for their craziness all the time. If that's true, then my place in heaven is secure.*

The empty elevator came quickly and she barely got inside before the door shut fast, almost catching her mane. She spun around to face the elevator's mirrored doors.

They are certainly more saved than I — maybe Needy even more so than Mother Blister. The thought of the one person, Ima, whom she'd paid to do her dirty work, having an iota of salvation never crossed her mind. Birdie's irrational thoughts came almost as fast as her fingers pounded the button to her deck.

27

While Lyon rested in his cabin until his time for dinner, Lionel went alone to the dining hall.

Their exploration of the *Desperation* had lightened his mood and given him a strut that made him look like a celebrity. However, he was not concerned about how he looked to the other passengers. Instead, his eyes took in the beautiful sight of fish-shaped ice sculptures and the astounding sight of men and women of all shapes, sizes, nationalities and countries. The sea of workers busied themselves bustling about as they attended to each diner's specific needs. The dining hall was huge and yet its elegance did not overpower the food's festive presentation.

As quickly as he'd arrived at the hall's entrance there appeared from nowhere the maitre d'. He was a dark-skinned man, short, somewhere in his mid-thirties, with a well-kept head of black shiny hair and a matching mustache. His badge showed he was from India.

"Welcome aboard, Sir. My name is Sunil. I will be your maitre d' while you travel with us. Please follow me and I will show you to your table."

Lionel followed Sunil to a table that was near the end of the dining hall. It suited him as it gave him an opportunity to observe the dining hall's activities.

Again, two servers magically appeared. One of them was a young woman with platinum blond hair. Her Nordic features were prominent in her green-speckled eyes. She was tall with a swimsuit-ready body. Her badge showed her as Inga from Sweden. She spoke slowly as though she thought no one at her table might understand her thick accent. "Good evening, ladies and gentlemen. My name is Inga."

As Inga introduced herself, gave them their menus, poured water, and explained the seafood-themed dinner choices, another waiter appeared and gently placed napkins on laps.

"Everything is just amazing," Lionel whispered excitedly to his server. "I don't know where to start," he continued. "Should I have the lobster and the lobster bisque or should I indulge in caviar?" He'd never had it and wanted to try a little sample.

"I'll bring you a sample."

He gave her his usual sexy wink. She'd obviously suspected he'd never tasted fish roe by the way she'd offered a sample to save him any embarrassment.

"Amazing, just simply amazing," Lionel repeated. While the others at his table let their palates salivate over the exquisite cuisine, he couldn't help repeating under his breath, "Amazing."

He was referring to the hauntingly beautiful woman who stood overdressed for the occasion and looked like a beauty queen in the hall's doorway. There was something different about her that awed him.

Lionel wanted to look away but found that he couldn't. At that instant, he made up his mind to get to know the woman. He couldn't remember the last time, especially since he'd given his life to God, that a woman took his breath completely away. And it was without any lust in his heart. *Why in the world would I come to dinner in this overpriced casual suit?* Meeting the beautiful stranger would have to wait until he changed. Would she wait?

Needy'd taken her time getting dressed.

There was no such thing as making a second first impression. Every inch of the brocade lavender Vera Wang cocktail dress hugged the right spots and downplayed the wrong ones. Her flat feet squeezed reluctantly into a pair of matching lavender three-inch pumps. She'd made sure that she put in the perfect-sized arch supports so that her feet wouldn't resemble Minnie Mouse's. She'd spent two months' worth of mortgage payments. It seemed right at the time because she saw it as an investment. An investment in her future shouldn't have a price.

Lord, I don't usually ask for much in the same way I'm asking tonight. The confident way in which she stood just inside the dining hall entry covered the deep insecurity that threatened to rise any moment as she sent her pleas to heaven.

She surveyed the elegance of the hall from where she stood and leaned her head ever so slightly to the side. Just in case her intended target sat out of her immediate sight she let her head tilt just a little the other way. Her auburn, upswept hair was store-bought but it wasn't the cheap kind that screamed, This ain't hardly real!

She suddenly had the strangest feeling that someone was watching her. In her fantasy whoever it was liked what they saw. They liked it as much as she did when she inspected her image in the mirrored walls along the outside corridor to the dining hall. *Thank you, Lord. You answered my prayer.* She smiled again. Even her reflection in the crescent-shaped mirror tiles along the door's frame looked pleased.

Before she could finish admiring her true beauty that stared back, she saw a bit of ugly approaching in the reflection.

"It's about time you got here." She almost broke a heel as she spun around. Needy's patience had soured, quickly, and at that moment, she didn't care who knew it.

"Would you please show some class?" Ima snapped under her breath. She'd worn a pair of hot pink, snag-a-man, five-inch spike heels and matching off-the-shoulder satin dress. She couldn't have run if she were on fire. She reached within snatching range of Needy and let her venom continue. "It's not my fault that my aunt got the best of you."

"Got the best of me? That woman is pure evil and having to stay in the same cabin with Birdie won't be a picnic. Why can't Mother Pray Onn stay with you? She's your demon aunt!"

"Stick with the plan, Needy," Ima replied,

strongly.

"I know what I'd like to stick —"

She was interrupted by the sudden appearance of a tuxedoed man whose badge read "Sunil." "I'm so sorry, Madams, for the delay. I will escort you to your table."

Needy and Ima had smiled the entire time they'd argued and hissed under their breaths. Sunil's swift arrival kept them civil. This time their smiles were genuine. They loved the idea of an escort to their table by a polite, handsome man who addressed them as madams.

Lionel hadn't heard a word said by either of the servers as they refilled his water glass and offered to grind fresh pepper on his salad. He still couldn't take his eyes off the woman as she entered with the head waiter and another woman. Both women walked as if they owned the ship.

"Are you planning on giving your order or will you be satisfied with just a glass of water?" one of the other men at his table teased. "I can eat an extra lobster tail if you're not having yours."

He was a much older, overweight, sun-deprived man. He'd watched the way Lionel's eyes had traveled to the dining hall entrance and trailed the two women who entered. It reminded him of his wanton youth.

"The way they prepare the snails and snakes are just the way you'd like them." The man continued to tease Lionel knowing that his words fell onto deaf ears.

The mention of snakes caused Lionel to give the man a strange sneer. "Who in their right mind would eat a snake?"

"You'll be eating one if you don't order." The man leaned in closer, moving the basket of assorted breads to the side. "My name is Harold Sugarman from Los Angeles, California." He offered his hand to shake as he continued speaking. "I'm not wearing a wedding ring and I see you're not either. I guess it's okay for a young single man to be leering."

"I'm not leering. I'm appreciating." Lionel gave the man a wink and added, "I know God is going to bless me with a good wife, someday, but —"

The man interrupted. "I think I know this speech," he said. "God will do it in His time, not yours. Isn't that what you were about to say?"

"Of course I was and I know He will. But you know I like to give God specifics from time to time." He winked again. "I'd specifically like to get to know that woman . . ."

He pointed to last area where he'd seen her walking. He looked from side to side and attempted to stand for a better view. She was gone.

The man from California saw the disappointment in Lionel's eyes. "You really do believe in love at first sight, don't you?"

Lionel didn't answer. He sat back in his chair and straightened the napkin in his lap. "Let's eat."

Ima had decided to go to the bathroom before being seated. When she came to the table she didn't like the look on Needy's face.

"What's the matter with you?" Ima asked.

"How are we supposed to see what's going on seated at a table near the kitchen?"

"I see what you mean," Ima said. She could see only the tops of heads from her seat. "Why didn't you ask them to change our seating?" she demanded.

"I did ask. Our head waiter, Sunil, promised to move us for our next seating if there is room."

Sunil must've seen the displeasure on the women's faces so he came over to reassure them of the ship's dedication to their pleasure.

"I promise you that I will do my best to

give you a more comfortable dining experience," Sunil said with a smile as he removed a tiny crumb off the tablecloth.

Ima looked up and gave him her promise as well: one to publicly remove his chest hairs, one at a time, with a rusty pair of tweezers on the bow of the ship.

She saw the sudden change in his expression and snapped her finger for him to lean in closer. "And, if you don't have chest hairs," she whispered, "wherever you have them it will do just fine."

The look of fear on Sunil's face removed all doubt that they'd have another table.

Birdie was almost fifteen minutes late getting to the dining hall. Once she approached Sunil and showed him her cruise card, his painted-on smile disappeared.

When Sunil saw where she was going to sit and with whom, all he did was point. "Over there, madam." He fled into the kitchen.

Birdie arrived at the table unescorted; she looked a mess. Her hair was still damp from her shower and there was a button missing from the back of her dress. No one would've ever guessed that she was the one with the money.

"What in the world happened to you? You look a hot mess," Ima ranted. "You're gonna make us look bad."

"How am I supposed to get a man with you sitting here looking like a charity case," Needy added. She turned up her nose as if Birdie had an unpleasant odor.

Birdie was still reeling from the experience with Mother Blister. She saw her need for a little churchy home girl sympathy was not coming. For the first time, Birdie let it all hang out.

"Needy, you show up out of nowhere and bum rush my cabin. You use up all the hot water to shower. You placed all your belongings in my closet space, and you left without so much as a goodbye." She was seething with anger and wagging her finger, as she looked from Needy to Ima before continuing. "Perhaps I need to get reparations from the two of you. You've been acting as if I was your personal money slave from the get-go."

"Get-go; did she just say get-go and bum rush?" Needy asked Ima as though she were offended.

"Did she just get loud with us and act like she didn't have any class?" Ima added equally indignant.

Wet or not, Birdie's damp hair suddenly started to fan out. She was about to kick the act of mutiny up a notch.

She turned her seat completely around and faced Ima, square on. "Yes, I said get-go, and bum rush, so what about it?"

Ima had never been the smartest or the sharpest kid in life's class — she'd used bullying to get her way. Instead of automatically slapping Birdie all up and down the dining hall, she reached over and grabbed Birdie's hands. She did it just in case Birdie was about to throw a slap in with her new-found bravery.

Needy realized that a fight wasn't going to break out when Ima gave Birdie a peck on the cheek instead, and a loose hug. Needy grabbed Ima's cup and sniffed it. Whatever Ima drank wasn't familiar to Needy. *I knew it would happen. That girl has lost her mind.*

By the time Ima finished hugging Birdie, pecking her cheeks and placing her fanned hair in its proper place, she had Birdie apologizing profusely as if everything since Eve ate the apple was Birdie's fault.

Needy sat there stunned. *That heifer is good!* Once more, Needy had found new respect for Ima. However, her feelings about Birdie's naiveté hadn't changed at all.

If any of the other diners noticed anything unusual, none reacted. Polite and soft conversation continued around the room. There were only two people watching the women's table, Lionel and Sunil. Each was in awe for his own reason.

While Needy, Birdie and Ima quieted down to a sumptuous feast of chilled shrimp and lobster claw appetizers, Mother Blister and Mother Pray Onn were up in the cabin about to bring the heat.

There was a thunderous outbreak in the old women's cabin and it scared Jai and Samuel.

As children back in Rwanda and Uganda, Jaiquist and Samuel were used to hearing the ferocious roars of heavy-maned adult lions proclaiming their dominence and protecting their territories.

Even as they escorted their herds of goats and cows through the dense brush in their native lands and stood for hours in the blazing sun, Jaiquist and Samuel were fearless.

However, when the two brave African men saw the looks on Mothers Pray Onn and Blister's faces at their first encounter, the men ran like scared rabbits.

"*Hatari!* (Danger!)" Jaiquist shouted as he pushed past Samuel hard enough for Samuel to spin like a revolving door.

"*Nisaidie, tafadhali!* (Help me, please!)" Samuel pleaded as he tried to get his balance.

"*Hapana!* (No!)" Jaiquist shouted as he ran down the corridor. He ran so fast his snow-white shirt looked like a streak of lightning against a night sky.

By the time Samuel caught up to Jaiquist at the end of the narrow corridor there was no room to pass. As they struggled, their legs tangled, causing them to trip.

There were only three other Owner cabin suites on the deck. The occupants of the other two suites were in the safety of the dining hall and had missed the battle. They were fortunate because the Mothers were about to sink the *Desperation.*

Jaiquist and Samuel had just arrived at the cabin when Mother Pray Onn stepped out from the bathroom. She'd taken a long, luxurious shower and because she'd thought she was alone, she'd seen no reason to wear a towel.

Mother Pray Onn had backed out of the shower naked as the day she was born and just as wrinkled. As she hummed one of her favorite hymns, as best she could, "I Come to the Garden Alone," she discovered that she wasn't. She'd come face-to-face with one of her many enemies.

Mother Blister had known she was way past tired as she tried to refocus. As far as she knew, raisins didn't walk or talk, so it'd taken her a moment to realize that what she'd seen was not a hallucination.

"What in the Sam Hill are you doing on this ship?" Mother Blister snorted. She tore the wig from her head. She had her legs spread, hands on hips, and was ready for whatever happened next.

"This is my cabin, and it ain't none of your business why I'm on this ship."

She didn't have on her glasses and she didn't need to. At that very moment, Ima's nefarious plan became clear to Mother Pray Onn, and she was livid. *Family: you just can't trust them. She set me up.*

Nevertheless, she continued her tirade against Mother Blister, pointing towards the balcony. "Besides, ain't ugly whales supposed to be in the ocean and not aboard the ship?"

"Don't forget whales eat nasty, slimy, arthritic shrimps!" Mother Blister towered over her. She would give as well as she took.

For the next few minutes or so, the old women traded insults and some threats. Not once during that entire time did Mother Pray Onn try to cover her nakedness.

Finally, they were so tired from arguing that all they could do was plop down on the sofa. Their aged chests looked like they were about to explode from overexertion. Yet, they continued hurling silent threats with pointed fingers and balled fists.

As tired as Mother Blister was she could take the sight of Mother Pray Onn's nakedness no longer. She leaned back, snatched one of the sofa's pillows and tossed it at her. "Cover yourself!" She leaned forward to get a better look and added, "And, put your teeth in. Your mouth looks like an old cave."

The pillow wasn't that large but it did cover up the front of Mother Pray Onn. She wasn't about to admit it but she was embarrassed; but more about her bald mouth than her nakedness.

"Don't like what you see, then get out!" She still clung to the pillow despite her boldness. "This is not your cabin. It's mine. It's called an upgrade," she informed Mother Blister.

"This is too my cabin. Those two ship boys bought me here. Would they bring me here if this wasn't my cabin?" She spied her luggage over in the corner of the sitting room and pointed to it. "That's my luggage, you senile old biddy."

Mother Pray Onn jumped up and snatched her glasses from a nearby table. She still held the pillow to cover her front nakedness and waddled over to the corner, giving Mother Blister the view of her sagging bottom. She knew her butt was uncovered. She did it on purpose so that she'd have the last word.

"Where's Needy's luggage?" Mother Blister asked, looking around the room.

"Can you possibly be that slow?" Mother Pray Onn mocked. She read the tags and was angered that she'd not paid attention when the luggage was delivered earlier. She'd thought that she'd outsmarted Needy, but apparently not.

Rather than explain what she meant, Mother Pray Onn left the room to dress and to plan her revenge.

While Mother Pray Onn was gone, Mother Blister sat and thought. *Needy is not smart enough to come up with this on her own. Birdie wouldn't do it.* There was only one person left. *Ima. I'm gonna kill her.*

When Mother Pray Onn returned to the room she knew by the fire that blazed in Mother Blister's weary eyes that she'd figured out what was going on. "I see you've seen the light."

"I'm gonna break your niece's neck," Mother Blister threatened.

"Oh, you can have her neck, but her behind belongs to me."

For the first time in many years, the two

old women had a common goal. It didn't matter that they'd served together on the church's Mothers Board. It mattered even less that they'd never agreed to a right way to hold a celebration or a fundraiser. They couldn't care less that they couldn't even agree on whatever day it was. Ima had finally done something that prayer or religion hadn't; she'd given them a common goal.

They were too angry to go to dinner. Instead, Mother Blister poured out the entire plan from start to finish, at least the parts that she could remember with any clarity. Mother Pray Onn added what she'd remembered Petunia telling her about Birdie's financing the cruise.

Somehow, they managed to piece together enough information from their faulty memories to form a plan. They had to keep repeating it because no sooner had they agreed on something devious than one of them would forget the details.

They were ready to put their own plan in motion. If they had to sink that ship to get to Ima, Birdie and Needy, they would. First, they needed to find Lyon Lipps before Ima did. He was going to have them as allies whether he liked it or not.

They ordered room service, took their

medications, read a passage from Mother Pray Onn's customized reworded Bible, prayed and then went to their separate bedrooms. They would need their rest to get their plan in action.

It was almost eight-thirty and the night air smelled salty.

Down on the inside lower deck the dining hall was as calm as the ocean that carried the ship. Most of the tables were empty because many of the passengers had left to enjoy the ship's late night activities.

Sunil instructed the servers to remove the place settings from the other tables as they impatiently waited for the remaining table of women to finish. They needed to prepare for a late seating.

The tired servers clanked dishes and even dropped a couple of glasses to get the women's attention. Nothing they did would make Ima and the other women budge.

For the first time since they'd boarded, Birdie, Ima and Needy relaxed. After the appetizers they'd traded appreciative looks each time a server appeared with unex-pected plates of seafood culinary delights. They'd dined on pork chops with fried green apples, marinated hanger steak with seasoned mashed potatoes, and seared tuna in coconut-curry sauce. They weren't accustomed to the ambiance of fine dining and when a bottle of Beringer Gamay Beaujolais Premier Nouveau wine was set on the table, they gulped it like flavored water. It was after their third glass that Ima excused herself as she felt the effects coming on.

"I wonder where she's at," Needy slurred, referring to Ima's absence. Each word she'd said sounded eerily strange to her ears, and she didn't know why.

"I dun no," Birdie replied. Her words ran together and her head began to nod. Her chin was about to land in the sugar bowl before she jerked up.

Birdie and Needy leaned over the table across from one another looking like statues connected at the foreheads. They wanted to move. They needed to move. They couldn't move.

He'd been seated at his table still sipping the remnants of a small demitasse when Lionel spotted one of the women from before. She was coming toward his table but passed by, and went straight out of the dining hall. He looked at the direction she come from, and finally saw the woman he'd seen earlier. His mood was automatically lifted and he was tempted to go over to the table, but he didn't. The two women had their heads together and were probably in a deep conversation. He wouldn't interrupt them. Tomorrow was another day.

As Lionel was about to push away from the table he spied Lyon among many waiting at the entryway to be seated.

"You made it down here. I wasn't sure if you would," Lionel said as he patted his brother on the shoulder.

"You seem to be very pleased. Was the food that good?" Lyon asked with a hint of suspicion.

"The food was simply wonderful and so is the entire dining experience," Lionel said as he motioned to the table in the back where Needy sat with Birdie.

"I think I see what you mean," Lyon said with hesitation. He really didn't see anything extraordinary about the two women that would cause his brother to become so enamored. And he couldn't be certain but something was familiar about one of the women Lionel had pointed out. When he mentioned it, Lionel laughed.

"Oh come on, Lyon. You know what they say, all white folks look alike." He didn't believe it but thought if he said something ridiculous, it would change his brother's mood. He could tell from Lyon's concerned look that it hadn't.

"Why don't we go back to my cabin and chat?" Lionel finally said. "I can order room service and you don't have to eat here alone. At least you won't have to do it tonight."

He steered Lyon away from the doorway to allow the others to enter and to show that it wasn't a suggestion. "We don't gamble and I'm sure that since we're on the ocean nothing on this ship will change overnight."

Lyon's gaze was fixated on the table. He alternated between wanting the woman with the long brunette hair to turn around so he could get a good look at her — and not. He was almost grateful to Lionel for making the suggestion to leave. Probably his exhaustion made him think that he knew someone who was obviously just another passenger.

As the other passengers filed through the dining hall door, Sunil met them with a wide grin. As each passed, he extended his hand, and did the same to Lionel as he departed.

"Have a good evening, Mr. Lipps. We hope you've had a most pleasant dining experience tonight."

"It was wonderful. Thank you so much. The service was excellent." Lionel's deep voice gave strong support to his words of praise.

Ima had stepped out from the ladies' room. She was just about to go back inside the dining hall to join the others when she thought she was hearing things. She'd recognized the same voice she'd heard on the phone when she'd called Lyon Lipps — it was only a few feet from her. There was no doubt. After all, she'd heard him addressed as Mr. Lipps. How many Mr. Lipps were aboard, particularly with that deep voice?

Instead of rejoining the others, Ima crept back inside the bathroom and peeped out. She saw two men pass. From their backs, they appeared to be about the same height and build. She should've gone inside the dining hall. How could she be sure which one was Lyon or even if these were the same men? He could've gone in the other direction.

Ima finally stepped out into the open. There was no one there so she reentered the dining hall. "Oh, this is just great," she murmured when she saw the conditions of Birdie and Needy. She ordered black coffee for them and waited until they sobered up.

While she waited, Ima thought about her other problem. She hadn't heard from either

her aunt or Mother Blister. *Either they've killed each other or they've had a heart attack from seeing each other.* She laughed at the thought and was almost ashamed. *I need to calm down. Needy said that there's more room in that upgraded suite than in the old cabin. They should be glad it worked out.*

She didn't have time to ponder more about what to do with the old women because Birdie and Needy were coming around.

"Come on you two love birds," Ima teased her companions as she parted their heads. "I've got to get you to your cabin."

28

It was well past midnight and into the second day aboard the ship. Millions of bright flickering stars circled the hanging half moon with lights that reflected off the water. The *Desperation* sailed quietly with only the noise from white-crested waves that kissed its sides from stern to bow. Everything across the ocean sky was still at peace.

However, inside the huge Owners suite, the senior hellhounds ran unfettered. Their mutual peace agreement hadn't lasted an hour before Mother Pray Onn tore into Mother Blister.

Neither of the two old women, despite their exhaustion, felt comfortable or trusted the other enough to close their eyes and sleep for very long. They'd sat on opposite ends of the long sofa with their eyes half-cocked. Drool seeped from the corners of their anger-twisted mouths. With their teeth on the coffee table within reach if needed, and uncombed wigs eschewed, their mood swings and memory lapses flashed like lightning. Stiffness from sitting stubbornly in one position finally forced them to take action.

"You are about as stubborn as a mule," Mother Pray Onn stated as she tried to massage the blood-flow through her numbed legs.

"Well, jackass, you'd know all about that, wouldn't you?" Mother Blister wouldn't back down. She felt spasms racing up and down her hips from the stiffness. She rubbed so hard she was about to remove the skin from them.

"Don't forget our Lord rode into town on an ass," Mother Pray Onn replied.

"Thank goodness it wasn't yours. We'd still be waiting for salvation."

Mother Pray Onn didn't blink or return the insult. Instead, she sweetly offered to make Mother Blister a cup of coffee. Mother Blister, forgetting that Mother Pray Onn never did anything sweetly, accepted the offer because she needed to stay awake.

While Mother Pray Onn plugged in the coffeemaker and set out the cups and saucers, Mother Blister went, again, into the bathroom.

Hours later as the sun traded places with

the moon the old women bickered again.

Mother Pray Onn had slipped a laxative into the coffee she'd served Mother Blister. She'd forgotten which cup was which and accidentally put the laxative in both cups. Of course, Mother Blister wasn't entirely innocent. When she'd gone into the bathroom, she'd found a box of Mother Pray Onn's bladder-control pads. She'd taken the opportunity to rip slits in several of them and poured water onto the rest.

They'd spent the rest of that night trying to out-race one another to the bathroom. Most of the time, neither was successful.

Despite the challenge of getting settled in the cabin and making sure that Needy and Birdie were nestled in their cabin, Ima had slept a peaceful sleep. The loll of the ship had rocked her until every nerve in her body relaxed.

She still hadn't heard from her aunt, so she'd take care of smoothing things over at breakfast. Depending on how angry her aunt was, she didn't know how she'd do it.

As she showered, letting the pelting water ricochet off her body, Ima hummed. She'd laid out a very revealing tawny-colored peasant dress made from gauze material that was sure to turn heads. *I might as well give*

Birdie her money's worth.

She let her mind retrace the events of the past night. Luck was definitely on her side. But Ima didn't know if she should be excited to know that Lyon Lipps shared the same meal schedule or not. Like most seasoned hunters, she loved the thrill of the chase. As much as she loved the sound of his deep voice, he was still going down.

Needy and Birdie arrived at Ima's cabin just as she was about to leave. Needy wore a lime-green, pinstriped, two-piece pants set. The jacket fell just below her waist and didn't accentuate her heavy bosom. She also wore matching sandals and a yellow floppy hat with a lime green sash. Her eyes hid behind a pair of large triangle-shaped sunglasses.

Birdie, despite her fashion debacle the previous night, also looked spectacular. She wore her hair in a ponytail and her makeup was perfect. She, too, chose to wear a two-piece pants set. The pink and chocolate-brown colors seemed to downplay her height. A pair of chocolate-brown open-toed sandals accented her pink pedicure.

The two of them looked like money to any that didn't know that Needy was definitely broke. Spending Birdie's money gave her a new appreciation for the couture look.

"I see you slept well," Birdie commented as she eyed, appreciatively, Ima's outfit. "Did I buy that?"

"Yes, you did." Ima took a couple of steps and twirled, giving them her best runway impersonation. "This is just a taste of what the rest of the ship will see." She, too, was impressed with what they wore but it wasn't in her nature to compliment another female.

Needy could care less. She'd seen Ima's show many times and the after-effects of the wine had given her a headache. She wasn't in the mood for pleasantries and let Ima know it. "I believe that half this ship already has what you have and the rest of it can see that same thing and for a cheaper price."

Ima had just begun her second spin when Needy's insults stopped her. She said nothing, choosing to file the insult away for a later time. "I guess you'd rather we rush to the dining hall so you can pack on more pounds," she said, innocently.

Needy knew she wouldn't win, so she backed down. She headed toward the door. "Are y'all coming? I simply can't wait to have my pounds brought to me and be called 'madam.' " She lifted her sunglasses off her eyes and smiled towards Ima so hard her teeth almost cracked.

Birdie tried to defuse the situation by asking Ima if she'd had any luck in finding Lyon.

"No, I haven't seen him." It wasn't exactly a lie. After all, she'd only heard a voice that sounded like his. Seeing a little disappointment seep onto Birdie's face, Ima added, "It's no problem. I'll seek him out after breakfast. After all, he still has to pick up the excursion passes I left for him."

Birdie's face lit up. "You're right."

As it had become their habit, they said a quick prayer for the success of their devious plan and left the cabin to have breakfast.

Lionel had just stepped onto the balcony when he heard the door to the cabin open. Lyon entered. His step had a bounce to it and his mood seemed more relaxed.

"I wondered where you'd gone," Lionel said as he came back inside, shutting the balcony door behind him. "You look good."

"So do you," Lyon replied. He looked at his brother and shook his head. "I guess no matter how old we get, we're twins and we will be on the same wavelength."

They looked like matching bookends, dressed unintentionally in identical white cotton outfits. To make matters worse, Lyon had risen early and visited the ship's barber.

Although Lyon's hair was cut just a little shorter and was now much curlier, from a distance it was still hard to tell the brothers apart. They laughed again and lifted their hands in their customary high fives.

Lyon had taken advantage of the breakfast buffet offered on the Lido Deck so Lionel left to eat alone in the dining hall. Lyon took advantage of the solitude by reading his Bible. With his heart and mind focused on meditating on the Word, he headed towards the balcony. The weather was humid but bearable. With the exception of an ocean liner in the far distance, he saw nothing but green water for miles.

Lionel saw her first. He knew it was she. She had her back to him but was with the same two women from the night before. It was open seating for the late breakfast so he chose a table that was close to hers but still a little off of the main aisle.

Lionel was robotic as he sat. He didn't mean to stare. But he was mesmerized by the way the sun's promising rays shone specifically on her and not the other two women. Was God trying to show him something? He couldn't help but feel that perhaps it was ordained that Lyon receive the free cruise, the bishop cancel, and that he would come along, too.

Ima was in the middle of one of her complaints when she saw him seated at a nearby table. She had missed his entrance so he had his back to her. However, she was almost certain that it was the same man from the previous evening. There was something about him that made him unforgettable. She could almost understand how he'd made such fools of the other women.

But Ima was determined not to be fooled.

"Are you okay?" Needy asked Ima, noticing she was distracted.

"Of course, I am. Why wouldn't I be fine? Just ask any man and he'll tell you how fine I am." She was rambling but she was also serious about how gorgeous she thought she was.

Both Needy and Birdie were facing Ima so they couldn't see him. She wouldn't tell them her suspicions until she was certain.

While the server took Birdie and Needy's breakfast orders, Ima's eyes peered intently over the top of her menu. She'd worn a pair of gray contact lenses, making her eyes appear almost mystical. Without letting her eyes move one way or the other, she took him in. The way that white cotton shirt hugged his bulging arm muscles and lay against his beautiful honey-brown skin

346

made it almost a crime to do what she was planning. However, she'd accepted Birdie's check and she planned to deliver.

Since it was the late seating and there weren't too many people in the dining hall it was possible to hear conversations from all directions. Ima directed her conversation towards Birdie and Needy but her ears were tuned to two tables away.

She heard him give his breakfast order and that removed all Ima's doubts. Ima picked at her food. Not one bite entered her mouth as she alternated between idle chitchat and spying on the nearby table.

Birdie accidentally dropped her napkin, and when she bent to pick it up, she saw him. It'd been a couple of years since their brief encounter, but from his profile, she was certain that it was he.

"My goodness. Ima, Needy, quick; look over there," Birdie urged, letting her neck stretch over her shoulder rapidly to make her point.

The urgency in her voice caught Needy and Ima off-guard. They looked at each other. Their eyes darted, questioning her sanity before turning back to her.

"What's wrong? Are you having a seizure?" Ima asked.

"You need me to shove a spoon down your

throat, so you don't swallow your tongue?" Needy asked, quickly reaching across the table at Birdie. She'd watched endless episodes of *MacGyver.* Needy clutched the tablespoon in one hand and a toothpick in the other like a surgeon ready to operate.

Instinct and the threat of Needy doing something stupid made Birdie try again to speak. She almost lost her balance but continued crooking her neck towards the other table. "He's here."

"Who's here?" Needy asked as her eyes darted, trying to follow the swift back-and-forth motion of Birdie's long neck.

"Lyon is sitting over there alone," Birdie bubbled. Her excitement mixed with her fears as she watched Needy jerk around to see.

Ima's face betrayed nothing. She'd wanted to be the first one to say she'd found Lyon and now, Birdie had accidentally blown it. *Focus, Ima, you need to keep the upper hand.* She turned slowly as though time was at her control. "You two need to get a hold of yourselves before you blow my plan."

By the time they'd all turned around, the table was empty. That time even Ima found it hard to hide her disappointment, although she needed to regain control. "Don't worry about it. At least we know that he eats the same time we do."

"It's open seating for the late breakfast," Needy offered. "We still don't know for a fact that it was him."

"It was him," Birdie interjected. "I'd know that piece of . . ." Her voice trailed as her ponytail became undone and started fanning. Every time she tried to speak, she got a mouthful of hair.

"Would you two please stop acting like you don't have a bit of class," Ima said as she secretly scanned the dining hall. Perhaps he'd gotten up to get something.

As much as they disagreed about whether or not the stranger was Lyon, they did agree upon one thing. It was time for Ima to earn her pay.

They knew for sure that Lyon had boarded, although they couldn't pry his cabin information from the purser. He was a freckled-face, pasty-colored man of about forty who held his clipboard firmly to his chest as though it were a bulletproof vest. The man's resolve was solid as he explained how he would not divulge any passenger information.

Ima had flirted. Birdie had offered money. Needy had gone so far as to try to distract the man by moving her oversized bosom in front of him, letting her breasts swing like thick branches. The purser would not budge. The women would never know that when he later went back to his cabin, he shared their failed tactics with his boyfriend. The men laughed until they almost passed out.

"This is the second day. We don't have a lot of time left to pull this off," Needy reminded Ima. "Birdie and I will check up on you later."

"I don't need you to check up on me. What I need is for you to stay out of my way." She'd started to say more but loud noises from outside the dining hall stopped her.

The angry sounds of complaints slowly filtered in. One voice rose above the fray. It was tinny and filled with barks, grunts and indignation. Another angry voice parroted the first.

Ima stood but she sat down quickly as though she wanted to hide under the chair. Birdie and Needy grabbed their purses and prepared to rush off. There was only one reason for the confusion.

The rat-a-tat-tat sound against the dining hall door confirmed their suspicions. Needy and Birdie glanced down at Ima for help. She looked as scared as they did. But there was only one way in and out of the hall, so there was no escape for any of them.

"What do you mean it's too late for us to eat?" She raised her cane and poked at the door several times to make her unspoken point.

"That's right. What do you mean it's too late to eat?" Mother Blister stood with a boxer's stance behind Mother Pray Onn. She looked like a shadow: a large one.

Sunil had barely slept the night before. He was used to getting by on just a few hours of sleep. It was just the second day and he felt as though he'd either worked a week straight or hadn't slept at all. Between the crazy women from the previous night and now these two contemptuous seniors, he was ready to quit. He would have if they hadn't been so far out to sea.

Sunil had no idea that the old women were serious about getting inside the dining hall. He didn't know that because of their feuding and overdosing on a laxative, they'd left half their body weight in their state-room's bathroom. One way or another they were going to eat. "Can't you see that she's old and needs nourishment?" Mother Blister pushed Mother Pray Onn almost into Sunil's arms. "Look at her, she's about to pass out. If she does, you'll be holding nothing but wrinkled skin and bones."

Mother Pray Onn was about to turn and stab Mother Blister with the tip of her cane but she'd caught on. She staggered a bit and then pretended to collapse, making it impossible for Sunil to do anything but catch her.

While the old women held Sunil captive with their demonstrations of hunger, Ima flagged down one of the servers who had just taken off his serving jacket. He appeared to be going off duty. He came over to see what she needed.

"When you leave, which way do you go?" Ima asked. She stood just so the sunlight from the portholes could shine through her dress, silhouetting her shape. She let her eyelashes flutter. Her eyes silently indicated that there was a promise behind the question.

The boyish-looking Philippino waiter could only imagine what would happen if he could hold such a beauty in his arms. He'd been at sea for a while, and earlier was admiring the darker woman's chest. However, the shapely, mysterious-eyed woman who obviously wanted him for her pleasure was coming on to him. She'd do.

"Please follow me." He'd thrown down his jacket on a nearby chair and walked briskly towards a side door opposite the kitchen. When he turned to make sure she followed him, he was surprised to see that all three women were coming. He quickened his steps as his heart raced with anticipation. If he played his cards right, he could save the money he'd planned on spending in a strip club when the ship docked in Mexico. That money he'd now send home to his wife and children.

No sooner had the server stepped through the exit door than the women raced down a nearby winding stairway. The server turned around again, eager to see what he was about to have, and they were gone. He stood gape-mouthed and questioned whether he'd been dreaming. He patted his pants pocket. His money was still there. It looked as though the wife and children would have to budget again.

By the time Hunter arrived, Mothers Blister and Pray Onn were yelling loud enough for a small crowd to gather. His brow twitched and his mouth went dry as soon as he saw them. He'd never imagined that the two old women would know each other. Yet, there they stood looking like a before and after ad, and they were screaming the "S" word.

"We're gonna *sue* this entire ship," Mother Pray Onn snapped. "And, I'm gonna start with you." She didn't know if she could sue or not and it didn't matter to her. "By the time I'm finished with you you'll never wanna see water again."

"That's right, we're gonna sue you," Mother Blister parroted. She'd become caught up and couldn't come up with an original thought. "You won't even be able to drink water or take a bath." She could tell by the slight smile on Mother Pray Onn's face that she was pleased with her input.

"Ladies, madams, please. What can I do to help?" Hunter couldn't stand to hear the word *sue*. He knew that it was a word usually followed by "you're fired." The sudden fear in his eyes did little to bolster his supposed confidence as he again tried to appease them.

"I'll take it from here, Mr. Sunil."

Sunil was very happy to leave Hunter with the grumpy and dangerous old women. He'd had enough of them and not enough sleep.

Again, Hunter thought he'd settled a conflict before any real damage was done. He escorted the old women inside the dining hall and left instructions for them to have whatever they wanted.

Mother Blister ordered eggs Benedict and

waffles along with an array of pastries and lemonade. She didn't want to drink anything dark, not even a glass of chocolate milk.

Mother Pray Onn decided after changing her mind several times on the chicken livers coated with garlic-flavored breadcrumbs and scrambled eggs along with a carafe of thick Columbian coffee. She was from the old school of thought of chasing a hangover with more liquor. She'd get rid of the effects of the laxative with more coffee.

Mother Blister had no idea that eggs Benedict meant that the yoke ran. She almost had a seizure when she pricked the middle with her fork. "Are y'all trying to give me a heart attack?" She snapped her finger at the poor server who had orders not to move until they were finished.

"Madam, what is wrong?" He'd given her exactly what she'd asked for and had to listen to the chef complain about it. "It is what you ordered."

"Oh, so now you're trying to tell me that I ordered my own heart attack?"

"Madam, I don't understand." He really didn't.

"I already got that high cholesterol that I'm taking medication for and you up here trying to make it higher."

"Madam — ?"

"Why are you trying to kill my best friend?" Mother Pray Onn chimed in. "She's already older than dirt. What's the matter, you can't wait for her to croak?" She couldn't wait to have her turn at him. She was feeling a little antsy and didn't know she was probably allergic to the garlic. She should've known because most witches are.

The more the server shook the more they tore into him. He only knew a few words of English and they were mainly the ones on the menu.

Mr. Hunter had barely returned to his desk when his pager went off at the same time his two-way did. As soon as he saw the dining hall extension on his pager he immediately turned it off. Then a frantic call for help on his two-way came. His two-way was shaking and crackling from the urgency. He turned it off, too. He'd deal with the consequences later. Whatever the penalties, they couldn't be as bad as having to deal with those two old women.

29

Cill and Petunia awoke startled. They'd completely forgotten that they'd spent the night in a nearby motel. Evilene had made it impossible for them to sleep until all the linens as well as Cill's bed were thrown out.

In the meantime they'd put a chain on the cat's flea collar and tied her to the tree out in Cill's backyard. She'd have to stay there until they returned in the morning.

On the way back to Cill's house they stopped at a local stationary store. They were told that for the price of ten dollars they could send a fax to the cruise ship.

"How long does it take the fax to go through?" Cill asked the man behind the counter with purple-spiked hair.

"Yo, lady. I think it takes about twenty seconds to travel through the atmosphere to wherever the ship is sailing," he said proudly.

Cill placed one of her tattooed hands on

the countertop and snatched the fax cover sheet. "Hey dude. You mean to tell me that I have to pay that much money just so this sheet can spend twenty seconds in the atmosphere?"

The sight of the pit-bull tattoos was enough for him. He pulled his sleeve down to cover his Pink Panther tattoo and told her, "I can just write the name over the top of the message and send it. That'll save you five dollars without a cover sheet."

"Then do that and stop trying to fleece us," Petunia said before adding, "Hurry up. We're on a mission from God."

30

The first port-of-call, Cozumel, Mexico, was about two hours away. Lyon was excited. He was going to surprise Lionel with the extra excursion ticket he'd purchased to visit the Mayan ruins.

There was a crowd waiting for the elevators so Lyon decided to take the stairs up to the cabin. He'd only gone two flights before he heard the commotion coming from inside the dining hall. Having learned the hard way in prison about running towards trouble, he was surprised that he'd stopped to listen. He cautiously walked towards the double doors that were ajar. He peeked inside.

The trouble came from two old women. Their heads were bobbing and they appeared upset about something. From the terrified look on the server's face, it appeared that he was the source.

Lyon determined that whatever was happening was none of his business and he was about to turn away. Suddenly one of the old women stood. She looked familiar.

It took Lyon a moment to put a name with the face. He was terrified.

"Mother Blister." He hadn't meant to say her name aloud.

He was certain it was her, the way she had her fist balled and her wig sliding to the side. He smiled slightly as he recalled a few times he'd seen her in action. *Nobody could throw down like that old woman. At her age she could probably hammer Mike Tyson with ease.*

Seeing Mother Blister also brought back the last memory they'd shared. He'd taken advantage of her and stolen her money. He'd done that awful deed after she'd offered him comfort. It was the kind of comfort that sometimes only a lonely older woman gave a younger man.

She'd stood over him while he'd slept. He'd been that confident to believe that she wouldn't discover the theft so he'd actually stayed the night instead of leaving. He'd awoken to profanity spat from her toothless mouth as she threatened to tear him apart.

It was pretty much the same way she stood now as she threatened the server. But he still couldn't turn away as he remembered with remorse the rest of that night he'd hurt her.

With a doe-eyed expression of false shame he'd cautiously risen from her bed with his nakedness in full view. In an instant, he'd reminded her of what she'd paid for and she quieted. It'd reviled him to have to go further than he'd done before but she was his current cash cow. He'd kissed her deeply in her bald mouth and told her how much he truly loved her. Just like all the other women to whom he'd told that same lie, she'd backed down and forgiven him with more cash. Shortly later, he'd gone to prison on an outstanding warrant and other charges of fraud.

Lyon willed his feet to move closer to the entryway. With his new life now securely grounded in Christ, he asked Him to help him to apologize to those women he'd hurt. There was no acceptable excuse not to do it because his opportunity stood on this same cruise and only several yards away.

Just as Lyon had summoned holy boldness to enter the dining hall, the terrified server bolted, trying to escape the second swing from Mother Pray Onn's cane.

Self-preservation pushed holy boldness aside and made Lyon turn to do the same. He'd apologize at another, safer time.

■ ■ ■ ■

Lionel looked again at his jeweled Movado watch. He'd just done the same thing only moments ago and it seemed that time had passed slowly. Lyon hadn't returned from wherever he'd gone and Lionel had tired of watching television. They were nearing their first port so the signal was too weak for programs using satellite. Only the ship's promotion schedule ran repeatedly.

Out of momentary boredom Lionel held a glass of cold soda in one hand and a pair of binoculars in the other. The pink stucco paint from the houses lining the Mexican hills seemed eerily close through the lenses. He could also see that several small tenders sat rocking in the ocean's watery arms while waiting for their passengers to come aboard.

Lionel set the glass down and stepped onto the balcony to get a better view. As he looked through the lenses and scanned the Mexican shores, she stepped into his view.

The strap around his neck that was clamped onto the binoculars was all that kept them from smashing to the balcony floor. She was in the next cabin and he'd not known. Was this another sign from God?

Just when Lionel was about to say something, she quickly disappeared from the balcony. He was going to have to be faster if he was to meet her.

Lyon rushed inside the cabin and out onto the balcony, interrupting Lionel's thoughts. He looked flushed.

"What's the matter? Is this heat getting to you again, already?" Lionel teased.

"You could say that," Lyon answered. He grabbed a cold soda from the lounge table, popped the top and went back inside the cabin. He didn't pour it into a glass, choosing instead to chug it from the can. "I came pretty close to the reintroducing myself to someone I made miserable in the past."

Lionel followed him inside. "You're kidding," he whispered as though there were others in the room with them. "On board this ship is someone from your past?" Just knowing how horrible his brother had treated some people, particularly the women, caused Lionel concern.

By the time Lyon had explained the sudden reappearance of Mother Blister in his life, the ship had docked. Lyon didn't have time to change as he'd planned. He and his brother were still dressed alike as they left their cabin.

When they filed through the long security line to disembark, Lyon was asked to remove his sunglasses. That was the only time he would. He'd already decided that he didn't want Mother Blister to recognize him until he was ready.

It had to happen, sooner or later, and Ima wished it'd been later, much later. Hunter appeared suddenly followed by Jaiquist and Samuel. They didn't look happy and that didn't make Ima happy. She'd made plans to spend much of Birdie's money shopping along the Mexican pier and didn't need the drama.

Ima had walked ahead of Needy with Birdie trailing behind. She'd raced ahead on purpose so she could have time alone to shop and plot. The sight of Hunter and the other two men made her quickly change her plans. She spun around and quickened her steps back to Needy.

"We've got trouble," Ima urged as she charged past Needy to blend in with the other passengers.

Needy didn't ask what kind of trouble it was. If it made Ima retreat then it was definitely too much for her to handle. She quickly turned and followed her.

Ima didn't think she needed to tell Birdie that there was a problem. She figured that if Birdie saw them going back that she'd do the same.

If Birdie saw Needy and Ima pass by, she didn't show it. However, she did see Jaiquist and Samuel coming towards her. Again, the two young men looked exquisite in their white uniforms and caps. It wasn't until they were practically upon her that she saw Hunter and realized that none of them smiled.

"G'day, Miss Tweet," Hunter greeted. The stern looks upon Jaiquist and Samuel's faces didn't change.

"Hello, Mr. Hunter." Birdie addressed him while she looked at the men; Jaiquist in particular. "Is everything alright?" She still hadn't looked at Hunter.

"I was actually looking for Ms. Hellraiser but I see she's not with you." He didn't bother to tell her that he'd seen Ima take off because he wasn't sure if she'd done it to avoid him. It didn't matter. He'd share his concerns with Ms. Tweet.

Hunter also hadn't noticed how tall Birdie was until he'd stood in front of her and asked her to please step aside so they could talk.

Birdie finally gave Hunter her full attention when he'd asked her to step aside to chat. She took that opportunity to stand closer to Jaiquist and Samuel who still hadn't moved or smiled.

"Yes, Hunter. What is it that I can do for you?" she asked. This time she was concerned. Meeting the two young men under these circumstances was not what she'd wanted. She hadn't figured out why she was so impressed with them.

"I have major concerns as well as complaints."

"Concerns about what?" Birdie asked. She couldn't think of anything they'd done that would cause concern. They did drink a little too much wine at dinner but they weren't the only ones, she was sure.

"I'm afraid it is about your other two traveling companions." Hunter said it with as much authority as he could muster. Just the thought of the havoc the women had raised already, and with five days still to go, nipped at his resolve.

Birdie thought about how fast Ima and Needy had raced past her and never said a word. "Let me please apologize for them," Birdie pleaded.

"We don't need your apology, Ms. Tweet," Mr. Hunter interrupted, "we need for you to keep closer tabs on Ms. Blister and Ms. Pray Onn."

For the first time since they'd stopped her, Birdie saw the looks change on Jaiquist and Samuel's faces. It'd gone from blank to fear at the sound of their names.

While Birdie took the brunt of Mr. Hunter's disdain, Ima and Needy stood safely in the corner under a dock canopy. There were several clusters of native Mexicans with bright-colored beads around their arms and necks. Some of them danced to the music of old guitars while others tried to harass the tourist into buying their cheap items.

"Thank goodness these Mexicans are short," Ima said as she stood on her tiptoes. She was nearly using the head of one of them as an armrest while she observed Birdie and the men.

"What are you talking about? Who are you calling short?" Needy didn't share her opinion because she was the same height as many of the Mexicans on the dock. She didn't have time to say more because Birdie was suddenly heading their way.

"She don't look too happy," Needy added as she hopped up and down trying to see over the head of one of the Mexicans.

"I'm sure that Mr. Hunter gave her an

earful," Ima replied.

"What did we do?" Needy asked.

"I'm sure we didn't do anything," Ima said loudly over the pleas from one of the Mexicans.

"Señora, mi sombrero, por favor." The man pleaded as Ima continued to rest her elbows upon his colorful straw hat, which left a dent.

Instead of apologizing, Ima flicked the man away like he was the problem.

"Then what could be the problem?" Needy wanted Ima to hurry and tell her so she could handle whatever was bothering Birdie.

"Don't be so dense," Ima barked. "If we haven't done anything then who do you think they'd be upset with?"

"Oh no," Needy's face soured. "Where are Mother Pray Onn and Mother Blister?"

"Exactly," Ima tersely replied. "Where are they?" She threw her hands up surrendering to Needy's innocence.

"Do you think they've been locked up in the ship's brig?" Needy wasn't sure if the ship had a brig. However, she did know those old women. They were incentive enough for the ship to build one if one didn't exist.

As usual, Birdie's hair had fanned out but

this time her blue eyes were the same color as the bulging veins in her neck.

"Why did you two leave me?" She laid a hand across her chest to slow down her heart and to keep it from jumping from her chest. In spurts, she continued. "You won't believe what's going on." Her hair was totally out of control. It was fanning and whipping at her face but she was determined to get her words out.

Ima stood looking at Birdie almost enjoying Birdie's hair attack.

However, Needy's thoughts of having their cruise aborted by two misbehaving seniors caused her to speak out. "They're in the brig, aren't they?" Needy asked. "I hope you didn't tell them that I was with y'all." She was not about to cut her man-hunting vacation short.

Again, Ima threw up her hands in defeat. Just once, she'd love for Needy to shut up and let her take control. "We already know about my aunt and Mother Blister." There it was. Out in the open with none of the built-up drama she'd wanted.

"How did you know?" Birdie asked. "Mr. Hunter said that he couldn't find either of you."

Again, Ima laid it out for them. "Have you seen those two old biddies together since we've boarded?

Birdie had just started to catch her breath when she seemed to lose it again. "I haven't seen Mother Blister since she went to the cabin, yesterday. And, I haven't seen Mother Pray Onn since we were back in Pelzer."

Ima continued as if Birdie had said nothing. "If we haven't seen them yet we know that they are now in the same cabin, you add it up."

Birdie's eyes popped as comprehension enveloped her. "So, what are we going to do?" she asked, nervously. "Mr. Hunter said if they caused any more problems that we'd be left in the next port to return on our own."

Needy turned slowly towards Ima. She was hotter than the Mexican sun. "Okay, you're the paid brains of this operation, what are you going to do?"

"I'm going shopping." Ima pulled a pair of sunglasses from her oversized bag and placed them upon her face. "Birdie," Ima turned and said, "I'm going to need a little more cash."

"Why?" Birdie asked while at the same time opening her purse.

Ima explained to Birdie, again, that the unwarranted prejudice of Birdie's people had turned her sweet aunt into the nagging hag she'd become.

By the time Ima again finished convincing Birdie that her people, the white race, were the basis for most of the world's woes, Birdie had given her another five hundred dollars in traveler's checks.

It was then that Birdie also decided that she would never marry and have a child with a white man. Reparations were too expensive and she wouldn't place that costly burden on her child.

Oh, that brazen hussy, she is too good. Again, admiration replaced Needy's anger with Ima. She could see the signs of total defeat on Birdie's weary face once more.

Further inland on the island, Lyon and Lionel anxiously began their tour. The Mexican locals had a nickname for the old bus that transported the ship's passengers to the Mayan ruins. The once-black, shiny tires were now bubbled, threadbare and gray. They called the old bus The Frankenstein.

The bus was painted a bright orange with splashes of a fiery red and dots of neon blue. It was aptly named because it looked like something out of an old horror flick. It struggled to make its way along unpaved winding roads and narrow paths.

Keeping the horror theme going was the

bus owner, a pock-faced Mexican driver named Hector. He owned the only bus service for miles. He looked much older than his forty years, with oily salt-and-pepper hair and two long sharp front teeth. As he sat in the driver's seat his back appeared hunched and he snickered for no apparent reason. He looked like a combination of Dr. Frankenstein's assistant, Igor, and a saber-toothed tiger.

Hector showed exceptional skill at steering the bus over the unpaved roads using just one crooked finger as the rickety old bus slowly made its way through several shantytowns. He also slammed on the brakes every few feet, causing passengers and their belongings to bounce around like beach balls.

Whenever the bus slowed down or stopped, several poorly dressed Mexican children with a plastic bag of peeled oranges in one tiny hand and another bag with small bottles of water in the other magically appeared. The brothers gave money to the little waifs that looked pitiful with their small hunched backs and crooked teeth. Remarkably, they looked like Hector.

By the time Lyon and Lionel reached the ruins they wanted to do a praise dance, throw their hands up to heaven and give

God the glory.

"Now that was scary," Lionel said while shaking his head and pointing back at the bus.

"It wasn't half as scary as that over there," Lyon responded pointing towards Hector who stood next to an old, toothless, hunch-backed woman.

"All I want to know is when does Quasimodo climb the tower and pull the bells," Lyon laughed as he gave his brother a high five. They quickly repented.

Although the ride to the ruins was something out of a horror movie, the trip turned out better than they'd hoped. The brothers climbed the many steps to several pyramids where they learned how human sacrifices were once the norm. They purchased colorful trinkets that were costly. No doubt the jewelry would probably break or turn colors before they returned home.

The brothers were finally in sync. They were relaxed as they took turns taking pictures of the fleet-footed iguanas, the colorful flowers, and the colorfully dressed native tour guides smiling pretty for the tourists.

The brothers played a game of "guess that language." Whenever they heard a foreign tongue spoken by a fellow passenger they'd try to guess the nationality. It was a silly game but it was relaxing.

By the end of their tour, the brothers were reinvigorated. Not even the dangerous ride back to the ship minimized their joy. It'd been a long time since they'd been so much in tune, so each lay his head against the other's and napped.

While Lyon and Lionel were touring and examining the ancient Mayan ruins, Mothers Blister and Pray Onn had gone ashore and tried to create new ruins with their antics.

"Oh, you gonna give me my correct change." Mother Pray Onn's tight gray bun literally tightened on its own. Her lips snarled and her eyes blazed as her glasses teetered on the tip of her nose.

"You'd better give her correct change, chica," Mother Blister parroted, not knowing the cashier's name but using a word she'd heard. She picked up several glass items to examine but not to buy. "She's in a bad mood, so don't push that little elf." She moved aside the sign that read Do Not Touch, and continued rummaging with her hands shaking.

"I gave you fifteen dollars for a twelve dollar useless piece of junk. You gave me three cents back!" Mother Pray Onn held the tip of her cane so close to the cringing Mexican clerk's nose that it could've poked another hole in the girl's nostril.

Mother Pray Onn continued to scream as she slammed down the change on the counter, coin by coin. The poor clerk continued to babble, not fully understanding why the old woman was so upset. And Mother Blister dropped one of the glass Mexican vases that had a price of two hundred pesos written in large black letters. In the midst of the chaos, one of the neighboring shopkeepers, hoping to quell the confusion before it ran off the paying customers, rushed to the girl's aid.

Using his limited knowledge of English, he shoved the still cowering girl to the side and spoke directly to Mother Pray Onn. "Señora, digame que paso aquí?"

Mother Pray Onn's cane tip hit his hand with a hard thud. The pain caused him to forget the English he'd meant to use, and he fled back to the safety of his shop where he could fleece the passengers in peace.

By the time the three Federales from the local police department arrived, Mothers Pray Onn and Blister were leaning against the counter clutching at their hearts.

"Oh Lord, I think I see Jesus," Mother

Blister pretended.

"I think I see Him pointing at me," Mother Pray Onn added, taking her cues from Mother Blister.

The two old women were so convincing the Federales quickly shut down the poor girl's shop. When she cried and protested, they threatened to lock her up if she didn't give the Mothers a choice of anything they wanted to take.

In less than thirty minutes, the two old women managed to drive a family-owned business of more than three generations further into poverty. It didn't matter that the poor girl had given Mother Pray Onn the correct change in Mexican money.

Fearing that the old women could actually make things worse for the town's dwindling economy, the Federales escorted them and their many free gift packages back to the ship. With the Mothers walking in the middle, the pint-sized marching Mexican Federales resembled a scene straight out of the Wizard of Oz as they climbed the yellow steel gangplank.

The Federales went directly to the security desk and asked to see Mr. Hunter. They felt it necessary to explain their position, and to ensure that the cruise line would continue doing business with the other shopkeepers.

They were willing to do whatever was necessary, even if they had to kick the poor girl and her entire family out of the country.

Seated at his desk inside his private office, Hunter leaned over and picked up the telephone on its first ring. As soon as he learned of passenger trouble ashore, he feared the worst. His alabaster skin sprouted huge bumps before he even heard the names Blister and Pray Onn.

Ten minutes spread into fifteen. The Federales huddled and rattled off one Spanish curse word after another. Their hands were tied politically, and they didn't need the bad publicity that came with arresting two old American women. But after seeing the scheming old women in action it came as no surprise when Mr. Hunter didn't show.

Just when they'd decided to abandon the old women, a way out of their dilemma dropped into their laps.

"I'm an old woman. I can barely hold a glass of water in my hand let alone in my bladder. I know y'all ain't gonna stand around and make me hold my water." Mother Blister leaned over and snorted at the nearest officer.

The Federale's hat seem to spin on his head as he cowered. He was instantly hypnotized as he watched the old woman's dark-skinned face flush as her feet moved side to side.

"I'm too much of a lady to tell you fools what I need to do. But y'all better hurry up because lady or not, at my age the only thing I can hold . . . is my cane." Mother Pray Onn wasn't about to let Mother Blister have the final intimidation.

"Lo siento, señoras." Another Federale pushed ahead of his partner. "Aquí," he continued as he pointed toward the nearest restroom.

As soon as the old women rushed off to use the bathroom, the police fled, leaving the cruise line to deal with them.

"Did you really need to use the bathroom?" Mother Pray Onn asked Mother Blister. She held on to the basin and cackled. "I almost believed you did."

"You know I don't lie easily," Mother Blister said as she put down her bags and headed towards an empty stall.

Mother Pray Onn stopped laughing, and started moving towards the bathroom door. "I've got to go back to the cabin. I just remembered something."

Mother Pray Onn had suddenly remembered that earlier she'd cut slits in Mother Blister's Depends pads when she was angry, yet about what, she couldn't remember. But

she didn't want to be around when Mother
Blister discovered the leak.

31

Back in her cabin, Ima looked at the expensive watch she'd bought with Birdie's latest financial contribution and smiled slyly at Birdie. She really didn't want to part with it but she needed a peace offering for her aunt.

Like most crows, she'll like this because it's shiny, Ima thought as she examined the watch and laughed.

"Well, I just wanted to let you know that I'm ready for battle," Ima said to Needy and laughed.

"I'd sure hate to be you," Needy quipped. She would give anything to see Ima grovel at her aunt's feet with a shiny trinket. "Are you going to her stateroom now?"

"Yes, I might as well get it over with," Ima answered. "You and Birdie might want to order something in or perhaps go up to the Lido Deck to eat. It may get ugly."

"What does that have to do with us?"

"I'm going to tell her that it was you and

Birdie who put her and Mother Blister in the same cabin."

"Are you crazy?" Needy snapped.

"Listen, somebody's gotta take one for the team. It should be you and Birdie. After all, I've got to ruin Lyon Lipps, and I can't do it if I'm injured or I can't concentrate." Ima plopped down on the sofa, looked at the stunned looks on Birdie's and Needy's faces and grabbed a cushion to muffle her laughter. She quieted down but still grinned until she thought her face would crack. She loved the drama.

"I think today ought to be the day you earn that money," Birdie said with authority. "I need to see some results."

"I'm going to do just that so I don't hear your nagging," Ima replied. "I'm going to follow him a bit and see what he likes."

"And then what?" Needy asked.

"Then I'll move in for the kill."

"You still haven't told us how you plan on destroying him," Birdie said as her hair began to fan to show her annoyance.

"You've paid me a lot of money up front and now you want details." Ima stood up to protect herself, just in case Birdie's erratic bravado became dangerous.

"Tomorrow will be the third day. If I don't see some results I'm cutting you off." Birdie didn't budge. She didn't know where or how she'd grown a spine and at that moment, she didn't care.

Needy couldn't believe what was happening so she grabbed a bowl of pretzels and sat down to watch.

"I'm going back to my cabin because evidently you've lost your mind." Ima was doing something she'd never done before: she was backing down and not with any believable dignity.

The move was not lost on Needy. She slammed down the bowl of pretzels and started for the balcony, but not before she let Ima know what she thought. "You're not my shero any more."

Ima didn't know how to respond so she didn't. Instead, she grabbed the box with the watch and her purse and stomped out the room.

By the time Ima reached her stateroom she was livid. No one had stood up to her like Birdie had in a long time. She was losing control and she didn't like it.

The fax lay on Ima's bed inside a white envelope with the ship's logo on the front. It only had her name on it so she thought it was probably a bill.

"Let Birdie pay this since she wants her money's worth," Ima snapped as she threw the envelope to the side.

She undressed quickly and headed for the shower. She needed the hard tapping of the water against her skin to cool off.

After showering she did feel better and began to sing. It was then that she decided that she'd go to the Karaoke Night and unwind. She was certain that she wouldn't run into any of the others there; particularly since they claimed to be so holy. Going inside a bar wasn't on their list of things they could do.

Lyon and Lionel came together inside Lyon's cabin. They'd changed and for the first time in quite a while they actually looked different.

"I like your new haircut," Lionel told Lyon. "Perhaps I should get my hair cut shorter like that and look more like a piece of man-candy."

"Perhaps you shouldn't," Lyon laughed. "The last thing you need is a bunch of pastor's wife-wannabes coming on to you because of your looks."

"Says who?" Lionel joked. "And can you please lay off the reference to getting a wife. You're really making me nervous."

"How do you know that I'm not prophesying?" Lyon asked with a wink.

"Then you'd be prophe-lying," Lionel answered. "On another note," he continued, "what are your plans this evening?"

Lyon picked up the ship's activity guide and tossed it to his brother. "I'm going to the Karaoke bar."

"Oh really," Lionel said with a raised eyebrow. "Why are you doing that?"

"No particular reason other than it's what I feel like doing."

"I'd go with you but I think I'll go to the bingo game. I understand the grand prize is about eight thousand dollars tonight."

"How do you know that?" Lyon asked before adding, "Should the good Reverend Lipps be gambling?"

"Probably not, but like you, I'm just going so I'll have something to do," Lionel replied, walking to the door. "And please do me a favor."

"What?" Lyon asked as he walked over to close the cabin door.

"Drop the reverend name while we're aboard. I don't want to make folks uncomfortable. They'll know by my conversation and my walk that God is in control."

Like most brothers will do, Lyon couldn't resist teasing Lionel. He started singing another one of his old favorite songs, "Control," by Janet Jackson.

The brothers laughed before parting.

Ima sat at a booth in a darkened corner of the Karaoke bar. Despite the low lights she wore a pair of large sunglasses. The glasses made her look like the star she thought she was.

She watched the other passengers stroll in. They were all ages, laughing, and mostly in pairs or groups. But she sat alone, which only made her stand out.

One by one the Karaoke volunteers went to the microphone. It seemed that each sang worse than the one before. Ima laughed with good reason and it felt good. At one point she laughed so hard she accidentally squirted juice from the drink she sipped through a straw.

"Come on now, that fella wasn't that bad," a man said as he approached her table. He tried to keep a straight face but failed. "I don't know if I could do much better," he teased.

Ima could see he was gorgeous even with her shades on, seated in the dark corner. All she could say was, "Excuse me."

He didn't bother to ask her if she minded if he sat at her table, he just did it. His sunglasses hid the pleasure his eyes surely revealed. *She's stunning,* he thought as he motioned to one of the servers.

"Please give the lady whatever it is she's drinking." He didn't ask her if she wanted another, he just ordered it.

Ima's quick tongue froze. She could say nothing and she didn't want to. He'd only stood for a moment but she knew he was tall. His hair was dark and wavy and just a little too short for her taste but hair could grow.

He watched her body relax as she sat back in her seat and watched him take control. "I'm sorry, where are my manners. I didn't bother to introduce myself."

"Don't bother," she replied but then smiled. "Let's not spoil things with names."

He was intrigued. "You like to play games?" he asked with just a hint of tease in his voice.

"I play very well and I don't like to lose," Ima said as she let her shawl fall off her shoulder. She wore a yellow blouse with spaghetti straps that looked like they'd pop if handled the right way. She let one leg extend from under the booth as if by accident to show her tiny but perfect feet.

He'd noticed the way she'd let her legs playfully escape the confines of her white skirt through a slit that seem to keep going way past the legal limit.

The waiter appeared and sat down a drink in front of Ima. She nodded her approval and turned her attention back to the handsome man who'd walked into her space unannounced.

"Just what am I paying for?" he asked her as he placed his cruise card into the waiter's hand.

"It's called a strawberry daiquiri." She sipped it slowly and said, "It's a virgin."

She'd said it in a way that caused them to laugh a bit louder than each had meant to do. It also caused the man at the microphone belting out a song to look over with disapproval. He'd thought he was thrilling the crowd until he'd heard the laughter.

The look on the man's face made them want to laugh harder but they nodded their apologies and turned their attention back to each other.

Without giving their names they spent the next hour talking about nothing in particular and laughing at those who tried to sing songs and couldn't.

Ima saw him check his watch. "Are you on a curfew?" she teased. Her eyes traveled from his strong hands to the bulging triceps that stood at attention under his shirt.

"No. But I don't want to take up all of your time," he said as he attempted to adjust his shades.

She wished he'd take the shades off but she hadn't taken off hers, so she didn't ask him to do so. Ima didn't mean to, but during the time they chatted, she found herself comparing his voice to the one that haunted her. The trouble was that there was no comparison.

The more relaxed she felt with the stranger the more she realized how foolish it was for her to concentrate on finding Lyon Lipps and his deep voice. She'd look for him tomorrow. Tonight she wanted to enjoy herself, and sitting across from her was what she needed.

The crowd was thinning and yet they sat engrossed as though they hadn't noticed or didn't want to. Finally, they had to gather their things to leave.

"Well, I've truly enjoyed sharing this evening with you." He seemed resigned to the fact that the evening had came to an end. "Perhaps, I'll see you again, Miss Won't Give a Name," he teased but was very serious.

"It's the same for me," she said with a hint of sadness, which she tried her best to conceal.

He quickly bent over and kissed her hand. What he wanted to do was ask if he could escort her to her cabin. He didn't want to seem presumptuous and drive her away.

Lyon allowed her to walk away and as she did he looked her over and appreciated her even more. He was surprised and delighted that he'd not felt an ounce of lust. "Thank you Jesus," he murmured and left a few moments behind her.

No sooner had Ima stepped onto the elevator than she ran into Needy.

"Where have you been?" Needy asked. "Wherever it was you certainly must've had a good time. You're glowing."

"None of your beeswax," Ima answered. Her nastiness was returning quicker than normal. She missed the stranger already.

"Excuse me for asking," Needy replied. "Save that nastiness for Lyon Lipps."

"When I find him he'll get what's coming to him," she answered. "I don't need a constant reminder," Ima hissed as she stepped off the elevator.

Ima entered her stateroom and slammed the door behind her. She flung off her clothes with abandonment. "Why did I have to meet a fine man tonight?" she said aloud. "I don't need this distraction."

She was lying to herself and knew it. The man she'd met was someone she knew she'd waited for all her life.

Ima grabbed a bottle of water from the cabin's refrigerator and drank it quickly. From the corner of her eye she spied the envelope she'd tossed earlier. "This is what I want to do to you, Birdie." She tore the unopened envelope to pieces. "You do your own dirty work."

Ima cried. She couldn't believe that a couple of hours with a strange man could change her that fast. She couldn't help herself. "There's no such thing as love at first sight!"

"She was gorgeous and her conversation was smart." Lyon was rattling but he didn't care.

"So now you do believe in love at first sight?" Lionel asked. He was just happy to see his brother happy.

"She just may be the one, as crazy as that may sound."

"What happened to praying before you leap?" Lionel said. "Of course, if it will keep you from tossing me onto the marriage train then I say go after her."

"Hold up. I didn't say anything about marriage," Lyon laughed. "I'm only saying that she may be the one who will cause me to reenter the dating game."

"Watch yourself, younger brother," Lionel

cautioned, "it's usually the hunter that gets captured by the game."

Birdie watched the starlit sky from a chaise-lounge chair on the Lido Deck. She found herself trying to identify several constellations and accepting the fact that she'd not seen so many stars in the sky since she was a child.

She ordered another soda, which she knew was bad for her complexion but she'd chance it. A waiter appeared and removed several drinks from her table. The drinks had appeared throughout the evening from various strangers wishing to meet her. She'd rebuffed them all as they sent her pieces of paper with phone or cabin numbers scrawled.

Birdie didn't know why but suddenly she felt more in control. She sank back in the chair and tried to pinpoint when it'd begun. She went over the conversations she'd had that day with Ima and Needy, the ones in particular where she'd fearlessly confronted them about one matter or another. She smiled when she recalled how she'd sent Ima reeling out the door with the promise of cutting off the funds if Ima didn't produce real results.

As she lay back with her eyes closed, reveling in her newfound courage, she became aware of another presence.

Birdie looked up and saw Jaiquist standing beside her chair. "Is everything alright, Madam?" he asked. "The buffet is about to close so if there is anything more you'd like to eat you may do so now."

Here was her opportunity to speak. All she could do was sit there shaking her head no.

So much for her new-found courage.

As soon as she heard the knock on her cabin door Ima kicked the ottoman out of the way and rushed to it. She tried to wipe her face with the back of her hand before she grabbed the doorknob. She wasn't sure how he'd found her but she was happy for his persistence.

"I didn't like the way you rushed away," Needy said as she practically elbowed her way past Ima and into the room.

Needy saw the pained look on Ima's face and stopped in mid-sentence. "Ima, what's wrong?" She'd never seen Ima sad. "Did something happen? Did someone hurt you?" Needy back-tracked. "Of course, no one hurt you. No one can hurt you, can they?"

"Will you please stop the inquisition," Ima

asked, caustically. She'd never admit to anyone that a man, stranger or not, was at the helm of her emotional rollercoaster. "I miss Evilene," Ima lied. She even surprised herself. She really hadn't given her pet cat a thought since she'd left Pelzer.

"Well since you don't have a man I guess it's natural to miss your pet," Needy said with as much tenderness as she could muster without breaking into laughter. "If that's your reason for the upside down smile then I'll leave you to it. I'm going to take advantage of Birdie's absence and shower."

"Okay." That was as much of an answer as Ima could give.

"I'm sorry that you missed the captain's welcome dinner tonight. It was fabulous, but probably not as much fun as you had at the Karaoke bar."

Needy's mention of the Karaoke bar caused tears to once again well in Ima's eyes.

Again, Needy misread Ima. "Listen, stop the crying. Evilene will be alright. How much trouble can happen if you have Petunia watching her? It ain't like Petunia has anything going on to distract her."

Needy didn't wait for an answer from Ima. She quickly left to use up the last of the hot

water for her shower before Birdie returned
to the cabin.

32

"Do you think she's opened it yet?" Petunia asked. She'd almost worn a path in Cill's living-room carpet. "Why didn't she call or fax or e-mail? She should do something."

"Ima ain't completely crazy. Even *she's* not dumb enough to go up against a man of God." Cill was trying to convince the both of them and not doing a good job.

"You know we're all going straight to hell," Petunia whined. "I don't know why I joined in with this crazy, vengeful plan."

"It was because he wronged you, too," Cill reminded.

The pawing at the door caught Cill's attention.

"Did you go outside and feed that crazy piece of fur?" Cill asked.

"No. I thought you fed her." Petunia threw her hands up in defeat. "Why do I have to do everything?"

"Wasn't she left in your care?" Cill stated

the obvious. "Unless you want to give Ima more bad news about her cat I suggest you take a handful of Kibbles and Bits and go outside."

"Are we supposed to feed that cat dog food?"

"Do you think that you'd mind sharing that deep dish cherry cobbler instead," Cill asked as she reached past Petunia for the casserole dish.

"Touch that and you and that feline catastrophe will be eating Kibbles and Bits," Petunia said as she snatched the casserole from Cill's reach.

"You need to go ahead and feed that pussycat instead of sitting here watching me. Don't you trust me with your cobbler?" Cill said with sarcasm.

Petunia didn't answer. She went to the window and opened it while she kept her eyes locked on Cill. "Evilene, come here kitty," she called out. With her eyes still on Cill, whose eyes were on the cherry cobbler, Petunia threw a handful of Kibbles and Bits out the window.

"Yeah, I trust you," Petunia said. She'd never looked away so there was no reason not to trust Cill.

"You do realize that the window is over the storm drain. Ima's gonna be real happy that you've thrown her cat's food down the drain," Cill threatened.

"She'll never know," Petunia said without confidence. "Evilene certainly won't tell her."

Evilene wouldn't have to tell her. Because when Ima returned home she would receive a bill from the Pelzer A.S.P.C.A. The bill would detail how they had to rescue the emaciated Evilene from the storm drain by removing a broken tree branch and several big boulders from Cill's property to reach the cat.

33

When Needy awoke sometime during the night she found Birdie still up wearing the same clothes from the night before. She was seated on the sofa with pieces of paper piled on her lap.

An old black-and-white western moved across the television screen with guns blasting and Indians howling, but Birdie wasn't watching and didn't seem to hear, either. Instead, her vacant stare seemed peaceful as she fingered several pieces of the paper.

"Are you okay?" Needy asked as she sat next to Birdie. It seemed that all she'd done for the past twenty-four hours was to ask someone how they were doing.

Birdie still didn't answer. Her mind was somewhere other than in the cabin's living-room and she still hadn't looked down at the strips of paper.

More out of curiosity than real concern, Needy picked up one of the pieces of paper.

And then she snatched several others. She read them one after the other with the same expression of surprise.

"Is there a Chippendales on this cruise ship? Why didn't you tell me about it?" She then started counting the slips of paper. "You've got some explaining to do." Needy started to slip a couple of them into her dressing-gown pocket but she didn't.

"I'm suspecting that all of these numbers belong to men." Still Birdie didn't answer her. "Is there something you want to share with me?"

Birdie was starting to freak her out so Needy got up and moved over to another chair.

"All the time I thought it was me," Birdie finally answered as though she'd not heard a word Needy said. "I actually thought I could do nothing, and I was selfish to think so."

"Okay, now I know something is wrong. And I want to know what it is?" Needy said. She was straddling the mental fence that lay between concern and curiosity, and she was comfortable with that.

Birdie finally turned to face Needy. "I had a chat with one of the crew members late last night."

"Ooh that sounds sort of low class but I

guess you take what you can get," Needy said with mock condescension. "Who was he and what craziness did the two of you get into?"

"His name is Jaiquist. He's from Rwanda." As Birdie let Jai's name and country roll off her tongue, she seemed to savor every vowel and syllable.

"Well did he bring the entire tribe to your table or something?" Needy asked as she pointed to the pile of papers in Birdie's lap. "I see a lot of names and numbers written and I don't seem to recall any Francois, Stephanolos, Enriques or Chesters coming over from the Motherland."

"These names mean nothing," Birdie said as she attempted to toss the papers from her lap into the wastebasket. "Men sent me drinks and numbers practically the whole time I was on the Lido Deck stargazing."

"And here I spent most of the evening at the captain's welcome aboard dinner. I'm chomping down nasty goose liver pâté with snooty folks looking down at me and all I had to do was look up at the stars and men's numbers would've fallen into my lap."

Needy was truly upset, but not enough to give back the slips of paper she'd taken from Birdie's lap. She slipped them into her dressing-gown pocket just in case the next night was cloudy and the stars weren't out.

"Did you know that in Africa there is an enormous amount of precious resources but the continent is literally dying because of the civil wars, AIDS and a high infant mortality rate?"

"I might've heard something in a public service announcement. What does any of this have to do with what you and the Rwandan fella did?"

The conversation was turning into a serious documentary chat. All Needy wanted to find out was the down-and-dirty and whether there was any dirt leftover that she could roll around in.

"I knew from the moment I laid eyes on this young man that my life would change." Birdie said the words calmly while her eyes blinked with excitement.

"And when did you meet this young man?" Needy asked, slowly. Birdie was starting to make her nervous. All of this sudden show of bravado and now a sense of social awareness were too eerie. "Okay, who are you and what did you do with my Birdie?"

"I'm tired. I need to get some sleep," Birdie announced without answering Needy's questions.

"It's five o'clock in the morning and now

you want to sleep?" Needy said as she gently pushed Birdie back onto the sofa. "Let's bond a little. Let's do our girlfriend thing. Let's order some wine. Let's do anything but go to sleep. I want to know what happened between you and this African."

Birdie shoved Needy's hand aside and went inside her room without saying a word.

While Birdie slept Needy was wide awake. She looked over at the television in time to see the Indians smoking a peace pipe with the white cavalry men. She didn't see the remote control so she had to walk over to turn off the television set. She saw the remnants of the pieces of paper that Birdie had tossed into the basket and fumed, "I've got to find a husband or at least a date on this ship. This whole doggone world is crazy. Everyone is making or getting peace but me."

Needy didn't go back to sleep and when the sun rose she was still seated on the sofa. She sat in the very spot Birdie had vacated, and hadn't budged because her pity party was in full swing.

She'd dug up from her past the skeletons from every male-related mishap she could remember. By the time Needy finished complaining to the universe about the unfairness of her life she was famished.

Needy didn't bother to shower. Instead, she wiped her face with a cold, damp washcloth, tweezed the long hairs from her top lip, threw on whatever was handy and headed to the dining hall for breakfast.

She knew Birdie was still sleeping but she was surprised to find out that Ima hadn't made it to the dinning hall for the open-seated breakfast. As much as she would've loved to give a blow-by-blow, detailed account of Birdie's obvious mental break-down, Needy was happy to be alone.

The dining hall wasn't crowded so she decided to sit at one of the smaller tables that were set for a party of four. She knew she wasn't looking as glamorous as she'd been the night before or even since she boarded, and she didn't care.

But then Needy sensed in her spirit that something was different or about to happen. The feeling came over her just as she was just about to lift a forkful of scrambled eggs to her mouth. That's when she peered over the fork and saw him.

He entered the dining hall wearing a pale blue open-collared shirt that left no doubt that he'd spent hours in a gym. His dark blue pants fit him like he was born to wear them. His stride was commanding and confident. Everything about the man was perfect.

As he neared, she realized that she'd seen him before in the dining hall at dinner. She could now see that he had flawless honey-colored skin. The hair was pitch black and straight like the Chinese man who made deliveries to her house.

The perfect man wearing perfect clothes was headed towards Needy as she sat with her fork in mid-air looking as imperfect as she'd ever been.

She looks different this morning, but I'm sure it's her, Lionel thought as he entered the dining hall. He noticed that she appeared a bit haggard but he'd looked that way from time to time when he'd not had enough rest.

Even though she was sitting down he could tell that she was a lot shorter than he'd first thought. He preferred his women tall. She was also heavier than he'd like but there was something about her . . .

He was also happy that she sat alone and not surrounded by the tall white woman and the gorgeous sistah with plenty of attitude, who seemed to block access. He laughed inwardly as he tried to reconcile why he didn't prefer the hour-glass-bodied woman with the beautiful smile and eyes. He didn't have an answer. He only knew that he was somehow attracted to a woman he'd never approach back home.

"Lord, I sure hope this is your will," Lionel prayed as he neared the table.

"Heavenly Father, what is up with Your timing? Please don't send this gorgeous man to my table while I'm looking like something the dog chewed on." Needy still hadn't moved the fork away from her mouth by the time the man arrived at her table. There was nothing she could do but watch him pull the chair away from the table and sit.

"Good morning," Lionel said. Her eyes were larger than they seemed from a distance. "I hope you don't mind sharing your table."

Needy placed the fork gently onto her plate and wiped her lips before answering. "No, I don't mind." She kept her answer short hoping he'd say something more. His voice reminded her of one of the late night radio deejays. It had the same bass tone that had lulled her into a romantic mood on many nights.

"I'll be back." That was all he said before he left to go over and check out the buffet.

As Lionel scooped eggs onto his plate, along with other breakfast items, he found himself praying. "Lord, all I can say is . . . Thy will be done. Am I supposed to minister to this woman? Is this why I'm drawn to her? Father if You don't reveal it then I'm totally confused."

Needy's appetite abandoned her, taking with it her last hope of finding a man on the cruise. She started praying, "Lord, if you wanted me to be a nun why didn't you just roll me in a habit and toss me into a convent? If I've done anything to offend Thee, then please forgive me. But don't tempt me, Lord, especially when You don't want me to do the same to You."

"I'm sorry. Please don't let me interrupt your grace."

He was back and he'd thought she was saying grace. For that much she was grateful.

The first five minutes passed and they slowly ate without conversation. However, they were observing one another. Everything was going well and then Needy accidentally belched. Her dark face turned almost gray with embarrassment. However, his belch was just as bad and it lightened the mood and permitted them to laugh.

From then on they chatted as though they'd known each other for years.

"Let me start over," Lionel said to Needy. "I'm known as the Reverend LL," he said as he extended a strong hand to her.

"You mean like LL Cool J?" Needy said with a smile. She was suddenly grateful that she'd plucked her top lip. If she hadn't it would've probably shaken like Jell-O from her excitement.

"Not quite. I'm no rapper," he replied. "And you are?"

"My name is Sister Need Sum," she answered.

"Do you, now?" he teased.

She caught the implied joke but she let it pass. "My friends and church members call me Needy."

Lionel silently rebuked himself, thinking that perhaps he'd been too forward with that last tease. "I'm pleased to meet you."

To Needy his voice sounded like what she imagined Moses must've heard on the mount when he wrote down the commandments.

"Where are you pastoring?" Needy asked. He was beginning to make her nervous. She was questioning him about things she didn't care about at that moment.

"I'm between churches at the moment. But hopefully I'll be accepted into a position when I return."

Before Needy could say any more the server appeared and began removing their plates. It was a dignified way of telling them

407

to get up so others could sit down. They caught the hint.

"Well Sister Needy, it's been my pleasure. I'm sorry I have to leave but my excursion into St. Maartens will leave shortly." He'd suddenly wished Lyon hadn't booked it so he could spend more time with her if she wasn't busy. "What does your day look like if you don't mind me asking?"

"I hadn't planned on doing much. Perhaps I'll visit the French side of the island or read a good book." She really wanted to latch on and follow him to St. Maartens but she didn't want him to know how desperate she was.

"Which dinner seating do you have?" He knew already but didn't want her to think he'd been stalking her.

"It's the same time as yours," Needy said with a wink. She didn't care if he thought she was stalking him.

They laughed and bade each other good-bye as they left the dining hall. He needed to work off the heavy breakfast, so Lionel took the stairs up to his stateroom. He never saw Birdie and Ima get off the elevator just as Needy was about to step on.

"Needy," Birdie said, "where have you been?"

"You'd better explain because this woman

woke me up too early. She was in a panic because you weren't in the cabin," Ima said as she pulled Needy out of the way so others could get on the elevator and Needy couldn't.

"Will you two please stay out of grown folks' business?" Needy laughed and said. "Whatever happens in the dining room stays in the dining room."

"What in the world did you eat?" Birdie asked.

"You ate too much cheese, didn't you?" Ima said. "You know you're lactose-intolerant." She said it loudly, and on purpose, so the other passengers would hear her. She knew it would embarrass Needy.

"The only thing I can't tolerate is your inquisition," Needy grumbled as she stepped onto the next elevator. Holding the elevator door open, she added, "Ain't you supposed to be killing somebody while we're on this cruise?"

Needy said it loudly so those same passengers could hear her. She knew it would implicate Ima should Lyon turn up dead or harmed.

Ima and Birdie stood gape-mouthed as the elevator door closed, and Needy smirked.

Immediately Ima became nervous when

she saw several of the on-lookers take out pens and paper. It looked like they were trying to make a sketch of her just in case something went awry on the ship.

Birdie took advantage of her whiteness, and left Ima standing alone while she disappeared into the crowd going into the dining hall. It was enough for her to pay reparations; she wasn't about to pay legal fees too.

34

Lyon swung open his cabin door and was surprised to find Lionel. For a moment he thought he was looking at his reflection in a mirror instead of Lionel in the doorway.

Lionel stood there wearing a cheesy Cheshire cat grin. It was the same silly expression that only last night he'd accused Lyon of having.

"Oh say it ain't so, Bro. Please say it ain't so," Lyon said as he wrapped an arm around Lionel to lead him out of the doorway.

"You were only supposed to have bacon and eggs. Drink a strong cup of coffee at the most, and perhaps enjoy a fat-drenched donut," Lyon teased. "Have a seat because I know I'm gonna need one, too."

It was that twin thingy, as they liked to call it, that told most of the story before Lionel opened his mouth to speak.

"I don't know where to start," Lionel said as he sat down.

"Translation . . . she wasn't what you were looking for, am I correct?" Lyon knew he was right but it would take the fun out of the questioning if he gave all the answers instead of Lionel.

"The long of it is that she's nowhere near what I've been praying or even hoping to meet," Lionel confessed. He seemed to almost apologize as if he'd sinned or disappointed someone.

"Is she that ugly?" Lyon asked. His concern was genuine but he kept the tease in his voice. "What did you do? Did you toss her back into the ocean along with the other sharks?" he added with a nervous laugh.

Lionel laughed too. He placed a finger over his lips as though he were about to tell a secret. "I've sort of left the door open where we can meet up again."

"Okay, that's a start. I guess she must be as tall if not taller than you?"

"No, she's about five foot three in flat shoes," Lionel said. He lay a hand midway across his chest to show where she'd reach if they stood together.

"You're scaring me now, Bro." Lyon got up and grabbed a soda from the refrigerator. He snapped back the tab and drank from the can.

"I noticed that she even had a little hairy

shadow just above her top lip," Lionel offered. "It looked a little sexy, almost."

Lyon needed to get up and change his shirt. That last revelation caused him to choke and the soda splashed from his mouth, sending the brown liquid streaming down his white shirt. It took a few moments before he reappeared and continued talking to Lionel.

"Let me recap our situation," Lyon said. He started using his fingers to count. "We have one old lady that I need to see and apologize to but am afraid to do so."

"Fear has no place among the people of God," Lionel reminded Lyon. "That's one woman out of many to whom you must make amends."

"I know you're right. Please keep me in prayer. But in the meantime there's the second woman." Lyon held up a second finger. "The beauty queen I met last night at Karaoke. She didn't seem like a woman who would let me get away with much. I like that. She's definitely a challenge."

"So is she wifey material?" Lionel asked. His mood was shifting to the lighter side as his brother lay out their situations.

"I'm not looking for wifey right now," Lyon reminded him. "I'm barely husband material. You know God's still working on

413

this old building."

"Okay, I can understand your hesitation," Lionel teased.

"Finally, we're down to your unconventional choice of a cruising mate." Lyon tried to stifle a laugh but he lost the battle. He started laughing so hard he was about to cry.

"I said she didn't look ugly or have a big wart on the tip of her nose. What's so hilarious?"

Lyon could hardly catch his breath. "You said that you were going to be specific with God about the kind of woman you wanted in your life."

"Maybe it was bad weather and the connection was weak when I prayed," Lionel laughed. "Or perhaps I cancelled out my specific choice when I ended the prayer with, 'Thy will be done.' "

"That was the deal-breaker. You gave God your list and He one-upped you with His." Lyon walked over to the balcony door and looked out. He then turned to his brother and said softly, "I betcha next time you'll enter the throne of grace with Holy boldness."

"Who said that I wanted to pray that particular prayer again?" Lionel stood and answered. "I'm rather curious as to what

God has in mind, if anything. I've not been an angel but I am certainly not praying for an unveiling of my life, if it can be avoided."

"You're not sounding like the Reverend L. Lipps that I know and love."

"And that, my lil' brother, is called growth." Lionel smiled as he watched Lyon's expression change. He knew his brother would think deeply about it.

Lyon and Lionel donned wide hats and shades to guard against the heat of the sun and possibly more. With cameras hanging around their necks, and their vouchers in hand, they left the ship to tour St. Maartens.

35

Most of the tenders had returned from the white sandy beaches of St. Maartens and St. Martins. The passengers laughed loudly as they exchanged details of that day's sightseeing tours. It was almost time for dinner so the line through security went quickly, as most wanted to change before they ate.

"So what's the plan for this evening?" Birdie asked Ima.

"It's been a long day. You don't have to hound me. I've got Mr. Lipps under control," she lied, but was surprised that Birdie didn't call her on it.

"Oddly enough, I really don't care anymore," Birdie said as she waved at Jaiquist. She'd spotted him balancing a tray of drinks with one hand, and pulling out a seat for someone to sit in with his other.

None of Birdie's strange actions escaped Ima. She had to admit to herself that as much as she liked Birdie's white money, she didn't want to see her flirting with a black man.

"You really have a thing for chocolate?" Ima said with sarcasm and venom dripping from each word.

"Not really," Birdie replied, "I don't think it's good for the complexion." She turned her stare from Jaiquist to Ima. "I certainly hope you're not thinking about biting into a piece of chocolate. You look like you've packed on about five pounds since we sailed." Birdie knew exactly what Ima had implied. Watching Ima's face turn almost blue from the sudden TKO was a victory in itself.

Before Ima could react Jaiquist appeared next to Birdie. If Birdie was Jane then Jaiquist was Shaka Zulu and he'd protect her just as ferociously as Tarzan.

Ima didn't know what was happening with Birdie but whatever it was, she didn't like it. The feeling of powerlessness was occurring too often and she needed to do something about it. She needed to do it quick.

Their two-day suspension from eating in the dining hall was over. Both Mothers Pray Onn and Blister had promised to behave if allowed to eat with the other passengers.

Because of all the pranks they'd played on

417

each other, they were tired, hungry and cranky. It took all the restraint they could muster but the old women managed to get through their dinner without one incident.

"Are you finished with your dessert, my dear?" Mother Pray Onn asked Mother Blister sweetly.

"Yes, I am. It was such a lovely meal. Don't you agree?" Mother Blister replied.

Mother Pray Onn nodded in agreement. And with precision they both dabbed their mouths with their napkins and prepared to rise from the table. There was a small red spot on each of the napkins that looked like blood. The old women had almost bitten a hole in their lips trying to keep up the sham. They inched their way into the hallway, used the bathroom, and then stood in front of the plaque that told the ship's activities.

Mother Pray Onn saw it first but it was Mother Blister who yelled it out. "Bingo!" And, off they went. They'd promised to behave at mealtime. They had not promised the same for other times.

"Do you think we'll have time to play and look for Lyon Lipps too?" Mother Blister asked as they waited on line to purchase their bingo cards, markers and chips.

"I don't see why not. How long do you think it will take us to take these old fools'

418

money?" Mother Pray Onn said as she cackled and pointed to a group of senior citizens milling around.

"Do you remember the old undercover ruse that the professional bingo players used to use back in 1952?" Mother Blister asked.

"Of course I do. I'm not forgetful like you." She was lying, and if she once knew, she didn't now.

"Watch it, Lucky Charms," Mother Blister hissed. She'd only asked because she couldn't remember how the ruse went. But it always worked.

"Don't be so sensitive," Mother Pray Onn warned. "Let's just play it by ear."

The bingo game finally got underway twenty minutes behind schedule. The activity crew kept in mind that most of the players were elderly so they allowed for the usual bickering, switching cards and hearing aid adjustments. That usually made the game late by five minutes. It was the craziness that Mothers Blister and Pray Onn started that took up the other fifteen minutes.

It had started when Mother Pray Onn found it difficult to remove the cap off the thick felt-tip ink marker. She'd rejected help from a young man seated nearby.

"I don't need no help from nobody," she

claimed as she struggled with the cap. "I can open childproof caps off aspirin bottles. I can certainly get this off."

"That's right," Mother Blister chimed in, "I've seen her take a childproof cap off with a claw hammer."

It took some doing but they finally got Mother Pray Onn to agree to use a black crayon instead.

The old women moved to a table way off to the side. They each had two bingo cards spread out in front of them. And they didn't bother to sit, choosing to stand instead to energetically mark each letter and number called on their cards.

The caller's less-than-enthusiastic voice kept rubbing Mother Pray Onn the wrong way. He'd start off by saying, "B," and then pause too long before he continued with "8." The bingo pot was almost five thousand dollars and she meant to have it.

"Okay, ladies and gentlemen," the bingo caller said, "we've called all the numbers but three. The rule is that only one more number can be called. Somebody must be close to having bingo."

He added more drama. He let his wrist wind as though he were playing with a yoyo before he pulled a number off the chute extending from the round glass bowl.

"O-75." He said it twice in case some of the players hadn't heard him the first time. "Whoever is the closest will win the five thousand dollar pot."

"It's show time," Mother Pray Onn whispered. She leaned back onto her chair and gave Mother Blister a half wink.

Mother Blister mistook the wink as a cue that she should start the ruse that she couldn't remember. She did the next best thing, she improvised. But she spoke up just as Mother Pray Onn was about to go into her routine.

"Oh my God!" Mother Blister screamed at the top of her lungs, beating Mother Pray Onn to the punch.

Suddenly the other players started fussing, cussing, and ripping apart their bingo cards thinking someone had won the pot. And, that's when Mother Blister followed through with another howl.

"I've got a cramp!"

It was too late. She and Mother Pray Onn were the only ones who still had their bingo cards intact. Under the glares and silent threats from the other seniors, the two Mothers strutted up to the table to collect their money.

"They did what?" Lyon asked when Lionel

tried to explain why he'd returned from the bingo game early.

"I swear I cannot prove it but I truly believe those two old women pulled a fast one." Lionel laughed and said, "I certainly wouldn't want to sit down at a poker game with either of them."

"I told you about the evils of gambling," Lyon said cheerfully. "I believe I'll return to the Karaoke bar this evening."

"Are you not going to dine?" Lionel asked.

"Not tonight. I've begun to eat too much on this cruise. Everywhere I turn there's a plate of fun waiting for me."

Lionel patted his flat stomach. "I know what you mean. We can't let ourselves go to pot because the food is free."

"What are you going to do?" Lyon asked.

"I'm not quite sure. I believe I'll explore the ship."

"Translation," Lyon said as he finished his brother's sentence, "you believe you'll go and hunt for your new friend."

"You know me well."

Birdie found Ima seated alone on one of the folding chairs on the Lido Deck. She was still wearing the same outfit from earlier so Birdie knew she was troubled about something.

"Didn't think I'd run into you here." Birdie tried to sound cheerful but she couldn't. Like Ima, she had something on her mind.

Ima's look was unsettling but it didn't have the usual meanness embedded. Yet, it was enough to make Birdie back off. "Look, I don't need to be here in your space. Whatever it is that's on your mind, either you can pray about it or you can marinate in misery. It's up to you."

"Why are you acting so spiritual all of a sudden?" Ima's expression hadn't moved although her lips had. "You go on a cruise and suddenly you pull out the courage and sass weapons. What's up with that?"

"What are you talking about? This is me." She pulled her chair closer to Ima's. Having courage didn't mean she wanted the entire Lido Deck to overhear what was said.

"This is not you!" Ima poked at Birdie but not as hard as she could have done. "You have money so you spend it like it's water. You believe everything that's told to you, but nothing that you feel inside."

"Where do you get your information?" Birdie asked.

Ima wouldn't be hushed. She continued her rant and still her expression had not changed. "One minute you want a black man banished to hell, and the next you're all over one who's straight out of the Serengeti."

Ima's expression finally changed. She was exhausted from the rant. She didn't care about the tears that tugged at the corner of her eyes. She really didn't care if Birdie went after one black man or a prison-full. In less than twenty-four hours she'd met and was entirely disarmed by one man. A man whose name she didn't know.

Through her watery eyes, Ima could tell she'd hurt Birdie. She knew the right thing to do would be to apologize. She didn't feel like doing the right thing. Instead, she leapt from her chair and headed towards the elevator. She was on her way to the very expensive cabin paid for by the very woman she'd just blasted for being so gullible. The woman she'd tricked into giving her anything she'd wanted. Now there were two women Ima didn't respect, herself and Birdie.

36

Petunia kept one eye on Evilene and the other on Cill. She was caught in the middle of their latest row and she was sure to be the loser.

Evilene had about sent Cill to the poorhouse quicker than Lyon Lipps had done Cill's sister. Cill had spent almost eight hundred dollars to get her bedroom fumigated, her bed and linen replaced, and the carpet taken up. Cill had spent every available cent she had, because Evilene supposedly didn't know the difference between her cat box and Cill's bed.

"You need to move out of my way," Cill snarled as she tried to circle around Petunia to snatch Evilene. "I've already spent a fortune faxing to that cruise ship. I don't have money to waste trying to replace stuff."

The cat had balled itself so tight, she looked more like a scared armadillo than a dangerous feline. Cill would need a spatula and a claw hammer to pry the cat away.

"Cill, leave that cat alone. She just misses Ima, that's why she's staying in so much trouble."

"If that fur-ball does one more thing to stink up my house it'll never see Ima or be able to lick its own behind again."

Evilene didn't have to be a smarty-cat to understand the venom in Cill's voice. Somehow it managed to wind itself tight enough to fit into a crevice in the corner.

"Look at what you've done." Petunia pointed to the trembling Evilene.

"Stop trying to suck up to that doggone cat. It can't understand what you're saying. And it certainly won't come to your defense when Ima gets that bill." Cill tried to push past Petunia to grab at Evilene. "That cat is going outside and that's that."

Petunia was smaller and quicker than Cill. She reached Evilene first and stuck out her hand towards Evilene so Cill wouldn't hurt the cat.

Evilene saw Petunia's outstretched hand as a threat and the cat did what any cat would when threatened. She unfurled and lunged at Petunia like a snake.

"Help me, Cill. Help me," Petunia hollered, trying to shake the cat loose when it struck again and clung to her arm.

"Just hold on," Cill said as she raced past Petunia and Evilene whirling around the room.

"She scratched me, Cill. That evil cat scratched me." Petunia was jumping up and down out of fear and pain.

Petunia and Evilene looked like they were part of *The Matrix*. Every move they made seemed to be in slow motion, appearing to be frozen in time, but it was actually lightning-fast.

Just as quick as Evilene had struck her blow, she released her claws from Petunia's arm and ran off to find more Kibbles and Bits.

Two long scratch tracks with specks of blood ran down Petunia's arm. "I might need a rabies shot," Petunia whined.

"You don't need a shot. I've got what you need to stop any infection," Cill said as she approached carrying her First Aid kit. She was concerned about Petunia and that Petunia would hear her laughing.

"What's that in your hand?" Petunia asked as she watched Cill tear open a small packet.

"Stop whining. It's just an alcohol pad to wipe your scratch."

It was Cill's turn to grab at Petunia and become one of the characters from *The Matrix*. They two-stepped around the room with Cill trying to dab at Petunia's scratches and Petunia trying to scratch Cill's eyes out.

In the meantime Evilene, fearful of all the pulling and tugging between Cill and Petunia, skittered off to try out Cill's new sheets.

37

Mother Blister took her turn entering the bathroom stall. It only took her a moment to stuff her half of the bingo money safely into her brassiere. When she came out she found Mother Pray Onn still keeping watch by the entrance.

"You got it tucked safely away in your First National Kitties?" Mother Pray Onn asked as she snickered.

"Oh yes. It's safely hidden between the folds of the twin sisters," Mother Blister replied as she patted her breasts.

Mother Pray Onn said, slyly, "I didn't know you had that much con in your old Christian heart. I'm impressed."

"You ain't too shabby either." Mother Blister's compliment was followed with a wide grin before she added, "You think you might be up to going with me on my next disability visit?"

"Why not," Mother Pray Onn said. "I can

show you how to run the slipped disc ruse."

"You'd really share your plan with me?" Mother Blister was surprised.

"Maybe I'll show you just a piece of it," Mother Pray Onn said, "but I'll have to pray on it first."

Two women suddenly pushed through the door, laughing. One woman entered a stall still talking as she closed the door. The other woman kept their conversation going as she pulled out a comb and brush from her pocketbook. Without so much as acknowledging the old women, she primped in a mirror, which happened to be too close to where the old women stood.

The interruption caused Mothers Blister and Pray Onn to pretend they'd been washing their hands. Each grabbed a paper towel, dabbed at their dry hands, and left.

As soon as they exited the ladies room, Mother Blister stumbled a little, almost bumping into Mother Pray Onn who walked a few feet in front. She wasn't sure if it was the excitement from winning the bingo money or if her heart raced because she was losing her mind.

Mother Blister looked around quickly. Where was Ima, Birdie or Needy when she needed them? Mother Pray Onn, as lethal as she could be, would be of no use to her now.

"What's wrong with you?" Mother Pray Onn asked. "You almost tore my heel from my foot." She stopped abruptly when she saw Mother Blister looking straight past her. She turned around and tried to follow Mother Blister's gaze but she saw nothing unusual.

"It's him," Mother Blister whispered. "He's standing by the elevator."

"There are three elevators," Mother Pray Onn said, "which one are you talking about?"

"The one by the Karaoke bar," Mother Blister hissed. She was annoyed that she was being questioned when they should have been leaving.

An elevator door opened and everyone but one young man got on it. "You mean the handsome young man with that pretty hair?" Mother Pray Onn asked as she adjusted her glasses to see better. "How would you know a fella that looked that good?"

"That's him," Mother Blister said quickly as she leaned over and pushed Mother Pray Onn out of view from the elevator.

"Quit pushing on me," Mother Pray Onn snapped. "Him, who?"

Mother Blister didn't try to hide her annoyance that time. "Lyon Lipps. It's him standing over there between that elevator and the doorway."

If Mother Pray Onn and Mother Blister were trying to be inconspicuous, they failed. When they peeked out from where they stood, he looked right back at them. Lyon Lipps had seen them, too.

The ship's library was nearly empty. There were two rows of computers for the passengers' convenience but only one was in use.

Jaiquist stood impressively by the library's entrance. He had a newspaper folded under one arm and a serving tray under the other arm.

When the last person left, Jaiquist quietly lay down the newspaper and the tray on a nearby table. He quickly closed the library door and went to the last computer in the back row.

Birdie sat waiting for Jaiquist wearing an oversized straw hat and huge sunglasses. When he came close enough she pressed an envelope into his hand, which he quickly secreted in his jacket pocket.

A man suddenly came through the door and headed towards an unoccupied computer. As if he'd not noticed the man, Jaiquist moved away from Birdie. He started arranging several chairs around a table close to where Birdie still sat.

"I can't seem to log on," the man called out. "Are the computers working?"

"Yes, sir, they are working. But they sometimes cannot connect if we're out of range," Jaiquist said, respectfully.

The man looked disappointed. He walked away. He didn't seem to notice Birdie at all or the fact that her computer was active.

"That was too close," Birdie whispered. "I'm not used to all this subterfuge."

Jaiquist continued moving a chair as he said, sadly, "Madam, in my country we need subterfuge to survive."

Birdie had no answer. Instead, she logged off the computer and walked away in the opposite direction from Jaiquist. She smiled slightly at Samuel as she passed him. He didn't look up but she could see his chin bob, indicating he'd seen her.

He'd stood silently during the entire time, behind the bar at the back of the room. As soon as Birdie left he went to Jaiquist and took the envelope.

Lionel had stayed behind in Lyon's cabin. As much as he appreciated the opulence of his stateroom, he'd found Lyon's cabin to be a bit more passenger-friendly.

From the desk, Lionel retrieved a pen and a pad. He placed them on the coffee table and opened his Bible. He flipped the pages slowly at first and then quickly. He knew the verses were in the book of Proverbs but he couldn't remember which chapter. He laughed aloud. "I'm supposed to know this book from Genesis to Revelation."

The scriptures had come to him during a brief nap earlier that afternoon. The words had been fleeting and when he awoke they plagued him. He was sure God was trying to reach him through His word. The pages in his Bible were smudged from thumbing through them and yellowed from his high-lighter pen.

He finally found the verse. Unlike the ones he'd studied and highlighted, this verse had no marks. And as he began to read he knew why.

Lionel began to read aloud, *". . . a man that findeth a wife findeth a good thing . . ."*

Inside the Karaoke bar the crowd gathered for the main event. There was a comedian who spent fifteen minutes trying to get the crowd to laugh. He'd only received a few polite giggles. The people were reserving their deep belly-laughs for the brave souls who'd dare to sing.

Ima and Needy sat at a table together and not because they wanted to.

Ima made it plain that she didn't want to sit with another female. "What if Lyon shows up," Ima complained. "How am I supposed to seduce this man with you sitting here looking like you're trying to draw flies instead of a man?"

Needy had worn a loud orange dress with huge floral patterns that made her look like a walking Rose Bowl float. She'd paid a lot of money for the dress and she was wearing it even if someone mistakenly pinned a picture of a scarecrow on it.

"Don't worry about what I'm wearing," Needy growled. "If you were all that then you'd have a man sitting with you whether it was Lyon or whoever."

Needy had put it out there. Neither of them was happy. Neither had seen the men who had turned their worlds upside down with only one meeting. They were taking it out on each other. They couldn't talk about it because they'd kept it a secret.

Ima and Needy continued sitting in silence despite the clamor around them. Yet every time someone entered or left the bar their necks swung in the direction of the door.

For the next thirty minutes, Needy and Ima sat and sipped on daiquiris. Needy ordered the virgin and Ima didn't.

His walk was a little unsteady and definitely unsure. There was no escaping.

Lyon walked slowly towards Mother Blister. With every cautious step he took, he prayed. He hadn't wanted to apologize to her in public but he must.

Mother Pray Onn was beside herself as she saw the young man approach. One look at Mother Blister's shocked expression told her everything she'd suspected was true.

"Have mercy, Bea Blister. You paid that young man to keep company with you. Didn't you?" Mother Pray Onn didn't wait for an answer. Instead, she walked away from Mother Blister and headed straight towards Lyon.

It was like a scene from a bad movie for both Lyon and Mother Blister. He wanted to turn away from the short old lady who seemed determined to meet him head on. Mother Blister wanted to snatch her back but couldn't move.

"How do you do, young man," Mother Pray Onn said. "I'm Mother Sasha Pray Onn."

She'd introduced herself in a manner that left him no place to run and no choice but to respond.

"I understand and can appreciate how you've tormented a lot of women with your good looks and," she stopped and used her cane to point towards his knees, "whatever else it is that you're good at."

"Excuse me," Lyon said. He was truly shocked at her nerve but she hadn't said anything untrue.

"You're excused," Mother Pray Onn replied.

She took him by his elbow and prodded him to the side to allow a couple to pass. He didn't resist. Mother Pray Onn tapped her cane on the floor and said with contempt, "I thought you were trifling when I'd heard that you took that skinny sack Petunia for a ride on your candy car but you've hit an all time low messing with my best friend over there."

"Who are you?" Lyon asked. He thought he was dreaming.

"I'm the one woman who can save your sorry behind, that's who I am."

"Please, I don't think we should be having this conversation," Lyon pleaded.

"I'm not interested in what you think. I'm saving your behind whether you want me to or not."

"I don't know what Mother Blister has told you," Lyon said.

Mother Pray Onn dismissed him by cutting him off in mid-sentence.

"My niece is going to kill you."

That stopped Lyon as well as shut him up.

"I know for a fact that there are several women who've hired her to stop your clock."

"And you would know this how?" Lyon was suddenly intrigued as well as fearful.

"You must be hard of hearing. I said my name is Mother Sasha Pray Onn."

Mother Pray Onn turned around to signal to Mother Blister to join them but she was gone. She'd have to handle things alone, but he was nothing that she couldn't handle.

Mother Pray Onn led Lyon inside a small alcove next to the Karaoke bar.

38

Birdie entered the cabin, immediately undressed and headed for the shower.

After she'd showered and dressed she sat down and placed her feet on the coffee table. She flipped through the pages in the folder she held and realized she needed to make notes. As she rose she spied an envelope with the ship's seal imprinted.

"This must've come while I was in the shower," she said aloud to herself. It was addressed to her. Just as she was about to open it she heard the soft knock at the door.

She opened the door to find Jaiquist, Samuel and M'gube. She ushered them in quickly. Ten minutes later, they left Birdie's cabin one by one and went their separate ways.

Lyon didn't want to believe what the old woman said but she knew too much for him not to. He shuddered as he listened to her lay out the plans that Birdie had paid for. He'd not realized that he'd hurt her that much, particularly since they hadn't really dated.

Birdie wasn't a casualty only because he hadn't had the chance to do worse damage; but he'd definitely wrecked the lives of Petunia and Mother Blister. And when he learned of what he'd done to Cill's sister, Jessie, he was crushed. He'd set those small fires using carefree and dubious kindling and now it'd become one huge blaze. He was about to burn but couldn't quite figure out what part Mother Pray Onn played. Why would she want to save him? He didn't have to wait long to find the answer.

"You wait right here and don't move," Mother Pray Onn ordered. "I just need to find out something real quick. I'm not going far."

"Yes Ma'am, I'm not going anywhere," Lyon conceded.

"You'd better believe it. I found you once and I'll hunt you down again," she lied. It wouldn't help her plan if he knew Mother Blister had pointed him out.

Evil knew evil. Even in the darkened Karaoke bar with her head slumped and her face hidden, Mother Pray Onn knew it was Ima. Of course, seeing Needy seated next to her made identification much easier. Who else but Ima would sit voluntarily next to Needy?

Mother Pray Onn motioned to Lyon, who still stood rooted in the alcove. She'd been on her feet most of the day and her bunions were burning so he needed to come to her. Putting her plan in motion became urgent. She wanted to hurry so she could remove her orthopedic sandals.

She tapped her cane to let him know that he needed to hurry. "Look over there at that third table."

Lyon leaned past her and looked inside. He saw nothing unusual or familiar. "What about it?"

"Do you see the woman sitting there in a dress that looks like a ghetto garden filled with beer cans, weeds and cigarette butts?"

He leaned past her again. He saw a woman, although he thought the dress was just fine. "I see her."

"Well that ain't the one that wants to punish you. It's the one seated next to her with her head down."

Lyon quickly peeked in again and that time he saw her as she raised her head. He looked inside several times to make sure that it was the same woman he'd met the night before.

An ashen pallor covered his otherwise flawless complexion. It was at that moment that he realized, and accepted, that whether he'd given his life to Christ or not, consequences always followed actions.

"Why would she want to take my life?" Lyon hadn't meant to say it aloud but he did.

"There ain't no murderers in my family," Mother Pray Onn answered with indignation. "She won't kill your body. She's out to kill your dreams and perhaps filet your finances," she added, proudly.

Somehow that revelation didn't make Lyon feel any better.

Mother Blister pushed open the cabin door hard enough to take it off its hinges. She was livid.

"That two-faced Smurf." She kicked aside an envelope lying in the doorway. "I'll fix her." She never saw the edge of the fax protruding.

Mother Blister headed straight for Mother Pray Onn's room. She started rummaging through several small packages on a chair. She found nothing that she could use.

Mother Blister raced into the bathroom and saw Mother Pray Onn's bottle of Listerine. "This will do just fine."

Mother Blister took the bottle of Listerine into her room. From her medicine bag she took out a Ziploc bag. In it was the powdered alum she'd brought along just in case she developed diarrhea.

"I forgot I had this." She'd only discovered that she'd brought it along after suffering through her laxative overdose the other morning. Her memory was in full effect now.

She pulled her glasses down onto the tip of her nose to better read the label: *"Soluble in water; has an astringent acid, and sweetish taste; when heated liquefies; and if the heating is continued, the water of crystallization is driven off, the salt froths and swells, and at last an amorphous powder remains."*

She was about to pour the powder into the Listerine bottle and stopped. "I've got a better idea." She quickly replaced the bottle to its spot.

And that's when she heard Mother Pray Onn enter.

"Where did you disappear to?" Mother Pray Onn asked. "I needed you to help me with the plan."

"I didn't expect to see Lyon. I figured Ima would've had him cut and quartered before the second day of the cruise." She controlled her anger despite her desire to wring Mother

443

Pray Onn's neck.

"Didn't we agree to partner up with him when we found out how Ima had tricked us?" She wanted to make sure that Mother Blister remembered or her plan wouldn't work.

"Of course I remember," Mother Blister replied. "I'm the first one to agree that revenge is best served when hot."

"I believe the term is, best served cold."

"You're right," Mother Blister said, slowly. "You're right about everything."

Mother Pray Onn took Mother Blister's concession as a victory. She sat her down and told her everything that had happened after she'd left.

"Did he really show remorse?" Mother Blister asked. "Maybe that's why he looks a little different now."

"Oh, he's definitely sorry."

"And he knows what Ima looks like?" Mother Blister asked the right questions but her heart was still in the wrong place. She wasn't about to let Mother Pray Onn get away with what she'd done.

"Are you tired?" Mother Blister asked sweetly.

"I'm not tired but my bunion is barking like there's an intruder lurking," Mother Pray Onn laughed while patting her throbbing bunion.

"I know what you need for that," Mother Blister offered.

"What?"

"Some fun, we need to have some." Mother Blister retrieved the wad of money from her brassiere and flashed it. "We need to hit the casino."

"Now you're talking my language." Mother Pray Onn quickly forgot about the bunion and reached way down in her tiny brassiere and pulled out her wad. "But first we need to stop by the Karaoke bar for the fireworks."

"Since when did they have fireworks at a Karaoke bar?"

"Ima and Needy are there, remember?"

"What about Lyon? Is he still there?" Mother Blister asked. As much as she wanted to punish Mother Pray Onn she wasn't quite sure if she was ready to face him. She hadn't told Mother Pray Onn everything and she hoped he hadn't either.

"She's what!" Lionel said. He slammed down his Bible, which was something he'd never done before. "I don't believe it!"

"I saw and heard for myself," Lyon said as he paced. "Those two women are friends and your new friend knows that my new

445

friend is out to get me."

"So the white woman you saw the other night is actually the one you were going to meet before we set sail?"

"That was Birdie," Lyon said. "I told you something wasn't right. I've felt it from the very beginning."

"Are you blaming me for this?" Lionel asked.

"Let me just calm down a moment before I say or do something that neither you nor the Lord can forgive."

"You need to quit pacing and drop to your knees. Why are you acting like these women have more power than God?"

"I don't know about those other women but I'm sure that little old woman, Mother Pray Onn, keeps God on His toes. She's not your typical church mother."

"Did you think that because you've accepted Christ that you wouldn't have to face any more tests?"

"Of course, I didn't. I just can't believe I've been set up. These are church women and if they're this devious, I don't stand a chance against the worldly women I've harmed."

"He's the same God with the same plan."

"Lionel, you're not standing in my shoes."

"Perhaps not, but I am standing beside

you." Lionel steered Lyon towards the door. "Let's go."

"Go where?" Lyon asked, letting his brother lead him.

"To face the enemy," Lionel answered. "I'd better take a weapon." He picked up his Bible.

39

Birdie hadn't known what to expect before she entered M'gube's small cabin. It was on the second deck and unlike the upper decks where the paying passengers stayed, her cabin rolled with the waves. It was all Birdie could do to keep from hurling.

The room was kept very neatly. There were two small single beds, a dresser, and a tiny bathroom with a shower. M'gube usually shared it with another young woman who was not on this cruise. Normally the ship would've assigned her another roommate but so far they hadn't.

But there was a peace about it despite the haunting photos of dust-covered children with eyes too large for their tiny faces. And then Birdie saw the same photos that had disturbed her when first shown by Jaiquist.

The photos were of poor quality but the subject was clear. They showed new mothers lying on dirty mats. They held their newborns, some still with their umbilical cords attached and untied. The vacant stares did little to minimize the pain of dead and dying babies.

Despite their surroundings Birdie could see that the mothers were mostly young girls. Some of them barely into their teen years, and forced to endure much more than their youth should.

M'gube watched Birdie and was moved by her honest compassion. She withdrew a small photo from her dresser and handed it to Birdie.

Birdie knew immediately that it was M'gube as a younger woman. In the picture, despite the surrounding misery, M'gube still showed an air of strength about her.

"I was only twenty," M'gube offered when she saw the questioning look on Birdie's face. "My baby should've survived as should have so many of the others."

M'gube's intuition told her that Birdie truly had no idea of the greatness of her sorrow. It was her turn to feel compassion for the white woman who held so much of her future in her hands.

"Madam, Birdie," M'gube said softly. "Please forgive my ignorance. From that moment on the Lido deck when you discovered Jaiquist giving me comfort, you've been so kind as to not divulge our relationship. I know you did so because Jaiquist requested it."

M'gube poured a glass of water and offered it to Birdie. She watched the teardrops fall from Birdie's eyes into the glass and didn't know if she dared continue to speak.

"I'm so sorry," Birdie said between sipping her water and dabbing at her tears. "If I had seen Jaiquist comfort you I would've not interfered. I wasn't spying — I thought something was wrong with you. I wanted to help."

"I know you were. We try to be very careful but we seldom have a moment when we can be together. And sometimes it is quite difficult for me."

Birdie nodded in agreement. That much she did understand.

M'gube picked up the picture of her baby again as she continued to speak. "It is forbidden in our country for Jaiquist and me to be together because we are of different communities. Even in these modern times, madam, there are customs to be observed."

"I'm so sorry," Birdie apologized again. "I can only imagine because I've never married or had children."

"Madam?" M'gube whispered. She was

confused. "I'm afraid we only have one thing in common."

It was Birdie's turn to be confused yet she was intrigued by M'gube's response. "What one thing is that?"

"I'm afraid that Jaiquist and I have married against our parents' wishes." M'gube conspired, trying to appear calm. "I see Jaiquist did not tell you everything?"

M'gube's revelation lifted the edge off the heaviness in the cabin's air, allowing each woman to breathe easier.

"It makes sense to me now. Jaiquist was also the father of your baby?" Birdie asked. Not that it would've made a difference at that point.

"Yes," M'gube said, simply. "And Samuel is my brother."

"And, the cruise line does not know this?" Birdie asked.

"No, madam. They do not and they cannot." M'gube suddenly lowered her voice as though they were not alone. "It is against the ship's policy to allow either siblings or married couples to sail together."

"It doesn't make sense," Birdie said angrily before adding, "and neither does letting mothers and babies die."

"Your generosity will go a long way in helping us to save new mothers and their infants."

"I cannot believe that for only five dollars both a mother and child's life can be saved."

"It is true, madam. All that are needed are sterile sheets, sterile scissors, sanitary pads, and the simple things that well-off countries take for granted. They were simple things that would've saved my baby." Her sadness returned.

"You know I went on the Internet and checked out that organization Jaiquist told me about."

"Sisters International," M'gube said.

"Yes. I found out as much information as I could. I went a bit further and e-mailed an old college friend, Akia Shangai, who lives in New York."

"You did that? Why?" M'gube asked.

"I'm about to donate a lot of money and I wanted to make sure that it goes where it is supposed to go and used for the purpose it's intended."

"I understand, Madam." M'gube finally beckoned Birdie to sit. "What did you discover?"

"I discovered that my friend, Akia Shangai, and the Sisters International organization share a common goal with The Links."

"I know about The Links, Madam," M'gube said. It was the first time Birdie had seen her smile.

"Akia e-mailed a portion of a press release. I'll read it if you don't mind." Birdie didn't wait for M'gube to respond. She pulled a piece of paper from her pocket and started to read aloud.

Currently, the World Health Organization is closely aligned with The Links for the Safe Motherhood Initiative. As active participants in the Maama Kit Campaign, Links chapters have purchased thousands of "Maama Kits" to help alleviate the problem of neonatal mortality.

"You can read the rest for yourself," Birdie said, handing the paper to M'gube.

"Thank you, madam." M'gube could do nothing to stop the tears and she didn't try.

"I should be thanking you, Jaiquist and Samuel," Birdie said as she handed M'gube a tissue from her pocket. "I was a mess when I came aboard."

"Why?" M'gube asked. "You seem to have so much, and —"

"I know what you're going to say — 'and I'm white,' " Birdie said. Her skin color seemed to make differences where she felt it shouldn't.

"No, madam," M'gube said as she attempted to explain. "I was going to say that you have so much beauty both inside and out."

Birdie felt uneasy. "I wish it was much more so inside."

She felt the sudden roll of the ocean as it bullied M'gube's small room. "What profits a woman to gain the whole world and not have Christ, fully, in her life?" Birdie murmured.

People were in pain all over the world. What right did she have to hold her supposed slight — against a man she hadn't dated — above any others' problems?

Right there in M'gube's room, filled with beauty and order alongside horror and disorder, Birdie felt her life change completely. The enormous check she handed M'gube was nothing compared to the gift the African woman had just handed her.

Birdie and M'gube had just said their goodbyes when Jaiquist and Samuel appeared.

"Madam, we can never thank you enough," Samuel offered. He'd been so quiet Birdie was surprised to hear him say more than two words at one time.

"You're more than welcome," Birdie replied.

Birdie then turned to Jaiquist and said,

"Jaiquist, you have a beautiful wife. Make sure that you do not follow in the footsteps of Abraham when he presented his wife, Sarah, as his sister."

"Madam, I do not understand," Jaiquist replied.

"Madam does not want either you or M'gube to present yourselves as available when you truly are not," Samuel said. He turned to Birdie and asked, "Is that the correct interpretation, madam?"

Birdie didn't answer Samuel; she smiled, instead.

"Can we impose upon you for one more thing?" Jaiquist said as he slowly closed the door before she could leave.

Birdie didn't know what to think or say. She was suddenly nervous.

"What more can I do?" she asked as both M'gube and Samuel came closer to where she stood.

"Back in his homeland," Jaiquist said, "Samuel is a Reverend when he's not sailing to make money for his family. We'd be honored if you would hold hands with us while Samuel leads the prayer."

They could see the tension flee Birdie's body. She almost went limp. "Of course, I would love to have a short prayer."

"I don't know how short it will be,"

M'gube said. "My brother Samuel is Baptist."

40

While Mother Pray Onn poked and prodded her way through the swarm inside the Karaoke bar, her companion in crime, Mother Blister, secretly placed Mother Pray Onn's name on the list to sing. She had done the down and dirty deed before Mother Pray Onn realized she wasn't walking behind her.

Needy and Ima still sat at their table. Ima looked a bit better but not much. She feigned surprise at seeing her aunt approaching.

"I think this might be my cue to leave you two to work things out," Needy said, pushing back her chair as she spoke.

"Stop acting so afraid. You're in this just as deep as I am."

"I'm not receiving combat pay; you are," Needy said snidely.

It didn't matter. Moses couldn't have walked through the parted Red Sea with as much determination as showed on Mothers Pray Onn and Blister's faces.

"I got your message," Mother Pray Onn said directly to Ima. She didn't even acknowledge Needy seated there.

"Did you get the gift too?" Ima asked, dancing around her aunt's implied nastiness. "I paid a lot of money for that watch."

"I got the watch that Birdie paid for and I gave it to one of the cabin boys. I told him to use it to chip the dirt off the toilet. And you can save your breath because I know about Lyon Lipps."

It was out there. Her aunt knew about Birdie's involvement and their plan to get revenge on Lyon Lipps.

"That's right, I know it all. Petunia blabbed before you even packed your bags to leave Pelzer," Mother Pray Onn sneered as she tormented her niece. "And, Lyon Lipps knows about you: checkmate."

Ima turned and looked angrily at Needy but Needy's gaze was someplace else. Needy wasn't sure if she'd had too much to drink or not. She'd ordered virgin daiquiris — perhaps she'd drank Ima's by mistake. Needy pressed her palm to her forehead. Her head felt okay. Any pain she was feeling was brought on by the unwanted arrival of those two cranky church mothers. She adjusted her wig on the sly, moving a piece of hair that had fallen over one eye.

Ima had followed Needy's gaze and saw the same thing Needy had seen. There stood two men, and they both looked like her perfect stranger.

She turned to say something to Needy and that's when she realized the reason for Needy's sudden upbeat mood that had lasted throughout the afternoon. Needy had probably met someone, too. She was sure of it because Needy had the same whipped look on her face.

Lionel and Lyon had entered and spoken to a passing waiter. They saw a couple that appeared to be leaving so they hurried over to claim the table. If they noticed Ima and Needy they didn't show it. They focused their attention on the small stage where someone was sacrificing their dignity in song.

"Let me order us some tea," Mother Blister said. "I know I don't drink hard liquor and I'm sure *you* don't," she said accusingly.

"I'd love a cup of hot tea," Mother Pray Onn said. She wasn't about to walk into Mother Blister's trap and have her blab to the Mothers Board if she took a drink.

While the old women waited for their tea

to arrive, Ima looked around for a way to escape. She didn't want anyone, not even her perfect stranger, to see her. It wasn't how she'd envisioned their next meeting. She didn't want all her skeletons falling out of the closet in front of his feet.

Lyon saw the waiter as he went over and spoke to Mother Pray Onn. Even in the dimly lit room he knew it was her. He also noticed that Ima still sat in that same spot. This time she had her head up and appeared to be less confident.

"There they are," Lyon said to Lionel. "And the smaller old woman is her aunt, Mother Pray Onn."

"Lyon, please don't tell me that the other old woman is the Mother Blister you've tried to avoid on this ship."

"I wish I could tell you that she wasn't, but I'd be lyin'." He smiled slightly. "No pun intended."

"All I can say is that it's a good thing you came to Christ," Lionel said. "I see Needy's seated there, too. I was looking forward to getting to know her."

"How can we get to know women we can't trust? God made His servants not to throw His pearls before swine. We need to kick the dust off and let it be."

"Hold on, lil' brother. Before we go that

far we need to confront them. I want to know why they felt the need to take things this far. You may have deserved some of their anger, but why me?"

No one saw Birdie when she slipped into the Karaoke bar. She found a seat near the kitchen entrance and was about to order a seltzer water when she spotted him — both of him. She thought she was finally losing her mind.

The waiter reappeared quickly with two cups of tea. Mother Blister gave him her cruise card and signed for the teas. She waited until Mother Pray Onn turned to chat with Ima and made her move. She emptied the packet of alum in the tea.

"Sasha," Mother Blister said, sweetly, "your tea is going to get cold."

Mother Pray Onn was taken aback when Mother Blister referred to her by her first name. But she let it slide and picked up the cup of steaming hot tea. Having those Hell-raiser genes kept her from burning her tongue as she emptied the cup in two gulps.

"Thank you so much, Bea." If she answered to her first name, then Mother Blister could certainly do the same. "I like us being on a first-name basis."

"I can't tell you how much I'm loving this

moment," Mother Blister said before she added, "Excuse me while I take a little break. You know how weak my bladder is."

Every emotion from fear to pessimism filtered from all four corners of the Karaoke bar.

Fear came from Birdie's corner, pessimism from Lyon and Lionel's. There was anxiety from where Ima and Needy sat, and satisfaction oozed from where Mother Blister hid and peered out.

The crowd had just booed the last victim and the deejay was setting up his equipment for the next one.

"Anyone who gets up there deserves just what they get," Needy said, nervously. She wasn't worried about being laughed at while singing but her dress choice was giving her concern, as well as where Reverend L.L. had disappeared to in the bar.

"You'd have to be a complete fool to put yourself out there like that," Ima added. She was referring to herself but wasn't about to let them know it.

A greasy-haired man with a bald spot and wearing a tuxedo suddenly appeared on the stage. "Okay, calm down ladies and gentlemen," he said while at the same time using his free hand to beckon them to laugh again at the last singer.

"We have a special request at this time. It appears that we have a star in our midst. At least, the request reads that she thinks she is. Please show her a little love as she comes to the stage."

He held the paper up to see it better before continuing, "Put your hands together for that little old lady from Pelzer, the incomparable Sasha Pray Onn. Sasha will be singing Outkast's hit, 'Hey Ya!' Give it up for Saaaasssshhhhaaaa!"

The crowd started looking around at one another while they clapped. No one appeared to know who the "star" was.

For the first time in years Mother Pray Onn sat glued to her seat when her name was called. From the stunned look on both Ima and Needy's faces she knew they had nothing to do with it.

It didn't take a brain surgeon to figure out who was behind it. And, since Mother Pray Onn had never been to medical school, she knew it had to be Mother Blister.

I should've figured it out the first time that gorilla in a dress called me Sasha.

Mother Pray Onn stood slowly, inhaling the euphoria of the applause. She switched her arthritic hips from side to side as she moved away from the table. The deejay had already started the track, and with the aid of her trusty cane, she used as much rhythm as she knew to shimmy to the stage.

No one knew it but two of Mother Pray Onn's favorite shows were Bishop T.D. Jakes' and BET's *106 and Park* rap music show.

Mother Pray Onn turned it out. She warbled and hyped the crowd with her geriatric version of "Hey Ya!" The crowd loved it and that didn't set well with Mother Blister. She became so enraged that she forgot she wasn't wearing one of her Depends. At the first urge to tinkle she had to rush off.

The crowd was on its feet and Ima was trying to find a place to hide.

Everything was going Mother's way until she got to the part where she had to sing, "Shake it like a Polaroid."

They hadn't meant to participate but they couldn't help it. Both Lionel and Lyon were on their feet. The anger was momentarily absent as they shouted, repeatedly, over the crowd at Mother Pray Onn. "Go ahead Mother Sasha. Shake it like a Polaroid."

And that's when the alum she'd drunk with the tea took effect. Everything was fine until she became caught up in her own hype. By the time she got out the words

"Heeeyyy . . . Yaaaaaaa . . . OHH OH . . ." her gums had shrunk, her dentures started clacking as they loosened and she sprayed spit in the faces and drinks at the surrounding tables.

By that time, Mother Blister had returned and when she saw Mother Pray Onn melting like the evil witch in the *Wiz,* she started laughing. By the time she got finished both she and Mother Pray Onn were embarrassed but for different reasons.

Birdie had enough. She'd started this odyssey of revenge and she was going to end it.

Birdie rushed over and grabbed Needy roughly by the shoulder. "Needy, come on. Let's get out of here."

"Are you crazy?" Needy laughed. "Do you know how many years I've waited for that old crow to get what was coming to her?"

Ima stood. She felt it was the perfect time to leave. For the first time since she could remember she didn't want to participate in drama.

With eyes wide open she'd walked straight into the romance trap. She, the hunter, was captured by the game. She'd heard about love at first sight but never believed in it. Now she couldn't get a grip on her feelings. She called it love but perhaps it wasn't. How

465

would she know? She'd never been in love. She'd certainly never felt whatever it was she was feeling.

Ima gently maneuvered her way through the crowd. She even apologized to a few who had taken offense at her impatience. Apologies were *not* in her make-up.

Ima had almost reached the door when she felt the touch on her shoulder. "You can't run and you'd better not try to hide."

The voice was still as commanding as when she'd heard it over the phone. She'd hung up because she wasn't prepared to hear a voice so deep, so sexually terrifying.

She still didn't want to face him but there were people now blocking the door to her escape. There was no way to avoid the inevitable but still she kept her head lowered as she tried to summon courage.

Ima exhaled and was about to turn to face her fear when suddenly she felt a tug on her other arm. She glanced to her side and to her horror, her perfect stranger had arrived.

In her mind, Ima's world was twirling out of control on its "payback" axis. The good things she wanted and the bad things she'd done were colliding. The man she'd found herself wanting now stood beside her. And there was no way she could keep him from hearing the awful truth from the man she

466

was trying to destroy.

"I've asked my brother, Lionel, to let me handle this situation," Lyon said, quickly letting go as if her body was too hot or unpleasant to the touch.

Ima was still experiencing an out-of-body moment when she turned. There was no emotion on her face as she looked at him.

"And I'm not about to let you hurt *Lyon* either." When Lionel saw that Ima was not going to turn to face him, he took a step and stood next to Lyon.

Just before Ima's Twilight Zone moment, Needy sat sipping the remainder of the drink Ima had abandoned. And she was determined not to pay Birdie any attention or leave just because Birdie had asked her to do so.

Needy was about to burst from laughter at Mother Pray Onn's humiliation. She'd just drained her glass when out of the corner of her eye in the dim light, she saw Lionel approach Ima.

"I'm asking nicely, Needy. Let's go." Birdie was adamant but it was useless. She hadn't seen what Needy had.

Needy wasn't giving up on her dream of finding a man without a fight. She brushed Birdie's hand away, almost toppled over the table, and rushed off towards the door where the brothers stood.

The situation was becoming totally out of control. Birdie couldn't handle things the nice way, so she decided that she had to meet her churchy home girls on their level.

"I'm turning the script over," she mumbled, trying to remember the phrase. She gulped down the last of her seltzer water to bolster her courage. She slammed down the glass and began to push her way through the crowd. "I'm about to shut it down," Birdie hissed.

When a few of the party people saw and heard the angry white woman mention shutting something down, they moved out of her way. With her hair fanning, her eyes blazing, and her fists balled, they thought she might just have the power to do it.

Just ahead of Birdie, Needy elbowed the crowd into making room for her to move. As she neared the door she saw Ima wedged between two men, both looking like her Reverend LL.

To Ima, the scene still looked and felt surreal. Her hazel eyes became the dreamy prisoners of the green ones that wouldn't look away. But why did the man with the deep voice address her perfect stranger as Lyon? And, why did both men look alike?

And, who in the world was Lionel?

"Is there a problem Reverend LL?" Needy asked. She'd left a few smashed toes and angry glares in her wake as she managed to shove her way to his side.

Ima didn't know when her voice returned but she heard herself say to Needy, "That's no reverend. He's Lyon Lipps."

"You must be drunk. I must be drunk. He's a reverend," Needy said as she pointed to Lionel. "And as for the one who looks just like him, well, I don't know who he is."

By the time Birdie rushed over they were all pointing and accusing in an unending circle of confusion.

"Hello Birdie," Lyon said, sheepishly stepping away from Ima as Birdie approached. "I'm sure this is not quite the date either of us expected."

And that's when Ima fainted into Lionel's arms and Needy ordered an alcoholic beverage called a Harvey Wallbanger.

They'd sat around the spacious living room in Lionel's cabin for almost ten minutes before anyone dared speak.

It'd taken some effort back at the Karaoke bar but they'd managed to get Ima somewhat revived, and Needy partially sober. At Lyon's insistence, Lionel offered his cabin as a place for everyone to gather.

Birdie and Lyon sat together on one of the two large sofas. Lionel opted to sit alone despite Needy's offer to share the other sofa with him.

Ima sat despondent on the balcony gazing at the ocean. When she'd come fully around, she was already in Lionel's bedroom. She'd gotten up and silently passed through the living room, heading straight for the balcony. No one seemed to care where she was going but Birdie. It was only after she'd reassured Birdie that she had nothing foolish in mind that Birdie unlocked the balcony door.

Needy saw her romantic chances slip away as she sadly watched Lionel, who appeared to be watching Birdie and Lyon.

"I have to accept responsibility for every demonic thing I've done to you and the other women that have crossed my path," Lyon told Birdie. "I'm through blaming it on my childhood. I was a dog and probably would still be one if Christ had not entered into my life."

"You've said that several times already," Birdie said brushing away his apology again. "There was no way I should've tried to do what only God can. It was wrong for me to judge you based on what someone said and then to pay to exact retribution. Even more so, it was ridiculous for me to buy into that dumb misery-loves-company theory, and to hang my happiness on a man and not the Kingdom."

This wasn't the first time since they'd started talking that she'd challenged him to let her accept her own part in the revenge plot. However, he seemed determined to stay remorseful.

Finally, Birdie took Lyon's hand and said, "Lyon, I've learned more in the space of a few days than I did in four years of college."

"I know I've learned a lot, too," Lyon agreed as his eyes swept past Birdie and out to the balcony.

"God has given us a purpose and a path to get there. But what you and I consider hard knocks are nothing compared to what is going on elsewhere in the world." Birdie's eyes began to moisten, but she knew she couldn't share everything she'd done since boarding the ship. To tell it all would only cause more grief and pain for M'gube, Jaiquist and Samuel. They'd been through enough already.

Before Birdie could explain further, Needy interrupted, loudly, as only Needy would. "Let me know when you're finished explaining the unexplainable," she said as she got up to use the bathroom. She saw her chances of getting closer to Lionel fade and it angered her.

As Needy passed Lionel, she couldn't be certain but it seemed that Lionel's eyes were piercing through her soul. But when she turned to look back, she found him still reading his Bible.

"What about Ima?" Birdie asked Lyon. He'd only shared that they'd met and they had an immediate attraction. He'd said nothing about where things now stood, and she needed to steer him away from any more questions about her own sudden change.

"She was willing to totally destroy a man's life for money and sport. What kind of woman would do that?" Lyon's voice was heavy with sadness. "I've given my life to Christ. Why would He bring someone into my life just to hurt me?"

"Only a woman who's never loved could do what she'd planned — but she had help," Birdie offered. "You *did* meet her aunt." She let the explanation hang in the air, knowing he'd get the meaning.

Needy returned from the bathroom and sat down in the same spot. She folded her arms and watched Lionel read his Bible.

The more she watched him leaf through the pages and listened to Birdie sermonizing, the more disturbed she became. She'd had enough. She moved to the edge of her seat and again spoke loud enough for all to hear.

"Tell me something, Birdie. Why are you over there trying to preach to that up-and-coming minister? We already got one preacher in the room." Her eyes darted toward Lionel who still refused to look up. "Of course, unlike you and me, he's perfect." Needy was at the point where she felt she'd already lost her chance so she was going to speak her mind.

Lyon quickly stood but not quicker than Needy. Needy was almost a big blur as she rushed over and snatched the Bible from Lionel's hands.

"Why don't I just see what a big-time, unforgiving, moralistic and hoity-toity man reads, while other folks are free-falling into hell?"

"Don't you ever snatch the Word of God from me again." Lionel's voice became deeper-sounding, almost like God would sound in person. "You don't know the first thing about me."

But like a tree planted by the rivers of Jordan, Needy would not be moved. "I know that you, Mr. Big-Time Preacher, don't have the right to read one thing in this Bible and then practice another."

"You don't know the Bible," Lionel said, harshly. "If you knew my God then you would've never aligned yourself with people who would hurt my brother! And that, my dear, is unforgivable."

"Is that a fact?" Needy said as she began to thumb through the Bible. "Well, let's just see what God thinks about your little interpretation." In an instant, she'd found the verse she needed.

"Psalms 25:11 says, 'For Your name's sake. O Lord, Pardon my iniquity, for it is great.' " She kept the place with her finger while pointing her words at Lionel. "In case you didn't understand it, let me make it clear; we are to forgive because we honor God's greatness when we do it!"

Lionel said nothing because he couldn't. It still didn't mean that he was convinced about her. And Needy saw his confusion in his beautiful green eyes.

"You don't look convinced, pastor." She opened the Bible again and found another verse. "Let's see how this one fits your smug mind."

"Colossians 3:13 and 14 says, 'Bearing with one another, and forgiving one another. If anyone has a complaint against another:

even as Christ forgave you, so you also must do.' "

Needy could almost taste the change in the room and it needed a little more salt. So she put on her chef's hat and added the flavor. "I know someone in this room knows what I'm talking about," she bellowed.

"Amen," Birdie said, smiling as she stood. She and Lyon walked over and stood beside Lionel as Needy finished simmering his ego. Birdie walked over because she wanted to support Needy. Lyon did it because his brother might need his help.

"I'm going to give you one more taste," Needy said as she straightened her wig with a quick flip before continuing, "because I really don't have a lot of time to spend with someone who's done nothing but sit here with his head in a Bible. Chew on this, Reverend LL. Psalms 34:8 reads thus, 'O taste and see that the *Lord* is good: blessed is the man that trusteth in him.' "

By the time Needy had finished reading the last verse, Lionel had stood. He approached her as though he was a lion stalking his prey.

But Needy wasn't just any old prey. Needy thought she'd just lost at the game of love and that made her dangerous. "What's the matter?" Needy asked as Lionel came closer.

"You need to read this for yourself? It seems to me that with all of your stylin' and profilin' that you must've read it from cover to cover already." She held the Bible behind her to avoid giving it to him. "How'd you miss those little tidbits?"

"Give me my Bible," Lionel ordered cautiously.

"No." Needy stood defiant. "I thought I was through but I've decided that I want to see what you've been reading while ignoring the real world."

Although Lionel was much taller and stronger than Needy, he wasn't faster. She ducked his outstretched arms and moved beside Birdie.

"Here Birdie," Needy said as she placed the Bible in Birdie's hand. "There's a page that's been folded at the top. Read it so that I can be blessed by the words that the good Reverend LL gave all his attention to."

"I don't think this is proper," Birdie started to say.

"I'm on the edge," Needy said as she and her hairy top lip quivered. "I ain't got much to lose. Read the words."

Birdie didn't doubt Needy so she quickly unfolded the page and began to read to herself while Lyon read over her shoulder.

"I'm waiting but not for long," Needy said

through clenched teeth.

Lionel turned and started to come closer so that he could take the Bible from Birdie's hands.

"Get back, Satan," Needy teased, but didn't smile.

The remark stopped Lionel in his tracks. He knew she was upset but he hadn't thought she'd call him the Devil. She had more fire than he'd imagined.

Birdie began to read aloud. "Proverbs 18:22, 'whosoever findeth a wife findeth a good thing, and obtaineth favour of the Lord.' "

Just like ducks in a chorus line, one by one, they looked at Lionel. There was an embarrassed look on his face as he stood there like he'd been caught with his hand in the cookie jar.

The words were like oxygen to Needy as they finally sunk in and resuscitated her dream. Perhaps all was not lost. She'd be happy to be his friend — to start off.

But no one moved, so once more, Birdie took over trying to clean up the mess. She didn't bother to cover her mouth or check for bad breath as she let out a loud yawn and said, "I think I'll be going. If there's to be no forgiveness given without reservation, then what am I staying for? I need to be among less perfect people."

"I'll see you later," Needy replied quickly as she gently started to push Birdie towards the door.

Birdie smiled and winked. "Are you sure you're going to be alright?" she whispered to Needy.

"I got this," Needy answered as she nodded towards Lionel.

"Goodnight, Reverend," Birdie said as she started to leave.

"Goodnight to you, too, Minister Lyon —"

But he was gone.

Still on the balcony, Ima had counted as many stars as she could. The law of reaping what you sow had finally caught to her. The anticipation of loving someone had felt satisfying but it had slipped away quickly. She knew it was her punishment. She'd said as many apologies, in her head, as she could. Though she hadn't heard the conversations going on inside, she was sure there was nothing left but more humiliation if she tried to leave while the others were still there. If she thought she'd survive the fall she would've tried to climb off the balcony to escape.

She was cold and the flimsy dress she'd

worn to seduce her perfect man now, like him, gave her no warmth. And the way things stood, he wasn't about to give her the time of day, either.

Ima felt something fall around her bare shoulders. She shoved it off angrily. "Just leave me alone."

"Have it your way."

Ima jumped up, knocking over the adjacent chair as she did.

"I'm sorry. I thought you were Birdie or Needy." She said the words *I'm sorry* aloud. It was like she'd taken her first baby step.

"I didn't want you to catch a cold. I'm not that inhuman," Lyon said. He knew he had to forgive but at that moment he was still struggling with his feelings.

"I'll be okay," Ima lied. She was as far from being okay as they were from Pelzer. "Where's your friend Birdie?" She, too, was angry, but for a different reason. She had another foreign feeling and it was jealousy.

"She left," Lyon said, keeping his replies short.

As if she didn't believe him Ima turned and looked through the balcony door and into the living room. She didn't see Birdie but she thought she was hallucinating again when she saw Lionel and Needy. They sat close together on the sofa and they appeared to be reading.

Lyon read the confusion on Ima's face and for the first time since he'd learned of her deception, he managed a smile.

"You needed to be there to understand."

She suddenly accepted his smile for what it was and it permitted her to smile also. "I don't think I would understand it if you showed me the video."

Lyon laughed hard and that time there was no struggle involved.

"I'm so sorry," Ima said as her face let go of her smile. "I've no excuse but I'm truly sorry."

"Let me explain to you about the problem with being sorry and remorseful all the time," Lyon said as he replaced the jacket that had slid off one of her shoulders. "There's no place for it in the ministry."

Ima looked confused because she was.

Lyon again laughed. He steered her over to the edge of the balcony and pointed to the sky. "For as many stars as there are shining I'm going to give you a reason to be happy, even if it takes me all night."

Ima took another first step that night. She thanked God for His forgiveness, His mercy and His gift of a second chance. And Ima meant it.

■ ■ ■ ■

Birdie had decided that she would visit Mothers Blister and Pray Onn before she turned in. But no sooner had she gotten off the elevator than she ran into Hunter, who looked like he was fleeing for his life.

"Do I have to ask?" Birdie said with a wide grin.

"No madam, you do not." Hunter doffed his cap and waited for Birdie to reenter the elevator as he knew she would.

"Are they still alive and kicking?" Birdie smiled and asked while she pressed the elevator button for the door to close.

"Evil will always live on, madam," Hunter replied. "It doesn't die, it multiplies."

Hunter and Birdie gave a sigh of relief as the elevator door closed and took them to safety.

Their exquisite stateroom looked a mess. There were drawers pulled out from the dresser and clothes strewn across the sofa and chairs.

"I'm not moving nowhere, you old cow. You move." Mother Blister picked up the last one of her bladder-control Depends pampers and threw it at Mother Pray Onn.

Mother Pray Onn caught it with the tip of her cane. And for the next few minutes the old women tossed it back and forth in a game of ping pong.

"You are a jealous old hag," Mother Pray Onn barked. "You were just mad because those young people liked me. I was the life of the party," she shouted.

"It ain't that hard to be the life of a party if it only lasts 'til 9 o'clock in the evening," Mother Blister shouted back.

"I don't care what you say, I had them shaking like a Polaroid!"

"You should care, cow chip," Mother Blister replied.

"Oh really, who's gonna make me care?" Mother Pray Onn quipped.

"Long term care, private care, dental care and eye care if you ever mess with me again!" Mother Blister threatened.

They were about to start round two when a persistent knock almost broke the door down.

"Now you've done it, you loud-mouth Karaoke hussy," Mother Blister screamed.

"Shut your trap and go in the bathroom while I handle grown folks' business."

Since she had to go anyway, Mother Blister snaked her way through the clutter and into the bathroom. Mother Pray Onn put on her best I'm Old and Don't Know Any Better face and opened the door. She came face to face with Needy and Lionel. The first thing Mother Pray Onn did was to check them for bruises. When she didn't see any it triggered her curiosity.

She was so short it wasn't difficult for Needy and Lionel to see the messed up room over her shoulder.

"I'd ask y'all to come in but we didn't get any clean-up service today. Mother Blister is too old to help so I'm trying to do all this myself," Mother Pray Onn said sweetly as she lied.

"That's okay. We just wanted to know if you'd like to come up to Reverend LL's stateroom. We're having bible study."

Mother Pray Onn saw the phone off the hook and understood why they hadn't called first. She didn't answer right away; instead she asked, "How is my poor sweet niece, Ima?"

"She's doing much better. As a matter of fact, when we left my stateroom, she and Lyon were out on the balcony," Lionel said smiling.

Mother Pray Onn whirled around and called out to Mother Blister, "Bea, hurry up and cut it short."

"Why?" Mother Blister hollered from the

bathroom.

"Ima and Lyon Lipps are out on the balcony in his brother's stateroom!" Mother Pray Onn yelled.

Instantly, Mother Blister hobbled from the bathroom with her drawers still down around her ankles. She stumbled into the room and spied Needy and Lionel standing in the doorway. They were looking over Mother Pray Onn's shoulder with shocked looks on their faces, but Mother Pray Onn didn't.

Without skipping a beat, Mother Pray Onn turned around and said, "Grab that Bible you brought from the dollar store. We're going to a prayer meeting."

EPILOGUE

The last days of the cruise went by quickly. Needy and Lionel lowered their guards and tried to get to know each other, as did Ima and Lyon.

During drama-free meals and quiet time on the Lido Deck, Ima and Needy learned that Lionel and Lyon possessed good business sense and were money-management savvy. The brothers owned the high-rise building they lived in as well as a fleet of limousines.

Ima and Needy tried to hide their happiness at hearing that the brothers were wealthy but failed miserably. Both women jumped up and started dancing. Needy danced the Laffy Taffy and Ima performed a praise dance, minus a sash and a streamer.

Lyon managed to do within a week what most men couldn't have done in a lifetime. He dampened Ima's fire with simple kindness and forthrightness, and asked for nothing in return. Ima was almost unrecognizable while they were together. She was so well-behaved, Needy wanted the ship's doctor to check her out.

The two couples flew back to Pelzer together. During their flight, Needy and Lionel realized that they truly wanted to become better acquainted and if God had other plans past that, then they'd be happy.

Lionel also concluded that he needed to withdraw his name from the pool of potential pastors of the Ain't Nobody Right But Us — All Others Goin' to Hell Church. It was partly due to his acceptance of the fact that he was not as righteous or as accepting of other people as a true pastor needed to be. That's what he confided to Needy.

He had, however, purposely left out that there was no way he wanted to pastor a church where Mother Pray Onn and Mother Blister would regularly test his faith. He was still questioning God about his current situation, and didn't want to jeopardize his chances of making it in. Those two old women has misbehaved so badly in his cabin until they'd almost caused him to cuss at the prayer meeting.

Mothers Blister and Pray Onn wound up having to use their ill-gotten bingo gains to pay for the damaged cabin. They weren't happy about it but decided to join forces to keep the money coming in. Old age and senility convinced Mother Pray Onn that she could make money singing Karaoke, and Mother Blister could continue likewise with her bingo scams. They even decided that at the next Mothers Board Anniversary they'd perform "Hey Ya!" as a duet with the rest of the mothers singing, "Shake it like a Polaroid picture," in the background.

Of course, Mother Blister, never one to miss an opportunity to one-up Mother Pray Onn, had purchased a video of Mother Pray Onn's Karaoke performance. She planned to show it at the next board meeting. It was a fact that she kept to herself as she laughed and plotted with Mother Pray Onn during the flight back to Pelzer.

Birdie found more than she'd bargained for during the cruise. She discovered that God wanted her to be meek and giving but not pathetic and unwise with herself and her wealth.

Birdie's friendship with Jaiquist, Samuel and M'gube would continue. She'd determined that she would place them in charge of philanthropic efforts to bring as many "Maama Kits" to Africa as her money would allow. The four of them would join with Akia Shangai to bring awareness to

Africa's neonatal crisis along with the need for more affordable medicine for people with HIV and other life-threatening diseases.

Birdie also discovered that she really liked Hunter's English accent. They became friends and promised to see each other again soon.

The flight from Miami to Pelzer was quiet. Everyone had gone through customs and the usual airport security without a hitch. The two old mothers had managed to behave and that made everyone sigh with relief.

One of the brothers' limousines was waiting at Arrivals. They offered to take both Needy and Ima home. However, the women declined, which shook the confidence of Lyon and Lionel. With a promise of a later dinner date the couples said goodbye.

During the brothers' ride, they admitted their confusion by the women's actions. By the time they'd arrived at their destination they were ready to return to the airport and insist the women come with them. Their new emotions were as foreign to them as the countries they'd just visited.

It took all the willpower they possessed for Needy and Ima not to chase after that limousine. They wanted so badly to remain with Lyon and Lionel. However, as much as they were infatuated with the two gorgeous brothers, they'd learned a thing or two. Those men would have to earn their love and respect.

Needy had a new outlook on life. She'd learned that there was someone for her despite her perceived imperfections. She appreciated that never once during the time she and Lionel were together did he disrespect her by ogling her oversized breasts. That alone did a lot for her self-esteem. She also realized that although she knew a verse or two from the Bible, she needed to put it into practice. And if Lionel was the man for her, he'd wait. A pastor's wife needed to know more than to quote a few scriptures.

Ima had a lot to digest. Lyon had not come on to her and yet she felt appreciated. Where evil thoughts had once constantly flooded her mind, she felt at peace. Ima was a mess. She needed to go home and just let the experience replay in her mind. Could this really be love? Or was she just being set up for more heartbreak? She decided that the only man who could truly help her did not reside on Earth. Ima determined that she was going to do what she'd heard before; she was going boldly to the throne of grace. She needed to hear from Him because never in her wildest imagination could she picture herself dating or marrying a minister. What could God be thinking?

Cill and Petunia arrived at the airport shortly after the brothers' limousine left. Ima and Needy recognized Petunia's old car. However, they didn't recognize the driver until the car stopped in front of them. Cill was driving. She wore a skull cap instead of her usual big Apple one. Her face had marks as though she'd been cut by someone having a seizure.

Petunia was more recognizable. She looked like a skinny mummy. She wore Band-Aids everywhere.

Just as Ima went around to the back of the car to put her luggage in the trunk, the car door opened. Without warning, a small black bag was tossed from the car. The bag almost landed in Needy's arms. Ima turned to rush back and was hit in the head by a box of Kibble and Bits.

Petunia's car raced away faster than it had when it was brand new.

By the time the shock wore off of Ima and Needy, Evilene had clawed her way through the bag. The cat strutted over to Ima, wound itself around her legs and purred.

Ima knew Evilene must've done something extraordinarily mean to intimidate

Cill, but she'd have to find out later. She reached down and picked up the cat while she gave Needy her cell phone.

"It's number one," Ima said, shyly. "Just tell Lyon we're desperate and we need him."

In the meantime the cabin crew prepared the *Desperation of the Seas* for its next sailing. They found the unopened envelopes containing Cill's faxes, warning the women about Lyon, and threw them away.

■ ■ ■ ■

A READING GROUP GUIDE
CRUISIN' ON DESPERATION

PAT G'ORGE-WALKER

■ ■ ■ ■

ABOUT THIS GUIDE

This list of questions has been created to encourage a group or individual to dig deeper — explore the heart of the book's content. These questions are designed to encourage interaction and discussion. Also, the following questions are **not** numbered according to chapter.

DISCUSSION QUESTIONS

1. One wedding set off a chain of nuptials in the summer of 2005 in Pelzer, South Carolina. Did it appear that the couplings described in the prologue were matches made in heaven? Why or why not? Scripture states, *"And they twain shall be one flesh; so then they are no more twain, but one flesh. What therefore God hath joined together, let no man put asunder."* (Mark 10: 8–9) Do you think God actually plays matchmaker? Support your answer with Scripture.

2. We first meet Sister Need Sum (Needy) as she imagines tearing a man's shirt off with her teeth. What impressed you most about Needy's spiritual response to her thoughts? Was she wrong for having those thoughts?

3. Oh Lawd Why Am I Still Single Club of the Ain't Nobody Right But Us — All Others Goin' to Hell Church was an

interesting mix of characters. Each woman in the group had serious issues. Still, they were drawn to one another for the sake of fellowship. What else, besides being manless, did they have in common?

4. The Apostle Paul stated, *". . . In the same way, a woman who is no longer married or has never been married can be more devoted to the Lord in body and in spirit . . . I am saying this for your benefit, not to place restrictions on you. I want you to do whatever will help you serve the Lord best, with as few distractions as possible."* (1 Corinthians 7: 34–35) Were the members of the Oh Lawd Why Am I Still Single Club devoted to the Lord in body and spirit, and serving the Lord with their very best? Or were they distracted? And if so, what were their distractions?

5. Why would Cill want to be a member of the singles group? She had no apparent interest in men or in getting married. What was Cill's main contribution to the group? Should she have been excluded? Please discuss.

6. Sister Birdie Tweet is the only caucasian member of the singles group. Does Birdie's race seem to make a difference? What did you think of the other members' treatment of Birdie?

7. What was your reaction to Birdie, Petunia, and Cill's confessions of knowing Lyon Lipps? How did you feel when they, with Needy and Mother Blister's provocation, decide to seek retribution? Do you think Needy overreacted? Have you ever been a part of a plot to get back at a man? Discuss.

8. What were your immediate impressions of Ima Hellraiser? Was it necessary to involve her in the plan to destroy Lyon?

9. Consider Mother Blister's affair with Slim Pickens. What made the relationship so scandalous? Were you relieved that she didn't have to "compromise" her "virtue" (or what was left of it) in order to get Slim to finance her trip? Do the same rules of fornication apply to elderly women and men?

10. The name of Mother Sasha Pray Onn evoked fear in Birdie. Do you think it was wise for Ima and Needy to put Mothers Pray Onn and Blister in the same stateroom? Were these two old dogs too old to learn new tricks, namely obedience to God?

11. Upon meeting twins Lionel and Lyon, which twin were you endeared to immediately? Which twin did you not like? Why?

12. Do you think Lyon should have followed the hunch of impending doom he experienced up until the start of the cruise?

13. The mayhem and foolishness caused by the unlikely alliance of Mothers Pray Onn and Blister left a bad taste in the mouth of the ship's purser, Hunter. Did they draw him to Jesus with their godliness or did their lack of godliness potentially drive him away from the Lord? What impression did those two leave about Christians? Did it matter?

14. When Ima and Lyon meet in the Karaoke bar, she decides to not exchange names. She chose to play a game. Why do you think that was the case? Moreover, Lyon chose to play with her, what does that say about him?

15. Jaiquist, Samuel, and M'gube are on a mission. How is their storyline tied to the outcome of the book and to other characters? What did you know about infant mortality and unclean conditions for new mothers in Africa, and the Maama Project before reading *Cruisin' on Desperation*?

16. What happens to Birdie? Was her change rapid or progressive, beginning before the cruise?

17. Lionel hits the roof when he learns that Needy and Ima were a part of a plot to

destroy his brother, which is understandable. However, he shoots first, and then asks questions. What does this say about his temperament and personality? Does he sound like a man ready to be a pastor and/or a husband?

18. Not even Needy's moustache turned Lionel off. In spite of himself, he is drawn to her — like a moth to a flame. Is this a likely or unlikely match? Who did the hook-up: God, or was it simply a case of mutual attraction?

19. Why is Lyon so attracted to Ima? Even after he finds out about her, he has so much compassion for and patience with Ima. Why is that?

20. The friendship between Cill and Petunia is already fragile but when Evilene, Ima's crazed cat, enters their lives the dynamics shift. How did the author use Evilene to teach these two bumbling women a lesson or two? What do you think Evilene got out of the deal?

21. Cill breaks down when Petunia reveals that she knows about the child Cill wanted to adopt. She had been holding in an incredible amount of pain. What can we learn about single women and their need to feel connected and have their own families? How is that often negated by

married women?

22. Ima experiences a crisis, which threat-ened her focus and mission to destroy Lyon. What happened to Ima? Will she be okay?

23. Throughout the book, references to faxed letters from Cill crop up. No one reads them and at the end, they are thrown away. What would have been the outcome had the first letter been read and heeded?

24. Who is the most transformed by the turn of events on the cruise? Who is the least transformed?

25. After the cruise, will the nature of the singles' group's meetings change or re-main the same? Will they even continue meeting?

A Q&A WITH
PAT G'ORGE-WALKER

Q: You've been writing about the antics of the Ain't Nobody Right But Us — All Others Goin' to Hell Church for a long time now. *Cruisin' on Desperation* is the third book featuring Ima Hellraiser and Mother Pray Onn. Is it safe to assume these characters offer an inexhaustible amount of material?

PGW: As long as the doors of the church remain open, there will be an inexhaustible amount of material. Judgment begins at the house of God and until we get it right we cannot tell the world how to worship or act. So, uh, yes.

Q: *Mother Eternal Ann Everlastin's Dead* is the first novel, and now *Cruisin' on Desperation* is the second, where you take the members on the road and away from Pelzer, South Carolina. First of all, is there really a

Pelzer, South Carolina, and second, where are you taking them next?

PGW: Yes, there is a Pelzer, South Carolina. I lived from the ages of nine through 12 in the small town of Williamston, SC. Pelzer was a nearby small town. Every time I tried to run away, I could only get as far as Pelzer. There was always someone in Pelzer who knew my grandmother, Ma Cile. They would pick up my little skinny tail and promptly deliver me back into the hands of Ma Cile who would shortly thereafter mete out justice. I promised that I would one day get back at Pelzer. On another note, the local Pelzer newspaper reviewed my books and loved them. I guess I placed them on the map.

To answer your second question: I believe the next stop is Las Vegas, Nevada, to see if what happens there really stays there.

Q: Why did you choose to let Ima, Mothers Pray Onn and Blister loose out at sea?

PGW: Those two argumentative old women, who are suffering from the fatique of menopause and the onset of dementia, are based upon real people. There were actually several senior citizens in my former church that were involved in a ménage à trois. For some reason they felt comfortable in sharing their details despite my obvious show of discomfort. I simply put them in a "what if" situation on a cruise ship and let them go. They were just as hilarious to me on paper as they were in real life. It was also a platform. I wanted to show how some religious people share the same space and circumstances yet act worldlier than those who claim no relationship with God.

Q: A Karaoke bar serves as the epicenter for many pivotal moments in the story. Many shifts in plot and changes in character development take place there. What was its appeal to you as a writer?

PGW: I love Karaoke. I've performed on cruise ships. I love the shift in personalities, etc., when people bare their souls in front of strangers. It's like watching someone with an open wound attempt to perform ego surgery, while one attempts to self-medicate with an act of embarrassment. The Karaoke bar was a place where there were no boundaries and freedom to change flowed like wine.

Q: How could two sweet old ladies like the

Mothers Blister and Pray Onn create such havoc on a cruise ship? Shouldn't they be more mature and guarded about their Christian testimony?

PGW: According to them, they've paid their dues. At their ages, they feel free to say and do what they wish. They are the epitome of not being able to teach old dogs new tricks. They only have a form of religion with no real basis in a relationship with God. And, those two old women have a bond. Although they're willing to torment one another, they still have each other's back when outsiders interfere. They have a love-hate relationship that is demonstrated at every Mothers Board meeting, choir rehearsal and any aspect of their church life.

Q: We know about Lyon Lipps' past as a lyin' (pun intended), thieving, womanizing ex-con. What is it that we do not know about Lionel Lipps' (Lyon's twin brother) past? Is he just too good to be true or what?

PGW: Lionel thinks he's the conscience and the keeper of his twin. He harbors guilt for escaping the unforgiving streets of New Orleans and not being able to save his brother from an undeserved initial jail stint.

Lionel is also very judgmental in his relationships with others apart from his brother. He also has a preconceived notion that he will marry someone who is as attractive as he is, someone that would make a suitable First Lady. No, Lionel is not too good at all and he shows his shortcomings in a big way.

Q: You gave Sister Need Sum an exceptional sense of self; girlfriend loves every roll of fat on her body, her hairy lip and her double-D chest. She is comfortable in her own skin almost to the point of being delusional. Was this an intentional development of her character?

PGW: Yes, it was intentional. Although the comedienne Monique preaches and lives self-acceptance, Needy could probably give her lessons.

Q: Gender-bending Cill is given an incredible gift in *Cruisin' on Desperation*. She is allowed to simply be herself and to operate in denial, thinking that no one notices her special proclivities. No one judges her at all but rather they seem to be waiting for Cill to get a clue. What purpose does this character serve in the story?

PGW: In most of my stories, there's always a character going against the grain. Jesus said He came to save not to judge. We must show love to those who seem to believe that God will accept behavior He's decreed as an abomination. We are not to judge, we are to allow God to do it. We are to show by example God's love and pray for those in such situations as that. Cill's character shows that we shouldn't accept people's behavior as the sum total of their being. None of us begin on the "good foot."

Q: Three words: Ima, Ima, Ima . . . Ima Hellraiser, mistress of darkness, receives her comeuppance in this story. Is this the beginning of a redeemed Ima?

PGW: Ima will eventually get it together. Just like most of my characters, Ima is based upon a real person. She's loosely based on my cousin Myra. I can reveal that fact because when I perform, and Myra's in the audience, I introduce her as Sister Ima Hellraiser. She loves it. However, Myra is saved now and resides in Greenville, South Carolina. So eventually, Ima Hellraiser will embrace salvation, too. But not too soon. The readers would revolt.

Q: *Cruisin' on Desperation* is obviosly not a how-to book for Christian singles. What are the lessons singles can glean from the story?

PGW: Christian singles should focus on their walk. The Bible says that we are not to be unequally yoked. If we seek the Kingdom of God, He will add unto us what we need; it may not be what we want (Lionel's dilemma) but it will be what we need. There are other numerous lessons of self-assurance, finding purpose and keeping God first.

Q: What does Mother Blister do with Slim Pickens when she returns from the cruise?

PGW: As long as Mother Blister's money runs short before the next check arrives, she'll continue fleecing old Slim Pickens. But he really does deserve it. ☺

Q: This past year has been exceptionally challenging for you. Your husband's illness tested your faith considerably and still you had a productive year professionally. How did you manage without losing your mind?

PGW: For whatever reason God seems to place challenges in my path when I'm working on a comedy story. I had a very difficult time writing when the first Iraqi POW's were taken. I couldn't find my comedy voice and the publishing company was very sympathetic.

However, when my husband was diagnosed with cancer in September 2005, I went through unimaginable pain. I was shocked, angry, depressed; and then the acceptance settled in and I went to work on calling up Heaven. I had Jesus on speed dial. Now on the other hand, my husband was the rock. He decided that God wasn't finished with what was required of him. I didn't want to leave his side and I turned down so many performances. The doctors had given him a year to live but I wouldn't let them tell him. Then of course, I had my own surgery two months after his diagnosis. But God being the author and finisher of our faith pulled Rob through. He is now in remission. I've lost about forty pounds and Brian has graduated and is about to enter college. My book *Mother Eternal* was nominated to be adapted into a film. I signed another contract with Kensington Books and the budget for the Sister Betty sitcom is in the works.

ABOUT THE AUTHOR

Pat G'Orge-Walker The First Lady of Gospel Comedy

Pat G'Orge (pronounced Gee-or-jay)-Walker is a former record industry veteran who has worked for several major labels including Epic, Def Jam, and Columbia. She has also performed with the legendary 60's girl group, Arlene Smith and the Chantels ("Maybe"), as well as with gospel groups. In 2003, G'Orge-Walker released *Sister Betty! God's Calling You, Again!*, followed by *Mother Eternal Ann Everlastin's Dead* in 2004. In between writing books and spending time with her husband Rob in their Long Island, New York, home, Pat is busy touring the country performing her sold-out One Woman Sister Betty comedy show.

The employees of Thorndike Press hope you have enjoyed this Large Print book. All our Thorndike and Wheeler Large Print titles are designed for easy reading, and all our books are made to last. Other Thorndike Press Large Print books are available at your library, through selected bookstores, or directly from us.

For information about titles, please call:
   (800) 223-1244

or visit our Web site at:
   www.gale.com/thorndike
   www.gale.com/wheeler

To share your comments, please write:
   Publisher
   Thorndike Press
   295 Kennedy Memorial Drive
   Waterville, ME 04901